DATE DUE

SEP 2 7 1994		
MAY 3 1 1997		
AUG 09 1997		
FEB 0 6 2001		
GAYLORD		PRINTED IN U.S.A.

DROWNING TOWERS

DROWNING TOWERS

George Turner

ARBOR HOUSE
WILLIAM MORROW
New York

First published in Great Britain in 1987 as: *The Sea and Summer* by Faber and Faber Limited, 3 Queen Square, London WC1N 3AU, England.

Library of Congress Cataloging-in-Publication Data

Turner, George.
  Drowning towers.

  I. Title.
PR9619.3.T868D75   1988   823   88-10550
ISBN 1-55710-038-1

Printed in the United States of America

First U.S. Edition

1 2 3 4 5 6 7 8 9 10

ACKNOWLEDGEMENT

This work was assisted by a writer's fellowship from the Literature Board of the Australia Council, the Federal Government's arts funding and advisory body.

CONTENTS

THE AUTUMN PEOPLE 1   *page* 1

THE SEA AND SUMMER 1   17
   1 ALISON CONWAY – AD 2061   19
   2 FRANCIS CONWAY – AD 2041–2044   21
   3 NOLA PARKES – AD 2044   61
   4 FRANCIS – AD 2044–2050   68
   5 NOLA PARKES – AD 2050   76
   6 FRANCIS – AD 2050   79

THE AUTUMN PEOPLE 2   85

THE SEA AND SUMMER 2   101
   7 TEDDY CONWAY – AD 2044–2045   103
   8 CAPTAIN NIKOPOULOS – AD 2044   114
   9 TEDDY – AD 2044–2045   122
  10 NICK – AD 2045   125
  11 TEDDY – AD 2045   131
  12 ALISON – AD 2044–2047   133
  13 TEDDY – AD 2045–2047   157
  14 NICK – AD 2050   175
  15 FRANCIS – AD 2050   182
  16 TEDDY – AD 2050   185
  17 NICK – AD 2050   210
  18 NOLA PARKES – AD 2050   221
  19 ALISON – AD 2051   224
  20 NICK – AD 2051   232
  21 TEDDY –AD 2051   236
  22 NOLA PARKES AND ARTHUR DERRICK – AD 2051   282
  23 FRANCIS – FROM HIS DIARY, AD 2056–2061   306

THE AUTUMN PEOPLE 3   313

POSTSCRIPT   317

'We must plan for five years ahead and twenty years and a hundred years.'

Sir Macfarlane Burnett

THE AUTUMN PEOPLE 1

1

The sun, high in early afternoon, sparkled on still water. There was no breeze; only the powercraft's wake disturbed the placid bay. The pilot's chart showed in dotted lines an old riverbed directly below his keel, but no current flowed at the surface; the Yarra now debouched some distance to the north, at the foot of the Dandenongs where the New City sheltered among hills and trees.

The pilot had lost his first awe of the Old City and the vast extent of the drowned ruins below; this was for him a routine trip. He carried hundreds of historians, archaeologists, divers and sightseers in the course of a year. His thought now was simple pleasure that the sun had power enough to have made it worthwhile to shed his clothes and enjoy its warmth on his skin.

There were not many such days, even in midsummer, and the southern wind would bring a chill before nightfall. Enjoy while you may, he thought, snatch the moment. And if that edged a little too close to hedonism for a practising Christian, so be it. He believed in the forgiveness of sin rather than in the possibility of his own perfection.

When this sunken city had reached its swollen maximum of population and desperation, a thousand years before, the sun had blazed throughout the four seasons, but that time was over and would not return. The Long Summer had ended and the Long Winter – perhaps a hundred thousand years of it – loomed. The cold southern wind at nightfall, every nightfall, was its whisper of intent and the pilot was happy to be living now rather than earlier or later.

Not every wall and spire of the Old City lay below the bay. The melting of the Antarctic ice cap had been checked as the polluted atmosphere rebalanced its elements and the blanket of global heat dissipated; the fullest rise of the ocean level had been forestalled though not soon enough to avert disaster to the coastal cities of the planet. To the north and northeast of the powercraft's position lay

3

the islands which had been the higher ground of Melbourne's outer suburbs, forested now and overgrown, but storehouses of history.

The other ruins, the other storehouses, part submerged, were clusters of gigantic towers built (with the blind persistence of those who could not believe in the imminence of disaster) in the lower reaches of the sprawling city. There were ten Enclaves, each a group of nearly identical towers whose designs had varied little in the headlong efficiency of their building. The Enclave now approached by the powercraft was one of the largest, a forest of twenty-four giants evenly spaced in an area of some four square kilometres opposite what had been in that far time the mouth of the Yarra. It was shown on the pilot's chart as Newport Towers, with the caution Erratic Currents, a notation common to all the Enclaves. These ancient masses, each more than 100 metres on a side, created races and eddies at change of tide.

Marin knew that what he saw were only the lower hulks of buildings which had stretched at the sky. Their greedy height had not withstood the eroding sea and the cyclones of destabilized weather patterns. Not one had endured entire; most were only sub-surface stumps of their hugeness, splintered jawfuls of broken teeth. It was difficult to conceive of them in their unpleasant heyday, twenty-four human warrens, each fifty to seventy storeys high and verminous with the seething humanity of the Greenhouse Culture.

He lived in a world where architecture favoured concern for surroundings, where stairways were thought of as an inconvenience and two-floor dwellings a rarity; processing conditions occasionally demanded excessive height in factories and these were bounded by restrictions of design and position. (It was estimated that in Old America some structures had approached a kilometre in height and there was much argument about the pressures that had produced such extravagance.)

He was bored with the Enclaves as such; there seemed little more to be discovered in their catacomb silence although today's fare seemed to find them a lifetime study. And not so much 'them' as a particular one.

He asked over his shoulder, 'Tower Twenty-three, Scholar? As usual?' and she agreed, 'As usual.'

The powercraft was a large one and the two passengers astern were sufficiently removed to speak quietly without his hearing, but he had the usual human awareness of being talked about, sensing the small alteration of timbre in the susurrus of speech.

4

The man asked, 'Does he always use the formal address? That must be the tenth time.'

'Always.' The historian was amused. 'The Christians are a punctilious lot, always polite but conscious of sanctity – not plainly apart but not wholly of the common herd.'

'Insulting!'

'No, only defensive. They feel themselves to be a rapidly decreasing minority as the contemplative oriental philosophies gain ground. And fools do tend to sneer at them.'

'Do you wonder? Anyone who thinks he can draw a line between good and evil is at best mistaken, at worst demented. The Christians as I understand them want to save mankind from sin without first understanding either sin or mankind.'

She smiled at him. 'Do you believe that or are you roughing out an epigram for your play?'

Because she had prodded a real weakness the actor–playwright contented himself with an enigmatic shrug; she had an unerring aim for small vanities and in the twenty-four hours of their acquaintance had made him aware of it. There was, for instance, his claim to Viking ancestry, based solely on his name, Andra Andrasson, though a strong Aboriginal strain coloured him unmistakably; the dark skin made it necessary for him to use a heavy Caucasian make-up for most roles and as a consequence he often went unrecognized in the public street. 'Who wants to be pestered by fans?' he had asked and had been almost able to hear her unspoken, *You'd love it*. Which he would.

Establishing the tutor–student relationship, no doubt. That was better than a predatory interest in a good-looking young man (thirty – er, – five is young enough); he had learned a healthy fear of footloose older women at first-night parties. This one, at any rate, was all tutor and chattily disinterested when not busily informing.

Lenna Wilson was not, in fact, wholly disinterested, merely unaroused – more accurately, a little disappointed. She had been properly excited at the request for consultation from one of the foremost stage personalities of the day and more than a little stimulated by his presence and his easy handsomeness. Then, on this first excursion, he had seized the chance to sunbathe and demagnetization had set in. In the nude he was curiously shapeless – *tubular* was her mute description – as though form were the gift of his tailor, and in movement he displayed little grace. Yet on stage he could mesmerize with a gesture, put on majesty, collapse into clowning or be instantly a nameless man in the street.

5

Well, each to his talent and hers was for history. She was as respected in her niche as he in his (though about one ten-thousandth as well known) and he had confirmed his knowledge of this by the string pulling he had done to obtain her agreement to coach him for a single force-fed week.

She said, 'Don't expect too much here. It's easy to be let down at first sight.'

'I expect to be horrified.'

'By empty rooms?'

'By ghosts.'

'That will need conjury.'

He sat up, speaking more loudly. 'Conjury is my business. I must call up visions before I can construct a play.'

The pilot looked over his shoulder as though he expected to catch a large theatrical gesture to smile at but saw only the set face of a man who took his work seriously and chose to express himself in metaphor.

Andra grinned quickly at him and said, 'In all this wreckage there must be a few ghosts on call.'

'Dirty, stinking ghosts, Artist, crowded, lewd and violent.' His urgent Christianity spurred him further than was wise. 'They were evil people.'

'Nevertheless,' Lenna said, 'they were the stuff of history.'

Marin, competent at his work, was also an academically ambitious man; his formal address of Lenna did not indicate respect, only a distancing. With the certainty of the indoctrinated he insisted, 'They were wicked – they and those like them ruined the world for all who came after. Scholar, they *denied* history.'

'Perhaps so,' she replied equably, 'but if history is to record the ascent of man it must also recognize the periods of his fall.' *Oh, dear, now we'll get the Garden of Eden.*

He was not such a fool as that and knew he had overplayed dogmatism. He pushed up a smile. 'In a few minutes, Artist, you will be able to question the ghosts for yourself.'

It was not much of a jest but it served to end discussion. He pulled the wheel hard over and the powercraft swung smoothly past two drearily tumbled steel and concrete monsters. The remains of broken walls that protruded above the water for a forlorn storey or two were black with the grime of centuries, pitted with friction and a thousand agents of corrosion; glassless windows gaped.

'Twenty-three,' said Marin, gliding them into the shadow of the tower that stood like a sentry on the northwest corner of the Enclave.

6

The building, Andra judged, was about 100 metres square and the water at this point – he glanced at the pilot's dashboard – was something more than thirty metres deep so that what remained, with only three fairly whole storeys rearing above the water, was a poor fragment of a once colossal structure. Narrow, shattered balconies ran completely round each floor and to one of these was hooked a sort of gangplank descending a few feet to a floating platform. Marin drew the powercraft alongside and grappled on.

'Best to dress, Artist,' he suggested as he shrugged into an overall. 'It is cooler inside.'

'Thank you.' Andra pulled on shirt and trousers while Lenna, fully dressed because she thought sunbathing an unproductive and dull pursuit, stepped overside on to the platform which rocked to her weight.

'That wouldn't ride out a mild storm,' Andra observed.

'The History Department provides a caretaker at each Enclave. The access floats are taken in when need be.'

'After all this time you still study these ruins?'

'There's no end to it. Divers find new and strange things, new study techniques demand constant scrutiny of the artefacts, fresh interpretations demand wholesale re-examination of the buildings.'

He was impressed. 'I'm told that your work in progress overthrows previous conclusions.'

Suddenly a tutor, she corrected him. 'Seeks to modify some previous conclusions about social attitudes of the Greenhouse Culture and to suggest that the Sweet/Swill cleavage was less complete than has been assumed.'

'That sounds the sort of information I need.'

'For your playscript?'

'For bridging characters. It would be difficult to present two totally separated strata.'

She said with tutorial orderliness, 'We must discuss it later,' and switched to picnic enthusiasm as she started up the gangplank, 'Come inside, it's absolutely fascinating.'

It was not a word he would have chosen for the naked concrete of the tiny apartment they entered through the balcony window. Bare rooms always seem small, constricted, but to Andra these were claustrophobic. There were three, each about three metres by two and a half, leading into each other, and two half-sized roomlets at one end. He thought that with some knocking out of walls it would make an overnight flat, a *pied-à-terre*, but not a place to live in. He hazarded, 'A two-person flat?'

7

Behind him Marin laughed without joy. Lenna said, 'It was intended for a family of four, but there was never enough room and soon no money for building. Seven or eight was common, often more than that.'

'In here! They'd live like animals!' The words were shocked out of him.

'Animals had more space – they were precious. Think of this: there were seventy floors in the completed tower and we estimate that 70,000 people lived in it.'

He stared doubtfully round the box of a room.

'That meant,' Lenna said, 'when you subtract areas for lightwells, liftwells and stairways, less than four square metres of living space for each individual and his furniture.'

Andra could not take it in. He imagined eight beds, with chairs and tables, wardrobes and shelves . . . an airship cabin would afford more space . . . 'Such poverty!'

Marin spoke like one who sees no need for shock. 'Throughout history, poverty was the lot of the common man.'

Lenna glanced at him with mild surprise. 'Yes, we tend to forget that. We see the monuments and forget the millions who starved to raise them.'

Andra shivered, not with cold. 'At least we have eliminated that from the world.'

'The interesting statistic,' she said drily, 'is the number of millennia it took us to learn how to do so, though it was always easy and we always knew it.'

She led the way from the flat into a dark corridor that ran the length of the building. A window at each extremity gave the only light save at the end where they stood; here a battery-fed standard lamp had been set up to illuminate some thirty metres of the length. By its light Andra saw that the cracked, broken, flaked-away walls had at some stage been painted; faint outlines and fainter suggestions of colour spread over every inch of wall space.

Hesitantly, peering, he asked, 'Murals?'

Lenna said, 'Of a kind,' and Marin, 'You'll see.'

She went ahead towards the window at the western end. 'We have managed to reconstruct a section of the wall decorations by computer-enhanced X-ray examination. Bring the lamp, please, Marin.'

The pilot brought the light down to the last doorway in the corridor, where it sparkled on a dozen metres of extraordinary glitter and confusion.

'They used paint, charcoal, whitewash, aerosol lacquers and

anything that would cling and then spread their designs one atop the others. Creative boredom.'

Indeed so. Andre could recognize nothing entirely, could only perceive hints of design emerging from a chaos of forms and streaks and splotches and dismembered spates of lettering. He studied the lettering, trying to extract words, and could not.

'Language has changed,' Lenna reminded him.

He told her irritably, 'I learned Late Middle English for the reading of Shakespeare originals but I can't recognize anything here.'

'Poverty, Andra. Education was one of the luxuries that went into the discard. Most of the late Swill neither wrote nor read. Those who did couldn't spell.'

The subject common to graffiti the world over appeared again and again in blatant crudity and total lack of draughtsmanship, but the finest example, drawn over all the rest and pristine in reproduction, graced the door of the corner flat. In brilliant, impertinent white a huge penis stretched most of the height of the door, balanced on a pair of gargantuan testicles.

'Strangely,' Lenna said, 'we know that to have been a child's joke. The most extraordinary snippets of information survive. We know quite a lot about the man who lived here.'

'That he was proud enough to leave this on his door?'

'We don't know what he thought. That's a problem in historical reconstruction, that we know what and usually why but so rarely how the people thought about anything.'

'Written records,' he protested.

'Those aren't thoughts so much as afterthoughts, and they generally show it.' She pushed the door open. 'We've tried to reconstruct this flat from scraps of information on a dozen tapes and files, but we still don't know the important thing about the Kovacs family, how its members thought from moment to moment. We can only extrapolate – meaning guess.'

She urged him gently inside.

His immediate reaction was that nobody in such surroundings could think at all. In the first room were two single beds and between them a roughly carpentered rocking chair; on one side, between the foot of a bed and the end wall, stood a small table which could unfold to some two metres and, leaning behind it, four pews folded flat. The floor was covered with a shiny, patterned material which Andra bent to touch.

'What is it?'

9

'They called it plastic linoleum. We had to manufacture a substitute – it wears quickly.'

Behind him, next to the door, a grey one-and-a-half metre screen filled the available space; below it an array of knobs and terminals was lettered with abbreviations he could not follow.

'Television?'

'They called it a triv; it was a general purpose communication centre. They hadn't advanced to crystal web projection. That's one of the few things we do better than they.'

Marin said sharply, 'We *use* everything better. We live better, think better.'

Andra spoke without looking round. 'Be a good fellow and give your spleen a rest.'

He moved to the next room. Here were two double-tiered bunks with a chair between and footlockers at the ends. On the walls cartoon pictures danced – anthropomorphized cats, dogs, mice and a large, fat-bellied, ineffably good-natured bear.

'For children?'

'Surely. Eleven people lived in this flat, most of them children. We suppose they slept two to a bed in here.'

Something essential was missing. 'Where did they store their clothes?'

'A short answer might be, what clothes? They had little beyond necessities. Probably they folded them at night and used them as pillows.'

He shivered again, unable to control pity and a creeping, unreasonable shame. At the same time his planning mind was creating a stage set – a full-width apartment with sections of the next one and at the other end the outdoor balcony – sliding walls, fold downs – the whole thing on turnover with the outer wall on the reverse, with crystal web illusion to give length and perspective – lifts, shifts, turntables, scrims, all in constant motion to allow actors access to flats above and below – and all alive with restless, shabby, desperate, pulsating life . . . odour stimulation to provide a discreet hint of animal sweat at moments of crowded energy . . .

The third room was comparative luxury – one double bed, one chair, one small cupboard, a table and, surprisingly, a bookcase.

'This was the only concession he allowed himself. A private room to run to.'

'Who?'

'Kovacs. Billy Kovacs. He was the Tower Boss, a man of great authority, feared and loved.'

Andra knelt to the books. 'Encyclopaedias, dictionaries, an atlas, children's primers. For teaching his children?'

'For teaching himself. He had vision of a sort. In an earlier day they might have called him a Renaissance Man.' Andra pulled at a huge, ancient tome. 'Don't. They're dummies. His own copies were dust long ago – they were old and dated when he owned them.'

The busy internal note-taker muttered to itself, Now *there's* a character I could play – gutter visionary – tall, tough, *no*, shuffling, slightly hunchbacked with raging eyes, *no*, stop being obvious, file it for later . . .

The two small end rooms were respectively a tiny kitchen and a shower recess with lavatory stool. 'No laundrapool,' he commented before the foolishness of that struck him.

Lenna made scrubbing motions. 'Kitchen sink. Rough soap and muscle power.'

'I can't take this in. I want to go outside. I'll look in again in a day or two.'

Marin said, 'Try to imagine the smell of eleven grimy bodies, meals cooking and a blocked sewer. The noise of screeching kids and desperate adults bawling at their nerves' ends.'

Andra went straight out of the place and back to the powercraft. In the density of the vision conjured by his creativity he was sweat-stinking, revolted, need-driven and guilty before the 70,000 ghosts of Tower Twenty-three.

2

The university had been built 1,000 metres up on the forward slopes of the Dandenongs, its south faces looking out over the foothills where the New City sprawled in smug comfort, over the islands which had been the outskirts of the Old City and, further, over the water which was its grave. Its low buildings camouflaged by trees, the university was nearly invisible by day but now, with the sun westering down to the horizon and searching out window glass, it could be detected in brilliant blazes under the green.

In Lenna's flat, on the southern rim of the campus, Andra drank her imported coffee – New Guinea Highland, Mutated, *very* draining on credit – and gazed out over the islands and the bay. After the afternoon calm it was visibly tumultuous, even at this twenty-kilometre remove, grey and streaked and ominous; closer, just outside the panoramic window, branches whipped and shrubs bent before the wind.

He was a Sydney man, new to this southern phenomenon of an evening gale which lashed the sun down into the water before dying away into silent night. 'Is it regular, every night?'

Lenna, fortyish and lazily plump, was content to take her coffee at ease in a lounger. 'Quite regular. In winter, longer and colder.'

'A trend?'

'Possibly. The meteorologists will not commit themselves. This may be a limited, minor weather cycle but it will take a decade of observation and measurement to be sure.'

'I saw animals swimming in the bay as we came back. Marin said they were seals.'

She smiled at his unwillingness to ask the obvious question. 'Yes. They are coming further north as the polar currents edge up the coast.'

'I've read – he hesitated with the uncertainty of the amateur before a more precisely trained mind, – I've read that the Ice Age could strike very quickly.'

'In historical terms, that's true, but quickly to a historian may mean a couple of centuries.' He looked ridiculously relieved, she thought, as though he had suspected it of waiting to catch him before bedtime. 'There will probably be a succession of cold snaps – very sudden and very cold, each lasting a decade or so – before the interglacial ends and the ice closes in. There's little chance that you will see it happen.'

'I don't wish to, I like the world as it is.' But he had been deeply affected by the towers and the sense of an immense past thirty or forty metres below the keel, brought face to face in his creative imagination with the vastness of changes that had metamorphosed a planet as mindlessly as cosmic eruptions destroyed and created stars.

Lenna said, 'We know this interglacial is approaching its end. The Greenhouse melted the poles and the glaciers, and those won't reform overnight, but the conditions that will finally recreate them will freeze the bones of the planet long before.'

'And humanity that has just struggled out of a second Dark Age will have its back to the wall again.'

'Don't be dramatic about history. We're very well equipped to endure a million years of cold. Our ancestors weathered an Ice Age in caves and animal skins, hunting with flint-tipped spears. I'll be surprised if we don't do reasonably well with insulation technology and fusion power. Besides, the equatorial zone will almost certainly be ice-free and temperate. An Ice Age is no great tragedy – it is in fact the normal state of the planet. We have knowledge and we have the Forward Planning Centres. We'll make the change smoothly.'

Outside, the sun vanished and the evening wind slackened perceptibly. The sky darkened. In the foothills, street lights made sudden patterns of habitation.

Andra made a short, trained, dramatic gesture to the scattered tower Enclaves fading into darkness. 'As I understand it, if I've followed the historical line correctly, *they* knew what was coming to them just as we know what is ahead of us. Yet they did nothing about it.'

'They fell into destruction because they *could* do nothing about it; they had started a sequence which had to run its course in unbalancing the climate. Also, they were bound into a web of interlocking systems – finance, democratic government, what they called high-tech, defensive strategies, political bared teeth and maintenance of a razor-edged status quo – which plunged them from crisis to crisis as each solved problem spawned a nest of new ones. There was a tale of a boy who jammed his finger in the leak in the dyke – I think it's still in kindergarten primers. In the twentieth and twenty-first centuries the entire planet stood with its fingers plugging dykes of its own creation until the sea washed over their muddled status quo. Literally.' She gestured. 'It's all there for you to read.'

Andra put down his coffee and crossed the the low table (solid ebony, he noted with collector's envy) where lay the eleven great fat folders titled *A Preliminary Survey of Factors Affecting the Collapse of the Greenhouse Culture in Australia.*

Preliminary! There must be 5,000 sheets here, a million words. Who could extract dramatic data from such a torrent? In the terms of his research grant he had just one week . . . Wondering how to put this to her without offence, he asked, gaining time, 'Was the Australian situation so different from that of the other continents?'

'Possibly better in many respects. I chose Australia for a laboratory specimen because I am here and because covering the world in comparative analysis would swallow my lifetime. Others can check my work against their observations elsewhere.'

Andra said shyly, exerting conscious charm to cover his wariness of tutorial pride, 'And I'm afraid that reading all that would swallow my research week.'

Sunk too far in the lounger, Lenna struggled to her feet, gasping laughter. 'Heavens, man, I don't expect you to read it. It's a specialist work; you'd need a general historical and technical grounding to get anything much out of it.' She picked out a single folder. 'I've marked passages here which should be useful, but there's no point in your attacking the whole opus.'

Thankfully he scanned the subtitle, forbidding enough: *The State in balance with the Sweet/Swill dichotomy*, but at least he knew what the words meant. 'Should I start on this tonight?'

She took it from him. 'Later, perhaps. There's something else I'd rather you read first.' She bit her lip, seeming at a loss for words, as though their positions were mysteriously reversed and she in awe of his special expertise. 'It is a less . . . *formal* presentation.'

Dear light of sanity, but she's written a bloody play and wants me to read it. Years of ghastly amateur scripts flooded his memory. But how could he refuse his assigned tutor?

'Actually,' she said, 'it's a sort of novel.'

Better, much better. He wouldn't have to explain to her that her coddled work was neither stageable nor rescuable. (Besides, he intended to write this play himself.)

She carried on breathlessly, 'The thing is, I want a popular audience. I haven't spent twelve years on this to see it buried in the data files for plunder by students in search of a theme. I want to correct the public idea of what our ancestors were like. All they have is folklore and guesswork and idiotic popular plays that can't get so much as the clothing right.'

He sympathized. He had appeared in some of them before he became Andra Andrasson who could pick and choose his roles, demand a Shakespearean revival and get it – and make it pay.

He said with automatic enthusiasm, 'That sounds just the thing! I'd love to read it.' It didn't matter how bad it might be so long as all the precise, accurate detail could be lifted out of it . . . 'You said, a *sort* of a novel.'

'I meant that it is not an imagined fiction. It is researched. All the characters lived and left records on tape and in data banks. There are descriptions, even pictures and police records providing detail.'

A true story. The artist's kiss of death. The terror of publishers' readers.

She said, 'The flat we saw today . . .' and trailed off, to try again. 'I've written it round the Tower Boss, Billy Kovacs.'

'You have?' His sudden vehemence startled her. She could not see the surge of images latent, waiting for the name to release them.

14

The Renaissance Man from the gutter.

Loved and feared.

From a crowded hovel in a termite heap ruling an immured nation of 70,000 suffering ghosts.

Teaching himself from old books while children screamed and scampered round his feet.

Fighting for – for what? – For some decency and order while the ocean rose?

A symbol.

'Where is it?' She found herself facing a man lost in a need. 'Give it to me!'

Back in his room his preparation amounted to no more than kicking off his dress shoes and piling cushions on the bed to prop himself for reading. A small voice at the back of his mind suggested that he had been overbearing, discourteous and precipitate in rushing off with his prize, but surely the woman understood devotion to an idea. Hadn't she spent twelve years on hers? In any case, said a more urgent mental voice, he had the book and could deal with hurt feelings later.

It was on a recorder block no larger than his palm which meant, presumably, that it was in final draft; he might have arrived just in time to intercept it. He slipped the block into its vent under the screen, took up the remote control, settled himself on the bed and set the scanner operating. The screen turned black and the first dull yellow letters appeared:

The Sea and Summer

A Historical Reconstruction

by

Lenna Williams

No parade of doctoral honorifics. He flicked off the title page and a cluster of Acknowledgments, passed quickly over the Contents – mainly uninformative proper names – steadied the first page of text in the frame and enlarged the image until at five metres he could read easily.

He was a thoughtful reader rather than a fast one, a visualizer who might take a full day over a playscript, creating each scene and movement as the dialogue set the author's dummies in motion. A novel was, to him, a playscript with more explicit stage directions.

The first short chapter was atmospheric stuff, nice enough as an introduction, a lulling of the reader into a specific receptivity. In dramatic form it would disappear altogether, replaced by lighting, music and subliminals.

The second chapter got smartly down to business. He recognized a screen-based technique at work, selective rather than consecutive. It seemed very simply presented . . .

. . . until he came without warning upon an attitude of mind, unheralded and unexplained, which balked his immediate perception. He thought about it. *It's no use saying we don't have social distinctions, because we do, but they tend to be lateral rather than vertical, a partitioning-off of equals. This Sweet/Swill cleavage is hard to take, too final, too artificial. But it seems central to the Greenhouse Culture.*

It made better sense when he came upon mention of the Fringe, the interface between the lordly and the lorded over. The Fringe did not figure in the popular folklore which concentrated on the savageries of the cleavage. Audiences, he admitted sourly, like their subtleties simplified; they demand intellection without the need for thought.

He rolled off the bed to hunt for the pens and pad which should be in supply, found them in a desk which unfolded from the wall, returned to the bed and made a note: *How did this division arise? Why no revolution?*

He read very slowly for two hours, making several pages of questions for Lenna. At this snail pace he would occupy two days ingesting this novel of ordinary length, stopping and starting and at length visualizing in enormous detail.

As his concentration flickered, he switched off. Visualization was the hurdle; he must study archive pictures of the Fringe houses, assuming they existed, obtain accurate details of dress and re-examine those decrepit towers at close range, perhaps dive to street level. Only with a grasp of background could he make Kovacs move amid the heaving squalor and latent violence of his time.

THE SEA AND SUMMER 1

1

ALISON CONWAY
AD 2061

When I was a little girl going to kindergarten we had the annual glories of the sea and summer. We brats – at that age we are all brats with angel smiles hiding the designs of demons – paddled from the beach at Elwood while the sun showered down bright splinters on the blue-green bay.

Summer! Paradisal time of cold drinks and coloured salads, skimpy frocks and games under the garden hose, days at the seaside with sunburn and jellyfish, sand and seaweed and lush wavelets of cuddling water. Playtime without end!

Yet every year there was an end called winter with lead-heavy clouds and storms on the bay, long woollies and cold mornings, rain on window panes and the fear that summer might not return.

Summer always returned. It was winter that faded imperceptibly from the round of the planet's seasons while magical summer grew humid and threatening and tropically wet. There were mild winters, then warmish winters, then short winters that merged into extended autumns without any real winter at all. Sleet and hail and frost became memories of 'the old days' and their occasional freak appearances disturbed us, menacing the new order of perpetual summer, perpetual holiday.

Lovely changes came to our gardens as plants were tricked by the falsehoods of the weather and some grew to extraordinary sizes. Roses like sunflowers, dandelions half a metre tall, pansies like velvet plates! *It's the extra CO_2* explained the neighbourhood know alls, *it feeds some plants but it kills others.* Which others? We saw no others; they had died off and gone away. They explained, too, that the CO_2 was a farming disaster, that the wheat belt was shifting south and being crammed against the coast and the old wheat belt was already a dust bowl, forcing whole populations to move and leave ghost towns whispering in an empty countryside.

Didn't they know it would happen? Oh, yes, 'they' knew; back in the 1980s 'they' were warned but 'they' were busy. 'They' had the nuclear threat and the world population pressure and the world starvation problem and the terrorist outbreaks and the strikes and the corruption in high places shaking hands with crime in low places, and the endless business of simply trying to stay in power – all to be attended to *urgently*. They weren't attended to; 'they' tried but the troubles were too big, too well entrenched to be amenable to sense or force – and the emerging troubles of the next decade had to be left until there was time, until feasibility studies could be made, the problems seen in proper context, the finance found . . .

Suddenly the next decade was here, with urgent new disasters and no sign of containment of the old. It couldn't all be blamed on the CO_2 but the saturation level surely helped. Helped us on down to misery and want.

How wonderful it would be now to wake one morning to a near-zero temperature and a wind of winter heralding the old world's return.

Instead we have the sea and summer. The sea is rising over the beaches of the world; the coastal cities face death by drowning. Day by day the water advances up the streets from the shores and rivers; our placid old Yarra was long ago forced over its banks by the rising tides. The coast roads have vanished and the lower floors of the tenements are uninhabitable.

The ageing woman has what the child desired – the sea and eternal summer.

2

FRANCIS CONWAY
AD 2041–2044

1

In 2041 the population of the planet passed the 10 billion mark. My life has been determined by the webs and progressions of numbers and this one impressed itself on me because it had been reached a decade earlier than the predictors hoped, and because it was sufficiently frightening for the how and why to be discussed by my parents, and probably by whole nations uneasily aware of their world closing in on them. But the how and why were beyond me and anyhow irrelevant to a six-year-old's concerns.

Teddy, three years older, pretended understanding, but Teddy always pretended understanding and I didn't believe him. As things turned out I should have paid more attention to his boasting.

Aside from my sixth birthday (birthdays were major events then) and my first sight of the sea (something of a non-event) the marker memory of that year is the shame put on me at school when the single talent that distinguished me from others was derided and shown to be a waste, a nothing. More of that in its right place; it had much to do with shaping my life.

But first the non-event, the sea which meant so little then but is now the hungry maw on whose lip we teeter.

2041 was a golden year. Dad would say that things had never been worse, that the whole damned human race was drifting to destruction, but Six-Year-Old had only to see sunlight on the grass to know that this was Dad talk, just as complaint about the meat ration was Mum talk.

These complaints were mysteries, anomalies, for Mum was all fun and laughter and Dad had a job and all was right with the world. Dad had a job . . . so we were Sweet. Not Big Sweet, only a sort of Middle Sweet, but certainly not Swill. Nobody knows how and when those two words twisted themselves into the language. We kids were born to the knowledge that Sweet had jobs and income while Swill lived on State charity. Even servants could look down on Swill. Actually, very few Sweet kids of the day had ever seen a Swill person; the ghetto lines were firmly drawn by the time we arrived. Nine of every ten of Australia's population were Swill and many other countries were in worse case. Living familiarly with such knowledge, the horror of it passed us by; it was the normal condition of the world.

Swill was only a word. Reality was *our* life, secure against fate. We had our own four-roomed house on our own standard block, with two metres of lawn strip in front and three metres of back yard and a share in the community satellite dish. We were the equals of any in our district and more equal than most because Dad owned a car.

Battery hovercraft, or indeed any modern private transport might be owned only by Very Big Sweet, but Dad was a member of Vintagers and loved the Old Bomb he had inherited from his own father, who had loved it for forty years before that. (In Grandfather's time, Dad said, everybody had a car. It's hard to imagine.) It was an expensive love. He spent most of his spare time tuning the engine, polishing the 'duco' or searching the hobby markets for parts; it was a 1986 model and one of only a few hundred petrol burners in the whole country. He drove it only once a month because petrol was unobtainable on the open market and he paid a lover's price for contraband; also, there was only one place in Melbourne where tyres could be laboriously retreaded and none where they could be bought. Mum grudged the cost of that monthly outing but enjoyed the little edge of superiority over the next-doors.

On my birthday I was allowed the choice of where to go on our outing and this year I, no doubt with some recent triv programme in mind, demanded a trip to the beach. Nobody showed enthusiasm and Teddy said with weary condescension, 'There isn't any beach.'

For once I knew better. 'I've seen it on the triv!'

'That's some other place. There isn't any on Port Phillip.'

Dad interfered. 'It's Francis's choice and we'll go to the bay.' He didn't seem to look forward to it.

Teddy decided to stay home. 'There's nothing to see. I've been there. I know.' He went through his routine of removing his attention but we knew that he would change his mind, boredly pandering to a younger brother's whim. I wasn't big enough to risk hitting him.

Usually our trips took us to the Dandenong Range at the city's edge, where from the middle slopes we could see its whole huge sprawl without at all comprehending the intensity of life and movement concealed in the concrete canyons. The various Swill Enclaves were easily visible, grim high-rise blocks towering over all the rest, ten close-packed groups of monoliths snuffling blunt

22

snouts at the sky. I did not wonder then how nine-tenths of the city's 10 millions could be squeezed into one-tenth of its area.

On this day Dad drove in the opposite direction. Road surfaces were still reasonably good in Sweet suburbs and we arrived at the bay quite soon. I saw why we had not come here before; as Teddy had said, there was no beach.

The triv plays often showed beaches with yellow sand sloping to brilliant blue water and children playing while their parents lay in the sun or under bright awnings. On the water there would be yachts with coloured sails and swimmers in the gentle swells.

What I saw was a street of houses like our own, save that one side of the street was simply a cóncrete wall stretching out of sight in both directions. Dad pointed to steps that led to the top of the wall and I got out of the car while Teddy sniggered. The wall was about two metres thick at the top and on the water side it sloped down and out about twice as far; it was a rampart. At the foot of it lay a metre or so of wet, greyish sand amid rocks and gravelly shingle and filthy mats of seaweed. Beyond these, the sea.

In the distance the water was blue but at the shoreline it was grey and unpleasant-looking and choked with more of the seaweed, which writhed in the tide like something not quite dead. And it smelt. Disappointment was too great; I cried out my anger to the sky: 'It stinks!'

Behind me Teddy said, 'Like a blocked sewer.'

It wasn't that bad, only a whiff really, but sewers were part of it. Dad and Mum had come up, Dad patting and stroking as he did when things were too wrong to put right. 'I'm sorry, lad, but it was best to let you see.'

A streak of obstinacy in me persisted, 'But there *are* beaches. On the triv.'

'On the triv,' he agreed, 'but not near the big cities. The nearest decent beach is two hours away.' He wouldn't admit it, but the car couldn't be trusted so far.

Mum surprised me by saying, 'This is Elwood and there was a beach here once. I used to paddle here. Then the water came up and there were the storm years and the pollution, and the water became too filthy . . .' She broke off, realizing that I didn't grasp any of this but Teddy followed on as if he knew all about it, 'It's the Greenhouse effect.'

'Only partly,' Dad corrected him. He always corrected Teddy as if it were important that he get things exactly right, as if he were someone special. 'The global temperature hasn't risen enough yet to cause all this, though the Antarctic ice cap has begun to melt and the sea level has risen very slightly, but changes in the weather pattern have laid us open to tremendous storms.' He lost track of what he was saying, and one thing led to another. 'I remember when the worst storm would only wash a few waves across the road. We didn't need an embankment. And there was a beach . . .'

I could always remember what I didn't understand and recall it later to fit in with new knowledge; I could remember absolutely accurately if it seemed worth the effort. I still can. Numbers and memory have been my salvation and downfall.

Dad recovered briskly. 'One day the ice cap will melt completely and all the coasts of the world will drown. Most of Melbourne will go under sixty metres of water.' He said it like a comment on something that didn't affect him. I did not understand but it sounded huge and memorable. I remembered.

'Not in our time.' That was Teddy, sure as ever.

That phrase haunts all our lives. It has been the cry of the people and of their politicians as well as of scientists who calculated the imminence of disaster and then sought reasons why it should not happen just yet. Refusal to believe is our surety that disaster cannot happen – at any rate, not today. And, every time, it does.

It was left for Mum to say, 'It must be terrible over there in Newport when the river floods.' Dad grimaced because the Swill Enclaves were not much mentioned in polite society; you knew of them and that was enough. But Mum went on, 'A high tide covers the ground levels of the tenements.'

She sounded sorry for the Swill and Dad said, 'Please, Allie,' in his *that's enough* voice.

Across the bay I could see the Newport towers, though not too clearly in the heat shimmer, three kilometres of grey obelisks. Teddy wondered aloud what the Swill would do when the water rose over their heads but Dad had declared the subject closed and would not answer. Perhaps he had no answer.

I tried to imagine the towers peeking through sixty metres of smelly water and millions of washed-out Swill swimming like mad, though I didn't really know what Swill looked like. Like us, I supposed, only ugly and dirty as in a triv play.

After that we went to the hills and had iced cakes and fruit drinks and watched performing animals at an Entertainment Centre and the birthday was saved. But the disappointing sea stayed with me as the reality behind a joyous myth – and later as destiny biding its terrible time.

2

I did not like Teddy but neither did I positively hate him. He drove me to fits of helpless temper, but they passed. We 'got on'. I think that he didn't bother to dislike me then, only saw me as a cross to be borne, a trial to his nine-year-old serenity. The worst of him from my point of view was his determination to monopolize Mum, to establish ownership. Dad he left to me; Teddy's unsentimental eye perceived weakness there before I did. I was welcome to the Old Man.

He was an engineering draughtsman, a designer of machine components, on a computer screen. Today it is hard to imagine such work being left to human fallibility but it was so. The occupation was classified as medium skilled and chances of promotion were slim but, as Dad put it, with 90 per cent of the nation – in fact, of the world – unemployed, it wouldn't pay to raise your sights too high. Memory of him has dimmed. I recall only a balding, worried man who made time to be a loving friend to me.

Mum was the lively one. If I loved her less than Dad, I trusted her more; it was to her that Teddy and I turned for decisions and permissions and the drying of tears. She sang songs and filled the house with the colours of joy; she charmed Dad's moods by teaching him dance steps on the little back porch until his two left feet brought them to a staggering halt in laughter and love.

Teddy resented her joy in anyone but himself; he would turn his back on their happiness, denying it. I think they were unhappy about it, but never mentioned it where we might hear.

But were they so unhappy with him? Teddy was the golden boy (a small thing, but he was always 'Teddy' and I the more formal 'Francis') with Mum's brilliant handsomeness. And Dad's moodiness. I bored him. When our rare open quarrels occurred he would circle his finger at his temple and call me 'figure farter' and stride off, leaving me raging and feeling obscurely contemptible.

It did not enter my mind that his contempt masked jealousy of my one talent, an inability to bear with my outclassing him in anything at all. I did realize that his needling was meant to trick me into explaining how lightning calculation is done; he believed that I wilfully withheld the secret from him, but I could no more explain it then than I could now.

How describe sound to the deaf, light to the blind? Numbers have shape, invisible but apprehended by the mind. Set *this* shape against *that* shape and together they make a different, *product* shape. The answers are always right because when the mind can see them it is not possible to be wrong. Do you understand? Nor do I.

It seemed a useless talent. Every adult had his wrist cally for instant answers or could use a triv terminal for complex mathematics; only quite old people remembered how to do sums with pen and paper. Dad wasn't yet that old but he did know how to work sums on paper, which was lucky for me – it made my future possible. My miniature talent – miniature because undeveloped – was at first unknown to myself. I supposed all kids could do as much if they wanted to.

Revelation came on the night when Dad dropped his wrist cally and stepped on it, cracking the microchip forme. He had brought home some figuring to do; he could have used the triv but he chose to call on Teddy to use his training cally, calling the sums while Teddy punched them out. They were simple sums – a child's training cally could only handle arithmetic – and I sat on the lounge-room carpet, turning my head from Dad to Teddy and wondering why Dad needed to ask and why Teddy had to punch keys for *easy* sums.

At last Dad called, 'Total one through eight,' and I, in a fit of showing off, said, 'Thirty-six,' before Teddy had a key pressed. Teddy paid no attention and carried on his mechanical addition, but Dad looked at me as though about to say something, then decided against it. I know now that he could do these sums by mental arithmetic (which is terribly slow) but preferred everything checked; he didn't trust himself always to be right.

It was Teddy who spoke first when he finished keying, and what he said was, 'You guessed.'

'I didn't.'

'Then how did you know?'

I didn't know how. I muttered, 'I looked at it.'

He sneered at my obvious attempt to lie my way out of a corner but Dad said, 'Add three through nine, Francis,' and I answered at once, 'Forty-two.'

Dad said, 'Check it,' and forty-two it was. I think Teddy would have put me to the torture in that moment; he couldn't bear what he couldn't emulate.

Dad asked, 'And you just *look* at the answers?'

I nodded while Teddy's lips formed the silent 'Bullshit' he didn't dare say aloud. Dad did not seem surprised; the gift is not unique and he was well-enough read to have come across mention of it. He gave me some more easy sums. Teddy refused to co-operate and

26

Dad ignored him. At last he said, 'One through twenty,' and all my expertise deserted me. I wailed, 'I can't see it.'

The trouble was that then I had no mental conception of a number as large as 100 (few people can in fact grasp the totality of more than six or seven objects at a glance) and the proper answer of 210 might have been incomprehensible if I could have seen it. Dad nodded as if he had expected something of the sort and asked if I could do division and multiplication, but I didn't know what they were.

'Tomorrow night I'll show you what they are. Then we'll see what you can do.'

Mum spoke from across the room. 'He's only a little boy, Fred. Don't push him.'

'Push? Allie, for him it's effortless.'

She pursed her lips and refused to argue in front of us but there was argument after we went to bed, with Mum saying obstinately that she 'didn't like it'. Then the door closed and we heard no more.

Mum was the social member of the family, and neighbours were on her mind when she objected to Dad's teaching me. Teddy was 'bright'; that was acceptable so long as we didn't make too much of it, but an aptitude for figures among people who couldn't add a shopping list without their callies would be seen as freakish, 'uppity', not acceptable. Yet Dad had his way. Mum pretended to take no notice and Teddy ignored the whole thing, so I was able to learn. Weak personalities get their way by being mulish.

Once I had grasped the idea that multiplication and division were only different ways of arranging the shapes they were over and done with. The 'large number' problem Dad dealt with by showing them to be as products of smaller, more accessible numbers. Fractions were hard to visualize except for the simpler ones and I sometimes balk still at fractions involving large primes, but decimals were a breeze and led at once to the table of logarithms which, once explained, I worked out for myself.

All this took a few marvellous weeks, with Dad warm and loving in our private world of numbers. Mum's disapproval moderated when my behaviour did not mutate into anything socially peculiar. Only Teddy blighted my pride. Each night when our light had been put out he would murmur words impossible in our parents' presence. Just loudly enough to poison my descent into sleep would come his goodnight: 'Fuckin' figure farter.'

He was telling me that beside him I was nothing and always would be. I cried but accepted myself as second rate.

Nevertheless I had every kid's dream of strutting it as the centre of attention, and this led to my downfall. In this my sixth year I left playschool for junior school, where we had to attend and learn instead of absorbing social morality by rubbing against each other's personalities in play situations. We discovered maps and the hugely meaningless size of the world. We were introduced to primers, though most could read after a fashion from deciphering the titles on the triv. We learned the tedious hooks and unions of cursive script, though few adults other than those in specialized occupations used it for more than random note-taking. (It emerged, in an aside, that Swill homes did not have word-processing vox-assemblies and we wondered how they would be able to do anything at all. There were mean legends about the Swill and such snippets fed them.)

Then there was the training calculator, the child's first simple cally. The first lesson was an explanation of the meaning of addition, followed by a practice session in which our fingers on keys demonstrated that two and two were for ever mysteriously four. Vanity overcame the herd instinct to lie low. I announced that I didn't need the cally and could 'do numbers faster than you punch the keys'.

The immediate response was scornful giggling from my peers and a demand that I prove my words, and our flustered teacher decided that the boast should be confirmed or exposed. She was probably only basically educated and out of her depth when I justified my bragging. More experienced assistance was needed to accommodate such genius.

For an hour of glory I was shown off to senior staff, adding and subtracting, multiplying and dividing as fast as the tests were devised. They applauded with tight smiles my innocence could not read. How could I know that these invincible adults, wrapped in wisdom, were all Teddys, hating to be upstaged, or that nobody, literally nobody, learned to figure in his head? When I mentioned logarithms the exhibition collapsed in grim silence and I was told, in a crash of reality, that I could now return to the classroom and learn the cally like everybody else.

In the playground at lunchtime the other kids paid me the full price for being the one righteous man in a world of vengeful sinners.

Then, at home . . . Teddy, in his senior class, had heard about what he termed my 'nightclub act', and now he rammed humiliation in my teeth with a taunting, 'Put you back in your box, didn't they!' Stung beyond caution, blind with self pity, I rushed at him, to meet a nonchalant straight left that set me howling on my arse in Mum's vegetable patch.

Mum murmured darkly that nobody listened to her advice and when Dad came home confronted him with the tragic outcome of his meddling. High words were followed by a sentimental session in which I bawled happily in Dad's arms while he explained that the world was full of people who wanted to drag you down to their level. I learned to hold my silly tongue but was always a fumbler on the cally keys, mis-hitting through sheer lack of interest in the slow machine.

In the next two years little happened in the small world of childhood. Living in a cocooned, cushioned 'four-room, free standing, smart suburb, 2.5 metre triv,' we were unaware of having been born into what an old Chinese curse considered 'interesting times'.

How interesting became evident when Dad was 'superannuated'.

3

I must reconstruct the background of that year of my ninth birthday, because 2044 was a pivotal year for the Conways. That Australia was in far worse case than could be measured by the fortunes of one obscure family did not impinge; a child has no grasp of impersonal disasters. The stretching of my country on the rack of history did not touch my snug youth.

Twenty thirty-three had been the year in which the pressure of world powers, helpless before the rocketing birth rate, forced us to give away a third of Australia's empty hectares to those ant-hordes of Asians squeezed from their paddy-fields by swarming fecundity.

Adult Sweet, with their comfortable lives hanging on knife edges of global politics, dared not protest against the coercion by the Great Powers – and so a number of dispossessed landowners, uncompensated by a bankrupt Treasury, vanished into the Swill and were heard of no more. The Swill, who believed that things could only get far worse before they failed once and for all to get better, showed little interest. Few had ever seen countryside, let alone the outback. Desert, drought and flies, wasn't it? So let the Veets and Chinks and Indons have it. No place for a white man.

Not much of a place for a yellow man, either; two-thirds of Australia has been uninhabitable through millennia, and to that area we admitted him. He set out to make it habitable and in a measure succeeded. He concentrated the weather-control techniques that

29

had been accumulating in cautious experiment for thirty years before and produced a torrential rainfall programme, which disrupted planetary weather until international outcry forced moderation. Then he poured megatonnes of soil conditioner and fertilizer into the ground and in a surprisingly short time polluted not only the coastal rivers and the water table but the artesian reservoirs as well. Potable water became as scarce in Australia as in those other parts of the world where expensive iceberg tows and desalination plants brought desperate economies closer to collapse.

By 2044 we accepted shortages as part of life; we were reared on interrupted supplies of water and power and of any food that could not be grown in the back yard. Our parents were inured to minor deprivations and we kids didn't know there was all that much to protest about.

Reference to a recent past without deprivations did not appear in school histories and rarely in printed sources (in any case, we had got out of the way of consulting printed sources) and certainly not in the sanitized trivcasts. I knew about the population problem, of course; everybody knew about that. But an annual increase of $1\frac{3}{4}$ per cent doesn't sound much, even when you work it out as doubling every four decades or so.

How should it when you are nine years old and living the good life?

About Dad: 'superannuated' was the word because 'sacked' and 'fired' had assumed meanings too nearly terminal. The lie that automation would for ever continue to create new employment died long before its full effects were felt, but automation proliferated as the only means of maintaining competitiveness; then, with 90 per cent of the planet on subsistence, where was the buying public for what competitiveness provided? The computer culture had its back to the wall but the working, salaried minority didn't dare look at the cracking wall. Who had a job was Sweet!

One day Dad came home early and silent and did not speak to us but went into the kitchen where Mum was preparing tea. And shut the door.

Teddy said, 'Something's up,' and slipped his shoes off. I followed him down the passage. Alone, I would not have dared to eavesdrop but small courage followed a leader. Listening, we learned something about our world.

Dad was explaining to Mum, in a monotone that stumbled and faded and ran into dead ends of speech. He was telling her how progress, magical progress, had squirted him from between its cogs as new techniques erased the human element from creative design. Given a base print and a specification, the new computers sorted millions of alternatives to spit out in minutes the optimum shape of a new component. An entire Department was 'superannuated' that day; in the places of eighty men and women, two processor screens brooded over untenanted desks. 'Superannuation' had once meant something like a pension. No longer.

Dad didn't seem able to stop; he went on and on as if for the first time he saw what had existed all his life. He puzzled over the way in which, across the world, thousands of men and women were tossed on to the job market every hour. And that was a buyer's market. No one *looked* for a job; infallible Central Data matched fortunate applicant to rare vacancy with disinterested precision. In a shrinking market few fluked two jobs in a lifetime.

The lucky 10 per cent – not necessarily the best but those whose capacities matched the requirement of the moment – were Sweet. For life, if their luck held. For the luckless there was the Suss – State Subsistence – the bare means of staying alive . . . in the Swill tenements. No government on Earth could provide better in the day of automated collapse; many could not provide at all.

He said these things until he had emptied his head of them. Through it all Mum did not speak and it was terrible that she found nothing to say. More terrible were the tears in Dad's voice. I had not known that grown-ups could cry.

There was a worse thing, the expression on Teddy's face. He had no pity for Dad, only a sneer for weakness.

Mum spoke at last, so quietly that we could make out nothing. We fled when Dad came stumbling out of the kitchen and slammed the bedroom door behind him.

Teddy dared what I would never have done – he went into the kitchen to ask, 'What's wrong, Mum?' as if it could be only some small daily affair. She continued preparing our tea with unthinking motions. She might not have heard him.

We went back to the lounge room. Dad's talk about Swill made no mark on my mind. That was about other people, not us. I studied Teddy's withdrawn face and wondered why he hated Dad so much.

After a while Mum called steadily, 'Come to your tea, boys.' We heard her knock on the bedroom door, and knock again.

Teddy said, 'He's sulking.'

Mum must have gone in then, so we tiptoed after her to see what they were doing. They were doing nothing, except that Mum couldn't stop shuddering at the end of the bed where Dad lay in the

31

red muddle of sheets and blankets and blood from his slashed throat.

Time slowed while I failed to comprehend this new thing – death. I floundered around an empty space in my mind while Teddy crept to Mum and she put out a groping hand to him. Holding it, he leaned over Dad, with *that* look on his face and screamed like a demon, 'Rotten coward!'

For the only time in his life, I think, Mum hit him, a wild, swinging blow powered by misery and lost love. He fell down, banging his head against the wall, and stayed there, blazing with rage. His rage was against her, something I had never dreamed in him, but she seemed to forget him at once and sat looking down at her hands as if there some message might lie. In Teddy's fury I recognized what must have lurked unformed in my mind, that his love for Mum had been only his need for notice; he loved only Teddy.

When my eyes wandered back to the blood I began to howl. Mum said in a quiet, ordinary voice, 'Do be quiet, Francis,' as though I had interrupted a train of thought or compounded a headache. She lifted her eyes to the empty air, to some vision past my guessing. She stared, I suppose, at the future.

In the morning she said little but had put stupor behind her. In the night she must have taken hold and seen what she must do.

She sent us off to school, most likely to get us out of the way and without thinking that the news of catastrophe might be there before us, in the lightspeed way of a community network. Like this: she had notified the Departments of Employment and Finance as the law required; they in turn had notified the Essential Services subsections and somewhere along the line a neighbour had been the Data Supervisor on duty. The news became at once local gossip.

No one at school referred to it openly; Sweet social conventions were based on a refinement of delicacy called 'decent considera-tion', but kids have their own cruel ways of making meaning plain. What mattered was not the suicide (that was perfectly understand-able) but that Dad had lost his job. The implications of this were gossip lollipops – the Conways were on their way down! Blatant avoidance of the subject kept it hot and visible.

Sympathy could not in 'decent consideration' be offered. Loss was private. A family should just drop out, vanish. Friends and neighbours should not be made to bear the pain – fear – of failure.

Codes of manners made painless the misfortunes of others; we ran gauntlets of barbed silence.

When we got home Dad was gone, the bedroom spotless and Mum prepared to talk again. (When did she weep, mourn, despair? We never knew.) She asked in the interested tone she kept for our small affairs, 'How was your day?'

I said, 'All right,' having no words for impalpable discomforts and inaudible jeers, but Teddy could always find words: 'Nobody called us Swill. Not yet.'

She said, 'Sit down,' and we sat while she spoke in a hard tone we would get used to. 'This family is not Swill and will not be. We cannot stay in this house but we will not be reduced to the tenements. Tell everybody that.'

The kids would have called that bluff without mercy; to them you were Sweet or you were Swill. Teddy went to the core of it: 'They'll say, if you aren't Swill why are you leaving?'

Mum knew what was unsaid, that neighbours as well as their young could be infinitely disgusting. 'Don't go back to that school. I'll arrange it.' And she did.

Next day at the Cremation Centre we saw the shamed thing, wrapped in black plastic, vanish through the automatic doors; impersonal music played from a tape that needed reclarifying. Bland relatives attended but no friends; friends could plead 'decent consideration' but in fact had already distanced themselves, as if our condition might be contagious.

After that affairs moved with speed. Once Mum had been allocated a place to live, everything could be done with triv calls to the proper Departments. Sales and Rental repossessed the house at the calculated market price, which left Mum in a raging mood because it was mulcted for small repairs which it claimed Dad should have made. 'Instead of polishing the duco,' Teddy said, unwisely, and her glare silenced him for hours.

She got a good price for the car by calling on the Vintagers who already knew its value. Strangers bought it; covetous friends stayed away. When Teddy sneered at their defection Mum took their part, saying that one must live with society as it exists; there was a saying that you couldn't touch pitch and not be defiled. Teddy said, 'They're superstitious, that's all,' and she replied, 'No, they're frightened. Any of them may be next. They don't want to think about it.'

That's another sentence that haunts our lives. It's a great shaper of history, that record of disasters we didn't want to think about.

Our new home was allocated by Housing computer search, based on Mum's statement of what we could afford, and she was very thoughtful when she learned where it was. She did not complain, because the computers gave the best available match between need and ability to pay, but the information shocked her.

She told us, 'It's closer to the tenements than I would have liked,' as if her new hardness had been pierced by a needle of doubt. 'It's in Newport.' I recalled the day at the beach and Newport in the distance and what she had said about floods. It wouldn't apply to us, though. That was only about Swill.

I had sense enough to keep a certain private excitement to myself. Kids whispered about the Swill but really knew nothing about them and the idea of proximity (safe proximity, of course) had a touch of adventure about it. I could not realize what the social disaster meant to Mum or the well of terror into which her life had fallen. Equally, I could not help but realize that the light and joy had gone out of her. They never came back.

4

We moved before dawn. The hovervan crew probably charged extortionately for running so early but Mum said she wasn't about to make a show for spiteful neighbours pretending to potter in their gardens while the corners of their turned-away eyes absorbed the thrill of another downfall. We travelled in the back of the van because what had been only money was now treasure for hoarding.

There was a long drive in darkness before the dawn caught us. Then, staring out from amid our boxes and furnishings, I saw vast grey towers rearing on either side as our route took us through the heart of a Swill Enclave. I held my breath in a fascination of fright and curiosity, expecting horrors, but there were only empty streets where nothing stirred, sky-stabbing piles whose windows were dark save for a very occasional light like a little star set in a concrete wall and such silence as tombs are made for. The millions of workless Swill slept, having nothing better to do.

From the Enclave we crossed the river into a middle-class district much like the one we had left. In the early light I saw, not far away, the palaces of City Centre, not repetitious monoliths like the tenements but mysteries of dawn-lit colour and form. Some day, I promised myself, I would visit City Centre, the grandest of all surroundings. (So, eventually, I did, to discover that the palaces were office blocks and heartless, bustling hives.) But now we passed it by.

The drive seemed endless and it was bright day when we saw our street. It was like nothing in my experience. The houses were all different. In our old street each house had its touches of colour and decoration but all were built to an orderly plan; this street was a jumble. Many of the houses were built of what I came to know as 'brick' and shared a common wall instead of being separated by fences, while others were constructed of overlapping planks of timber on which paint had faded and cracked. There were slate roofs, which I had never seen before, and what I learned were 'tiles', and others of unbelievable corrugated iron all warped and loose and rusted where the paint had flaked away. There were iron-roofed verandahs instead of awnings and some of these loomed right on to the footpath with no garden space at all.

As if she saw into my mind Mum murmured, 'This is a very old part of Melbourne. Some of these houses were built over a hundred years ago.' She was apologizing.

It was depressing. There were few garden trees and no nature strip in the footpath, which itself was asphalt (also never seen before), holed and uneven, while the gutter was formed of big, squarish stones. All the windows were narrow and secretive; the street and everything in it was shabby and untidy, having given away pride.

Our new house was brick, its two halves separated by a passage with a front door in the middle. We were to have only half of it – three rooms to ourselves and a share in kitchen and bathroom – and small rooms made it much less than we were used to, In front was a verandah with a wooden floor whose planks were broken in places and a strip of garden overgrown with weeds, uncared for.

The owners, an old couple, watched us from the verandah like a pair of scruffy birds, with that look of grubbiness which so often comes unfairly to the old. They exchanged words we could not hear with expressionless faces, pretending they were not assessing us for the squeezing of extras.

Teddy, as usual, found words. 'It's a stinking slum.'

It was not quite that but its time was running out; only two blocks distant the tenement towers cut the sky. We had missed Swilldom by a thrilling hair's breadth. Thrilling? Swill horror country was also triv serial adventure country from which brave policemen or brave young scientists or brave and muscular footballers rescued beautiful girls held captive for purposes not fully understood.

As the vanman lugged our belongings on to the footpath I saw the first live Swill person in my experience.

He leaned against the picket fence, quite still except for his gently moving jaws. He was about Dad's age, middle forties, but lanky and fleshless as if his bones stretched his skin; he didn't look starved, more as if his body held only what was useful to it. He was narrow – face, nose, pointed chin – and he had no expression at all; he simply looked and didn't seem to care whether he saw anything or not, and chewed. Triv thriller lore identified him as a 'chewer', addicted to a vice not mentioned in respectable suburbs; the schoolkid legend had it that chewing turned your skin yellow and you went blind and your tossle fell off.

He was neither blind nor yellow and didn't look as though anything might be missing, but his shirt and trousers and old canvas shoes were so filthy that Mum would have thrown them out. He was unshaven, his brownish hair fell raggedly over his forehead and neck and he looked as if he would smell.

Also – a terrific touch, this – he wore a knife at his belt and this in triv lore made him a local gang leader. (Curiously, half correct.) But why was he here? The triv rule was that Swill came into Sweet areas only in marauding gangs, but I saw no gang. Ours was a corner house and I peeped round into the next street to make sure.

He spat a gobbet of grey stuff across the footpath into the cobbled gutter, so I had my first sight of the masticated, half-digested 'opiate of the unwashed' and my silly breast seethed with the exciting wickedness of it. (Disappointing to discover later that the 'chew' is an almost harmless mild narcotic with few side effects.)

Teddy hissed at me, 'Stop looking at him! He stinks!' Even Teddy couldn't smell him at five metres but he turned his back to register contempt.

The chewer had sharp ears; his eyes were instantly aware and the narrow mouth widened to grin some contempt of its own. Then, to my hypnotized ecstasy, he closed one eye at me in a ferocious, entrancing, conspiratorial wink.

Then Mum called me to help carry some loose things into the house; the vanmen lumped the heavy furniture inside and we inspected our new home.

Mum said nothing but I might have cried if I hadn't been afraid of Teddy's sneering. There were no built-in cupboards or shelves, the walls were dirty and the ceiling was cracked; the floors gave underfoot and the triv was an old, half-size model from years back. After our big double-glazed windows and fadeless paint this was a prison. Through the three rooms our furniture lay in a clutter of mattresses, dismantled tables and chairs, broken crates and bursting parcels, and my dejection lay among them.

Mum paid the men, the hovervan hissed away and we were alone with our fate. Not quite alone: on the verandah the ancient couple hovered, knowing a scene yet to be played and humiliation awaiting us.

But the first humiliation was theirs, when the chewer moved at last to turn his head over his shoulder and say to them with flat emptiness of feeling, 'Piss off.'

They fled into the house, scarcely waiting to gasp in unison, 'Yes, Mr Kovacs.'

Mum had been conscious of him all the time, knowing what he was and why he waited, but refusing to look at him. Now she looked steadily but I saw that she was frightened. (This is a great puzzle in childhood, this discovery that the invulnerable adults share our shameful weaknesses.)

The chewer levered himself off the fence and for all his savage dirtiness did not look like the murderous Swill of the triv plays. He looked like a thin, strong, rather ordinary man who needed a bath. He slouched to where we stood beleaguered in a strange land, two little boys whose mother's arms crept round their shoulders, and nodded, confirming some secret deduction and said, 'You don't know a thing, Mrs Conway, do you? Not a bloody thing.'

Mum's fingers tightened on my flesh but she said nothing, not even to ask how he knew our name.

He said, 'I'm Billy Kovacs. You'll get to know me. PR.'

With a sort of last-ditch courage Mum said, 'Public Relations,' in the voice she used for dirty habits.

He shook his head and smiled and his whole face changed. I *knew* he was good. 'Protection Racket, Mrs Conway. Call things by their names, then no mistakes.'

His voice was what we called 'common' but he didn't speak Swill the way the triv actors did.

Mum said, 'Go inside, boys,' but Kovacs said, 'Why don't we all go in?' and when Mum hesitated he went on, 'Mrs Conway, we got to talk sense and your boys better hear it. What they'll hear is what can keep them alive that much longer. Maybe you, too.'

That was the first hint that the schoolground tales might have some truth in them. Mum caught her breath a little but nodded and he followed us inside. Mum hated him because he was a threat and Teddy despised him as he despised anyone who did not fuss over

Teddy, but I felt already the stirring of hero worship for tough, dirty Billy Kovacs who had winked his way straight into a small boy's heart.

In the lounge-room Teddy and I sat on the sofa where it had been dropped in the middle of the floor. Mum stood by the narrow, unclean window, fidgeting and forlorn, and Kovacs perched on a crate with his legs crossed under him, which is awkward if you aren't used to it. It crossed my mind even then that perhaps Swill places did not have much furniture and so they sat on the floor. And now that he was close, he *did* stink – of chewey and sweat and plain dirtiness.

He poked a thumb at our piled-up stuff and said, 'Too much furniture.' Mum hadn't wanted to leave anything and we would be pushed for space to move between the chairs and cabinets and little tables. 'You should've sold it. Know why?' He let the question hang until our mouths dropped with waiting. 'Because the Swill – that's people like me, lady – live just down the road. They hear you've got all this nice stuff and they think how *they* can sell it. Over your knifed guts if need be.'

He was matter-of-fact; it was everyday stuff, like sunrise. Mum stared out of the window, pretending not to be frightened but her voice said otherwise. 'It isn't like that. This is the Fringe but it isn't Swill. You're trying to put your price up.'

Price? More Swill lore?

'It is like that, lady, and your price was fixed before you got here. I know what's in your bank and what you can pay.' That shocked her; her face fell apart as he told her exactly the state of her account. 'So you can pay your way for a couple of years, maybe three or four if you're careful.'

Mum tried not to cry. 'How could you know? The banks – '

Kovacs's grin opened wide, like a friendly shark that might gulp us down with the greatest goodwill. 'Accounts can be tapped if you have the right connections. Like the coppers.'

Blunt statement of the corruption sometimes hinted at in the triv plays was excitement for me but for Mum it was a pit open at her feet. She had always claimed that the scriptwriters exaggerated everything.

'Call it co-operation, lady. You had police protection while you paid taxes, but now you've got no income and you draw Suss and to the coppers that makes you Swill.' Mum's instant anger rejected that and beside me Teddy made a spitting sound like a cat, but I could tell that Kovacs was being hard so that we would remember. 'Swill don't pay taxes, so the coppers don't know you – unless you do something silly like join a protest against food prices or power blackouts or – ' he paused, then said as if it had just occurred to him, ' – child prostitution. That includes young boys.' I wasn't sure of his meaning but Mum's face was ugly with fright. 'Protesters get noticed and next thing their brains get splashed on the footpath. What they don't get is protection against theft or violence or pack rape. For that you have to come to the gutter shit – me.'

Teddy yelled, 'Don't you talk like that to my mother!' To give Teddy his due, he was always brave, though now he was red in the face and shaking.

Kovacs pretended to be puzzled. 'Like what, sonny?'

'Words like – ' He shut up and I couldn't stop a giggle at how he had nearly been tricked into saying it himself.

Mum knew she had to make some stand. She said in the voice for visitors she didn't know very well, 'It doesn't matter, Teddy. Mr Kovacs is trying to help. In his fashion. Still – ' at last she looked straight at him, ' – we can do without Swill language in my home.'

Anyone else would have apologized but Kovacs gave her a surprise of a really strange kind. 'Shit isn't Swill talk. You wouldn't understand gutter Swill if you heard it. That stuff they feed you on triv plays is prettied up but shit is proper English. From the Middle German *schiten* and before that – '

Mum was so furious she broke in on him. 'I've heard there's no lout worse than an educated lout.'

He flung out his arms and legs like someone applauding a tremendous joke or like a great laughing spider who had the three of us in his web. Then he curled the long legs back under him and laid his big, bony hands on his knees and the laugh was over. 'I'm not a lout, Mrs Conway, if it suits me to act one, and I'm not educated neither – *either*.' We would become familiar with his trick of self-correction, his effort to be what he was not. 'I went to school when they still had real schools for Swill kids, not the pigpens they run now. So I learnt – *learned* – to read. Maybe one Swill in ten can read, the older ones. I've got books, like a dictionary and encyclopaedias and that sort – if you have to know, I stole them – and I read them because knowing a few things is useful in my work.'

But that stuff was all on Data Central, so why did he need books? Wondering, I noticed what had escaped me before, something as daunting as being lost in the dark: there was no Info terminal on the ancient triv. We weren't hooked in to Data. We would never know *anything*.

'Work!' Mum's contempt was brave. 'You blackmail the helpless!'

Kovacs was unmoved. 'Blackmail is a dirtier word than shit and I give value for money. That's what I started to tell you before young Galahad got all upset and wanted to fight me – I think.'

He had Teddy summed up from the start. I have never worked out whether Billy was an intellect blunted by environment or just a thug with flashes of insight.

He went on, 'I was saying about pack rape,' and Mum muttered again that he exaggerated but she was only talking up her courage. 'You think so, lady? It happens every day. The teenagers are the worst. People die in the towers and in Fringe streets like this one and it isn't old age that kicks 'em to death and cuts 'em up with blades fixed in the toes of the clogs. You better believe it.' His voice was no louder for its burden of horrors, only harder against our ignorant resistance. 'The newscasts won't tell you, because why? Because Sweet don't want to know and the State likes Sweet that way. Anyway, who cares what happens to Swill?'

Some real hatred broke through, something of black hatred for facts of an existence inconceivable to us.

'Swill are nothing because they do nothing because there's nothing for them to do. It costs the State money just to keep them alive. How long can that last? One day the State will begin killing them off because it can't afford them any longer. They'll be wiped off the books and respectable Sweet won't have to go on hiding from their own guilt.'

His voice shook but his talk was beyond me; the Sweet life had fenced off the world he knew. I suppose it was not new to Mum; with her it was that knowing something is not the same as *realizing* it. I think, too, that Kovacs reached her in a way he had not counted on because she said quite softly, 'You were telling us about your work,' as though there could be an understanding that took no note of Sweet and Swill.

It took him by surprise. The muscles of his dark face relaxed in a flash of gentleness. 'So I was.' The flash went as fast as it had come and he was performing again. 'It's my lecture for the new kids at Swill College.'

Perhaps the flash was not entirely gone; the jokey tone helped him make a new, foreign place of the world, in no way jokey.

'About coppers – police. The State's broke. You know that. Most of the world's broke.' I had to grow older before I understood the simple and obvious way this had come about but Mum and Teddy seemed to know. 'How to keep order when you can't pay coppers?

Well, we've got a big, useless army, same as everybody else's got a big, useless army – that's part of why they're all broke. So to get some use out of it, some go into training barracks in the Enclaves, where they can stamp hard on trouble and save coppers' wages. There's no coppers' beats in the Enclaves, not one! You with me, lady? There's only soldiers pretending to train for street-fighting and getting some real good training at it – when the Swill start a riot or a protest or that. But the police, the coppers? Well, law guards property, so the coppers look after people with property – the Sweet. There's no copper law in the towers, only a soldier's boot in the guts for the stroppy. But you know all that.'

He was challenging Mum to say that in her Sweet isolation she had not known. I didn't then grasp the idea of deliberately not knowing something, of keeping it down out of the sight of your mind or of looking at facts in a special light that dimmed out the savagery. Only now, years afterwards, can I recognize Billy's head-on assault as a strategy designed to teach before ignorance could undo us. We could not have understood then that all this, from a filthy and stinking stand-over man, was powered by a kind of love.

'You know, but it's never meant anything to you. Rape and theft and murder are part of being Swill. Who cares what they do to each other so long as they don't get loose among the Sweet?'

I noticed that the Swill were 'they' to him. He claimed to be Swill but in his mind he was something else. What else? He was a divided man.

'You get the picture? No, you don't, because it's only half the picture. Swill are dirty and violent and ignorant but they aren't all rotten. Most aren't. They don't like living with louts – your word – who rob and terrorize, but they don't have a choice, not even your little Fringe of a choice. So there's us. PR. We keep a sort of order, but we look after them that can't look after themselves. There's more helpless, silly people than you'd believe. So PR people have to take risks, up to our lives and our families' lives. That's why we take pay. We don't skin you but we take something and we do look after you, specially the kids. The system works about as good – well – as you'd expect and it'll cost you ten dollars a head every Monday.'

It didn't sound much to me but it was a stomach blow to Mum. To *pay* to live safely in a rundown rat-hole, from a bank balance that must some day vanish. All she said was, 'Or else you send your thug collectors round.'

41

He told her with awful gentleness, 'We stand between you and thugs. If you don't want us we stay away. After a week of us staying away you won't have a chair to sit on or a bed to sleep on or a virgin son.'

His bony face had a sad little smile for my open mouth and Teddy's glare, while Mum opened the purse that had lain within his reach the whole time. He stretched a long arm to take the notes and I saw her flinch from the blunted fingers and nails bitten far back.

He was still talking, explaining. 'You Fringe people, not Sweet any more and not quite Swill yet, are hard to look after because you don't know anything and won't believe when you're told, and because you live in separate houses, thieves can get at you without noise. So we have to patrol and that's expensive. A lot of men. A lot of PR.'

He put the money in a pocket inside the waistband of his pants, behind the knife sheath. That meant that he couldn't count on being safe either.

Mum tried desperately. 'There must be police in the Fringe. It isn't – isn't – '

'Isn't Swill? Near enough to. There's an arrangement. Coppers stay out of the towers except with an escort of soldiers. On their own they'd be murdered. But we tip them off about things they can handle better than us, like if we want a bad mob broken up and put away. Then they come in with troops. That way they get a good image with the State and maybe a quick spot on the news: "Dirty Swill fixed but good!" So they tip us off to little things we need, like your bank figures. They don't like us, we don't like them, but it's a system.'

He uncoiled again to stand down from the crate. 'I'll look in later to see how you're going.'

He waited for Mum to say something but she turned to the window as if freedom might be out there. His face twitched, perhaps with pity. He thought of something more: 'You kids! Stay away from the towers! If you get into any trouble, you yell for Billy Kovacs. Nobody else, only me. I'm your number two dad, and don't you forget it.' He grinned at Mum's back like a naughty boy. 'Yours too, lady.'

Mum stayed still as if she hadn't heard. That didn't worry him; what wiped the grin off his face was Teddy saying, 'You're no father of mine, Ratface.'

Mum cried out, 'Teddy!' and came to stand between them, terrified. I was scared, too, but I couldn't help thinking that 'Ratface'

42

was exactly right, for his skull with all its bones centred on the long, pointed nose.

He only looked down at Mum with a wholly different smile to say, 'Got spirit, that one.' I felt ignored. He said to Teddy as if no insult had passed, 'You'd be going on twelve. Been Tested yet?'

Teddy's decisions to hate were final; he turned his back. Mum said tiredly, 'He's twelve. He's been Tested.'

I hadn't known and this was big news, because only kids showing Extra promise were Tested. How did he know that Teddy had been listed? He asked, 'No letter yet?'

'Not yet.'

He said to Teddy's back but with no enthusiasm, 'Good luck, kid.'

It was typical that Teddy's arrogance should rise above his resentment to try to put Kovacs down. 'There's no luck in the Test. You're Extra or you're Swill meat.'

Kovacs said then the only thing I ever heard him utter in spite. 'There's plenty of Extra heads with Swill hearts.'

Then he went away.

Mum spoke to Teddy with menace born of fear. 'Don't you insult him again, ever!'

'I hate him!'

'We need him. For a while, at least.' As if the words scalded her tongue, 'He is trying to help.'

'For money! What about when the money runs out?'

She must have thought of that but could only say, 'We'll worry then. Be glad of protection while we have it. He is an evil man but we need him.'

Teddy turned on me. 'Francis doesn't think he's evil. Francis likes him.' Teddy had frightening penetration. 'He thinks Ratface is a terrific hero.'

He was, as usual, right.

So, in a way, was I. But that is hindsight. Just then I was more disturbed by what had happened to Mum. In half an hour she had grown old.

5

So much had happened, yet it was not quite nine in the morning. Mum shut herself in her still unsettled bedroom; it must have been a horrible time for her, with every fear come true and every inadequacy exposed.

That left us with nothing to do and long hours ahead, and idleness led to the single most frightful experience of my life. With Kovacs's warnings fresh in my ears, I nudged catastrophe on that first day.

For a while we explored the unlovely house, observing windows nailed shut, lighting fixtures without elements and taps that drooled rusty water in a mean trickle. Our rooms had not been swept out for us, much less cleaned, and the kitchen reflected its owners who to us seemed dirty, decrepit and indefinably wretched. In fact they were simply old, despairing and frightened of life.

A small back yard held a square of patchy lawn and some dusty geraniums. Teddy said, 'Disgusting!' and brooded. He was no company. I went back through the house to hang over the front fence. The street was wide, with old, broken traffic-light standards on the corner, so it must have been busy once, but in half an hour only a single commercial hovertruck whoofled past; the road surface would have shaken Dad's car to pieces. In our old suburb the local council would have poured a new surface; I thought perhaps Newport did not have a council. (It did not.)

Few people were about. Why should they be? It was too early for shoppers and no one with work to go to would live here. Those I saw were neat, like shabby people making the best of what they had; nobody at all came from the direction of the towers. The city might have been dying though the triv news said it was growing like a mad thing.

I slipped out to peep round the corner for a glimpse of the tenement towers only two blocks away, the haunts of fabled brutes and horrors. I would not dare go close but I could go a little way because the houses in the two intervening blocks were Fringe, like our own.

So I went a little way, drawn by the unknown awful, a little way and a little way, meeting nobody – until I stood on the last street corner of safety and the first concrete monster reared over me, a hundred metres away across the road. I gazed, daring no further.

Round the foot of the huge tower was a grey concrete skirt of emptiness, so that the tenement stood in its own hard, empty space. At close hand it held no threat; it was only drab and disappointing. A few ragged people hung around the bare skirt and I heard the clack of wooden clogs; otherwise there was only a closeted hum as if life lurked somewhere, not declaring itself.

Boredom might have sent me home again if I had not heard the noise of kids playing, laughing and calling out, distant but coming closer. Soon I saw them.

They came running, perhaps a dozen of them, all about my own age but ragged and dirty. They wore neither shoes nor clogs; only their voices made sound as they came in a rapid wedge down the middle of the street at the concrete's edge. It was a chasing game of some sort. The one in the lead ran with arms and legs pumping and the pack squealed at his heels, one bigger boy with long legs closing to tag him.

The quarry screamed when the bigger boy hit him over the head with a clenched fist and tripped him with a kicking foot. It was not a game but a hunt, my introduction to violence in fun.

I stood ice-frozen as the prey vanished in a struggle of kicking bodies, kids crowding each other for the chance to maim. An abominable screaming continued until the biggest one jumped on the victim's belly, when it stopped.

I expected them to run away then, horrified by what they had done, but they only strolled to the cement skirt, chattering and excited. None of them looked back at the kid squirming on the roadway. Game over. What next?

What next was apparent when the big one noticed me and said – I heard him plainly – 'Fu'n Sweet!'

My clothes, of course. I wore enough quality on my back to feed the pack of them for a week. He called out something like 'Wosher nyme, Sweetie?' in a voice rawer and flatter than any triv actor's imitation. He jumped the gutter and my petrified throat could barely gulp as the pack swarmed after him with hunting whoops. I expected to die.

My idiocy unfroze and I turned to run.

And ran straight into a hard body and a hand that held me while I shrieked in new and more urgent terror, then turned me round to face my pursuers. I thought I was being delivered to death, but the hunt had halted in mid-street.

Uncertainly the ragged kids looked to their leader while he tried to appear a wise captain calculating the risk, but he was all show. In a gesture that reduced him from fiend to snotty kid he poked out his tongue at the iron giant who held me. Then they all turned back, swaggering, making believe to be neither defeated nor afraid.

Over my head my rescuer snarled, 'Stoopid li'l bassud! Washer doon 'ere? Yer gonno sennis?'

That is the best I can make of his appalling speech. He had his father's rat face and bone-and-muscle body but not his rough, hard kindness. He shook me and it hurt, and grunted at me, 'Onna street in 'em glads!' and more in his dreadful Swill whine, telling me to wear overalls and go without shoes and to get myself home and stay there. (I found out later that he didn't always talk like that; Billy had taught him better. 'Local colour' he called it.)

At first I could not speak for gratitude; godlike, he had shown his face and the enemy had fled. Then I bawled, with relief and horror, that they had killed the other kid.

'Ner. Li'l bassud's awri. Toes dun 'urt. Clogs 'd a dunnim.' And in fact the battered kid was on hands and knees snivelling and whimpering, crawling and dragging a leg, but alive.

Then the god brought his free hand from behind him and slid his knife into its belt sheath. PR or not, he had taken no chances with the small foe. Here was a lesson: grown-ups could be afraid of children. That kid was lucky to be alive. So was I. The god thumped me, and not gently, in the direction of home and swore his dad would half kill me when he reported how stupid I was, and so laid a new terror over my day.

That was Allan, Billy's eldest boy, murdered two years later trying to break up a gang rape, when he was just twenty.

At home I said not a word. Teddy would have scarred me with contempt; Mum would have been distraught. I spent an hour dreading the coming of Billy Kovacs and the power of his punishing arm, until Mum appeared and set us to helping her arrange the rooms. After a while I fancied that Kovacs might not come again that day, or even the next, and disaster deferred might shrink to nothing.

He did come, after tea, and I fled to the twilight of the back yard, but he came after me. Instead of taking off his belt and laying into me he ran his fingers through my hair and said, 'You were lucky, eh?' And of course I blubbered in shame. 'Not just lucky, Francis. Allan was there because I told him to be around – because silly kids are more trouble than silly grown-ups.' With my streaky face buried in his stomach I noticed that something was not as it had been, but conjecture ceased when he commanded, 'Stop bawling!'

I stopped. Billy had that effect when he wanted to.

'Don't go near the towers again! Not ever!'

'No, Mr Kovacs.' I meant it. My deepest intention was that I would never go near the Swill or their dwellings. If my social education suffered, my skin would stay whole.

He put his long spider's arm around me and his breath smelt faintly of the acid-sour chewey. He said a strange thing, 'You may be special. Not Extra, but – Your mum says you do figures in your head.'

I muttered, 'Yes, Mr Kovacs,' luxuriating in forgiveness.

'Well, we'll see, maybe.' I did not ask what we'd see; I was busy with my earlier dim perception. With the brashness that only a child can get away with, I said, 'You don't smell bad any more.'

He shook with soundless laughter until he was able to say between splutters, 'A man doesn't have to stink all the time. It just helps to show new people what they've come to.'

It was not the last example of the lengths he would go to earn his weekly dollars.

I saw now that his hair was groomed and parted, his face bonier than ever in shaven cleanliness and his patched clothes newly pressed.

We never again saw his fully redolent Swill persona though he took to dropping in every day. Mum thawed and learned to trust him but Teddy loathed him. I found him a fine number two dad. How many kids have an *accessible* hero?

6

Days became a fortnight and Mum did not mention school for us. We pretended glee but in fact were bored to petty quarrelling, stuck in the house. The fact was that she had no idea where to look. It did not occur to her to ask Billy; his unlikely knowledge of the derivation of 'shit' did not qualify him as an educational authority.

There were a few shops in that part of our Fringe district that bordered the Sweet area, away from the towers. In the quiet of the morning we were allowed out to buy a news-sheet in which Mum read, with concealed yearning, of her lost world, which was the only world of news columns. News did not happen to Swill. Billy's explanation of that was: 'One bashing's much like another. No class about Swill murders. Not to disturb nice folk with that stuff.'

There was also a duplicated sheet issued by others who had fallen into the Fringe and now spent their lives complaining about it. It fell stealthily on doorsteps by night, with items like '. . . More than 100 unreported Swill murders every week . . . Children starve when their food is stolen by bigger children – or by heartless adults!'

Mum, resisting knowledge, would ask, 'But is this true?' and Billy – acting as a sort of schoolmasterly family friend, but still collecting his dollars – would tell her that wasn't the half of it.

'But surely it can be stopped. The soldiers – ' She could not understand that the Swill-based garrisons were gaolers, not police-men.

Billy would ask with his ferocious grin, 'How?' and read her a lesson she refused to accept. 'Too many people and not enough resources to give everybody a useful share – not anywhere in the world. And the poorer they get the more get born and what can you do about it? Wipe out poverty? How? Easier to wipe out the people.'

Mum ignored the monstrous coda. 'Equal sharing – '

'Equal arseholes, lady! There isn't enough of anything to be equal with. Equal shares would mean everybody in equal poverty – till somebody re-invented business and cornered the food market. It gets worse, not better.'

'And when it can't get any worse?'

'The killing will start.' He said that so calmly, as if it were a future everybody knew about, that it became nearly believable. 'Remember kangaroos, when the hunters used to shoot them to keep the numbers down? The cull, they called it. Then it came that there wasn't enough feed for us *and* the kangaroos and they culled them right out. Just like that, some day we'll cull ourselves – when there's not enough feed. Your boys could see it happen.'

His sharp eyes brooded, but the cull was an aberration of his otherwise practical mind and we didn't want to argue over some distant tomorrow. Minds wiser than ours paid no attention to future enormities; if you didn't look, they would dwindle away. We did not know that other yet wiser minds had considered food, birthrate and poverty for three generations past and found only monstrous resolutions.

If we had known, what of it? We had enough to eat.

The period of inertia ended with a letter, Council of Advanced Education dramatically black on the envelope. Mum laid it on the table and Teddy was afraid to touch it; its contents could intoxicate or slay him. Finally he said, 'I feel sick,' picked it up and went outside.

Mum asked me in a very cool tone, 'Do you know what being Extra means?'

'You go to a Special School.'

She told me in the tight voice of somebody reading a set piece, 'Extra is a Latin word, it means outside. An Extra has intelligence outside the ordinary.' Her tone became desolate. 'Teddy may be Extra.'

Teddy had never seemed all that clever. Smart-alecky, if that counted. But he kept so much to himself there was no knowing. I asked, 'Would that make him Sweet again?'

I thought, too late, that Mum would snap, 'We are not Swill, Francis,' but she said only, 'Yes, Sweet for ever.'

An anger in me protested, 'He can't even do sums!'

She managed a laugh. 'Doing sums isn't very Extra. It's a talent, not a – a superiority.'

Teddy came back with no expression at all on his face and said, 'I passed. I'm Extra.'

After that neither Mum nor he knew what to say, until she asked, 'When do you go?'

'Next Monday.' Teddy didn't often make jokes but for once he tried. 'It'll save you ten dollars a week.'

She smiled as though that was a terrific thought (it would also lose her Teddy's share of the Suss) and said she didn't think Billy would mind. Then more silence.

Teddy broke it. 'I'm going to put in for Police Intelligence Recruit School.'

Mum looked unbelieving but my egocentric innocence saw that a sort of super-copper could be a useful prop to the family fortunes. We could have 'arrangements', like Billy's.

There was a queer moment when Billy was told of Teddy's Test result. We were all in the lounge-room, Teddy as usual refusing to acknowledge Billy's presence, working on a puzzle supported on his knees. Mum told the news, hovering between pride in her son and superstitious fear for his fortunes in a profession none of us understood.

Billy repeated, 'Police Intelligence . . .' in a sort of affirming irony, and his role-playing could not supply warmth to his, 'Congratulations, kid.'

Teddy looked up without speaking; his face blazed a contempt that words could only have diminished.

Billy nodded to the unspoken message and gave his answer: 'You're wrong, kid. I do matter. All the Swill matter. You'll find out.'

Teddy left on the Monday without fuss. Mum was upset because he was going to dormitory school and would not be home at night, but he who had insisted on being the centre of affection now wanted no demonstration; she would move to pat an invisible speck from his shoulder and he would avoid the touch. I knew what danced in his head that he dared not let her know: *I am leaving this demeaning place.*

The council's hoverbus, with its Knowledge Is Power motto in bright scarlet across the bow, floated over the wrecked macadam to rest at our gate. Its door folded open. From the windows the young faces of the month's intake considered Teddy, jealously appraising.

His stiff goodbye was almost a flight but he could not avoid Mum's embrace and kiss. 'Don't forget to write.'

'Of course not.' But his eyes were on the bus.

'And come home every chance you get.' She remembered that in our other suburb proud Mrs Urquhart's boy had visited often twice a month. 'We'll want to hear all about it.'

'Of course.' Briefly he returned her kiss and hurried into the bus. I might not have been there. As the machine lifted he waved but his sight was fixed on far places.

He did not write; he did not come.

Mum waited and did not complain; since Dad's death she had worn armour whose joints rarely showed. She wrote to him – and again. Soon an official envelope came.

'. . . psychological gulf between Edward Conway's status training and his unfortunate family circumstances . . . social tensions implicit in his consciousness of Sustenance connections . . . proper balance to be maintained with new relationships . . . our reorientation demands on the child are severe and parental feeling should, in fairness to him, take second place . . .'

It must have seemed to her that in the name of love her life was being butchered.

I have to admit that Teddy's absence did not depress me.

She showed the letter to Billy, having no other confidant. She spoke to none of the neighbours; they kept to themselves anyway, and the two scarecrows in the other half of the house hardly dared to address someone so friendly with Mr Kovacs. Billy's influence was a mystery to us then, but real enough when it came to getting things done.

I heard only one remark from him about the letter: 'Don't cry over him. You've got one son in Sweet heaven, so your life hasn't been wasted. And he isn't stupid. In the end he'll make up his own mind who he sees and who he doesn't.'

Such tough comfort appeared to help her, if only in setting a goal of waiting.

Billy couldn't help me when I asked how the Extras lived; the intellectual life was beyond his imagining but he had an opinion to offer when I wondered what the State wanted with them: 'The superbrats? Insurance. So they'll know who not to kill off. Heaven's an exclusive place.'

My ears had conditioned themselves to close automatically when he got on to that raving cull stuff.

7

In the end it was Billy who badgered Mum about schooling for me, telling her in his gritty way that having an egghead in the family didn't justify leaving the other one Swill-ignorant.

She could only ask, 'But where?'

She should have known that Billy had settled that before he raised the subject. I imagine she had her ideas as to why he paid us such loving attention as he did, and deduced his motive as a patient courtship, but it was long-sighted opportunism that set him to furthering my education.

His complicated contacts had located a school in our Fringe area, a small privately run place catering for those lower-income Sweet who might easily be phased out of their shaky status but held on as though tomorrow might not come. When Mum asked about fees he was vague, saying he might be able to 'swing an arrangement'.

The arrangement was, of course, already swung; he saw no need to explain to Mum that the goods – myself – had only to be produced for assessment.

On the day he took me to the school he was in Swill rig. He didn't actually smell but he was unwashed and unshaven and his hair might have been combed with his fingers. In rumpled and greasy clothes he was better than the filthy spider of the first day but less than the novice gentleman he tried to be in our lounge-room. I saw with surprise that he was not really the menacingly tall man I accepted him as being but only a little above middle height, that his powerful presence was put on and off at need. The presence that day was rat-faced cunning; in a triv play I would have spotted him at once as con man and thief.

After all these years his personality still eludes me; all his pretences except the foredoomed gentility seemed real in the acting. Perhaps they were; some actors claim that the role 'takes over'.

The school was some twenty minutes' walk from home, on the edge of a proper Sweet suburb, a biggish two-storey house with the wrought-iron balconies of another age. I could hear kids playing somewhere behind, out of sight.

My sense of propriety took fright when Swill-rigged Billy made for the front door and I suggested that we go round the back. He grinned his con-man's grin. 'Servants' entrance, eh? But I'm not a servant, kid, I'm the boss. You'll see.' And he banged the shiny brass knocker.

The lady who opened the door was Sweet, thin and grey and prim, but under the primness was the beaten wariness I learned to recognize in the small Sweet as their hopes died. She said to Billy, with a decent woman's disgust, 'You might at least have washed. And you're late. Mrs Parkes has been waiting ten minutes.'

'Then she's ten minutes older with bugger all to show for it. This is Francis Conway. Francis, this is Miss Pender, your headmistress. In you go, lad.'

Miss Pender led the way. I followed with new-boy shivers, but Billy's big hand comforted while it urged me on.

In the office, by the windows, sat the woman who must be the waiting Mrs Parkes – hard-edged, middle-aged, cool-eyed with a no-nonsense sheen over all. Extra-Bitchy Sweet, I decided, which was unfair. She was in fact a sympathetic woman who happened to run a business, not quite honestly; she needed her professional hardness.

By her stood a man who had to be Very Big Sweet – assured, tailored like a jewel, soft-fleshed but nasty-tough under it. The woman surveyed me with casual interest. The man grunted, 'Looks like any other brat.'

Billy, standing just inside the door, said, 'That's part of his value,' in the rasping whine triv actors use to pretend Swill, but the man gave no sign that he heard. Some Sweet had begun to believe that Swill weren't really people. Or perhaps he knew fake Swill when he heard it and wasn't to be conned by game-playing.

Billy leaned against the wall where he could see all of us without seeming to be part of the meeting. He threw me a quick wink but Mrs Parkes saw it and made a moment's study of him. Miss Pender seemed to have no function; she sat at her desk and listened.

Very Big Sweet came over and took me under the chin, turned my face up to suit him and said, 'You figure in your head, eh?' and did not wait for an answer before he accused, 'And you think you're really somebody, eh?'

With one question requiring yes and the other no, I was dumbstruck. He leaned down to me, smelling peculiarly of roses and aromatic leather, and hissed, 'What's 17 into 1,274, eh?'

Though he frightened me, this was too easy; my numerical reflex was shooting back at him before his mouth closed: '74.9411764705882352 all after the decimal point repeating.'

He controlled surprise, but I saw it. 'Write it down.' Miss Pender gave me a piece of paper and a stylus and I jotted it down while he checked it on his wrist cally and grudgingly admitted me right.

Billy said to the air, 'Try something that'll stretch 'im, Boss,' and was ignored. (Billy could do arithmetic with pencil and paper, saying it was necessary for a Swill businessman; the Very Big Sweet probably could not.)

The Sweet read out two ten-digit figures to be multiplied together; he didn't know enough to set a tricky sum. Mrs Parkes shook her head in mock amazement at the little boy bubbling his snappy answers but I knew she was not putting me down, particularly when she gave Billy a slight nod of approval, recognizing him as a real person with a part in what went on. When she smiled at me I wanted to please her; smiles had been rare since Dad died.

Then she spoke and the Very Big Sweet shut up and we saw who was boss. Except perhaps Billy, who always had his own ideas about who ran things.

She gave me sums of another kind. I guessed they dealt with goods and prices by the style and the long sequences to be collated in a single answer. The ability to remember and reach back was important, not the easy figuring. She had the answers ready and checked every step.

At the end she said, 'It took me six hours to work those on paper.' An obvious question jumped into my head but Billy stared hard at me and I shut my mouth. Mrs Parkes said I was very good, 'Quite good enough.' Then she asked, 'Will you work for me for an hour every week?'

What had this to do with going to school? Not knowing what to say, I looked to Billy. His rat face fell into the gentlest smile I had ever seen on it as he told me, in that dreadful fake Swill accent, 'You can say no if you don't want to do it.'

He knew me better than that – I would have figured all night for a smile and a pat. Of course I said yes.

His smile twisted slightly as it faded back behind his mouth. I could not know that he was having uneasy second thoughts, last-moment uncertainties about his scheming, almost hoping that I would make up his mind by refusing a potentially dangerous game. I closed the door on escape with a word siphoned out of me by kindness.

'That's it,' Billy said. 'Now yers got 'im.'

Mrs Parkes spoke as if of ordinary things. 'Please drop that unpleasant dialect, Mr Kovacs. The connections who found me for you told me all I need to know about you. And the unwashed touch was unnecessary.' She smiled thinly. 'But I appreciate thoroughness.'

Since he only gazed at her with blank eyes she had to prod him with a question: 'Are you selling the boy's brain or his soul or both?'

'Neither.' The sound of his normal voice took some of the play-acting out of the air. 'I never seen – saw – a soul and I don't sell people. *He* is selling a bit of talent for an hour a week – while he still wants to.'

'And you?'

'I see fair play and fair pay. I know what he's worth to you near enough to set a price.'

The Very Big Sweet broke in, 'State's sake, Nola, he's just a Swill crim with a bumboy.'

Billy said explosively, 'No!' but Mrs Parkes paid no attention to either of them. She crooked her finger to bring me to her side, looked into my eyes and turned me to face Billy. 'What is he to you, child?'

I had never thought about that; a child doesn't think about what *is*. Grasping at an answer I said, 'He's my number two dad,' which made her eyebrows rise and her lips twitch and brought a disgusted grunt from the Very Big Sweet. I saved the moral day by adding, 'He looks after Mum and me,' creating a safer but equally wrong impression.

'Does he, now? That's not for me to – ' She asked instead, 'Do you love Mr Kovacs?'

'Of course. He's my number two – '

'Yes, yes.' Her eyes were on Billy. When I looked it was too late; he had put on his blank stare. But she laughed aloud. 'Damned if you aren't a doting second-string father after all!'

He growled at me as if I had betrayed him in some way, 'Piss off outside, Francis. We've got business to talk.'

Miss Pender made her one ladylike contribution: 'It might be best if I take Francis to his classroom,' and bundled me out before the interesting part began.

When he picked me up after school, Billy would not say much. When I asked, 'What will I have to do?' he answered, 'Be a schoolboy.' His tone, usually so downright, was unsure and I guessed there was something not straight about the arrangements. That gave them an attractive, romantic aura, like an adventure.

As for the school, I don't think it amounted to anything scholastically but I stayed there for several years and learned nothing to do me any harm. It was outside school hours that fascinating affairs came into my life.

As we walked home that afternoon a light rain fell, what Mum would have called a Scotch mist. There was no shelter in the residential street but it wasn't heavy enough to worry about. 'It'll get heavier,' Billy said. 'The river was up a bit this morning.'

There had been river-flood scenes on the triv the night before, with stranded cattle and people on rooftops with water up to the spouting, but that had been away somewhere in the country. Rejecting a connection of events, I said, 'That wasn't our river though.'

'It was. Same one, further up.'

My mind slipped back to the birthday and Mum talking about Newport. Where the Swill would one day swim like mad. 'Does the water come in at the ground floor?'

'Sometimes. Where did you hear that?'

I explained and asked because the vision was unclear, 'Isn't there a wall?'

'A bit of a one. They must have thought it was high enough. Or they wanted the money for something else.'

I asked, 'Does it stink?', which might have sounded irrelevant but Billy said, 'When it goes down, the mud stinks. Like dirty shithouses.'

'I've never seen the river. Is it big?'

'I can't tell, kid. I never saw any other one.' He was saying that he had lived his whole life down there in the towers, seeing nothing else. He should have found a way out. Surely there was a way out.

That conversation might have taken an informative turn if he hadn't grabbed my arm. 'Listen!'

There was a distant, murmuring sound like a cat purring in its dreams. He said, 'The bastard *is* up!' He had me half running, half dragged, until we came to our street and the purr was a deep roaring at the bottom of the hill on the other side of the towers. 'Is that the river?' He nodded.

Now a wind rose from nowhere and heavier rain came down, cold and stinging; in seconds we were drenched. He pushed me through our gate. 'Tell your mum I've got to get home.'

He was running, waving *no* as I shouted, 'Come in and get dry,' the soaked shirt and trousers sticking to his bones.

When I told Mum, she said that the river must be flooding and that he had his family to look after. Family was something he never talked about; he kept his affairs in separate boxes, one kind of life here, another there.

'Where is the river?'

'At the bottom of the street, more than a kilometre away.'

'Can it come up to here?'

'No.' Then she amended, 'Not yet. One day, perhaps.' And, tiredly, 'Everything in the world is perhaps.'

It rained for hours while I wondered if there was water rising in Billy's tenement flat. (It was not. His quarters were on a higher floor; the 'family' he looked after was 70,000 strong.)

He came round very late that night. I was in bed but I heard Mum say, 'Dry your feet on this. You needn't have come back tonight. Francis told me about the interview.'

I could not hear his answer; his voice was dull and tired. She asked, 'Are your family safe?' and again he muttered.

When they came in to see me his clothes were muddy, his shoes jammed into his belt and his trousers rolled up to his white, bony knees. I guessed that the water was not very high, that the Swill weren't swimming. He sat on my bed, smelling faintly of chewey, while Mum hovered, motherly and apprehensive, and he told me what instinct had suggested, that the morning's happenings were secrets. 'You don't tell anybody about Mrs Parkes. Not anybody!'

'I don't know anything to tell.'

'You will. I'm taking you to her on Friday night. And you don't talk about it! Specially you don't mention it to the other kids at school. Understand?'

I didn't, quite, but I said, 'Yes.'

He pressed, 'Do you know why not?' and I had to shake my head. 'Because they won't believe what you tell and they'll make fun of you. Or maybe they'll repeat it at home and their parents'll make trouble.'

'About me being able to do figures?'

He reached a long arm to gather me in while he said, 'Because they can't stand for people to be better than them.' I had stopped thinking about Dad but that brought him back. 'You're going up, Francis, and they won't like that. They'll take out spite on you.'

I wriggled round to see his face. 'Up?' But he was watching Mum. 'Do you mean out of here?'

Still watching her, he nodded. 'But not yet awhile.'

'Away from Swill?'

'One day.' Perhaps he felt the leap of my heart. 'Does that mean a lot to you?'

'Yes, Billy,' I said.

'Then you know better than to talk. Ever!' He turned my face up. 'You made a hit with Mrs Parkes.'

56

'I only said I'd do sums for her.'

Mum was in a flutter, unusual in her. 'I hope this – I wouldn't want him – '

Billy gave her his special smile for getting his own way. 'And I wouldn't let it happen.' What he said always went with Mum, even when she suspected it wasn't above aboard, which it often wasn't; she had fallen into trusting him.

I asked the question that had bothered me during the interview: 'Why did she take six hours to do her sums? She must have a cally.'

The answer to that was a lesson in the deviousness of the world, introducing me to the idea of a State that took money from its owners under the name of taxes, duties, excise and levies. He did not say this was unjust but I found myself on the side of Mrs Parkes who wanted to evade these impositions and who had been nice to me.

'But Finance Squad coppers can trace cally and comp operations, even recreate them after wipe-out, so they always know what money people have. That makes it hard to keep two sets of accounts without getting caught. But if she has a cally that spouts answers without using a key or a chip, she can write them on bits of paper. And who looks for records on bits of paper any more? Besides, it can be microfilmed and hid – hidden – in a dot in an old book. So only you and Mrs Parkes will know what's on the bits of paper.' He gave me a play punch on the jaw. 'Get it?'

'Yes,' but I was hazy. As time went on I got it very well but now I was concerned with my own prospects. A fine future at some distant remove was all very well, but, 'Will I get a present or something?'

'Or something, and plenty of it.'

After he went, Mum whispered, 'I'm sorry Francis,' and I answered, 'I'm not.' She was worrying her heart out at having sold her son into a child labour racket. For an hour a week! That bothered her more than any whiff of illegality.

After she had gone to bed I puzzled over the flood pictures on the newscasts; they never showed the city, only the country. It was true, and in some way sinister, that the Swill were rarely mentioned on the news.

I put shoes on and sneaked quietly into the back yard; in one corner I could climb the fence and see down the street past the towers. The moon was high and shining like silver on a mirror which should have been the street leading down to the towers. But the mirror rippled. I was seeing water that had risen from the river and was only a block or so distant. The street slope was gentle and we did not seem to be very high above the flood.

I watched for what seemed hours, waiting for the water to climb the footpath and our fence, but it came no nearer, and finally sleep got the better of entrancement.

In the morning I could see right down the street and the water had gone. Mum explained about flash floods that receded as fast as they came but the triv carried no news about it. She said softly, 'Poor Billy.'

But what about poor Francis? I understood Teddy's triumph in escape and my determination was reaffirmed that I would never fall closer to the Swill than this house on this barely safe corner. Instinct suggested that Mrs Parkes held the key to the future, that Billy had lifted me higher than he knew.

8

Though Billy could speak reasonably good English when he tried, he never mixed with Sweet. For one thing, they would never have let him near them; they saw Swill as beggars and criminals, which was near enough to the truth. So there was painfully much he did not know, and it showed sharply when he called to take me to Mrs Parkes.

He brought a parcel of clothes with him and used my bedroom for changing. 'I couldn't wear this stuff down there – half Newport'd be sniffing after what I was up to.'

When he appeared, dressed for the Sweet streets, even I knew it was all wrong and Mum asked, 'Where on Earth did you get those clothes?'

Misunderstanding, he told her bluntly, 'Stole 'em.'

She must have been laughing inside but not wanting to hurt him. 'What sort of Sweet do you want to be taken for?'

'Little Sweet. Workman, like gardening or cleaning.'

There was no way round telling him, 'Billy, the grey denim shirt is right but nothing else is.'

He said defensively, 'I had to take what I could get,' angry as a kid caught in a boast. 'What's wrong, anyway?'

'The jacket, to start with.'

'Everybody wears leather jackets. You see 'em all the time on the triv.'

Mum said gently, 'The triv is deceptive. Workmen wear plasti-leather. That jacket is real leather, tailored. It would cost a fortnight of unskilled wages. You might wear it to a sporting event.'

He sat down, unable to argue. 'What else?'

'The trousers. Workmen wear a heavier weave with belts, not tailored waists. And green shoes are for dancing. You might wear a cap going to work but at night you would have a blue or black beret.'

He said flatly, 'So I've buggered it.'

Mum hesitated over something she would have preferred not to say, and in the end said it: 'Fred . . . my husband . . . was about your height. A little heavier . . . I kept some of his clothes for the boys, for later on.' I thought she was going to cry but if she did it was in her own room where she kept Dad's clothes in a trunk. She brought out the heavy trousers he had worn in wet weather, a plastic jacket I remembered from country drives, a plastic belt and the cheap beret he had worn for polishing the duco. She said, 'It's only sentiment. You might as well have them.'

Everything was slightly too big for Billy's narrow frame, but when he squared his shoulders he looked passably right. Dad's shoes were too small for his long bones but Mum painted the green horrors with brown Plastidye and said they would do well enough at night.

He muttered the resentful thanks of hurt pride, but Mum laughed at him and said he'd made her face enough hard facts and how did he like his own medicine? He laughed a bit and said he didn't and things were all right again until she thought of something else. 'What if some policeman is suspicious enough to question you? Are you carrying a knife?'

He patted his armpit and Mum held out her hand. 'Leave it here.'

'*No*, lady. Oh, no.'

'Carrying a concealed weapon is a criminal offence, in Sweet territory at any rate.'

'I know that. It's – ' He did not seem to know what it was, but said, 'A man's naked without his knife.'

Mum lost her temper, just a little. 'That's Swill talk! You're trying to be Sweet. What's your story if you are questioned, with a knife in your shirt and my son in tow?'

It was a shock to see Mum outface him. He opened up his shirt, unstrapped the sheath and threw it on the table. When he spoke, it was not about the knife. 'I don't like you thinking about me as Swill. I try, don't I?'

Now Mum blushed, the fiery red of detection in snobbery. 'I don't think of you like that, Billy!'

Of course she did. How could she not? He knew. 'Yes you do.' He took my hand. 'Come on, young Francis, there's Sweet money for the picking up.'

The scene troubled me. Billy reduced to temper because he did not know the right clothes to wear and to bitterness when a woman laughed at him was less than the hero I cherished. He did not step down from his pedestal that night but he stood less securely atop it.

When at the end of a quarter-hour walk we took a public hovertram and he tendered our fare, he said, 'Me and the kid,' instead of 'one and a half,' and then stumbled over the street name of our destination, so that the driver had to work out that he meant Cholmondeley Street. When we sat down Billy muttered, 'Chumley', to himself as if he didn't believe the difference between the spoken word and what was written on his piece of paper.

I had hoped we would go through magical City Centre but our route circled it and all my eyes gathered was a skyline of buildings like dominoes with bright window spots. I could have cried with disappointment. Billy leaned near to whisper, 'You never been there? Me neither. I never been this far out of the towers since I was a kid.' He was as rapt as I.

That was incredible. My lovely Billy had never *seen* the world he tried to juggle in his fingers. Worse came when he said, 'You watch for the street sign. You spell it like this.' He gave me the scrap of paper with the name in clumsy capitals. 'My eyes's not so good lately.' He was nervous, making mistakes and not correcting them.

I asked, irritably because I resented imperfection in him, why he didn't get glasses and he smiled the sad version of his smile that always melted my tempers and asked, did I know what they cost? I did not, and felt ungenerous, but I wondered what he did with all his stand-over money. (In fact it went to his indecently large family.)

When we got down at Cholmondeley Street we were in the sort of world I had glimpsed from Dad's car when we drove to the hills, a world of huge houses set in gardens that would have held a dozen of our Working Sweet blocks, houses with two floors and not prefabricated like ordinary houses, houses brilliant with lights outside as well as in.

Mrs Parkes's place was immense. I counted twelve windows across the ground floor, all alight behind blinds, and wondered what she did with so many. Instead of going to the front door we took a side path off the drive and I asked why we were going to the servants' entrance.

'Because this time we're servants.'

Everything conspired that night to show that Billy was not the eternal boss man he made believe to be, and to show me that idols cannot be trusted.

3

NOLA PARKES
AD 2044

That night, in my private office at home, the first impression of young charm wore off. The boy seemed now to lack personality; his talent became the only interesting thing about him. He was then a skinny nine-year-old, good-mannered and properly cared-for but suspicious and withdrawn, only timidly responsive to a kindness. It was hard to see why Swill-tough Kovacs spent affection on him except as a golden-egg layer.

Francis was obviously got up in his best clothes. A mistake: that age is more relaxed when a little scruffy and grubby. At the school he had been animated because he was showing off; here he was nervous, unsure of himself now that the performance was no longer a game.

There was a weakness in the entire transaction – Francis's ability, or lack of it, to hold his tongue. For that I had to depend on Kovacs's watchfulness and authority. My continued success in position and influence hangs daily on the silence of dependants whose livelihood hangs in turn on my patronage. The few who *know* could ruin me just as I could, with a simple dismissal, toss them down to the Swill towers. There was this also, that the collapse of my small empire would bring down greater ones with it. Commerce was a network of deceit, secret understandings and outright fraud. The State auditors knew it, but what could they do short of dismantling the last bastions of an economic system already moribund?

I trusted Kovacs because I must and because my fact-finders guaranteed him in remarkable fashion. A chameleon, they reported, an ignorant man stuffed with unexpected knowledge, a reader of encyclopaedias, a trivia gatherer. On the other hand an intriguer, a tactician and, when necessary, a thug. Also a devoted family man and a dedicated lecher. In spite of, perhaps because of all this his reputation among the Swill was for dependability and strict honesty. In this the police, of all people, concurred.

What should be the physical appearance of such a man? Cesare Borgia in Swill reach-me-downs?

Not at all. Tonight he was a delight, an oddity, certainly dressed in borrowed plumes and aping swagger to demonstrate command of the interview. In the view of an old hand who knew how men and women ticked, he was out of his depth. I decided to ignore him for a while, a deflating process.

I said, 'Good evening, Francis,' smiling with what genuineness I could bring to the boy's tension.

He muttered, 'Good evening, Mrs Parkes,' and might as well have said, *I don't like it here.*

'Are you well?'

'I'm all right.'

'And your mother, I trust?' What nonsense! His tension was feeding itself to me.

He said with an edge of surliness, 'She's all right.' I barely caught the quick tightening of Kovacs's hand on the boy's shoulder, but Francis reacted with precision. 'I mean, she's very well, thank you, ma'am.'

Number Two Dad says, *Mind your manners!*

What now? Offer a chocolate?

With inspiration, as if it were the obvious conversational gambit, I said, '12,598 over 73?'

He did not so much answer as begin churning, '172.75 – ' It was the right tactic; with his attention turned on himself he relaxed, ' – 342 – '

'Stop, Francis, stop!' He ceased obediently, smirking slyly at what he judged my inability to keep up with him. I said, 'Never more than three decimal places unless I ask for more. You'll flood me in numbers.'

He misunderstood. 'I can remember them for you, ma'am.'

'That could be useful. Are you ready to start work?'

'Yes, ma'am.' He behaved now as if we shared a joke. So that was it: performing Francis was your equal while small boy Francis was a wary, curled-up creature.

I said, 'Sit in the big chair,' and both of them glanced at it. I saw the thief in Kovacs appraise it – timber frame and genuine leather, indecently opulent, *very* expensive.

Francis said, 'I'd rather stand,' and explained, 'Like answering questions in school.'

Kovacs stepped silently away from the boy, redundant, made to feel it and sullen about it.

'Why don't you take the chair, Mr Kovacs? We'll be ten or fifteen minutes.' Dismissal. The rodent face glared for an instant before he perched on the edge of the seat. I could have bet that he had never sat on such luxury in his life.

In a few seconds over twelve minutes we did a week's work in separating the facts of my business from the taxable fiction. When I said, 'That's all, Francis,' he showed disappointment, as though he had been only warming up, but he went to Kovacs, who put a proprietary arm around him.

A genuine feeling. Strange man. Now it was his turn. 'Mr Kovacs, I must speak with yoou.'

The rat face pointed, sniffing at meaning. 'Yes.' It was the first word he had spoken.

I pointed to the doorway. 'Through there, Francis, you will find books. Choose something to read for a while.'

His face lit with pleasure – good! but he looked to Kovacs for permission, granted with a flick of a nod. At the door he said, 'I like old books about when they had adventures.'

Adventures! Gone with the ravaged forests and culled beasts. We had survival, action and danger on the stock market, but no adventures. Romance was gone away. My mind reeled back to walks in rain forests now chopped to chipboard, to swimming in bays whose blue water had turned grey and foul, to being young in a world of wonders with no prescience of it being torn down around you . . . preserved in old novels.

Kovacs asked, 'What do you want, ma'am?'

Yesterday, I should have said. 'I need to be sure of the boy's silence. And yours.'

It was no more than a feeler, a hope that he might have something to offer, but his offended, upward glance said I had disappointed him with a foolishness. 'There's no way to be sure of that, ma'am. We all take the same chance on a greasy footpath.'

I said, 'I suppose that's true,' knowing myself clumsy. No one can guarantee another's silence; psychodrugs can lift any knowledge out of any head. It was a daily risk grown familiar but not therefore discounted, a skeleton at every feast, recalling mortality.

Kovacs stood and the movement carried his message that we spoke as equals; for a second I saw what enemies might fear in him. He was not a big man but he projected an animal forcefulness; better fed, better housed, better treated in a better world, he might have been a power as humans go. As it was he had the physique of a ferret and, they had told me, a mind to match.

'I never break my word, ma'am. That's how I stay alive. Not natural honesty, just good business.'

I believed him at once, but he was crossing psychic swords with me and my nagging, fundamental class consciousness could not brook challenge from the gutter. It was necessary that he understand the nature of power.

'If I had reason to doubt – ' I said, and let the unspoken drag out its implications.

He asked with exemplary politeness, 'What would you do, ma'am? Have us killed? Sounds like triv stuff but I bet it has happened.' I had been worse than clumsy, stupid. Yes, it had happened, though not through me; there were unpleasant stories of the covering of exploded intrigues. He was a most patient, explaining man. 'Ma'am, you haven't got the hard guts for it.' And of course I hadn't. 'I can get killed any day in line of business, it don't worry me none.' I was given a surprising glimpse into his pretensions when he frowned and corrected himself: 'It does not worry me.' I did not dare smile; I think I wanted really to pat his hand and say, *That's right*. 'Suppose,' he said, 'we take each other on trust, then neither gets worried enough to do anything silly. Anyway I'm a businessman and it pays me to protect you.'

That was the rock-bottom argument that should have stopped me before I started. Now it gave me a chance to turn the talk from the awkward lessons he was reading me. 'And I expect the businessman will want payment in cash. Credit would be of no use to you.' A credit voucher in Swill hands would cause instant suspicion of theft.

'Swill get no credit, ma'am, even for good intentions.' He had managed a final flick as the subject changed. 'Not much cash, either, except they steal it.'

'Mrs Conway – '

'She still has her Sweet credit rating in bank deposit, but if Data says she's got no income she can't make more deposits.'

'Well, then?'

'Goods, ma'am. To eat or wear or be used up some way that won't be noticed. You can pay the boy's school fees – nice lady taking pity on Fringe kid – and we can use small change, like for fares to get here. Otherwise, goods.' He unfolded a sheet of paper and held it out to me. It was a list in an awkward but clear script. So few of them could write more than their names.

He saw my surprise. 'We had proper Swill schools once. Remember? But we weren't called Swill then.'

He was probably not as old as I and the difference between us lay bare before me in a shock of guilt. Involuntarily, words jumping out of me, I exclaimed, 'How did we come to this awfulness in a single generation?'

He took the question seriously. 'We didn't, ma'am. It was coming a long time, a century. What the politicians called the Greed Syndrome, that they blamed others for while they had both hands in the till.'

It was the catchphrase of three decades back – the pursuit of wealth, the survival of the wolf; the sapping of the money system as starvation mounted, and starvation mounting as population soared and food became the plaything of graft and international blackmail; statesmen and philosophers and bleeding hearts all helpless against *I want, I want*, as the Earth's resources were sacked to shore up the illusion of an endlessly expanding economy. Ideas and ideals flourished on the intellectual stock exchanges but stood not a chance against *I want* that became *I must have in order to survive*.

Three millennia after its invention money had become the tiger which could be dismounted only in bankruptcy.

'Something wrong there, ma'am?'

I had stared at the list without seeing it. 'No.' I read a little and asked, 'Is this serious?'

'It's not a joke, ma'am.'

'Groceries, toothpaste, pens and slates, scratch pads, soap. Soap!' His quiet gaze seemed to consider me as some ignorant oddity. 'Can you actually not get such things?'

'Some but not enough. They're luxuries.'

'Soap?'

'Soap. You don't realize, do you? You've got this – ' his wave embraced the house, the city, all my kind, ' – so you don't know, don't think.'

'You shame me.'

I meant it but he was genial. 'No need for that. If you gave away all you've got it wouldn't make a dent in the poverty. We can't change anything so we join the greed game, both of us. You're in too deep to stop and I play to stay alive. I'm as bad as you.'

He did not say, *You, rich Sweet, are as bad as I, Swill scum*. The inversion, assuming me naturally corrupt, was worse than the outright insult. I am corrupt; I faced that long ago. But it hurts to be told. I returned to the list. 'Pens, slates, scratch pads. Why, on Earth?'

'I've got five kids, three to twelve, besides the big ones.' Good God – *floreat* Swilldom! 'I try to teach them. But I need books – to teach me, I mean, so I can teach them. I can't steal what I need – I can't get near where books are without starting questions.'

Sympathy shook me almost to tears of pity and respect for such useless courage. 'I'll get what you need. Don't steal. Don't do anything you might be caught at. At least,' and here I tried to set sentiment at arm's length, 'not while I still need you.' That tickled his pragmatism and I felt that we had reached a point of mutual regard. 'How do I get these things to you? You can't very well carry them off in a parcel.'

'There's ways. Now I've seen the area I'll work something out. I'll tell you next time.' Hesitantly he gave away a fraction of his method? 'I've got connections with Little Sweet, delivery drivers and that.'

Interesting, but something I had better not know too much about. I supposed a blurring of caste at the lower levels of income earners, those with relatives on both sides of the line, for instance . . . 'You haven't asked anything for the boy.'

'I'll ask his mother. I had to see the setup first. Next time.'

'But you have asked for yourself and yours.'

'Little things. Testing the delivery line.'

'A general and a planner. Is this all?'

'All for now, ma'am.'

I would have liked to have him stay and talk about his strange world – but ours was a business association. I called, 'Francis!' and he came at once, holding a book close to his chest. 'What have you there, child?'

Unwillingly, perhaps fearing that I would take it from him, he exposed the cover. *Peter Pan*. An old, illustrated edition I had won at school. For essay writing in another world, another culture.

'Do you like it?'

'Yes, ma'am.' With a struggle he overcame doubt and reserve. 'May I finish it when I come again?'

'Take it home. Bring it back next week.'

He broke into an unexpected, excited liveliness, thanks foundering in a clutter of words. To calm him, I asked, 'Would you like to take home something for your mother?'

Reserve returned. He muttered, 'I don't know.' While I tried to think of a gift small enough to fit a pocket, his manner took a startling turn. He said mutinously, 'How do I know what she wants? Why doesn't Teddy get stuff for her? He's the Extra.'

Kovacs ejaculated, 'Francis!' For all his hard dealing he was emotionally simple; a man with such a gaggle of children should have recognized sibling rivalry when it squalled at him, but he was merely shocked at bad behaviour. He could dote as he pleased but I decided then that I disliked Francis. I have not changed my mind in the years since.

'Never mind,' I said, and to Kovacs suggested, 'A woman appreciates good underwear. Even when nobody else sees it.'

He did not rise to that bait, but with all those children bedraggling his home life it would be surprising if a man of his reputation was not finding in Alison Conway an outside solace. I have read that poverty breeds puritanical moral codes to defend the family solidarity, but I do not quite believe it.

When he left, I felt mentally mauled, second rate in the face of such determined efforts at clear sight. But at least I knew and respected what I was dealing with. We could treat as equals.

4

FRANCIS
AD 2044–2050

I never felt the same about adults after that night. I was earning things for Mum and Billy that they couldn't get without me, and it changes everything when you see that they have weaknesses and you have strengths.

I was only nine. Adults underestimate children.

The next few years were quiet, as though a time of adjustment had ended. There were no adventures or highs or lows. At school I made no real friends and on Friday nights Billy and I went to Mrs Parkes's house – after a while I was able to go on my own – to earn our luxuries. That was about all.

Home was more comfortable though we couldn't risk showing our advantages. Keeping clear of the neighbours probably made them more curious than they might otherwise have been but our only regular visitor was Billy (whose presence held tongues at bay) and Mum made sure that the old couple never came into our half. She would tell me that such contacts could only drag down our social level, but I think the neighbours would have protected us out of sheer greed if we had shared some of our luck.

I could not then articulate what I was beginning to perceive, that when the gap between the rich and poor is vast and the middle ground the haunt of an endangered species, snobbery was a defence against terror. The Sweet had to believe in their superiority or admit that they tore their possessions from the fingers of the Swill.

And so we did. We might as well admit to being animals fighting for what we can get. Keep eyes and ears open and there will always be opportunity of profit, influence and security. What you don't grasp, another will. Billy's PR dealing taught me that. Mum said he was a good man doing his best under harsh circumstances, but in fact he was a parasite with a single grace: he looked after his friends.

Teddy did not exist. If I mentioned him, Mum said, 'I don't want to talk about him.' She had to be tough to keep from falling apart but in her heart she bled.

The only other thing that recurs to me from that time is that *Peter Pan* became my favourite book. Mrs Parkes let me keep it. It told of flying into a world where life was an adventure and every adversity was finally an occasion for triumph and joy. Heady stuff for a lonely boy living on the edge of the rubbish tips of his culture.

I was eleven when Billy began staying overnight, sleeping in Mum's room. He kept clothes there, too, because sometimes he had a clean shirt at breakfast and his clothes hung with ours on the drying line. The old couple said nothing; they were too scared. To me it meant nothing. I was incurious about other people's relationships – even the dirty jokes at school had only a removed meaning, the reality of fairy tales. I did see that they had reached a new sort of intimacy, a private talking that switched off when I entered the room, but I did not have a prurient imagination. I must have been a pretty limited boy.

I knew what they were up to, in a hazy fashion, but it did not impinge until Mum delegated to Billy the 'man's job' of explaining to me 'the facts of life' and he stumbled through the sexual catalogue with dumbfounding vagueness. There was nothing new in it, only a connecting-up of disparate schoolyard jokes and speculations; the scribbles on the lavatory walls fell into a pattern. Masturbation, it seemed, was unsatisfactory rather than forbidden and would not, after all, stunt my growth.

It was one more proof that Billy, however successful as a PR man, could also be bumbling and inept. Mum would have done it better, but she had begun to make casual acquaintances in the Fringe shops and to slip into the prim attitudes of the not-quite-Swill who clung to the fairy floss of their lost affluence and the behaviour patterns defining 'woman's sphere' and 'male responsibility'. She laughed at their middle-class morality without seeing that it was hers also.

Visiting Mrs Parkes lost piquancy, became something of a chore. Others offered for my talent but not many were allowed occasional use of me. She and Billy had the sense not to be greedy where too many contacts could leave traces to be detected by computers that 'talked' to each other and pursued anomalies clear to the prison gates.

Since it was impossible that my attendance should go unnoticed in her house, at least by servants as well as unexpected callers and even hovertram drivers, I became her distant nephew in whom she took a philanthropic interest so that my family, fallen on 'discouraging' times, should not feel deserted and ignored. There really were people who soothed their Sweet consciences by playing Lord or Lady Bountiful, and the social delicacy of the time prevented more than superficial questioning of my status.

What I dreamed of and hugged to myself was that I was on my way up, away from the revolting, fearsome tenements. In time I would be wholly Sweet again.

Kids adapt to change so quickly that they forget that the world was not always as in their present moment.

One change frightened the wits out of Mum and most other people and caused some overnight rearrangements of Billy's operations. In response to awesome shifts in the world's economic structure the State froze bank accounts, allowing only business firms to make financial transactions, and then only on paper. A temporary measure only, it was announced. Until national liquidity was restored. For a time those who earned must live on their earnings.

It hardly touched the Swill, who lived on coupons and vouchers, but made a huge difference to Mum who had nibbled each month at a bank account suddenly non-existent. Nobody believed that the State would or could repay what it had grabbed. Nor did it. Many Fringers not quite fallen into the Swill now tumbled all the way and more than a few Sweet suicided in the face of social obliteration.

Mum and Billy were lucky, having me – Mrs Parkes made sure we did not suffer. I knew how much I mattered in the home but did not dare assert myself. Billy would have belted the hide off me now he was practically my stepfather.

More by association than by application I had learned the distinguishing formulae of share transactions, tax dodges, undeclared earnings, international money-buying and the rest of the language of fraud and understood vaguely that money as such was losing meaning in a world geared to poverty.

The Third World (a concept whose meaning has been lost) had, before I was born, renounced indebtedness to the West (another dubious term) and driven money into a no-win situation wherein the Third World had to be shored up financially by the West because it was the West's profitable junk market. The idea of selling to people who bought with money lent by the seller lest the system collapse was more than idiotic; it was the final self-criticism of a system that could exist only by expansion and when expansion ceased for lack of markets must eat its own body.

This was only a part of what was happening to the world but was the most visibly urgent part. Wealth was in the hands of a few and governments were hunting down the sequestrators of wealth before *they* should hunt down the governments. The only strategy of power was to place the entire planetary population in the position of poor relations, fed on what could be salvaged from the necessities of armament equality and the maintenance of a crumbling technology in which research and development shrank as they became too costly. Once there had been a 'space programme'!

Over this desperation presided a monstrous joke, the ravenous armament factories belching out weapons, which became osbolete on the very design screens and must be replaced in the moment of production . . . for a war nobody dared start for fear of nukes and an industry nobody dared stop.

The Australian State – and the world – stalled for a time. Time for what? There were only stopgap answers.

I was fifteen when the money system collapsed worldwide.

That, in a single sentence, records the passing of one of the fundamental human-invented systems, private-sector capitalism. It died because it had reached its limits. The poor – that is, most people – could buy only necessities and disaster struck manufacturers when necessities became, inexorably, luxuries. The dumping ground of the Third World no longer yielded even a miser's profit.

Money did not actually vanish but became a thing of promises and acknowledgements and recognitions of debit and credit held in the guts of the new molecular storage units. The commercial Sweet had spent months preparing for the changeover to what might preserve some standard of living or drive it to final chaos. I suppose it was saved in this country (others fell into conditions worse than beggary) but that may mean just that we had become used to the poverty line. Cash money went out like a passing itch. With forgetful speed it became *convenient* to present an allocation card at a State Distribution Store, see it computer checked to assess the balance of your provision-reserve, be told your entitlement of what was available, make your selection and then start in on the serious calculation of what remainder you could afford to squander in the free-choice section. Home logistics – the calculation of supply, necessity and limited pleasure – became the new game for Swill with simple arithmetic skills.

I recall Mum explaining to Billy that Russia had adopted a similar mode some decades back and had predicted that the rest of the world would come to it. He was shocked, and asked, 'Is this communism, then?' 'Communism' was a dirtier word than any in the four-letter range.

She told him, 'Heavens, no! Communism is only an idea that has never been tried – except perhaps by the Pilgrim Fathers for a very short while, and they were happy to backslide as soon as cash became available.'

For all his hungry reading there was a lot Billy didn't know – he had to be told who the Pilgrim Fathers were.

My one worry was with Mrs Parkes's situation, but she had made her assessment when she saw the change coming, and maybe had inside information, for her network was higher-reaching than Billy's and no more licit. With the change she moved, as it were, sideways, from the ownership of an import–export firm to the direction of a State sub-department, handling the same products. It was a smooth operation and she was one of several to accomplish it. The State helped, knowing whom it wanted, probably knowing who robbed it and preferring efficiency with 'bonus deductions' to muddling honesty.

My calculations changed from cash to kind, frustratingly complex when values were assessed in terms of consumer demand instead of ability to pay. Knowing what a thing was worth required more art than knowledge; the continued use of money terms, still the easiest way of expressing comparisons, was an exercise in abstractions.

Absurd State errors occurred, usually through faulty programming. Billy told horror stories, mostly second-hand, of Swill communities starving through computer error when Deliveries provided tonnes of salt instead of reduced protein, or some such stupidity, but the newscasts reported only the odd comic mixup that had no serious consequences.

There were thin times for some while the system ironed out its creases. In an older day such occasions might have been marked by mass protests and blood in the gutters, but nobody now believed in a better future – better to face life at subsistence level than die by useless violence. That may be a conclusion of hindsight, but at fifteen I saw pragmatism as the common-sense way of solving social problems. I still do.

Total State control made little difference to Mum and myself. Both of us were rediscovering our personal lives and this is always what matters most to any of us. We were growing apart. It's all very well to talk about natural affection and love and the rest of it, but behaviour comes down ultimately to conditioning and advantage. Once you recognize the selfishness motive you begin to see things as they are; what we do 'for others' we do because it suits us, because we get pleasure or because we are constrained. In the end it's all personal profit and loss. Love (using the romantic term for it) can make you forget everything you ever learned about human beings – and later on you pick yourself off a rubbish dump of misery, then look back and see how you let yourself in for it by forgetting that love, for lover and beloved, is total selfishness, the ultimate *I want*.

I had a few schoolyard crushes, but little good they did me; morality was in one of its cycles of prim virtue among the Sweet. Some Fringe girls were less restricted, or perhaps more fed up with the greyness of Fringe living, and between us we learned the tearful rules of the game. I have forgotten most of their names and would be surprised if they remembered mine.

Mum and Billy stopped pretending. When he moved in permanently I wondered what was the position of his wife and family in the tower. Did he give them his spare time as he once did us? He was a contradiction, a sentimental man without moral standards, and that's an optimum combination for free-lancing sexuality.

I had outgrown hero worship and become immune to him; he was good company in his half-wise way but limited in his outlook. His disordered reading was only a picking at bits; his mentality and world view were pure Swill. How Mum put up with him I don't know; pleasure in bed doesn't explain it. I couldn't ask about it; what they shared with each other was taken away from me.

Billy began taking part of his Parkes rake-off in high-class wines and spirits, and he and Mum drank together of a night. They didn't get drunk – Billy would never risk that – but it was part of their loving, something more I could not share. I didn't want to share it. I was seeing them without illusion and soon with less affection. I understood how Teddy could go off and never come back. I saw Mum as she really was, a good-hearted woman, courageous in her way but finally weak. How else could she have accepted Billy?

Beyond the PR gloss he was just a criminal. He stole when he could and was involved in 'removals' of people he called 'bad types', who may have been no more than competitors to be got rid of. I can't say I ever really disliked him; we were better off with him than without, but his sentimental efforts to 'be a father' to me were embarrassing.

I was growing up while Mum was growing down, making herself Swill when she took a Swill man. This was proved to me the day Mrs Kovacs came howling about her rights.

She was grey-haired, fat, ugly, and vicious as the hungry gutter cats. Billy couldn't be blamed for preferring Mum.

I opened the front door to the knock and there she was, meaty-armed and monstrous in dirty overalls and sandshoes, with evil, angry eyes. She said nothing, just pushed me out of her way and almost walked over me – she must have weighed 100 kilos – and into the lounge-room where she screamed at Mum in a Swill argot we could scarcely follow, working herself up for violence. It was sheer luck that someone had warned Billy, so that he came in only half a minute behind her. She wasn't afraid of him and made it plain at the pitch of hoarse lungs; he had practically to fight her out into the street, and she left bruises on his face.

After that I simply had to cut free. If I stayed in that house I would fall to their level by sheer pressure of environment. They were dangerous to me.

Another influence tipped my feeling, a comparatively small thing.

I woke one morning during the 'winter' months feeling cold. The power had failed, which was nothing unusual; it could fail at the hint of an overload, or without it. There was talk of new power plants but they were always being built, never in operation. No money! So we suffered at the dip of a thermometer. Mrs Parkes had a heat pond out back . . .

My bladder got me out of bed, to find the lavatory blocked and stinking. (A job for Billy – he didn't care what he tackled.) It would have to be the back lawn. Shivering in slippers and dressing-gown I stepped into the back yard and into something new and strange. The ground, the plants, the grass were filmed over with frost, like the food in the freezer compartment of the fridge.

Outdoor frost I had heard of but never seen. It was beautiful in a way but frightening; there was satisfaction in dissolving it away in a warm stream but none in the cold air nipping at nose and fingers.

The house was cold and Mum was making breakfast on a smelly oil stove, a bit of junk Billy had found somewhere, and I put my fingers near to warm them. Mum said, 'There was always frost in winter once,' as though it had been a pleasure; she had taken to remembering 'old days' when everything was somehow better though it sounded worse.

Billy came in, in shirt sleeves, looking as if cold did not bother him, and I said, 'I thought it was getting hotter all the time.'

'So it is. World average is up 4½ degrees since 1990.' It was the sort of trivial exactness he picked up from his reading, like a bird pecking at the pavement. 'That's the Greenhouse Effect,' he said, as if nobody had called it that before.

Mum began, 'I remember – ' and cut it off as she heard the words coming too easily, too often. 'There used to be argument about that. Some said temperatures couldn't rise more than 2 degrees because then the air would be saturated. Others said it could go as high as 14 degrees and melt the southern ice cap.'

'The ice cap *is* starting to melt. That water in the bottom of the street isn't all flood water.'

I objected that it would take more than a piddling 4 degrees to melt the polar cap and he said that it was 10 degrees higher there. He couldn't explain why; there was always a hole in his reading that stopped him from knowing anything useful. Anyway, the met stations said the oceans had risen 30 centimetres overall.

It was my turn to start, 'I remember – ' and not continue. I remembered millions of Swill swimming like mad, and stopped at the thought that most of the Big Sweet lived on high ground well above the coastline and the river. Did they know facts that we did not, facts not discussed on newscasts or in triv plays?

And there was this morning's cold. If the temperature was rising, how . . . ? Billy had the answer among his jackdaw bits. A volcano had blown its crater 5,000 kilometres away and filled the air with dust, so there would be some temporary cooling.

At school the heating was off but came on at midday when it no longer mattered. At Mrs Parkes's house it would have been on all the time . . .

I thought how it hurt to go into her house and see not just beautiful things but clean things, new things, unbroken things. What we had at home was cramped space, blocked sewers and the tattiness of neighbours and neighbourhood. And now the sea moving up the street. I could perch on the fence and see it in the distance, reaching up at the tenements before it ebbed back into the bay. Closer, closer, and one day not to ebb at all?

It was time to get away from the dirty, dangerous Fringe.

NOLA PARKES
AD 2050

Francis at fifteen was little improvement over Francis at nine or twelve. I did not glean much from conversation with Kovacs but could see that the boy had outgrown his young love for the man; tiny touches of resentment, unconscious facets of attitude, peeped out. I suspected, too, that affection for his mother had waned, that he loved little beyond himself and my hoarded books. I had to remind myself that his home life must be deadening, his social life arid, confused and driven by Swill fear.

He rarely displayed much wisdom but could move effectively when crowded; he always managed to slip from between contending issues. So I suspected that circumstances were forcing him when he made his natural, logical and, I was sure, dishonest request.

He lingered, one Friday night, at the end of our accounting session instead of making impatient getaway to my library shelves.

'Is there something you want, Francis?'

He had become a good-looking boy who would be handsome and poker-faced. He was capable of a charming smile, but rationed it. He offered me the beginning of it now, the twitch of a smile in process of becoming. Very appealing. Wasted on me because I was unable to like him. He was with me still because his talent and his silence, of which he knew the value to both of us, had become indispensable.

'There is something, ma'am. If I could – It's just that – '

His teenage acting was unpolished, the hesitation too calculated to display the poor young man who knows his place but trusts in the stern but just older woman. He had only bad triv scripts to learn from. Hesitation should be followed by a rush of words. It was.

'I was thinking, ma'am, that I could be more use to you if I was on your proper staff. If I lived in Quarters. You could call me when it suited instead of having to save everything up for Friday.'

The idea had at times presented itself to me. It would enable me to pay some debts of obligation by farming out his talent in small, regulated benefices – bribes and thank-yous. I had mentioned the farming-out idea to Kovacs, who had been nervous of Sweet areas outside his knowledge, game enough but afraid for the boy if a move misfired.

'Have you talked to Mr Kovacs about this?'

The question took his planned dialogue unprepared; his mouth opened and closed. At length he shook his head, sensible enough to be truthful where he knew I could nail a lie.

'Why do you want to leave home?'

He answered instantly, 'Because I hate it,' dropped his eyes and his voice in decent reluctance to complain of personal matters. 'Mum's got Billy now. All the time. Like a husband, I mean. They don't want me around.'

I knew that Kovacs had moved into the house and he had been cheerfully open about it when I referred to it as a reminder that I kept my eye on him. Being curious about Mrs Kovacs, I was told bluntly, 'I look after her and the kids, I love 'em all. But for bed games you can't go on pretending after twenty-five years. You have to be honest.' Honest! Billy Lecher had charm and was as common as dirt. I could have told the presumably contented Mrs Conway that he sowed his seed lavishly in the course of his PR activities and was known around the gutter as Billygoat. He had the morality of a teenager mixed with a genuine capacity for love (in his fashion) and respect for his responsibilities. Certainly his zest for living cut across the Swill legends of misery and resignation.

But who knows the hearts of the tower dwellers? We don't want to know. I understood Francis's need because, like anyone on the secret knife edge, I shared his fear of the depths.

I said with some dryness, 'You don't look neglected, Francis.'

'Oh, I get enough to eat and that – it's just that they don't care any more what I'm doing. They don't even ask.' Silly! He should have guessed that Kovacs asked, often. Came the predictable punch line: 'They wouldn't notice if I wasn't there.'

He deserved sending off with a flea in his ear, not for his ingratitude, because fewer children are grateful than their parents hope, but for the blatant attempt to use me. Still, there could be advantages . . . Automatically, in line with the mental processes of years, I looked for compromise and found it.

'You can join Staff as a trainee warehouse auditor.' Placement Data would complain but could be overruled. The boy's face was a study to treasure; it had not occurred to him that a move to Quarters necessitated the creation of a real job. 'There will be time for you to continue your special work. And to go to school.' I had expected *school* to cool his fever but his face approved the word.

'You *want* to study?'

'Yes, ma'am.'

'For what?'

'To go to university, ma'am.'

He had surprised me. 'It can be arranged, in time. But to what end, which degree?'

He shook his head, not knowing, saying a little desperately, 'There must be something.'

'Something essential?'

He nodded fearfully, knowing that I saw clear through him.

'Something so necessary that it will save you for ever from falling into the Swill?'

That was cruel, for it was a perfectly good motive. But reason enough for lies and ingratitude?

I allowed myself an unjust mockery. 'On present trends the whole planet will be Swill soon enough.' Plainly he did not recognize the possibility, was impervious to the world outside himself. I moved to remind him of it. 'You can move into Quarters next week, but – ' How his head came up, wary of conditions! ' – but I will not have you desert your mother and Mr Kovacs. You will spend your weekends at home.'

It was obviously a setback but he knew better than to protest or comment. He was sufficiently upset, when I sent him away, to forget to take a book.

I regretted my need of him. The young brute had not spoken a word about the future for his mother and Kovacs, probably had not thought of them, but I meant to see to it that he found his responsibilities pursuing him up the ladder of escape. Deductions from his vouchers would augment the Kovacs contribution I had no intention of stopping. Francis must pay for his self-seeking.

We all pay for our self-seeking.

6

FRANCIS
AD 2050

I had expected refusal, to have to make the attempt again and again until I succeeded; even the qualified success was a triumph. Mrs Parkes recognized my value to her; the rest was just conventional family-style thinking. And her kindness was remote, more like good manners than goodwill; her true thought was hidden.

When I got home Billy was out somewhere, which suited me. He was hard to lie to. He would not try to trip me up but simply look and walk off, leaving me soiled and ashamed even when I was in the right.

I told Mum that Mrs Parkes had decided to put me on Staff, that it meant promotion and bigger rewards – and that I would have to live in Quarters.

Her face went quite still. With scarcely moving lips she said, 'So both my sons are successes.' The oblique reproach upset me so much that I blurted out what I had meant to keep to myself until I had thought about it, that the Ma'am wanted me to spend my weekends at home.

She relaxed like someone who had started at a shadow.

She had lost much of her figure and complexion of her Sweet days though she looked better than some of the Little Sweet frumps in the Ma'am's big office at City Centre; she was filling out and would get chubby, her skin was roughening and would become lined. Still, she was not soft and helpless and she had Billy. She smiled now after the ugly stillness and said, 'You must make your way, but don't leave home.'

'But some day, when I grow up – '

'Time enough then. But not yet, Francis. Not yet.'

Her gentleness rocked my determination; in that moment the future could have resolved itself differently. Yet I knew that I must be resolute or be lost. I kissed her and went to bed, leaving her to tell Billy.

I expected hard questions from Billy when he came to breakfast in the morning, half-dressed as always with only a spit of a wash. I had grown used to his slovenliness but now I saw it again as repellent and gutter cheap. He might drag Mum down but not me.

All he said was, 'You got a lift-up, eh?'

'Yes. It means more work though.'

'But good pickings in Quarters.'

'Maybe. I don't know.'

At the stove, pouring tea, he said, 'It's what you wanted.'

'In a way.' I did not recall ever saying what I wanted but Billy's intuition could be troubling.

If he was probing, Mum stopped it by saying, 'If he's to have two homes he'll need more clothes.'

He sucked his tea with the slight slurp he never conquered. 'That's the Ma'am's worry. She wants him, she sets him up.' He stared hard at me. 'Right?'

I hadn't thought of it. 'I suppose so.'

'If you sell yourself, see you get a proper price.'

Sell yourself was sour; I had the feeling of being tested without knowing what for, but comforted myself that it was just Billy's habit of distrusting every move until he understood it thoroughly.

On the Monday morning when I left to start my first week in Quarters he said, 'We'll see you Friday night, then,' and my guilt suspected irony.

It did not occur to me that Billy, whose only business with the Ma'am was picking up the weekly fee, rarely seeing her, did occasionally talk with her as part of what he fancied to be his responsibility as number two dad. Had I known I would not have dared to carry out my plan. I always feared Billy even when I loved him.

A senior house clerk saw me to my room in Quarters, a compact combination of bedroom and lounge-room (what old novels called a 'bedsitter') with a full-sized triv and a full range of terminals and accessories, a small refrigerator and utensils for preparing snacks and drinks – luxury for the body, privacy for the mind.

The clerk, an uninteresting little born bootlicker, said, 'A Fringe boy can strike it lucky, eh?'

I hadn't realized that all of them knew where I came from and I snapped back at him, fast, 'The Fringe boy wasn't lucky. He made his opportunity.'

He clasped hands in mock admiration and whinnied, 'My, but we *will* get on in the world, won't we?' and hurried off to tell his section about the uppity new kid. It was a poor start but I didn't care; I had blessings to count.

. . . The beginning of a life of my own making . . . an ambience of intelligence and sane living . . . an education I could not have obtained as a Fringe boy unable to afford it (actually, unable to reveal the existence of the means to afford it) . . . a kindly Ma'am and a simple cover job . . . luxury, position, protection in return for a few hours of service a week . . .

I was mistaken. For the next three years I worked like a driven horse.

The 'cover job' was real. I spent four hours a day in the warehouse, learning the logistics of government supply while a secretive part of my brain put together an infinity of two-and-twos to discover just how the Ma'am operated her network of subtraction and accountability. I spent six hours a day in school, in special tutorial classes set up by the Ma'am for her own children and a selected few of the junior Staff. It was there that I met Lottie Parkes, only a few months younger than myself. But more of her in its proper place. I had also to keep my room spotless and take my turn at rostered duties in Quarters, like cleaning the community rooms.

I worked a twelve-hour day before I called a moment my own and the first week brought me close to tears, but in time the pace became a practicable routine and the days as manageable as though my life had been spent in commerce. At the end of that first week, though, I could not get home fast enough for two days of lounging and lazing.

Mum and Billy found my woebegone account matter for laughter and talked about 'facing realities' until I could have spat in their silly faces. Their insensitivity glorified my nest of privacy in Quarters. When I left on the Sunday night I took a few private things with me, not enough to arouse suspicion, enough to prove to myself that I was cutting loose from the empty past.

On the following weekend I took a few more.

On the fifth weekend I stayed in Quarters. The break was made.

Many Staff had no homes outside Quarters, so meals were served as on other days; I would lose nothing by not going home. Mrs Parkes would not approve, but she rarely came near Staff Wing of a weekend. She would find out eventually but with luck this need not happen until the separation had established itself. I need only behave quietly.

The luck ran out immediately.

81

Lottie, of all people, spotted me. I had not known that she was in training to succeed her mother and that one of her apprentice jobs was to monitor the kitchen stores and weekend catering. She saw me at Saturday breakfast but paid no attention, so I thought no more of it then.

Lottie at fifteen was in her chrysalis stage – too fat, a little owlish and serious, playing strenuous games in hope of achieving the figure which later fell into neatness of itself – but she was nobody's fool. She was a rapid learner, had her own bright talent for music and was not impressed by my arithmetical acrobatics, but we got on well together in class – it's possible that the ma'am had told her to make me feel at home.

I felt at home without anybody's help, but Lottie was a comfortable sort of girl and we chatted in class breaks, but socially we were rungs apart, so it surprised me later that morning to answer a knock on my door and find her on the threshold. She asked without preamble, 'Does Mother know you're here? You aren't listed.'

That was a body blow. I shook my head uneasily.

Lottie said, 'She'll be furious when she finds out.'

I knew that, but asked, 'Why should she?'

'Because she promised that man you would go home at weekends.'

She did not move to come in and I was too shaken for the courtesies. 'What man?'

'I think he's a Swill.' She smiled like someone with a secret. 'Don't tell Mother, but I think he's nice. In a rough sort of way.' (Good God!) 'I didn't think Swill were like that.'

'They aren't,' I told her, 'and neither is he. And look, I won't tell the Ma'am if you don't say I'm here.'

That wasn't any sort of a bargain on her side but, still half girl and half woman, she liked the idea of small intrigue. She said, 'Secrets!' with a finger on her lip, and went away.

She told, of course. Not right away but fairly soon.

The Ma'am sent for me one Monday morning. 'You did not go home at the weekend.'

'No, ma'am,' telling myself unhappily that I was not frightened.

'Or for the three previous weekends.'

'No, ma'am.' Timidly. I dared not be brazen with her.

'Why not?'

With a sensation of stepping off a cliff I gathered my little courage for the fall. 'I didn't want to, ma'am. I don't want to go there again, ever.'

She surveyed me in the strangest fashion, not as if I had done something wrong but as if she was seeing her handiwork and blaming herself, and to herself rather than to me she said, 'Nothing to be gained by forcing you.' Then she asked, 'Are you happy here?'

'Yes, ma'am.' I meant it. I was half silly with happiness because she was not about to crush me.

She fiddled with the things on her desk, making idle patterns, then sighed and said, 'Go back to your work.'

I was at the door when she spoke again. 'You are throwing away love. Do you know what that means?'

I could risk boldness. 'No, ma'am. There is no love there.'

'Do you think that?' I was wary of a faint distaste in her tone, but all she said was, 'You lack gratitude.'

'No, ma'am, I don't lack.' I had to make some sort of a stand. 'But do I have to be grateful for ever while the chances pass me by?'

She seemed to look at me without seeing me while her thought went out and round and back again. 'Perhaps,' she said, 'it is best that you remain here, where I can see you. So that you do not make *silly* mistakes.'

She looked down at her desk. It was dismissal.

In later, cooler mood, I had second thoughts about her last remark. The scene could not be replayed or altered; it was a warning against something that eluded me.

Lottie came to see me. She had been crying. 'I didn't mean to tell. I didn't, Francis, but she knew anyway and that man was here.'

If he had wanted me back he hadn't got me. Why should he want me? Mum nagging him?

Well, it was done with and Lottie was getting ready to cry again over her hapless treachery. She needed comfort and I was in giving mood. Besides, I liked her and her charm was beginning to flower.

THE AUTUMN PEOPLE 2

Andra woke early, which in his life's experience meant that his mind was busy and telling him to get on with the pursuit of its obsession; sleep would come when necessary, when exhaustion dropped him into it.

He had left the curtains wide and from the bed he could see a square of sky, morning-grey with as yet only a promise of blue, flecked with wisps of cloud whose eastern edges were scarcely tinted pink. The colours warmed and deepened as he watched.

In the grey half-dark of his room he fashioned his obsession, the armature on which the theme of his play would be built. Its shape was a man lounging in a dark corner, chewing slowly, grinning familiarly, defying completion. Andra stripped the clothes from him, striving to see the body, to discover what muscle could be plated on to bones covered with a minimum of fat, to observe the resultant cording of surface veins, to manipulate the stance, holding spine and pelvis in pivot and balance for swift and easy movement. Sure now of how the man moved and stood, he built the clothes back on to the frame, observing how they fell and creased and fitted.

The face was difficult. Ratface! The nose insisted on too much elongation and tended to wrinkle at him, snuffling over too-sharp teeth. A difficult visualization.

Entrancement was broken as the wall screen shrilled for his attention. He sat up, swearing damnation as his mind-figure vanished, and scrabbled for the remote control to shut off the noise, refusing the call. It began again at once with Lenna's voice overriding the signal, 'Don't shut off, Andra. Please answer me.'

He yelled at the screen, 'Do you always get up in the small hours?'

'It is after seven. I thought that – '

So it was, and full daylight, the room bright with early sun; time had raced by while he built a man out of shadows.

'Yes, yes, it's all right. I was working.'

'I'm sorry I interrupted you.'

He said pettishly, needing a small dart, 'So am I. What can I do for you?' and was glad she had not opted for visual. And what did *she* look like at this hour, before the day's disguise was dabbed and patted into place? Like a self-possessed tutor, of course; only handsome actors looked like destiny's bad joke at sunrise.

She said, with a hint of placation, not quite all tutor, 'You could breakfast with me. You may have questions.'

'Plenty of those, but I had thought of a meeting later on.'

'Not before tonight, I'm afraid. I have my regular lecture and tutorials as well as administrative duties. After today I will not be so busy.'

She was saying, without undue emphasis, that she was prepared to give her time now and he could like it or leave it. An accustomed autocrat, he submitted unwillingly, reaching for a shred of histrionic charm to grace his voice. 'That's kind of you. Please forgive my abruptness. I'm usually a late riser and not at my best at sparrowcrack.'

'Who is? In half an hour, then?'

'Yes.'

He heard her take a breath before she asked with a return of the timidity that afflicted her as an author of fiction, 'How much did you read?'

'Part one, to the point where that beastly child cut the ties with his home.' She would expect more, something heartening. 'Strange. Interesting. Evocative.' That should be enough to hold her for half an hour.

'Ah.' The screen switched off with a discreet hiccup. In the corner Kovacs flickered briefly to cover his mouth with bony fingers, aping the gentility he could not command. *That* would require work not to raise laughs in the wrong places.

He keyed for outside temperature – 9 degrees, fairly average for early morning in these cooling, weakening summers; 22 later, the forecast promised. Jacket and heavy trousers, he decided.

With a quarter of an hour to spare he took a turn round the lawns and found his memory assaulted by the morning scents of shrubs and flowers and cleansed air. He was rarely up so early, certainly never outside so soon; the fresh world was a return to childhood.

This southern edge of the campus was served by the South Hill Escalator that ran 400 metres down to the river bank. The drop provided a huge vista of the city far below, patches of bright fog still snug in its hollows, and beyond it the islands in the intricate delta of the Yarra, and beyond again, the sparkle of blue-green sea and a soft white line of horizon mist.

A solitary figure on the rising section of the Escalator grew improbably into Marin, dressed only in shorts and a thin shirt as though temperature were the concern of lesser breeds – non-Christians, for instance. Andra, preparing to rein his temper and treat insolence with suave good humour, was greeted by a breezy boy (would he be nineteen? twenty?) who wanted to show him round the campus and was disappointed at unwillingness.

'Perhaps after breakfast, Marin. I don't rouse much enthusiasm on an empty stomach.'

'You won't rouse much on the Scholar's breakfast. Coffee and a crust! We could go to the Communal afterwards and eat properly.'

Surprised, Andra asked, 'Are you also breakfasting with Miss Wilson?'

'Yes, she buzzed me to come up. She had a suggestion that should interest you.' He took Andra's arm familiarly while preserving protocol address (strange boy!). 'Look across there, Artist.'

He pointed out over the New City, over the islands to a hump still dim in the morning, some twenty to thirty kilometres away. 'That's the only Enclave that was sited high enough never to have been flooded. It's cut down and broken by storms and erosion – and probably by hasty building practices – but the ground floors are more or less intact with their internal divisions. So are the promenade skirts. You can actually walk the street between the towers.'

Some enthusiasm there. From the corner of his eye Andra sought and found a genuine glint in the boy's expression.

Said Marin, 'The Scholar suggests that we visit them this morning. Or in the afternoon, if that suits better. She feels that you should see them.'

'Then I suppose I must.' And what of *his* needs, *his* routines, *his* habits of work? She would say, with tutorial smile: *All in good time, Andra; now, first you must* – But he had begged the grant, hadn't he? 'This afternoon,' trying not to sound driven and mutinous.

'Straight after lunch? One o'clock, say? At the boat? It will be worth it. There are sections in the book where it helps to have the reality in mind.'

'In the book?'

'The novel. She said you had begun it last night.'

'She did?'

'That's why she called me for breakfast.'

'I see.' He saw nothing at all but thought the sense would appear in time. 'Have you also read it?'

'Of course.'

Of course! 'How did it impress you?'

'I am not a judge of literature, Artist.'

What luck that Christianity had little to say about literary criticism. 'Did you enjoy it?'

Marin's boyishness deserted him in favour of the moralist. 'It pleads for a lenient view of the Greenhouse people, yet scarcely an action in the story is less than venal.'

'Ah.'

'But it holds the attention. It is a weakness of the flesh that – ' a change of tone heralded a thumping piece of moral pronouncement, ' – that one is fascinated by the contemplation of wickedness.'

'Yes, indeed.' Prudently he refrained from suggesting that acquaintance closer than contemplation had its attraction but asked, carefully because unsure what might cause the boy's prickles to appear, 'Am I permitted to ask why Miss Wilson gave you her book to read?'

It seemed not to be an intrusion. 'I think she wanted to broaden my mind, as the saying is.' He swept an arm to gather in all the Old and New Cities. 'She wants me to see these from various viewpoints. She once described Christianity as too narrow a slit through which to watch the world.'

'I would agree.'

'I suppose that professionally you must. Your profession, Artist, mirrors the world but does not explain it.'

Andra suppressed an impulse to hit him, while admitting privately that an encounter would most likely leave him bruised and bloody; the Christians had never been a peaceful brood. Hadn't their founder caused a riot in a temple, wielding a scourge? And brought 'not peace but a sword'? (A good line, that.)

'She also said,' the boy continued, 'that to understand evil it is necessary to see it through the eyes of the evil-doer. In some part her book is an attempt to do that. It is very instructive.'

Andra considered this ground altogether too treacherous. 'It is time we went to breakfast.'

Breakfast for Lenna was truly coffee and a crust – well, toast spread with some kind of sugarless, diet-conscious viscosity – but for her guests there were eggs and stewed fruit and containers of salt and sugar, which she did not touch.

Andra could not forbear remarking that Marin did not offer a grace.

'How could you know, Artist? Noisy prayer is not a badge of virtue.'

Serves me right. Stick to what you know, Andra.

'My time is limited,' Lenna said. 'Would you have urgent questions, Andra?'

'Several dozen that can wait on developments, one that I would like to settle before continuing. The total cleavage between Sweet and Swill puzzles me.'

'It was never total, as you will see in later chapters.'

'There was the Fringe, but that seems to have been something of a buffer zone.'

'It was exactly that, designedly. Each Enclave was surrounded by a Fringe zone and a ring of open parkland, and each Enclave had a strong military post in its heart.'

'So it was a tyranny?'

Marin suggested, 'A master–man relationship? Keeping the Swill in their places and letting them know it? It was not quite so.'

Lenna turned on him her wholly tutorial aspect. 'If you have perceived that much – '

The boy said with a touch of wariness, 'I have done some ancillary reading also.'

'Then tell me what you have understood.'

Marin chewed pensively as he sought an entry into complications. 'The idea was not oppression but preservation. The Sweet, educated and by and large the most competent sector of the population – with the usual leaven of time-servers – were necessary to adminster the State. With the collapse of trade and all but essential industry the Swill became a burden on the economy, easier and cheaper to support if it were concentrated into small areas.'

Andra asked, 'Are you saying that they built the Enclaves and herded the unemployed into them?'

'No, no. It happened almost by accident. Sweeping changes always seem to arise without planning – taking advantage of them comes later. By the turn of the millennium the employment position was so bad that governments everywhere were forced to build high-rise apartments to accommodate the people supported by the State. They knew high-rise was socially a poor answer; the previous half-century had proved that, but with two-thirds of the people on pension or dole the financial situation was desperate. With populations rising, the people could not be spread over the countryside. Productive land had to produce, and Australia had never been a fertile country. So the Enclaves grew. By the end of the second decade they had become recognized as a mode of existence and the State organized itself around what had become a fact of living.'

91

He glanced at Lenna, not quite prepared to ask *How am I doing?* but heartened by her nod. Andra thought it sounded like a prepared speech: am I present at a viva voce? He said, 'Everybody thought it a good idea and settled comfortably down? A place for everything and everything in its place?'

'Not at first, Artist. Nothing human is so simple. The Sweet were no problem to the State – they knew that the Computer Culture was on its way out of history and that the Greenhouse disruption of weather and agriculture was the final blow. They knew that present comfort depended on toeing whatever line the State decreed, and the State played on their fear of poverty. The Sweet became a sort of aristocracy, graded from servitude to power.' He added, as if it summed them up, 'The hectic culture of decay.'

'And the Swill?'

'*They* wanted nothing to do with the Sweet. They despised them.'

'Now that needs explaining.'

Marin shook his head. 'I am not sure that I understand, either. Scholar?'

Lenna set down her coffee and rested her hands on an invisible lectern. 'In a classless – at any rate, a casteless society, it seems an irrational attitude, but throughout history it has been a psychological refuge of the poor to denigrate their so-called betters, to satirize their excesses and manners and behaviour and pretend *they* were above such an artificial existence. The Swill thought of themselves as the *real* people and sublimated their envy by aping contempt. They pretended they wanted nothing to do with them and Enclave existence ensured just that. In a couple of generations the Swill founded a whole new culture, based on necessity, self-preservation and lack of information.'

Andra pushed a piece of eggshell round his plate. 'It makes no sense. There must have been envy and anger.'

'Of course. Bitter envy and anger. The contempt was a pretence, a shelter to make poverty bearable, even honourable, and so make pride possible. It is a historical commonplace. You might check with a psychologist.'

'No, that won't be necessary.' (But he would do it.) 'But why did no leader arise to take them out of the Enclaves and sweep the Sweet out of existence? They had a human tide of numbers.'

Marin offered one of his fits of gnomic wisdom: 'Revolutions begin in the universities; the streets breed only riots.'

'I distrust aphorisms, lad.'

Lenna said, 'He has a point. It is close enough to truth for the exceptions to be very noticeable. Revolutions have commonly brewed for decades before erupting – the two great revolutions of the Late Middle period, the French and Russian revolts, simmered through a century of intellectual argument before demagogues arose to begin the killing. Without intellectuals to stir them, the poor tended to accept their condition and devise philosophies to make it bearable. Occasional tensions caused outbursts of rioting which were controllable because they were mostly uncentralized and unplanned.'

'Most controllable,' Marin pointed out, 'when there was a military detachment with the firepower of an army sitting on the doorstep. It was also possible to drive rioters indoors by spraying unpleasantness from the air. And the parklands made it visibly unwise for large numbers to try to cross into Sweet territory. I think they called them zones of fire.'

'Yet you claim it was not a tyranny.'

Marin threw a plea for help to Lenna, who explained: 'Force was rarely necessary. The decay of the State's ability to service the towers properly caused the rise of the Tower Bosses. These were at first gangsters pure and simple, but a few men of vision gained the upper hand in some towers and established the pattern of small states within the State. The police and the Political Security executive saw the value of this and encouraged it by opening the corrupt lines of communication you read of last night. They gave the Swill a measure of contentment by letting them run their own affairs as far as possible. The other thing they did, with a nice sense of political management, was to convince the Tower Bosses that only a condition of status quo could preserve a collapsing civililization. They had a saying – don't rock the boat. Fifty years earlier it might have been good advice but the senior men who were steering the boat knew it was already too late. One can only suppose that they persisted in the hope of a miracle.'

From the mooring in one of the delta's confusing byways the Enclave was at first awesome, majestical to people who did not find great height a necessity of building. Eleven floors of the nearest tower remained, more or less, dog-toothed against the skyline, in two places riven clear to the ground. Looking up the slope from the powercraft it was impossible not to see this vast relic in terms of mightiness and eternity and the infinite sadness of silence.

Marin led the way up the path through weeds and low shrubs. There were signs that trees had been cleared away to allow the first overwhelming vision from below; they had been cleared, too, from the 100-metre concrete skirt surrounding the first tower and from the flanking roadways. The remainder of the Enclave had been left as the forest claimed it. Andra counted nineteen giant walls rising over the trees and there were possibly others timeworn below the level of the green. All in all, the seagirt Enclaves had fared better, their bases protected from cyclone and polluted rain.

The power of growing things confounded imagination. Little fresh top soil had formed on this man-made clearing but the roadway had for all practical purposes vanished under weeds, shrubs, trees, native grasses. The huge concrete skirt, like a shield round the foot of the building, had been forced into humps where trees had made power-ful passage to the sunlight, cut and sliced and shattered where grasses and growths as fragile as wild flowers had heaved themselves through tiny rifts to create crevasses.

Yet a ruin is a ruin, a toppled remnant, and its final statement is failure. In Andra's effort to imagine the Enclave pristine and soaring – brilliant with sun on windows, noisy with the crush of life in the streets – it survived only a breath or two before settling into hangdog decay. It became ugly, monotonous and dead.

He poked interestedly round the ground floor of the first tower, cleared of rubble for inspection, observing the layout of stairways and corridors, liftshafts and lightwells and the various maintenance rooms. Everything was dismayingly compact. Space had not only not been wasted by the architects but made to accommodate more than such restricted spaces should – the tower interior was claustrophobic. The buildings had been strikingly self-contained; Marin identified garbage disposal, sewage treatment, air conditioning and other ser-vices from the fragments of machinery remaining.

'Most metal was salvaged and re-smelted once the new technologi-cal era began. They took whatever could be used.'

Andra mused on history repeating. 'Their ancestors – *our* ancestors tore down much of the Roman Colosseum for building blocks.'

'That still exists. These scarcely do though there's not much sal-vageable from poured concrete.'

'You are interested in history?'

'In some history, Artist. I plan to write the history of the Christian churches.'

Andra's heart sank; the subject lay in wait behind the most inno-cent, distant remark.

Marin continued, 'The Scholar is helping me.'

'You are a student?'

'In part time only.'

'Please tell me why a very senior professor assists a part-time student.' He had had to scratch and claw his way past obstacles to obtain her limited services; only his professional reputation, in his sphere as high as hers, had gained him a hearing.

'Professor Wilson is my great-aunt.'

Nepotism flourishes. He said jealously, 'You are fortunate.'

'Yes, Artist,' Marin said smugly, aware of privilege. 'She does not do so very much with me because I have a regular tutor, but she locates obscure Data Bank references for me and plays me tapes from the Late Middle period. And discusses historical theory. And she let me read her novel.'

'Hardly as Christian history, I imagine.'

They turned about and started down to where the powercraft lay. Andra was pleased to have the ancient monsters behind him; the inspection had been useful but the ruined silence in the end oppressive. What further detail he might need for the creation of his play could be obtained from holograms and reconstructions.

'I think,' Marin said, still smug on the subject of Marin, 'that she would subvert my faith if she could.' As a simple fact, as if it were not a defiance of earthly powers, he declared, 'But I know my strength.'

At any rate, Andra decided, you believe in it however little you know it. He prodded, 'The novel?'

'She wished me to see that virtue can exist without a religious basis.'

'And?'

'I perceive some virtue in her characters and remember that their actions were those of real people. Most of them in that day were nominally Christian but pagan at heart, so their virtues achieved nothing, having no firm foothold in a faith. Their virtues becames vanities, lacking humility.'

'I haven't observed much humility in you.' Andra could have bitten the words off his tongue but felt better for the small release.

'As you say, Artist.' Carefully noncommittal.

Some silence brooded as they made their way downhill and Andra cogitated what olive branch he might offer this prickly young man.

Marin's curiosity saved him the trouble as he asked tentatively, 'Concerning your play, Artist?'

'Yes?'

'Have you some definite form in mind?'

'Not yet. No form. One thing only – Kovacs. So many facets to the man. A play needs at least one character who is wholly individual.'

After a few paces Marin said with quiet innocence, 'I would have imagined that the Artist would realize that all people are wholly individual.'

Fair payment. Andra held back a smile: let the boy count coup. 'I should like to play Kovacs.'

Marin, a few paces ahead, balked in his stride and half turned back to him. 'You could hardly do that.'

Andra offered coldness to chill the air, the real ice of the expert challenged at the heart of his being. 'And why not?'

The sound of an arrogance to match his own had its effect on Marin. 'I mean, Artist, that – uh – how can I put it? The physical terms are different.'

Andra, seeing the trouble, unfroze a little, not much. 'So?'

'Kovacs was a thin man where you are broad. His face was narrow and pointed to the nose, seeking, prying. His bones showed through his flesh.'

'Look!' With his palms Andra clapped his ears close to his head, pulling back the skin of chin and cheeks. He dropped his shoulders and hunched them forward, taking 10 centimetres from his breadth. With eyes narrowed, face thrust forward and cheeks sucked in to elevate the bones, he misquoted in a sly, cajoling voice, '"This Cassius hath a lean and hungry look."'

And so he had – in daylight, without the distance of the stage, without make-up or the false skins of illusion.

Marin muttered, 'I apologize, Artist. You could play anything.'

'Anything human,' Andra told him and stubbed his toe painfully against a stone in recognition of vanity. Marin's damned Christian God, he thought, was listening.

Through Lenna's window a red sunset laid glamour on the campus and the city as Marin gave his version of the afternoon's inspection. It had little reference to Andra who found it disturbing to hear young enthusiasm turn, sentence by sentence, to bigoted morality and end with, 'It is easy to pity them but in the end they were a wicked people who brought their world to a wicked end.'

Lenna, still in tutorial grey, suggested gently that in the face of the insurmountable they had done their best.

'Strength without virtue! It wasn't good enough, was it?' He glanced out of the window, threw history overboard and exclaimed that the day was nearly over and maintenance remained to be done on the powercraft. 'Goodbye, Aunt Lenna,' To Andra's surprise he kissed her. 'I'm sure we'll meet again, Artist.' And he was gone, running, to beat the sundown.

Andra said, 'That is the first time I have heard him address you familiarly.'

'Sometimes he forgets his reserve. Mostly he is terrified that others will think he gets his tuition by my favour.'

'Does he?'

'Not altogether – he is a very good student. I admit I help.'

'Sooner or later he will have to choose between morality and reality.'

She laughed. 'That's easily said, but which is which? Should I brew tea?'

'Please do. I was wondering this afternoon if God allows your nephew to chase girls.'

She laughed. 'Most busily.'

'I'm pleased to hear it. No conflict there between morality and reality?'

Busy with pot and hot water, she said, 'I don't ask what goes on in the powercraft by night. I shouldn't want to be the cause of a holy schizophrenia.'

Down below, the foreshortened figure of Marin jog-trotted to the Escalator head; otherwise the campus, busy when they had come up from the river, was almost deserted; the evening gale was not dangerously powerful, but powerful enough to discourage unnecessary exposure – the city retired indoors for its unruly half-hour. As Andra watched, its approach was heralded by a dimming like a light veil over the distant sea; outside the window the branches bent in their first gentle swing.

'And I,' he said, 'would rather have his moral dilemmas than those of the two graceless sons of Alison Conway. Did those desertions actually happen?'

'Yes. She kept a diary which was preserved in one of the time capsules.'

'A nasty pair.'

'You may change your mind about that – they were products of their time. Family bonds had been loosening for three generations before they were born, there is plenty of evidence of that.'

'Love disappearing in a pragmatic culture?'

'Not at all.' She set out cups and small biscuits. 'Changing its meaning, perhaps. Love was always a word that covered too much territory, from loving a spouse to loving a hobby or abstract justice, and the emotion-mongers of popular entertainment portrayed it as everlasting and exclusive. In a culture under stress the truth could not be concealed by sentimental fluff. The Greenhouse people learned to appreciate love without glorifying it.' She paused, eyes searching the table distractedly for something elusive. 'Sugar, of course! Your poison.'

Andra thanked fortune that his life was not dominated by God or diet. With love and stress he was on better terms.

'There's a stress missing from your novel, one which anyone as self-centred as Francis would have felt strongly – the threat of nuclear war.'

Scooping tea into the pot, Lenna said, 'Nobody seriously believed in that by the time the towers were built.'

'Is that your thesis or accepted historical wisdom?'

'Accepted. Our popular drama and literature make much of it but in fact it dropped out of the contemporary forms early in the third millennium.'

'Yet one imagines it as a shadow over the world right to the end.'

'It was always a possibility but not a major terror. The mass of people simply stopped thinking about it. We do that, don't we? We suppress the consciousness of sin, the awareness of a limited mortality, the possibility of accident, the discomfort of tomorrow's unknowns.'

'A fatalistic philosophy?'

'More like complacency. The major nuclear powers, America and Russia, recognized an inherent stability in their stand off as custodians of a power that raised greater problems than it could ever solve. They conducted a century-long quarrel about each other's motives and it appears in retrospect that both recognized that while they talked, however strong the language, they and the planet were reasonably safe. Without formal agreement they frowned on small states and terrorist groups that had access to nuclear arms and kept them more or less in order by divisive intrigue and financial threat.'

'Only more or less?'

'More than less. There were attempts to use fission bombs for terrorism and blackmail. The users were eliminated. Quite ruthlessly. They dwindled to one-day excitements on the newscasts. Nuclear weaponry became a technique of postponement, as good a solution as any in a basically neurotic culture. Nuclear physics would not go away but it was kept on the top shelf, out of the reach of the children. The world got on with the business of starvation and selfishness.'

Andra complained that she made it too simple.

'Why isn't a simple answer good enough? The nuclear threat was never absent from international dealings but it ceased to be news. It dropped further from sight when the space programmes ceased for sheer lack of finance. They reached the level of expertise where the cost of minute advances becomes astronomical. The satellite threat decayed and vanished.'

'But there must have been an underlying awareness – '

She became brusque. 'Of course there was. They simply became used to it. Do *you* worry about the Long Winter?'

Surprised by the change of direction he reacted without proper thought. 'Should I? It's a long way off.'

'And therefore unimportant? And is it so far off? There's no agreement on that and no solid knowledge. Our evening gale may be the first sign, who knows? Some say the Winter can come very suddenly – a series of cold snaps and it is here to stay.'

'That's all could-be, could-be. There are planning bodies – '

'At government level?' She sounded angry with him. 'It's somebody else's business, so why be concerned? Is that it?'

'What would my concern achieve? I'm no scientist.' He observed himself ill-temperedly waving his half-full teacup at her, an actor fallen out of his role and improvising at second-rate level. He set it down quietly and turned the game back to her. 'What do you suggest my attitude should be?'

She waved her teacup in mockery. 'The attitude of an artist, self-absorbed and using his vanity for the delectation of audiences.' Quickly she hurried across his resentful astonishment: 'Keep up as well as you can with the scientific information and you could be able to think usefully if the time for action should arrive. Otherwise, live as suits you. Be like the Swill, aware but unworried.'

She thought he stared into his teacup with a silent vengefulness, irritated by her mockery. In fact he was preoccupied by a technical consideration that historical knowledge would not resolve: the removal of the nuclear threat would make dramatic flow in his projected play easier to manage with one less pervasive concern to reckon with – *but* modern understanding of the period, fed by romantics, had it otherwise. How, then, explain it to an audience in a snatch of dialogue taken on the run, unemphasized, not projecting from the action as an explanatory pimple but arising naturally from a passing scene?

He muttered, 'It needs thinking over.'

'Your attitude?'

With most of his attention removed from her he said, 'No, theirs,' put down his cup and stood to leave. 'I'll do some more reading and see what suggests itself. Goodnight, Lenna.'

His going was not uncivil, merely sudden. He was already removed when the moment of thought closed in; the rest was only the body trailing after it.

She wondered, did she behave like that when immersed in her work? She probably did. It was mildly unnerving to see it in somebody else.

THE SEA AND SUMMER 2

7

TEDDY CONWAY
AD 2044–2045

1

They Tested me, written and oral, all through two days. *Easy* questions! Easy for me because I was confident. Others stammered and wondered if the obvious answers hid traps, hesitated and made wrong choices. Teddy wasn't other kids.

Being Extra wasn't the thing – I had always known I was that. What counted was getting away to the Special Schools where I could forget my family existed. Other kids had fathers and brothers but I had a Second Grade Design Engineer and Francis. Dad was as weak as piss, whining about the way things were going wrong while he threw our money away on that useless car; Mum couldn't stop him though she had twice his guts and brains. And Francis! Lying, snivelling, pilfering little shit, sucking up to Dad as if that could get him anywhere! When he discovered his tiny talent – how to count without using his fingers – you'd have thought he was Einstein, when in fact he was so clumsy he could punch wrong answers on a cally.

I didn't hate them. You don't hate what you've got used to, you put up with it, but I knew I'd get nowhere until I left them behind me.

Mum wasn't so bad. Wasn't bad, that is, until the night Dad cut his throat and she showed that when the chips were down she was as hopeless as Francis. She *grieved* for the man who had ruined us because he couldn't hold a job, and when I let fly with the cold truth she hit me.

I said nothing while we made the shift to Newport and settled into our slum, because I knew my Test report would come soon. Then – away!

What finally killed goodwill in me was Kovacs. He was something new in low bastards, a fleshless animal under a face sharp enough to bore holes in you, with soft brown eyes pretending that what looked out of them wasn't the soul of a rat. Blackmail, murder, theft, extortion – you could back him to be the local champion. He was cheap from his second-hand clothes to the Swill voice that he tried to curl round human speech as if that disguised the accent of the gutter.

Mum didn't even pretend to resist him; when it came to the trial she was as weak as Dad. Kovacs walked into the place and sat down and purred and she let him. As for Francis, he took a crush on the man that soured my stomach, following him round with eyes like swooning stars.

I refused to speak to the Swill animal when I didn't absolutely have to and he never tried to make friends or stand over me. He was the kind without real guts but I just wasn't big enough to take him on.

You can see what they were like and why I had to get away.

The pity is that you can see also what I was like.

Bastard Kovacs tried to sneer down my success, unable to bear the idea of anybody being out of his class. He had the sense to stay away the morning I left.

I felt, after all, a tug at leaving Mum, but there was nothing else for it. What could she offer that Kovacs would not drag down and degrade? Francis, I didn't think about.

The hoverbus was full of kids, all strangers to each other, trying to make conversation. The girl next to me said, 'Hello.' I said, 'Hello,' and let it go at that; I wanted to be alone with my relief and my visions of the future. What did I expect? A spectacular ushering into a ceremonial hall staffed by smiling adults welcoming us into the life intellectual, a jovial welcoming speech from some dignitary followed by . . . by what?

There was no ceremonial hall or welcoming speech. The bus didn't so much as run through City Centre but drove into a huge iron shed so old that rust was eating through the paint, with sets of parallel tracks sunk into the cement floor. One of the kids whispered that it was an old electric tram depot, but none of us could remember tracked trams.

Other buses were there with some 300 kids. Desks lined one wall with an unsmiling adult at each, not giving a damn for our intellects, having no speech of welcome ready and wanting only to be rid of us as fast as possible. Questions, data checks and the handing over of a large, heavy carryall stamped with a number: 'That's your squad number and this is your bus number. Find your bus and stay with it. If you have to go to the toilet, tell your driver. Questions?' About what?

My squad of ninety-six bright but suddenly up-anchored brains began to settle into small groups. Inevitably there were outsiders whom no group wanted or who did not yet want a group; it suited me to stay solo. Time to pick acquaintances after casing the field.

One of the girls approached the driver where he waited at the wheel – I suppose she wanted the toilet. We could not hear what was said but we could see that she was shocked out of her dithering wits and that she went off where he had indicated in a visible flutter. When she came back, a flurry of scandal flew through the squad as only scandal can.

'She could hardly understand the driver. He's Swill!'

It is strange now to think of our reacton to that scrap of information, from prudish outrage to thrilled curiosity. A real Swill! Tame, one hoped.

His presence, though, was a puzzle. A Swill with a job was a contradiction in terms; we could make nothing of it. (He was a plant, of course, an entering wedge into our ideas; the Schools did nothing without intent.)

When finally we were herded into our seats each bus raced off in a different direction. I refused to concern myself about destination. The thing was, to accept what came with aplomb proper to an Extra mind. What came at the end of a two-hour run was a huge field of stubbly brown grass stretching away to distant canvas tents. We piled out at the driver's Swill-voiced direction, trying to look as though we were not actually following orders from scum, and clustered in dismay under a blistering sun on an empty road through untold hectares of naked *countryside*.

It turned out that not one of us had ever spent a night under canvas. What confronted us was cultural shock.

Across the field – to us it seemed closer to scorched waste – came a solitary man, taking his time. Arriving, he waved to the driver with a friendly, 'Take it away, Larry,' which Larry did, carrying civilization with him. The solitary man grinned at us like a shark coming in to bite and said, 'Welcome home.'

We looked towards the tents and were silent.

He said, 'I'm your Squad Overseer – head tutor, if you prefer that. You will address me as Mr Nikopoulos and call me Nick behind my back only so long as I don't catch you at it. Now pick up your bags and follow me.'

This is the right place to tell something about Nick, saving complicated explanations later on.

He was Greek, of course, but Australia had been home to emigrant Greeks for more than a century; as a nation we had more mixed blood than was worth the trouble of sorting out. In any case, you could no longer tell the immigrant stock from the convict strain because the mixture was evening out. Nick was different in being third-generation Australian without intermarriage, pure Greek with black hair, brown eyes and the nuggety body of his peasant ancestors.

To me, on that blazing day, he was a malevolent, over-muscled oaf with authority that must be deferred to. He was part of our transfer to a barbarous scene denying the expectations Testing had built into us and, in the way of transference, he became the focus of blame for it.

He was authority without explanation or reason. We had read of the old military juntas, the Nazis, the Red Kremlin and the rumours of such systems still at work in our modern world; they formed the undercurrent of suspicion that divided nation from nation and made patriotism the necessary defence of freedom. (You don't question that sort of thing at age twelve.) Nikopoulos's assumption of unquestionable authority stirred these in our minds; his mild order translated as, *I'm the boss and I tell you, move!* We had never been treated so in our psychologically sanitized schools.

He was, though we did not discover it until much later, a Police Intelligence Officer who resented these comfortless tutoring secondments as much as we did.

I disliked him on sight, disliked his dark face, his animal physique and his neutral, tell-nothing Australian voice; so obvious a Greek had no business to sound like one of us. Dislike turned quickly to animosity.

That changed in time, but it was a slow process.

The tents were a long kilometre from the road, a kilometre of peculiar hell. Remember that none of us was over twelve, that we were toting heavy bags given to us at the depot as well as our own luggage and that our private luggage contained in nearly every instance about twice what had been recommended in the written instruction. Outraged mothers saw only ineptitude in an instruction stipulating one change of socks and underwear and no extra shirts and shoes and stating that toiletries would be provided. One kid actually had a blanket roll; several carried portable trivs. Many had two suitcases instead of the required one, so the depot carryall made a serious encumbrance.

There was a general move to pile the carryalls in a heap with the idea of returning for them later, but Nikopoulos scotched that. He said, very courteously, as though it were not a sick joke, 'I realize that a conscientious parent can be troublesome, but now you must resolve the trouble, out here and alone with your baggage. Remember that the carryall contains overalls and basic clothing and that no time has been allotted for a return trip. You must make your decisions at once. Follow me.'

He started off and never once looked back.

So there we were – case in hand, smaller case clamped uncomfortably under left armpit, carryall in right hand and other matters dependent on ingenuity – staggering over the pathless stubble. Under a furious sun.

The bunch shook itself out into ninety-six sweltering units covering 100 metres from stumbling leaders to complaining tail. I was lucky in having only one suitcase – though it was heavy enough with gadgetry I fancied as necessities – and in being strong for my age. I knew I would make the trek, however uncomfortably.

Early on I passed the girl I had snubbed in the bus. She had her cases open and was trying to cram the contents of both into one. She was plain, cheaply dressed, probably no better off than the Conways, and I said, 'I can stuff some of that in my pockets if you like.'

She squealed furiously without looking at me, 'Stuff yourself! I don't need any help.'

She was close to tears and obstinate with frustration, so I left her to it.

The trek became a trail of discarded belongings, entire suitcases as well as two portable trivs, the blanket roll, items of clothing and a small golliwog.

Nikopoulos strolled, aware of jettison and distress but not turning his head. He waited by the first group of tents, until we were all assembled. It took some time. Then he said, 'Those who discarded what could be done without showed decision in a situation of necessary choice. Those who struggled to bring all they had showed determination. In an unreasonable world the Extra needs both.'

One among the ninety-six, a girl, said quietly but clearly, 'You bastard.'

'Now that's no language for a lady! Would she care to declare herself or would she prefer the anonymity dictated by good sense?'

Get you coming or going.

'I said it.' It was the girl who had told me to stuff myself. She was raging and had been crying. Her voice, her accent, was different from what I had been accustomed to; I could not place it.

Nikopoulos gave her his shark's grin. 'You prefer courage to good sense?'

'It don't take courage to talk back to you.'

'It *doesn't* take courage.' The correction galled her as it let me place her socially. *Declassé*, the Sweet would say, a long-term Fringer with standards slipping. 'It does, though,' he said, 'take more anger than logic. Cowardice, properly judged, may be a survival trait.' Then, confrontation suavely turned to profit, he said, 'You will sort yourselves out, four to a tent. For that you have five minutes, which should obviate unnecessary fiddling over who shares with whom. At the end of that time a siren will sound and your stomachs will warn you of another survival trait.' He pointed out a marquee some distance away. (Everything, we discovered, was some distance away.) 'Questions?'

Someone asked, 'When can we pick up the stuff we dropped?'

'Threw away. Why should you want what you threw away?'

By that time he had irritated me so much that I stepped forward to say, 'We don't have to give reasons for wanting our property.'

He nodded affably. 'No, you don't. But when will you find time? Your day is closely scheduled.' He glanced at the sky. 'It hasn't rained here for two years and surely won't today, and no wind is forecast, so the gear can stay there until you find time, make time, scrounge time to fetch it. I assure you none will be stolen. You have now four minutes in which to choose your tents.'

Bedlam. After four minutes of chaos a siren cried like something dying and hunger hit like a blow below the belt, but everybody had thrown his or her gear in somewhere.

They gave us a civilized meal and plenty of it, and when we got back to the tents all the dropped gear had been collected and laid out for easy identification. First the lesson, then the dollop of jam. Basic stuff. Nobody was mollified.

Much, much later I concluded that the purpose of the morning's exercise was mental preparation for all sorts of seeming unreasonableness which would eventually make reason. We were being told: the world isn't the place you think it is; it is neither rational nor just.

2

We spent twelve months in that camp. The training and schooling seemed like helter-skelter hard work but was in fact a sorting out of potentials. It was much like military training, without weapons, on the physical side. We turned out daily with the sparrows and washed in a creek five minutes trot away; during the day we did as much physical training as school work, with emphasis on team games. On some nights there was, surprisingly, dramatic study. If I detested the days I loved the nights of Shakespeare, Ibsen, Brecht (no moderns, you notice), the arguing over character and meaning and techniques. It seemed irrelevant but was not.

Our tutors, both men and women, took us in groups of six, so learning was intensive and personal. They were friendly but remote; they gave out the conventional come-to-me-if-you-have-problems, but their tents were pitched so far off that the matter had to be damned urgent for you to sacrifice the time needed to find them.

Out of syllabus hours we were left to ourselves. Really to ourselves. Nobody inspected tents or read lectures on behaviour or called 'lights out' or cared if we missed a morning dip in the creek.

The result was at first tumultuous. We were Extra, superior and aware of it. The tents were hotbeds of tension with everybody trying to be top brain, the weakest driven to fits of self-pity. Yelling matches flourished night and day, with kids flouncing out of their tents to sleep on the ground rather than associate with pseudo-intelligent pigs, tears of rage and a few fights. Sometimes we stopped the fights, sometimes we egged the warriors on, the girls as bad as the boys. I was no better or worse than the rest.

For ten days we saw nothing of Nikopoulos – the tutors seemed uninterested in how we behaved out of class. Lateness and inattention were the only crimes.

On the tenth day the squads assembled at the tutorial area (most of the teaching was open air) and were left to wait; when we talked we were told to shut up. We waited for half an hour.

Nikopoulos turned up, strolling, all the time in the world on his hands, looked us over and said, 'I have seen your tents. You live like animals. I have heard your noise at night. Animals display more social conscience. You behave like your own idea of the Swill you despise. There is some excuse for them.'

Then he strolled away and the day proceeded as usual.

No threats, only a sneering blow at the snobberies and fears we had been reared in. Our social studies had begun with self-examination.

From then on Nikopoulos took to wandering round the tutorial groups, listening a while and then taking over with his personal injection of the unexpected, tying one or other of us in knots and wandering off again, destruction accomplished.

He picked on me one day and what happened was extraordinary, though only I knew how much so. He caught me in one of those moments when my mind was astray on an excursus of its own and when he called my name I came to with a rush but had not heard the question.

He said quite mildly, 'Pay some attention, lad. I asked why the twentieth-century engineers laid down such a fine system of roads and then let them fall into disrepair.'

Upset at being caught wool-gathering, I snapped at him, 'They didn't let them run down. We did.'

I thought he might snap back but he said only, 'That's right, we did. We ruined their fine and very expensive roads. Why, Conway?'

I brushed that off. 'What do hovercraft want with roads?' My tone was plain rudeness. This outdoor tutorial setup was primitive and comfortless and I disliked him.

He said, 'Bicycles might use them.'

It had to be a trick remark, not possibly serious. The only people using bicycles were the rare countryside Swill who wobbled around on rusted frames with solid tyres cut from the detritus of tips and dumps; you saw them sometimes in triv comedies. You couldn't imagine city people on them – a man on a bicycle had no dignity, no sense of how ridiculous he looked.

My face must have said most of that because Nick became ironic. 'Not bicycles? Our fathers rode bicycles.' His stare demanded comment. I was the fish on today's grill.

Vanity and resentment are a destructive combination. I said, 'There's been progress since then.' He couldn't know that the word *father* had called up an image of my own feckless parent on such a machine, elbows stuck out, face red with effort, knees pumping.

He asked, 'Is it progress to lose something useful?'

How many of us have since recognized that question as a lever jammed under our ignorance of the world? I crashed blindly into an answer. 'They were crude. Besides, people had cars.' Confusion had entered somewhere, propelled by my father's shade; logic was lost in a maze of reactions. 'They had everything they didn't need. They killed each other with their cars. They killed hundreds of people every day with them. I know. My father had a car.'

My mind was a chaos of pitfalls centred on my father forever rabbiting on about how things had been better . . . I went cold in the hot sun because control had been lost as well as logic and I felt the squad withdraw from me.

110

Nick seemed unaware, concerned only with a line of argument. 'Perhaps your father thought that private transport had advantages. Did he never tell you that?'

Some part of me withdrew, like the squad, so that I was able to listen to my anger and my cracked voice screaming at him, 'Who cares what he told? He told me shit! He didn't have guts for the real world. He killed himself!'

In the silence a distant kookaburra laughed, which was possibly fair comment, but the squad stayed quiet with eyes on the ground. They had seen where I joined the bus in Newport and now observed the value of intelligent social stratification – it took a Fringer to create a situation beyond protocol and good manners. I thought of that while my disjuncted tongue made a last comment, a casual coda addressed to memory: 'There was blood all over the place.'

Nikopoulos was inhuman; he carried on as though Edward Ellison Conway did not exist, simply switched his questioning to another victim and carried on his intention of upsetting the squad's view of history and human endeavour.

I waited for the bird to laugh again. I could have joined in to mock the problems of a stranger in an unexpected land. I had just rid myself of one of them. I had admitted the nightmare of Dad and spewed it out for ever.

3

At the end of the second week there was a three-day break for home visiting. I stayed in camp. What would have been the point of going back? I was never lonely, never short of internal resources.

Authority with its big capital A was unhappy about it but didn't argue too hard, even seemed to understand in its remote way. Eventually a letter was written, with my agreement. It was a dishonest letter but its meaning was plain. A clean break causes less pain.

Less pain to whom?

4

Each day after the first fortnight half a dozen of us were called to private interviews with Nick, and the things that bastard of a man had ferreted out about us were enough to make you believe in the evil eye.

One of his jobs was the preparation of progress reports on each of our ninety-six. Many years later, when I could look back without wincing, I was able to track down my file and record some extracts (illegally), to learn in partial fashion how a twelve-year-old intellectual vulgarian developed into if not a good man at least one who could carry his shames as learning experiences.

Here is one of Nick's progress tapes, made some two months after intake, spoken in the flat, tired voice of a man striving to keep emotion out of an emotional activity:

10 August 2044.
Subject: Conway, Edward Ellison.
Classification: Extra, B Grade.
Progress summary and comment: 2.

General: Little overt change. Conceited, reserved, making acquaintances but no friends. Poor team worker; wants personal recognition, looks for applause then pretends to ignore it. Lonely but not admitting it, possibly even to himself. Psych Section advises family relationships crucial to his stable development; for comment, see Addenda.
Physical: Stocky body type, muscular. Unsuitable for high performance athletics, ideal for endurance activities. Should develop excellent combatant physique.
Educational: Mathematics poor. (Sibling rejection of brother's freak talent?) Romantic view of science; enjoys fancy extrapolation and forecasts but little laboratory bent or interest. Word skills excellent; strong interest in literature and acting. Repeat, acting.
Expressed preference: Police Intelligence Operations. More a romantic than an intellectual choice but successful training is possible. Personality traits make total failure also possible.
Overseer's addenda: I feel that his short period of Fringe residence hardened incipient attitudes and his world view. Obvious diagnosis is profound self-dissatisfaction not yet realized. Psych suggests I persuade him to visit home regularly but his resistance is strong; his readiness to connive at that prevaricating letter to his mother was no small thing. I wish Psych had the job of persuading him.

Rejection of mother and brother might succumb to time and pressure but Kovacs is a stumbling block. The police report on Kovacs is interesting. He is a Tower Boss with brains and ability and enough sense to operate within his limits. Some contradictions: a family man and a libertine, an extortioner with a penchant for generosity, a thief and con man and probably a killer who protects his tower with a pragmatic morality which includes police-informing on opposition elements. Will fight but would rather plot. Some attempt at self-education. An updated Renaissance *condottiero* – a thug with brains – carving out a gutter kingdom? Physical appearance unattractive but strong sexual charm. Represents to Conway everything despicable in the Swill stratum, but is on a solid footing with Mrs Conway as family friend.

How to get the boy home – *willingly?*

1. Move Kovacs out of area? Out of the question; too valuable as Tower Boss.

2. Move the Conways to another Fringe. Too much opposition from allocation departments with eventual refusal on policy grounds.

3. Enlist Kovacs's help with the boy? But how? Delicate, touchy.

4. Shatter the boy's world view and rebuild.

3 and 4 are the most delicate and risky but also the most productive if the boy is to have a career.

A long-term project might be to bring Kovacs into active participation; this kind of Swill alliance is slippery on sociological and psychological grounds but might be attempted as a long-range goal. Should be considered.

My major problem with this boy is his thoroughly unlikeable personality, with few openings for sympathy. He is unhappy but clamped tight. It is hard to *want* to help him.

How far ahead he planned and how deviously! I did not know that his rank was Captain, Intelligence, and that his secondment to instructional duties was in the nature of the change said to be as good as a rest. Some sort of occupational joke.

8

CAPTAIN NIKOPOULOS
AD 2044

Teddy Conway grew into a tough, intelligent man from a tough, intelligent little bugger of a kid. He wasn't the kind whose middle name is Trouble – they're usually easily handled – but the kind you can't get a grip on while the outside of his mind is so smooth and seamless.

I never despair of reaching any brat – and Extras can be nastier brats than most – but it took me longer than it should have to realize that all the clues to Teddy were in that second report. In fact my entry into the inner Teddy began when I called him for routine interview shortly after it was dictated.

He was one of those who always swaggered into the tent, miming self-possession, but he couldn't restrain his curiosity (thinking it veiled) from scanning the fittings.

Every intake began by believing that the tutors' tents were a front for hidden furnishings and equipment for orgies. They were not to be fooled by plank beds exactly like their own or the plain desk with vocorder and intercom and no other visible gear. All façade, they reasoned. There must be screens, mikes, direct-access terminals . . . They accepted only gradually that the tutors lived much as their charges did. How else could we enter the day-to-day working of their minds?

I let him decide that there were no careless clues exposed for him to pounce on, then said, 'You've been fighting.'

He knew I wouldn't accept sullen silence, but the sullen, 'Yes,' was as useless.

I said, tiredly because this was a regular grind with Teddy, 'Yes, *sir.*'

'Yes, sir.'

Why not, *Yes, you bastard,* and be done with it? 'What was the fight about?'

Explaining a blind rage is never easy; he muttered that it was a private matter.

'It wasn't. What happens in class is public. Your drama tutor agrees. Is she right?'

'I suppose so . . . sir.'

'So do I. Again, what about?'

How account for rage and shame that had to be released but put him in the wrong and was anyway too great for the cause? He started grudgingly, 'We're doing *Macbeth* – '

'I know, and I know you enjoy drama class. Come to the heart of it.'

He squared his chunky body and stared at my adam's apple as if planning damage. 'It was the dagger scene: "Is this a dagger that I see before me?" There was an argument.'

He dried up, needing help. I said, 'There always is about that scene. There's always someone who wants a prop dagger floating in mid-air, all silver-gilt and menacing. To shock the eyes of the groundlings.'

Oh, cunning Nick! The misquotation found a mark in his surprise that this authoritarian oaf knew enough Shakespeare to play verbal games. From a different play, too. Since I was now talking his language, I kept at it. 'And why not? Banquo's ghost appears later on, played by a real actor, so why not a real dagger?'

His tongue wagged obediently, fighting over the class argument. 'But that's because in Shakespeare's day a ghost could be real. Macbeth *sees* Banquo though nobody else does – ghosts could do that. I mean, the people thought they could. But the dagger is only in Macbeth's mind. He doesn't even see it clearly, that's why he asks, "Is this a dagger – ?" '

It's marvellous how a little enthusiasm can charge a mule's face with life. 'And so?'

'You don't have a dagger on stage. He *acts* it. He makes you see it as he does. A sort of vision.'

If the expression limped, the thought was valid. I asked, 'How does he do that?', which was unfair, and I made it more so by demanding, 'Show me!'

Beth Castle had said the boy's skill was considerable, but falling into character in drama class, with everybody keyed up and the air already smelling of another world, is very different from doing it from a standing start in a sweaty tent with a gimlet-eyed so-and-so challenging you to justify your thesis. He got the first line out and dried up in that total, terrifying blankness that is the actor's dread.

I went round to the front of the desk and took pose as Macbeth, hand outstretched to ward off horror, eyes peering into a corner of the tent. 'Like this?' And I let loose with 'Is this a dagger that I see before me?' in the hollow tones of an escapee from an echo chamber.

It must have been excruciating but he let me get to 'And on thy blade and dudgeon gouts of blood' before he interrupted me in sheer outrage 'No, not like that, Nick!'

That was *lèse-majesté* but it was not a moment for cavilling. 'What am I doing wrong?'

He frowned and fulminated like the ghosts of all the great directors since Stanislavsky, 'You're *acting* all the time. The audience has to be looking for the dagger, not watching you! Their eyes have to be behind yours, looking out. You have to stay as still as possible.' He was in flood, laying down technique to a clumsy understudy. 'You can move when you say "Mine eyes are made the fools o' the other senses." You can turn your back on the vision there, but in the new direction there it is again. You say "I see thee still", but this time there's blood on it and it won't go away because your mind keeps it there. You say so: "There's no such thing; It is the bloody business which informed thee to mine eyes." So you can't use a real dagger.'

A fine run, Teddy, but now back to earth – to tent and tutorial ogre. 'Show me!'

Show me he did, taking the speech with the least possible body movement save for that one turn, speaking it not loudly but like a man talking distractedly to himself. It wasn't great art – you don't get that from children – but it showed enough to set me thinking. He really *saw* the damned dagger. The rhymed couplet at the end defeated him as it has defeated Macbeths for centuries – there's no way to speak it that doesn't tear the magic.

I gave him the nod of applause without extravagant compliment and asked, 'Is that how you did it in class?'

Sullenness returned full strength. 'No . . . sir.'

'How, then?'

The young bugger took his revenge with a straight face. 'More like you did, sir.' The *sir* came easily as an act of impudence. 'I hadn't had a chance to prepare it.'

'But you've spent time preparing it today. Why?'

'Because last night I got it wrong.'

'And they laughed at you?'

If, as they say, looks could kill . . . 'Yes . . . sir.'

'So you hit the nearest set of teeth.'

'Yes, sir.' Without regret.

'Belonging to Squadman Graves.'

'Yes, sir.'

'An enemy?'

116

'No, sir.'

'Simply the nearest. And he hit back?'

'Yes, sir.'

'Naturally. Who won?'

He looked mulish. 'Nobody. They stopped us.'

Oh, dear me, watch out next time, Graves! 'If they hadn't, who would have won?'

'I would.' Conscious of unseemly bragging, he modified it. 'I'm stronger than he is.'

'Maybe, but when you hit out at the nearest, what if it had happened that the nearest was your tutor, Miss Castles? Would she now have a split lip?'

Seeing the pit dug for him he admitted unwillingly, 'No, sir. I would have controlled myself.'

'Hitting a tutor is not permissible but a smack in the teeth for Graves is?'

Humiliation is to dig your own grave, then be forced to crawl into it. 'No . . . sir.' *Sir, you bastard.*

'But forbidden violence is sweet, eh?' It was time to bring forward a plan I had designed for him and a couple of other hotheads. 'As from next week you will attend an additional night course. Three times a week. Judo.'

His blank face told me he had never heard the word. Why should he? Teaching martial arts had been banned for thirty years. (But Police Intelligence teaches them. Very nasty.)

'It is a course in the philosophy of non-violence allied to the art of self-defence. You will learn how to protect yourself, which is essential in a policeman, but also how self-defeating violence can be. You will be given mental training in repressing violence in yourself. What does all that add up to?'

He wasn't slow. 'Self-control, sir.'

'I will be your instructor.'

That didn't go down well, so I passed to the next matter, where I expected strong resistance. 'Your mother wants you to visit home.'

He looked murderous, no other word for it. It hit me so hard that for a moment I lost hold of the situation and said something untrue and stupid. 'So does your brother.'

He said baldly, 'I don't believe you.'

He didn't care how I might react. He wasn't angry; he was frightened and fighting for his freedom. It was an extraordinary impression to gain from a kid. I was knocking too suddenly on his secrets, yet too far committed to stop.

With the special grace that favours blunderers, he helped me. 'That creep wouldn't look at me if I was dying.'

That disposed of Francis. 'Your mother – '

He cut me off, not so much with rudeness as to prevent unwanted urgings. 'She knew I wouldn't be going back.'

Her letters to the Department had said differently. 'Did she tell you that?'

He gave me a brat's brazen, eye-to-eye look. 'You can tell. You can always tell.'

'Tell what you prefer to believe.'

'Maybe.' Bluntly, challengingly, slamming that door.

'Did she beat you?'

'No.' Then, with unforgiving spite, 'She hit me once. Anyway, I'm not going back.'

I said, 'There's nothing to stop you,' and by blind chance struck gold.

'Yes, there is. Kovacs.'

I had known of the aversion but not the power of it. 'Billy Kovacs?'

He was shocked. 'You know him?'

'I know about him.'

He didn't care for that; nobody likes being told that Authority fingers his private existence. 'He's shit.'

'That word only means you don't like him.'

'He's a criminal.'

'Can you prove that?'

'He takes my mother's money. A stand-over Swill bastard.'

'He looks after your mother and Francis.'

'For ten dollars a week each.'

'He gives value.'

On the edge of tears he asked, 'How would you know?'

'It's my business to know. Everything about the Conways is my business, so I know he looks after them.'

He sulked. 'Nobody asked him to.'

'Without him you would all have been mugged, robbed and left in the gutter. He earns his dollars.'

He changed his ground, whining slightly. 'He hangs around Mum all the time. He's always there.'

Like that? My information hadn't included that. It was worth a shot in the dark. 'You're afraid he'd kick you out?'

'No. She wouldn't let him.'

So there was trust yet. 'Yes, mothers are like that, forgiving. In any case you should be grateful to Kovacs.'

'He stinks.'

He meant it literally and it was almost certainly true but it gave me the opportunity to plant a dart. 'The towers can't always get enough water. If they wash they may still have to put on sweaty clothes because there isn't enough water to wash them as well. What Kovacs smells like isn't what he is. And he's been good to you.'

'He's Swill shit.'

It would have been a pleasure to smack his head, hard. 'That's prejudice talking. He could teach you a lot.'

'Why would I want to know Swill stuff?'

'As a Police Intelligence Officer you would. Nine-tenths of the State is Swill.'

That was a fact that steadily refused to occupy Sweet minds; not only were the implications too dark but their social training rendered the Swill almost invisible. The idea that there could be Swill Extras would not have occurred to any of them – even Fringers were suspect. To have been told then that ninety-six Swill kids occupied a similar camp in another part of the State would have disorganized their thinking as a contradiction in terms.

Teddy produced his own rationalization. 'That doesn't mean living with them.'

'Why not?'

He said, 'It couldn't,' because it was not possible, then swept his eyes round the tent like something hunted as he tried to dodge the idea that perhaps it was. He let out a long, hopeless breath and said, 'I can't.'

Can't go home, he meant, because he had made his stand and didn't know how to back off from it.

I let the matter drop for the night. Slowly, slowly . . . But his climb up adolescent Calvary was not yet done. I asked, 'Who's your best friend here?'

He moved his shoulders minimally up and back. I was annoyed by his shrugs and hesitations and evasions and becoming aware of an angry bias in myself. But once started you must make some sort of finish.

'No best friend?'

He played his game of attacking instead of admitting. 'Do I have to have favourites?'

'No. Nor do you have to be generally disliked.'

The damned shrug again. 'That's their worry.'

'Teddy needs only Teddy?'

119

If he had defied me with *Yes* I might have hit him and to hell with the consequences, but he said smugly, 'They don't approve of Fringers.'

'Fringers in other squads have established themselves.'

He was not to be put in the wrong. 'Why do I have to join the mob? Is that what being Extra is for?'

'Join the mob, no, join the team, yes. PI doesn't favour lone-wolf supermen fighting crime singlehanded. The turnover in lone-wolf supermen is too high.'

More sulks. 'They don't behave like intelligent people. They're still kids.'

'So are you. None of you will behave like intelligent people for a year or two yet. Get the idea out of your smart head that you can look down on anybody. You're a B-Grade Extra, not up there with the pick of the bunch.'

It shook him badly. We rarely told squadmen their gradings because it fostered internal élites, but here the need justified it. It was cruel but not gratuitously cruel. He didn't know that occasionally we have to throw one back but that we fight hard against sending a good mind to rot in hell. Failed Extras tend to end up as drowsy chewers in the towers.

The blow taxed his capacity to absorb; he had conceived of himself as the most mature mind in his group. (In some not altogether pleasant way he possibly was, depending on your definition of mature.) He was a sorry boy when he asked the obvious, 'Who are the A Grades?'

Name the competition! 'I won't tell you. Just remember that there are better minds than yours quite close to you who choose not to make pigs of themselves over the way they can out-think your tantrums and snide cracks.'

I had to pay his resilience. He asked with real dignity, 'Can I go now?'

'*May* I go now, *sir*.'

He repeated the words, white and raging. The difference between us lay in my hiding it better.

'No, you may not. I have more to tell you. A mediocre intelligence can outclass its betters by using itself to its full capacity. You aren't mediocre, but you have betters. Top minds can fall into traps of sterile intellection while lesser ones search out what they may accomplish. You have talent for language and drama. Think about it. You have also an open sesame to life experience many others have not, and one day you'll go home and study Billy Kovacs.'

It was too soon to decide what had got through to him but something had, because Teddy Conway was in unlovely twelve-year-old tears, the sniffling tears of a smallish lad with no handkerchief in his pocket who could only stand still and brave it out.

'Goodnight, Teddy.'

He went without answering and I did not call him back; you can have quite enough of that sort of minuscule showdown. Besides, my part in it had been no copybook operation to pride myself on.

9

TEDDY
AD 2044-2045

That night may have marked a turning point of sorts, but how do you tell? At the time I hated his unholy guts for prying at the covers over my mind.

He was right about Mum, but what could I do?

He was right about Kovacs, but I wasn't able to accept it. That took years.

He was right about me, too, and I knew it, but knowing made no difference. You don't decide, *I will turn myself into a better person*, and do it, like a Godstruck church-freak. Change is a life's work that has to look after itself.

I thought that out, consciously, as I loitered across the paddock back to the tents.

To reach my tent I had to pass the sandpit with the parallel bars and acrobatic gear. In the bright moonlight I could see someone practising back flips from the bars to the trampoline – very dangerous, a potential backbreaker, forbidden by the gym instructors. It could only be Carol, the bitch who had told me to stuff myself when I offered to help her, all on her intense little own in the moonlight, exercising her pointless talent.

She had tried to make up for that day (short of apologizing, which kids only do under pressure) and annoyed me by always speaking when she passed by. A compulsive friend maker. Her persistence annoyed me and her distorted, long-time Fringe vowels annoyed me.

It was two years, when we were training back in the city, before the penny dropped (what did that old phrase originally mean?) and we became, cautiously, friends. And another six before we married. I get that out of the way now because there's no room here for the peripheral history of a courtship.

That night it was too late to do more than stare ahead as I skirted the sandpit, and of course she saw me. In the middle of a double somersault she would have seen me. And, being a friendly idiot, she called out, knowing why I would be coming from that direction, 'You look as if Nicky ripped strips off you.'

As greetings go it was sympathetic but I grunted, 'Shut your face, shithead,' and made sure she knew I meant it. I knew she sat perfectly still on the side of the trampoline as she said to my back, 'You spoilt, spoilt bastard.'

After Nick it was too much. I had to walk the dark in circles for ten minutes before I could be certain that my face carried no streaks of tears.

Nick must have known what he was doing that night; he never handled me so roughly again.

How it affected me is hard to say. You don't observe change in yourself; new attitudes always seem to be what you were developing towards anyway. Other people say nothing until the change is made, when they start in with, 'When I think what a rotten little monster you used to be – ' and you can't see that you aren't still basically the *you* you always were. You are, but have learned to handle the beast better.

I have followed the changes, in some degree, through Nick's reports. Here is one from my eleventh month:

8 May 2044
Subject: Conway, Edward Ellison
Classification: Extra, B Grade
Progress summary and comment: 11

General: Great improvement. Recognition of equals and betters has replaced conceit by a determination to excel, often just as objectionable. Still basically a loner but less ready to reject advances. Unable to go home, by his own connivance, he has accepted the necessity to fit himself to social circumstances.
Physical: Continuing improvement, particularly in acrobatics and martial arts. Team attitudes still poor; basic to personality.
Education: Maths much improved; dislikes subject but resents being worsted. Still little interest in sciences. Some talent for mechanical maintenance and repair. Earlier interest in drama taken fresh turn (see Addenda.) Developing interest in modern history; hooked by differences between received and actual truths.
Addenda: Drama coach says boy has become useless in conventional theatrics. Has conceived a style of 'realistic' acting involving total absorption in character, out of key with interpretative role-playing demanded by scripts. He claims a

script demands only character 'highlights' and leaves out everything not shown on stage, whereas real characterization must include what is not shown. He says people in real life hide the reactions scripts force them to reveal, that an actor cannot convey humanity while he is required to 'portray' instead of 'project'.

I have seen him demonstrate his theory. He did ten minutes – from scratch, unscripted – of a schoolboy cheating in an exam, caught and ejected. Solo performance, mime, with a few words when 'caught'. It was dull because it was the real thing, not dramatized to underline psychological implications and cunning insights. This could be an ideal undercover talent. Later I will introduce him to true spoken Swill; then we'll see how good he is, how assimilable into the repellent unknown.

Prognosis: Right for Police Intelligence. Undercover? Must wait and see.

I suppose that from his vantage – overhead and twitching the strings – it was easy to reduce a boy to a set of simple factors and push him in a desired direction. Since his direction was also mine, well and good.

And if it had not been mine? Fruitless speculation, but I would never have become reconciled to him in my heart if I had not recognized, deep down, that we worked to a common end and that all his subversion was a prelude to building. Most of my troubles were rooted in bloody-minded resistance to admitting myself less than perfect.

10

NICK

AD 2045

The kids knew that all tutorial classes were recorded for later discussion by the tutors. Born into a data-collection society – which means a surveillance society, however gently disguised – they took it for granted, yet the sessions could be ding-dong affairs with little guard on tongues, much as in family life. Which, when you think about it, is very much a surveillance society.

In the twelve-month camp which the tutors called the Stations of the Cross they tried to gouge out pointers to the kids' basic thinking. Essays are no good for this – too considered and too given to expected answers. I preferred to set a subject for dissertation, allow a few minutes for thought, then plant the kid in front of the squad to make what impression he or she could. Nerve-racking for some, an exhibitionist opportunity for others.

One topic, 'How good were the Good Old Days?' made for Conway a peculiarly private exercise which tutor conference labelled the work of a condescending, histrionic, intellectual little shit. Which was near enough.

There was more to him than that and my private session with him, later, took us a lot further forward. He wasn't his sassy self that night but met my eyes meekly, with the glimmer of a self-conscious smile, hopefully ingratiating. I had seen it so often on kids waiting for their speeches to be shredded that I nearly failed to see it as out of character – he usually met critical sessions head on and unrepentant.

I said, 'Drop it.'

He gave me puzzled surprise, instantly repressed, a squirm of discomfort and a 'student' voice protesting with prim correctness, 'I don't understand, sir.'

'I've never hit you, Conway, have I?'

That stopped his acting. The idea was unthinkable. 'Of course not!' Shocked, defiant, and no 'sir'.

'There might be a first time. What are you playing at?'

He recovered at once, not believing me (not realizing that he should have believed me) and answered brassily that he was 'exploring'.

'Exploring what?'

'How they feel – the rest of the squad.'

'About me?' It was blinding cheek but interesting.

'They're afraid of you. That is, some of them are. I was being one of them, finding out how it felt.'

'How does it feel?'

He gave his trademark of a shrug. 'Uncertain. A short-of-guts feeling.'

'Are you perhaps confusing short-of-guts with simple good manners?'

'I don't think so.'

'And you aren't afraid of me?'

Expecting a blunt *No*, I was made to wait while he thought about it. The answer was fascinating. 'Not of you but of what you could do if you wanted to. That's what authority is, isn't it? The power to make people afraid?'

Like most definitions of human activity, it was half right – the wrong half. I prodded, 'You make it sound like something we should do without.'

'No.' At thirteen he had developed a furrow of concentration. 'Sometimes one person has to give orders and everybody else obey, even if they don't want to.'

'If you don't want to you risk punishment?'

'That's what's wrong. You shouldn't be punished for disagreeing.'

'I don't think that happens too often.' In this camp, it didn't, but in much of the disintegrating world, held together by despotic strength, it happened, happened, happened. 'Punishment is for acting out your disagreement to the point of being a nuisance, perhaps a menace. Is that wrong?'

'I suppose not – yes, it is wrong. Authority shouldn't be only a threat of punishment.'

Good lad. 'What should it be?'

'Understanding. Correcting. Gentle. Needed.'

I was fairly sure then of his future. 'One day,' I told him, 'I will remind you that you said that.'

Closing the subject while he still wore his surprise, I pressed the start key to set his recorded dissertation on its bullish collision with the subject: 'Romance is one thing, history another. Romance makes history palatable by making it pretty; real history is dirt and famine and plagues. The legend of the good old days has always been a way to justify disliking something.' The taped voice had a quality of

126

patronizing certainty at variance with the usual Teddy sullenness. 'Moving closer to the present we find the same romanticizing urge – '

I cut it off. 'What the hell did you think you were at? Preparing a political speech? A manifesto?'

Challenged he would always tell the truth. 'I was addressing a crowded hall – the Historical Society or something like that.'

Role-playing. 'Why?'

'It makes it easier.' He took his time for exact expression. I had learned to wait. 'It was the theme – only obvious things to say. And you always know just how the squad will react. It needed to come alive.'

'For them?'

'For me.'

Now, isn't that what role-playing is about? 'So you adopted an authoritarian lecturer persona, with prestige to give weight to your lightest word and some tizzied-up language to match.'

'That's about it.'

Now for a touch of cruelty. 'How does it sound outside the spellbound hall, delivered to just you and me?'

He flushed. 'Crappy. Pretentious.'

'Good word. Try putting in a *sir* now and then.'

'Yes, sir.' This still happened at every session.

I set the tape going again.

– as with my father, who lived his life in a rosy past. He owned a motor car, a survival of the personal status era, which he would not give up although its breakdowns wasted our income. His past was paradise and all new things were rotten. If he were alive today he would be crying that the new coupon system would end in the complete collapse of currency – *Dad knew better than you think, Teddy-boy. Two years from now, or three or five . . .* – and trying to tell us that it was better when you were always calculating how much interest you had to pay and checking your account and working out service charges and worrying about your loan extension and afraid to spend because your financial roof might fall in.

As Dad's did. He was quoting the State's propaganda from the triv breaks, the comfort-pap that the coupon system is easier and safer and isn't waiting to pounce. He was, in fact, calling the population sheep who only wanted their problems offloaded. He was pretty near right.

Yet in his own lifetime the deadly streets were made safe to walk in, data networks made information available worldwide in seconds, the average height increased by 5 centimetres, the lifespan by seventeen years and the IQ average by six points. Listening to him made it plain that the good old days were just nostalgia in the minds of discontented people who didn't remember properly.

I stopped the tape. 'Well?'

He was judicious about handing down an opinion. 'The English expression is good.' For his age, yes. 'It sounds a bit high-flown, I think.' In fact it sounded contemptuous and unforgiving, as if someone ought to suffer for it. He concluded, 'But the idea is right.'

'Is it, now? Do you still think, after all your history classes, that you can wipe away the past as a failure? We're here, aren't we? How did we manage it? We didn't. Our stupid, dirty forefathers got us here.'

Again the pause and a small, dissatisfied sigh. 'Perhaps I should do the speech over again, sir.'

'No, we'll erase the tape.' I did so. 'Your list of modern values praises quantity of activities with no mention of quality.'

'Do you mean that people were happier then, that the past really was better?'

'How would I know? I wasn't there. The recent past may seem worse than today but the people living in it might not have agreed. It was different. People make the best of what they have and are happy or unhappy. Our fathers loved life and the world and left their records to testify to it.'

I caught the flicker that meant he was going to bowl me up a smart one. 'What might the Swill think about that?'

Smart enough but right into my hands. 'You think they must be unhappy?'

'Wretched.' *Wretched Swill* was a cliché of the day.

'That's their physical condition compared with yours. It doesn't describe their hearts, which aren't wholly unhappy.' His look of patient tolerance got under my skin. He *knew* Swill couldn't possibly be happy like – like *people*. 'You've never moved among them.'

'How could I? But we're told – '

' – by those who haven't moved among them either. There's joy and laughter in the towers, even contentment. As much as among the Sweet, anyway, which isn't too much.'

I wasn't getting through. A central belief was being contradicted. He said with stonewall impudence, 'I don't think I understand.'

I snapped at him, 'You'll see for yourself one day.'

That was stupid of me and I would pay for it. It was far too early for such information, but now there could be no retreat.

'*Sir!*' That was rejection beyond mere refusal to understand.

'I said you'll see for yourself.'

'Go among them! What would I want down there?'

Down there . . . 'To do the job you have opted for. To gather intelligence.'

It was revenge for all the frustration he had given me. (Oh, delirious triv serials, where Intelligence operatives penetrate the Third World jungles, parachute into secret China behind portable jamming screens, creep across the ocean floor into the harbours of the Gulf States . . .) Among the Swill! That sort of job!

I should have been ashamed but was not. After eleven months of improvement he was still a pest of a kid.

He snorted, 'What could you learn from *them*?'

'If, perhaps, the present is better than the past.' It was time to cut it short. 'Goodnight, Teddy.'

He resisted dismissal. 'But how – how?'

So the idea had made a small impact. 'With difficulty at first. By becoming one of them in your mind. A job for an actor.'

He protested, 'I can only act what I know. Swill aren't like us. They're – ' he saw disaster but his tongue was too far ahead to be halted, ' – animals. I don't know how to be an animal.'

He waited warily for the fire to fall but I said only, 'Yes, you do. We all do. Think about it.'

A whole conditioned lifetime rebelled. 'I'm not the Swill kind of animal – dirty, criminal, ignorant.'

He needed an unfair jolt, below the defences. 'Change the way you think about them. Like this: if the Extra Test had been introduced thirty years ago, it might be Billy Kovacs sitting here trying to teach you sense. His wasted brain is probably as good as yours.'

What should have been outrage emerged as sulky complaint. 'No matter what, you always come back to him.'

'Just as one day you will.'

'No!' Explosive, furious.

'Yes. Eventually. Goodnight, Teddy.'

'I want to – '

'*Goodnight.*'

His sudden calm was not capitulation. His shrug said, *I'll get nowhere with this goon*, while his look said, *But it isn't finished.* 'Goodnight.'

'Sir.'

'*Sir!*'

I was left alone with my mistakes. This conversation would be all through the squads by midnight and in a day or two I would surely be carpeted for jumping the curricular gun. So much for the cool intellect of the instructor, always on top of the exchange.

11

TEDDY
AD 2045

Carol was at the sandpit; she always waited for me, practising the flips and twists that were refining themselves into mathematical lines and whorls of grace. How had the waiting come about? Memory does not say; it had crept up on us as such things do.

I told her the whole interview. The one thing I shared with Francis was an actor's talent (not after all so common among them, either) for verbatim recall. At the end I said outright that I didn't believe him. 'They wouldn't waste Extras on Swill.'

Carol was less sure. 'If Nick said it – '

No gainsaying that. What Nick said always turned out to be right. That was the one shining thing about Nick, that his most outrageous ideas made eventual sense; his resentable statements shook down into truths to be swallowed. She said pensively, 'Perhaps not for all of us. I couldn't go there, I couldn't act it.'

Nor could she. She was a rotten actress, striking poses and using words as if meaning hadn't been invented. And Nick hadn't said *everybody*, he had said *you*, meaning me. 'It could be only those who opted for PI.'

'But that would mean me, too. And I couldn't. It's you because you're a good actor.'

She had tapped into my vanity. The situation reversed itself and I saw my part as someone very useful, possessed of a special talent which allowed me to do what others could not. For a visionary moment I did what I had said I could not do and moved into the mind of the only Swill I knew anything about, stretching my snake's body along the fence, chewing while I watched the foolish woman and her kids coming down in the world, calculating what could be screwed out of her, summing her up while my forked tongue selected a point of strike . . . I felt the dirty clothes and my unwashed lousiness, the skin stretched over my narrow face, the champ of my jaws and the thin, sharp soul looking out at prey . . .

This was what Nick had promised *me*. The unacceptable glorified itself into need. I had been thrown the challenge to roll in muck and come up undefiled and I was the one who could do it. In his prodding, undercutting way he had promised me the most extreme use of a talent. I saw him for what he was, a shaker of minds until the crusted rubbish fell away and the cores were exposed.

That all this added up to an exercise in flattered vanity did not matter. From opponent Nick became my accomplice.

The alliance withered at birth. Some years passed before I so much as saw him again.

While I preened myself on self-discovery Carol spread my gossip round the tents where it was received with degrees of credence, disbelief, tolerant guffaws and outright fright, according to type. In the morning, when the squads assembled, it caused nervous questions to be asked of tutors. The questions caused a flurry of embarrassed, conflicting, time-serving replies which culminated in an unscheduled conference of tutors at midday. Then Nick was silently gone and a new senior in place. It was accepted that my wagging tongue had precipitated Nick's downfall (the tutors spoke only of routine replacement) and I achieved among the squads a shortlived notoriety as a man to be wary of, a throneshaker not lightly to be crossed.

The tutors observed me with stone faces and pretended that nothing out of the ordinary had happened.

At the end of our year – bronzed, filling out, shooting up, bursting with health – we were transported back to Melbourne where we were broken up into our final training allocations. Carol and I, with a dozen others, were ushered into the Police Intelligence Recruit School, where our first and most unsettling shock was the discovery that we formed exactly half of our cadre.

The other half were Swill.

Our presence upset them as theirs demoralized us. We glared at each other across a barrier of social incredulity. Neither half realized, had been capable of realizing, that this was the climax of the long undermining of preconceptions.

One thing we Sweet discovered very soon was the reason for our twelve months of living hard: it had been to bring us up to physical scratch. Those Swill kids had been street fighters while we still played in kindergarten.

12

ALISON
AD 2044–2047

1

I was educated, well-bred, socially competent. I was well read, worldly wise, mentally balanced. I was a wife, a mother, a social success. I was safely middle class, safely married, safely ensconced. Safely safe, safe, safe.

My husband killed himself and overnight I was a nonentity, an indelicate presence without income or status, expected to have the decency to slip quietly from sight. But I prided myself on courage and a practical mind. It was the courage of the cornered rat and the practicality of the tamed goat with no alternative but to accept its tether, but for a few days I played the heroine, tigress mother with cubs at her breast, competent handler of problems, indomitable facer of fortune fallen to ambiguous status but retaining Sweet pride and Sweet assuredness of right and wrong.

Billy took all that from me in half an hour. I faced up to him (so I thought of it) with tough acceptance of the inevitable, ceding what must be ceded so that my boys might live in safety and keep pride in themselves. In fact I surrendered every point because I didn't dare do otherwise and worked up a fine mixture of hatred and contempt to shore up my role of suffering heroine.

He wanted me. I recognized that from the beginning and was fool enough to think it gave me power over him so long as I never let him take me. That was the idiot psychology absorbed from triv romances. It was not I who dangled him at cunning fingers' ends but he who soothed me gently into my place in the society of the gutter, never moving closer until he was sure that I saw myself without distortion and saw him, too, as he was.

His patience was monastic. It was powered by love, the one impulse I did not credit in him; through two celibate years I knew he wanted to climb into my bed (among, I found, any number of other beds), never dreaming that he might want, need, more than that. I didn't credit Swill with a capacity for love. Worse, I didn't credit myself with the capacity for love of a Swill man. (One who already had a wife and family of twenty years' standing!) When the caste nonsense collapsed I hardly noticed its going.

I have never fully understood Billy. Billy in love is thoughtful, kind, infinitely gentle, superior in strength and devoted in sharing them. Billy detected in weakness, deviousness or, most painfully, in loss of face through lack of education or social nous, is spiteful and childish. Billy away from those he loves is a two-faced schemer, a thief, a brawler, a stand-over man and – I am fairly sure of this – a killer. He is also the essential law in his agreed area of Newport Swilldom. I love him. Let that stand in lieu of total comprehension.

Is he a variant forged in the unique Swill fires or are there more like him, a contradictory breed thrown up by the pressures of a decaying culture?

Teddy's desertion hurt bitterly, but he and I had seen each other clearly on the night when his father died. Also, I was still numbed by disaster, buffered against shock. Billy was bewildered, unable to understand that families can crumble as the myth of 'natural affection' is exposed; a Swill family is indivisible, a tribe, proof against internal hates and dissensions. Teddy confirmed his opinion of the Sweet as essentially self-serving. Not altogether wrong.

He said, 'He'll be back. He's gone off all cocky to stand on his two feet against the world, but just wait till the world's worked him over. He'll be back.'

No. I could see him in solitary tears but not crawling home in defeat – he was too proud for that.

'Fuck pride,' said Billy. 'It wears off or it gets knocked off. He'll come home when he sees straight.'

Motherhood involves a lifetime of mixed self-deception and clear sight. I had no illusions about Francis as a selfish, deceitful child but my inner foolishness trusted his weakness to hold him at home where love and security lay. The fact penetrated only slowly that love and security lay in the gift of the Swill protector from whom I bought them for weekly dollars.

At first I saw his affection for Francis as an exploitable foible, a kitten softness at odds with his big cat menace. I sold Billy short in our early dealings. He was a blemish to be borne, a coarse servant cheaply paid at a few dollars, a discomfort but one that I could manipulate. There's vanity! I convinced myself that I employed and directed a dangerous thug bound by unrequited sentiment to me and my son. Oh, I knew that Francis adored him, but schoolboy crushes wear off in time. (And so his did. He got over Billy and he got over me, too. But that was later.)

One adapts so easily. The years that began in terror and loneliness settled into a housewifely round of making ends meet. When we had relearned the pleasure of small amusements there were as many good times as bad. This came of Billy's caring while my attitude towards him slid, almost unperceived, from angry disgust to reserved tolerance, to amused friendliness, to open dependence, to –

– To the night he 'put the hard word on me'. That was his blunt description of what he thought of as a declaration of love – I recall it with a twitch of the heart between exasperation and laughter. So he 'put the hard word' on me and I dissolved into the passion that had waited at my shoulder for the stirring of the senses.

Billy thought Francis disliked the arrangement; the boy said nothing but the bond between them loosened. So Billy said. I, schoolgirl-silly in my new adoration, did not care what Francis thought – he could forfeit a trifle of the comfort of his heart in favour of mine. After all, he had to grow up.

I wonder at my love for Billy, as if I were an observer amazed at my willingness to fall into the Swill embrace. A scrap of old aristocracy whispers, *nostalgie de la boue*. I accept that. I was happy.

That is enough of me. It is Billy I need to tell about.

He knew so much of what he called 'the real world', meaning the towers, and so little outside them. He saw education as a desired tool but had little idea what it was or how to use it; he came unwillingly to understand that his magpie accumulation of facts was not an education. It was hard for a man in his forties to face the thought that much of his effort for himself and others was founded on muddled ideas. That he rose above anger and resentment and came to me for instruction is a measure of the man he might have been in a fairer time. (Swill men do *not* take instruction from their women; my position in his life was, to his observant peers, quirky and questionable.)

At first I used superior knowledge as a stick to beat his complacency – it's a wonder he didn't hit me, a greater wonder that his devotion survived the temptation. His grim self-control warned me in time that he suffered me because he needed knowledge as a – I nearly wrote, 'as a flower needs the sun', but that won't do for Billy – as a dog needs its dinner, in blind hunger.

Yet he knew and understood matters that had existed under my nose for years without my seeing them. As in the case of the newscasts.

The subject came up one night as he lay in my arms. Because he was absent so much on business that I preferred not to know about, most of our intimate talk took place in bed, where this dominant male liked to be nursed. A psychologist might make something of that.

This was a night in the aftermath of a storm tide that had pushed the river back for miles. The lower streets had been submerged for a full day of dangerous undertows and conflicting currents, and the Tower Bosses had been worked to their limits through forty hours of organization and rescue. The very young and the very old were a heavy responsibility in flood time.

As always when his body and mind had been tested beyond decent endurance there was a running-down period before sleep, as though he needed equilibrium before resting. He talked of split-second rescues and disgraceful desertions, of rigging rafts out of unlikely salvage, of a baby afloat in a caulked crate and a distraught grandmother stumbling and squawking after it with little concern for the child but a great and noisy terror of the father who would thrash the skin off her for carelessness.

At some point he said, 'But we're better off than the Gold Coasters up north. They have cyclones, great whirling bastards that can split a tower. Kill hundreds at a time.'

'Not any more,' I told him.

He twisted his head to look up at me. 'How so?'

'The weather control people found out how to make cyclones wind down before they reach full strength.'

'When was that?'

'Oh, years ago. I remember reading about it. Taming them increased interference with rainfall and weather fronts but it was the lesser evil.'

'You're sure?'

'Of course. Do you think it couldn't be true?'

With his cheek back on my breast he said you could never be sure with those bastards who made the news and then unmade it to suit. 'Like the bushfires. When do you see triv news about bushfires? About whole farms wiped out and country centres burned – and those are Swill centres mostly. When did you last see that? And when will you see today's flood on the triv, telling how many were drowned and how many lost every bloody thing they owned because there's no rescue service any longer? Or how we set broken bones in the tower corridors when the State meds can't cope? You won't.'

I thought with a disturbed wonderment that all this was true. In the Lucky Country we had no disasters. None, that is, in public. We had incidents, bushfires that were 'contained', torrents that 'subsided', droughts whose effects were 'minimized'. Other continents existed in permanent catastrophe, stalked by calamity, starvation and death as ruined ecologies reeled under the patternless weather conditions that drowned and buried at seasonless random. The northern hemisphere, we were told, suffered more than the southern. That had always been true, the palaeontologists said. In the southern hemisphere we remained the Lucky Country.

Was it so? Really so?

Billy said, 'Anyone with half a brain knows the news is cooked – them that still have a triv that works, that is. You Sweet don't think, because you're not allowed to. You've got to be kept calm to run the State – or think you run it. No upsets for you about people dying when they don't need to, no desperation about safety and death and food and shelter. No truth because then you'd start thinking and half of you'd drop dead with fright.'

As usual he had startled me with a possibility and then run it down with overstatement. Conspiracy theory now, that old bogey. I said, 'Somebody has to know the truth in order to suppress it. It would leak out.'

'It does. Rumours. Say, did you hear about . . . ? Then forgotten because nobody gets all the facts. When it's only a talk game it doesn't matter if a bit of truth slips through. Who'll notice?'

'It couldn't be done.'

Quite spitefully he nipped my breast. 'Hitler did it and Stalin did it and Churchill and Nixon and that was only in one century.'

Him and his damned bits-and-pieces reading! 'Perhaps they did but that isn't to say . . .'

To say what? Why was the news always good or, at worst, only trivially disturbing?

'It *is* to say, Allie! Sweet pay taxes and make the State work as properly as the rickety thing knows how and so the State lets them think they're being looked after. Tell them how bad off everybody else is and they won't make trouble for their protectors, see? Same with the Swill – make them understand it's no good rioting for more of anything because there *isn't* any more, and anyhow they're better off than poor bastards in India and Siberia. Trouble everywhere except at home! You can bet the other countries do the same.'

Quite suddenly he went to sleep and I lay unmoving, finding what he had said as hard to refute as it was to believe. And – this is the proof that he was right in essence if not in detail – my thought as I too drifted off was that it hardly mattered any more; we had made this world and it was all we had. There was nothing to be done about it. Fred would have believed him – he had died of an overdose of truth.

For an instant I was terrified. Then sleep came.

As often happened in this pillow talk, a curious thing Billy had said was lost among the words but in the morning it emerged while I brewed tea and made toast with the lumpy bread the State bakeries packed with God knows what to make it 'stretch'.

Billy slurped his tea – I never could cure him of that – wearing only underpants while Francis, neatly dressed for school, sipped and silently disapproved. He hated Billy's morning slovenliness but I was foolish enough, and I suppose enough in love to see this primness as a holier-than-thou phase of adolescence.

To tell the truth, Billy in the morning is no sight for the sensitive, lounging scruffily half-naked until tea and toast 'set him up' and he is ready to shave and dress. His metabolism refuses to deposit more than a minimum of fat and his muscles hang like blobs on a stick-man frame. Neat in his clothes, in undress he is like something slapped together from a child's constructor set. Lank hair droops over a narrow face to meet black shadow of a fast-growing beard, and I imagine I thought as on a thousand other mornings, *God knows he's awful – and I'm a damned lucky woman.*

Still, his frowsy presence over chair and table allowed me to think I saw how the poor lived. We were, of course, better off. We had all we needed . . . and at that the shock words surfaced. I asked, 'What did you mean last night when you said "for them that still have a triv that works"?'

'Did I? That's what I must have meant.'

'Everybody has a house screen. It's in the building code, like windows and running water and sewerage.'

'So?' He scratched his stomach as if that might help and Francis looked delicately away. 'And then they break down.'

'Well?'

'That's all. No more screen or no running water and a stink in the sh – bathroom. Unless you've got a right fixer in your tower.'

'But all you have to do – ' I remembered tales heard in Sweet days but not credited.

Billy's big eyes opened wide while he mimicked, 'All you have to do is ring Triv Complaints and a technician will call as soon as one is available. But he's never available.'

'I've rung and had him within the hour.'

'You were Sweet with a husband paying taxes that bought service. For Swill the man doesn't come round, the screen stays dark and you do your viewing with the neighbours, until theirs goes dark too. But the man never comes.'

I said nothing because I would be afraid of a home without a screen. So much depended on the screen and the ancillary terminals, though our present one was not fully equipped. I had often wondered how people coped before triv.

Francis, young and ghoulish, asked, 'What about the bathroom? I mean, when the flush won't work?'

Useless to protest that this was no subject for the breakfast table; Billy always made sure that Francis got necessary answers, and they talked over me.

'They put up with it till a few more clog up and the stink gets bad. Then Complaints listens and sends a man. And I have to provide a guard for him.'

'They're afraid of a plague?'

'I don't know about a plague but they don't like it when everybody gets the shits and it spreads.'

I laid down my toast with a lost gentility's revulsion and even Francis corrected him with his own repulsive pedantry, 'They contract diarrhoea.'

'Do they ever!' He grinned at me. 'OK, then, diarrhoea,' filing the word for use with queasy stomachs. He was proud of his ability to match his spoken English to his company, from Swill to 'classy', but could muddle his styles sadly.

Francis was not to be put off. 'Why do they wait so long? And why don't they fix the trivs? Where we lived before, they always fixed everything. Even here – '

The fact hit both of us in the middle of the sentence: that we had never had a Complaints serviceman in this house because we had never lodged a complaint. Little things went wrong, but either Billy fixed them with a sort of man-of-the-house enthusiasm or he took the faulty item away and replaced it (best not to ask how) or had it repaired.

Billy frowned like Francis over homework, meaning that his knowledge was entering an area of uncertainty. 'We reckon they haven't got the trained men.'

'They could train thousands in six months.'

'They'd have to pay wages.'

'Of course.'

'What with, Allie, what with? If there was money to pay for what people need there wouldn't *be* a Swill. The State's broke, Allie. I think the whole world's broke. If I could get at the sort of information the Sweet can get I'd soon know, I'd be able to work it out. Don't *you* know?'

Yes, I knew, but I had never seen the need to assemble the knowledge into a pattern of cause and effect. The planet had been insolvent for a generation or more, what with the repudiation of the Third World's debts, the awful consequences of the weather changes we called 'climate creep' and the bankruptcy of an unemployed mass living on the crumbs of existence . . . I knew but it was a knowledge of the faraway: *I* did not starve. It would smooth itself out because somewhere out there the world's economists were twisting theories of money and resources into new shapes and making the circle of credit – that is, taking in each other's washing – go round and round in a pretence of doing the work of non-existent national reserves.

This was common Sweet knowledge. The world was planning its way out of bad times; there would be years of hardship, perhaps decades, but also an ending to them. Common knowledge yet Billy did not know it, could not get at the information.

I knew at last what it meant to be Swill. (So I thought; I was only beginning to know.) These, the greater part of the population, were kept in ignorance, conditioned to live in hell and not ask why. They were not told what might upset them, confuse them, start them thinking . . .

Dear God, conspiracy theory now! I'm as bad as Billy. Back to earth, girl, before the rabid paranoia bites you.

Francis was fitting an unfamiliar phrase into his vocabulary. 'Would a right fixer be a Swill man who can do a Complaints job?'

'You've got it, boy. There's five in my gang – group. My tower's the best off in the district.'

He rarely spoke of his 'group' and the mention of technicians altered my hazy idea of its functions, but I still thought 'gang' was the truer word.

Francis asked, 'Where did they learn?'

Billy grinned ferociously. 'They're Sweet who lost their jobs and dropped into the Swill. All kinds. I've got one who can fix trivs, if we get him the parts.'

He meant steal the parts but he liked to preserve a veneer with us who formed the genteel aspect of his life, God help him. I have often wanted to cry for Billy but I have never laughed at him. It is heartbreaking that anyone should look with envy on our rags of vanished sophistication.

A few days after this the world exchange system collapsed. All money was withdrawn from circulation. It was a coup of sorts, carried out by the major powers, another throw in the game of keeping the planet feebly moving.

I was alone in the house when the news broke in a special newscast full of reassurance and an air of taking it in one's stride, together with details of how the new coupon issue and home-budgeting regulations would make life less complicated. I sat down and wept without knowing precisely why. In a clueless foreboding of the end of all things? After wasting time over that, I set about the daily business of cleaning our rooms, preserving normality in the face of the unknown.

The old couple, with whom I had finally come to a sort of arm's length sociability, knocked for admittance and were distraught all over my lounge-room with fears even less choate than mine. Their sole tetherstone was Billy and the hope that my intercession would work for them. Mr Billy, they chattered, would know what to do.

Mr Billy had no idea what to do, indeed no clear idea of what the death of money meant. He confused it with communism, which Swill doctrine equated with black evil. It took a night of explanation, increasingly woolly as his questions bared my ignorance, to lay that ghost.

After all the tears and fears nothing devastating happened. The planning had been excellent. We adapted to new methods of getting and accounting and came to think them an improvement. They became habitual. Habits are safe and cosy and we form them quickly.

The world rolled wearily on down.

My memory lacks a sense of order. I try to pin down these years and only dredge up incidents dominated by Billy, though in some things he deferred, almost begged. I was his slut and mother, he my satyr and brat in a muddle satisfactory to both.

That he had a wife and a grown family did not interfere with my contentment; the mind looks where it wishes, not where it should. My taking to alcohol may have been the physical expression of guilt glossed and ignored.

No, no, I did not take to drink in the grand manner to become a sodden hag, but I looked forward to sharing a bottle of wine with Billy in the evening where once I would have preferred a decent cup of tea. An occasional packet of Ceylon came with the loot from Mrs Parkes but imported tea was not easily got even via her corrupt tentacles; a good class of wine was a more frequent gift.

We did not drink until Francis had gone to his room at night because he viewed the bottles with suspicion, having a mind full of triv drama showing Swill in drunken stupor. Billy's insistence that drunkenness was commoner among Sweet than Swill (who could obtain mostly 'home brew') did not convince him. We told each other that he was growing up, navigating the difficult years between boy and man; his growing introspection did not warn us that not only was trust dying but love also.

2

Mrs Parkes was generous; it would be graceless to say that we went short of anything that mattered. She gave us quality foods, replacements of linen, special clothing and the little things that make the difference between subsistence and some pleasure in living. What she did not give were the basic items of cheap clothing, groceries and so on that could be obtained for the issued coupons. This was good sense but heralded a great change in my habits.

When money died I went to our post office, a few blocks away, to draw the first issue of the new basic coupons and joined a long queue of faces I recognized but could not name. It was an almost silent queue – Fringers are an asocial lot.

Most received their booklets with the same deadness of spirit that marked their faces, but there was an occasional outcry laced with fear. A woman cried out, 'But I can't shop there!' and became hysterical and an unexpectedly present policeman ushered her outside. I thought, *So even the shops we use are pre-determined*, and was irritable until I saw that for proper rationing of quantities the arrangement was inevitable.

I got my coupon booklet. The cover was stamped NE4, the code for the shop with which I was to deal. I checked the wall map where others also peered to see which dreary shop was indicated. A man I knew by sight turned away and, catching my eye, spoke to me for the first time. 'No need to look – it's the same for the whole street. They've tipped us in at last.'

I didn't believe him until I had checked. It was true.

It was frightening. Then it was not, because Billy would fix it. My Billy would never allow . . .

Now the truth about Billy, learned by degrees, as manipulator and fixer.

His strong-arm hooligans kept a sort of order in his tower area by methods the police could not use without risking civil war and the killing of policemen; in return he was made privy to certain 'contacts' and could depend on a blind eye being turned on his errors of judgement. Let me translate: my Billy kept order in his tower by carrying out ruthless vigilante justice. He worked sometimes in covert co-operation with the police and was, in blunt terms, an informer. The informing was confined, more or less, to tipping off the police as to how they might, with the help of the soldiery, manage a large scale round-up that was beyond his resources, but he was not above putting an enemy out of play where his own means failed.

It says something about the human ability to improve on virtue that this style of tenant vigilantism developed from the very effective Neighbourhood Watch system sponsored by the police in the last century.

There is no point in pondering Swill morality. *Informer* has always been a dirty word although there are obviously situations where only informing can prevent atrocities. When I once found the nerve to question Billy's methods he heard me out, then read me a sermon on survival of the fittest. The end of it stays with me: 'The fittest isn't the strongest. If I depended on strength I wouldn't last a day. Fittest isn't what you are, it's what you do with what you are.'

It meant, unflinchingly, being a thug who was also a police toady and messenger boy. That was what he was; what he did with it was – the best he could for his tower.

I did not fully appreciate these things when I pointed out the impossibility of my shopping in Newport Northeastern Four and he said sharply, 'You'll have to if you want the stuff.'

We were at the tea table and Francis became urgently tense when I named the distribution centre. I said in the flat voice I used when it was necessary to withstand Billy, 'I can't go there and I won't.'

'Then you'll go without.'

I tried desperately, 'Mrs Parkes – '

'You'll not use Mrs Parkes. Or think of it.'

In my cowardice I must have looked at Francis because he squalled – the only word for it – 'I wouldn't go down there! Not for anything!' And he poured out a garbled story about children kicking another to death in the street and himself being saved by Billy's boy, the one who had been killed in some brawl a year or two before. 'Billy knows about it!'

Billy did know. 'The kid wasn't killed, wasn't much hurt. You got a fright, that's all.'

But I was shocked out of all good sense and ranted at him like a harridan at his expecting me to venture –

He stopped me with a yell of anger that must have terrified the old pair in the other half. 'For fuck's sake, woman, shut up! Give me a chance to think.' He added sullenly, 'You've got to learn, that's all.'

'That's all!' I mimicked furiously and saw his face and wished I had held my tongue. I thought that surely one of his grown-up sons could do my collecting for me but had no courage to suggest it.

There was no lovemaking that night. I was frightened, resentful, humiliated and everything unbearable, and he was impatient with what he saw as unreasonableness. He kept explaining, 'I'm not bloody God. I can't get the shop location changed. It's all worked out by Data Central on a map grid that doesn't know anything about Sweet and Swill. It just knows what shop is nearest to your address.'

When I bawled, 'They're trying to make me Swill!' I thought he would hit me. Perhaps he should have.

He said, 'Swill is when you think you're Swill. I've lived all my life down there and I'm not Swill.'

When it suited, he would claim to be Swill and proud of it, but he really did think he was a cut above his station.

Later, when I calmed down, he reasoned with me. 'You've got the wrong idea about the Swill with what your parents taught you and the bloody rubbish on the triv shows.'

'Those things happen! Don't tell me they don't happen.'

'But not all the time and not everywhere. The Sweet are just as bad behind their closed doors but you don't see it. In the towers everybody lives on top of each other and you see everything. You see every lousy, stinking thing people do to each other and because it's under your nose you get to thinking that's all there is in life. Well, it isn't. Most Swill people are as decent as you or me.'

I didn't dare laugh. He went on, 'They don't think the same way as you but that doesn't make them worse.'

'Then why must you have your vigilantes?'

'To keep bad from getting out of hand.' Then he turned his back and would not be coaxed. I lay there feeling ignorant and a mite stupid.

3

In the morning he went off as usual with no word of where he would be or what doing but, most unusually for him, with a laconic, 'I'll be back about eleven.'

So he was. Poor Fred would have created drama out of having rearranged his world in order to find time for me but Billy said, as though I should have expected it, 'Get changed and I'll take you down to NE4.'

That was terrifying but I knew that if he had thought it through, it was what would happen.

I said stupidly, 'You mean *dress*?' For Swilldom?

'The oldest stuff you've got. What you put on for dirty jobs.'

I tried to joke. 'Those old trousers of Fred's? With the knees patched?'

'They'll do.' He meant it. 'No make-up, not even powder. Just do your hair properly, like a Swill woman making the best of herself with nothing to help.' Then, enjoying what he knew would shock me, 'Don't wash.'

My resistance of the night before might never have existed, which meant that it had better not be revived. So I dressed like a dowd in a dead man's trousers (tightly belted and rolled up two inches), an old jumper and a pair of worn-down shoes, and was sure I had overdone it – Allie the Footpath Floozie with Her Man Who Done Her Wrong – but he nodded Good enough. (*Just what a feller requires of his girl.*)

My immaculate suitcases and shopping bags were richly unsuitable; he found me two big, grubby paper sacks like cement bags. I gathered that carrying was woman's work. 'Come on,' he said.

'But what about you?'

'What about me?'

'You're *dressed*. You're neat and smart while I'm got up like an old clothes pedlar.'

"S'right, but I'm Billy Kovacs. I'm Somebody around here. I've got to keep up appearances. You'll see.'

'While I get around in castoffs!'

He sighed that great male sigh that has slithered down the ages, the one for the stupidity of women. 'The hags in NE4 don't know you. Later on you can slap up a bit but first they have to get used to you. If they pick you for a stuck-up Sweet gone sour they'll give it to you hard – pick the shit out of a Sweet woman slumming among the Swill. Get me?'

Uneasily, I got.

In the street he took my arm and walked on the outside of the footpath (Swill have a standard of manners long forgotten by their betters) and accompanied me with the seriousness of an equerry. I was occupied at first with keeping a straight face, sure that with a Tower Boss for escort no wickedness could touch me.

There were few people at the Fringe end. I tried not to notice that those we passed knew Billy at least by sight and examined me as closely as they dared without giving offence – to him.

This street into which I had never set foot ran downhill from the Fringe, into the heart of the Swill Enclave. There are twenty-four towers in Newport, housing nearly 1¼ million people – an average of eight to each three-roomed State flat, a figure that fundamental panic refused to confront as abominable. The nearest was no more than 300 metres distant, soaring like Babel to a height of despair. To reach it we had to navigate a footpath long ago collapsed into rubble.

Then it seemed that in a dozen paces we crossed an invisible limit of the Fringe and were in the seething gut of a vast, disgraceful city.

The Swill slept late but once awake they poured from their huddling places into the light. Each tenement tower was a blunt shaft assaulting the sky and round its base, like a dancer's skirt, spread 100 metres of concrete desert. If those huge spaces had not existed the people would have packed the roadways in an immovable mass.

People! I had never seen so much gross humanity at one time. What I had thought of as crowded streets were free passages beside this heaving of bodies. That was a first, loaded vision that gave way slowly to seeing that the crowd moved with purpose and the ease of custom. It lost thereby nothing of its monstrousness.

Because it stank. Across the width of the roadway it stank of sheer dirtiness and sweat. With a foot on the kerb I would have stopped in returning terror of the Swill myth if Billy's hand had not forced me on. We crossed the broken, traffic-less roadway and stepped on to the huge concrete skirt of the tower.

I passed into that condition of mental shock wherein the senses operate and the body feels but the will is paralysed, confronting the bogey of my upbringing, the unimaginable presence of the Swill.

I saw without immediately understanding that in the packed desert of flesh a sort of territoriality ruled. On the featureless concrete bodies sat or lay, for the most part browned and half-naked to the heat, like figures in a contagious dementia fancying themselves sunbathing on some dream lido. Through and around

146

them others walked tracks that by mysterious consensus remained open; the penned herd seethed with its own impenetrable order. More than that, this mass with nothing to do and nothing to look forward to was not a Slough of half-human Despond, morose and inert. It lived. Its corporate body was vital and its disparate minds were at work.

As mine was not. I moved in an observing, camera-eyed stupor because Billy forced me.

NE4 was somewhere beyond the tower, in another street; we had to cross the desert of flesh, through the sickening stink of humanity, of clothes and bodies that smelled of squalor. This mob at the foot of its tower was refuse ejected to pollute the air.

My one coherent thought was that if one of these ragged dwellers touched me, knocked against me in its passage, I would scream out my panic. It did not happen. Groups divided, stepped aside; contact was avoided. It came to me that we were given passage by people who knew Billy, greeted him at every second step and made way for the Tower Boss and his – whatever they thought me. They did think of me. Every eye raked me. It may have been the scrutiny that brought me round for, quite suddenly, my terror receded to a nervous tension and I was able sensibly to take in what I saw.

I had braced myself for monsters and there were none here. Dress them, wash and brush them, and who would know Swill from Sweet? Theirs were the faces of men and women, eager or reserved, intelligent or dull, no more, no less. Their opened mouths told another tale, not only by the uncouth dialect of which I caught barely a word but by the brown fangs, broken stumps and sucked-in lips over no teeth at all. *But dentistry is free!* Horror replied: *These are not the dispossessed; they are the abandoned. The man does not come round.*

I was appalled by the irrational number of extremely old people, wrinkled, decrepit and unsteady – surely centenarians to have lived to such physical failure. Then I remembered how the aged Sweet are cared for, maintained by anti-decrepitants and cosmetic medicine; these hordes of ageing Swill were not so old, simply beyond the expensive love of the hapless State. They were what I might become in a decade or two. I looked away.

Among the younger folk there was enormous noise, shouting, a deal of coarse joking, even some restricted horseplay. But there was also music, some singing of songs I had never heard to groups who listened and applauded, accompanied on instruments, most of them flat-toned and home-built but some expensive (stolen?) and played with the natural talent that cries out for tuition. There was a sense, fully alive, of an established culture – I don't mean of art but of a way of life accepted and understood, defying dirt and the ambience of the gutter.

Each thing I saw convicted me of ignorance of a whole world I had taken for granted like all my gossip-fed kind, a world quarantined by Sweet fear, State expediency and the gulf of birth and circumstance. But the enclosing smell and Billy's hand, protecting, reminded me that the eye is not enough. Below the exteriors lay real demons. His changeling self was one of them.

Beyond the skirt, on the actual roadway, the congestion doubled and redoubled into a moving, dodging mass, too thick for the swift, lithe manners of the skirt. My fear returned in helpless flinching as Billy held my elbow to drag me through the throng with a forcefulness I would not have dared for myself, too fearful of attack by an infuriated harridan or a simple beating aside by some unseeing male. Then the huge sign of NE4 loomed overhead, most of its lightstrips rotted or peeled away. We passed under it and inside.

A whole city block . . . cut into corridors by shelves of goods . . . think of a Sweet supermarket ten times enlarged . . . crammed with shoppers as no Sweet venue ever was . . . *crammed*, overpowering.

My instinct was to run from the press of sweat and carcases but Billy's clutch drew me to one of a dozen queues waiting to enter the shopping area, one person entering as another emerged from a checkpoint. Deafening noise was squeezed by walls and ceiling into a clamour that drowned the rattling of overhead trolleys replenishing the continuously raped shelves. The stench of bodies was insupportable. My imagination faltered at thought of their world of rust-rotted pipes, blocked ducts and the man who never came round.

I said, 'I'm going to be sick!'

'You aren't!' That was an order, a threat. I took pains to control the retching. I mean *pains* – anyone who has done it will understand.

Inching forward, we entered the cave of rationed necessity. My idiotic Sweet apprehension of a struggling mob, feral in determination to snatch items from under each other's noses, was just that – Sweetly idiotic. The shoppers moved slowly, eyes on the shelves, reaching to grasp and claim while moving with the dreary line. A sort of flaccid accommodation seemed to be the rule, the habit, less deliberate than politeness, less positive than law. Nobody moved against the flow; who forgot or failed to observe an item, forgot or failed. My mind observed in some spasm of note-taking that where anarchy would have been instantly disastrous a pattern of behaviour had evolved.

So what of the triv dramas and the back-fence rumours of Swill viciousness? Plodding in the endless queue, I recalled fuzzily that jungle law is an accumulation of practical behaviours. Beasts of a dozen species gather at sundown at the waterhole, each in its protective group, without conflict or fear; by day, predators and prey congregate in view of each other until the moment comes for just one to be cut out and killed. There is order, understood. NE4 was the waterhole. Outside . . . best not to assume too easy an understanding.

Women ahead of me cast over-shoulder glances – I felt myself stripped, pawed, assessed. I might have said something stupidly offensive to their ears if Billy had not turned blank eyes on mine and ever so slightly shaken his head.

Two women behind me calculated totals and the number of coupon points required for this item or that, and I was shamed that these trudging hags could run rings round me, round most Sweet, in mental arithmetic. In a tribe without callies it was a survival talent.

I was learning, learning, almost forgetting the purpose – to acquire goods for the home. I tried to watch the shelves and ply my shaky addition and subtraction. At snail-pace we moved up aisle and round corner and down aisle, scanning every shelf. I made an incompetent mess of that day's foraging, partly through lack of preparation, partly because I did not know what was available (little, and that basic), or where in the endless shelves it might be found. At least the stink became less apparent as the nose surrendered.

People were openly curious about me, most with a cautious eye on Billy. He relaxed just once to whisper in my ear, 'The more that remember you the better.' Remember me as being under protection. The gallant escort did not, however, carry his lady's parcels. She carried one swiftly filling bag and another slung over her shoulder on a cord. The peacock strutted beside.

At the checkpoint (magic-eye check, automated gates, no smirch of human hand) the bags were emptied and repacked while I shivered in case my undependable addition had overspent our coupons. My figuring *was* wrong, though under, not over, but in any case I should have known that Billy was keeping his own score and would not have let me compromise his standing by making a public fool of myself.

Outside, we fought our way back through the press, I with a heavy bag dragging at my shoulder and another clasped in my arms, he with lordly push and shove to make a way for his pack-horse. I would not have believed that a week's purchases could be so unmanageable.

In the comparative freedom of the concrete skirt we moved well into the sitting, lying, singing, muttering, playing, self-absorbed mob before Billy staged a grotesque demonstration. (He told me later that he selected a place where some of his friends and thugs were close enough to hear as well as see.) He stopped, turned to me with calculated formality, took the bag from my arms and said loudly, in the Swill jargon I rarely heard from him, 'U'll giv y' and, luv.' Around us heads swivelled. We moved on at once, he with his arm about my waist, a mutter of comment rustling in our wake. God knows how many scrutinized our progress and noted the breeding points of Billy's publicly proclaimed mare.

Take away nightmare and the sweating stops. When we left the towers behind and he asked, 'Well?' I was able to pretend a sort of judicious balance. 'Not what I expected.'

He was not fooled. 'Couldn't be, could it? Afraid?'

'No!' He was silent. 'All right, then – sometimes.' I had been scared witless. To prove the steadiness of my mind I said, 'I thought I saw a group acting out a story, a sort of street theatre. I would have liked to watch.'

'Another time. There's always something like that. If we'd stopped today they would have gathered. Staring.'

'At me because I was with you?' Hot news! His grin was offensive. 'Anyone would think you are an important man.'

'Not just a guttersnipe, eh?'

'That's not fair. You know I didn't mean that.'

'No? Well, I am a guttersnipe. It's just that I'm an important one. To them, that is.' A frown settled like a mask on his narrow face. 'You don't seem to catch on what it means to be a big man in the towers.'

He made me feel inadequate and unobservant. I tried to joke my way out of it: 'This is where Francis would ask, "Then why aren't you rich?" '

He said, 'I am. I've got respect and authority and people depending on me and contacts that make me able to look after them. That's rich, isn't it? You're rich, too, but you won't know it while you think Sweet.'

He was telling me of a foreign country, forcing change on my view of the world. He said, 'I'll come with you twice more. That'll make it official. After that you're on your own. Don't go anywhere except to the store and you'll be all right.'

As if I might! I reached home in dismal contemplation of that weekly future.

At once he was on his way out again. I asked, whining a little, 'Do you have to go?'

He gave me the head-shaking half-grin that meant I was not using my brain. 'How many people live in this street, all of them Fringers on their first day into the Swill?'

My hysteria of the previous night had prompted him to organize a new style of operation. He had fifty men and women fighting through the crush, hour after hour, teaching terrified Fringers not to be afraid. Schemer, thief, liar, informer, lecher, he yet believed in earning the respect paid him and that order and kindness were the responsiblity of those who could generate or enforce them. The morality was beyond me. For years I found it hard to credit that men and women existed with an ingrained need to preserve essential humanity no matter what the cost in work and danger.

The moral cost troubled my schooled beliefs about the sanctity of this attitude or that convention until Billy said, 'The Sweet wiped you, didn't they, for getting poor? That was the rule you broke. Where's the morality in that?' Another time he said, 'The only people with morals to spare are the ones who've never seen the world straight.'

'The world can't be wholly wicked.'

'It's worse, it's stupid.'

I suggested, needling, 'Violence is stupid.'

'It don't prove anything, that's for sure, but it's only stupid when you come off worst. That's bad planning.'

You can't win against a stand-up comic.

4

In the third week a few men greeted me as we crossed the skirt. I could scarcely make out the words behind the thick accents. What sounded like, 'Daichums, Billy,' was finally identified as 'Good day to you, Mrs Billy.' I giggled over the quaintness of 'Mrs Billy,' to find that it was not quaint to Billy, who told me stiffly, 'Mrs Kovacs is someone else.' He did not often remind me of her existence.

Inside NE4 a few of the women nodded a distant acceptance. Two or three murmured the ritual greeting and I replied as instructed, 'Daicher.' I was not required to know their names unless they offered them; the system assessed strangers gradually. Mores had to be learned.

In the fourth week I went alone. My heart was in my mouth but might as well have stayed in its proper place; I was not raped or robbed or submitted to indignity. My path had been smoothed with such exactness that soon I acknowledged greetings with something like gaiety.

In the store I noticed a skinny, narrow-faced boy about sixteen years old who never seemed far from me that day. I had never seen Billy's sons but I suspected that he had detailed a family apprentice to this minor surveillance. The boy never met my eyes but neither did he let me out of his sight. Once he stopped to speak with a vast jelly of a woman, one of those unfortunates who collapse into middle age with a surge of weight into elephantine arms and thighs. She may have had good looks in her day but they had vanished into greying hair and eyes sunk to glittering from heavy cheeks. She was marginally better dressed than the women about her, less patched, less faded – and clean. So was the boy. She stared ahead as we passed each other, I patrolling up one side of the aisle, she foraging down the other, but I was sure that she saw and summed up every inch of me. If there had been anywhere to run I would have run.

Late that night Billy said as he played little boy with his pointed nose nuzzling my breast, 'You saw Vi today.'

It was the first time I had heard her name. Vi – Violet. For that mountainous woman! It was unfair of fate. 'I thought it might be she. She must hate me.'

'Why?' He did not lift his face to ask. He was simply curious.

'Any woman would.'

'That so?' He was ruminating, not making fun of me. 'She does all right. Gets everything she wants – well, just about. She's got position and a family. Why should she care?'

Were things done so differently in the towers? Or was he totally insensitive? No, he was not that. Whatever he was, I had no intention of surrendering him to a wife. His view of morality became more intelligible: it is something you practise when you can afford it, and I could not afford morality.

She did care. She invaded the house one day in a murderous rage and I had no courage to face her. Billy arrived – my shabby white knight – while she raved and I cringed and he manhandled her out of the place. I wish I could forget my cowardice. Guilt does that to you.

Perhaps I represented her last outcry against what time and uncontrollable glands had done to her, for everything I heard of her thereafter showed her as intelligent and very self-contained.

Then Francis went away with a lie on his lips and did not come back. Billy tried to comfort me. Poor, clumsy Billy. He was not often clumsy but he had given love to Francis and knew that comfort was not possible. An unsuspected rejection can be devastating and degrading.

I wept for my failure as a mother. In time I ceased to care. That isn't true: caring does not cease, only drops to the rubbish heap of the subconscious, and rots and festers.

5

'Winter' had become a name for a few weeks of the year when one perspired from effort rather than from humidity and the crowds in NE4 smelled – not sweeter, nothing could achieve that – less powerfully. As the global temperature crawled upwards a fraction of a degree each year, our once temperate and now subtropical State fluctuated between extremes of drought and torrential flood. The farms were ruined by both.

The Swill measured disaster by the food deliveries. Sudden dearth of cereal or occasional mild glut of potato, vanishing of sugar for a month or so, midsummer rationing of milk or – most infuriating of all – trial runs of staple-substitutes which neither substituted nor in any way appealed.

'Winter' meant warm downpours drowning the State as though a stuffed atmosphere had discharged an overloaded gut. On the tower skirts children danced in it while their elders muttered knowingly about the Greenhouse as though the word equalled understanding. Then the river would rise and a surge of filthy water overflow its banks. When there were ocean storms, river and tide would battle it out in the streets and the ground-floor apartments. I would recall my blue sea of delight in summers of glory – recall it with, occasionally, a useless tear.

One night, after both my sons were gone and Billy was off on some unmentioned and perhaps unmentionable business, I slept alone while the rain drummed and the wind howled in my dreams, though the dreams were of bright yellow sand like a strip of gold under a smiling sun and a small girl in a scrap of costume, ecstatic in the lapping shallows.

At some hour of the night the sea came up out of the delta to lap at my doorstep, but my windblown dream knew nothing of that. It had never before risen so high, even in beleaguered Newport.

In the morning I noted that the rain had ceased and the sun shone, made myself a cup of Mrs Parkes's tea and sat drinking it, half concerned because Billy had not come home, half enjoying myself *not* bustling to make his breakfast. From the wall the news bulletin chattered about the confluence of an unusually high tide driven by gale winds and a flash flood powered by cloudbursts over the Baw Baw Mountains. The ground floors of the towers, I thought, would be stinking messes of mud and rubbish with the unfortunate salvaging what they could in this fresh access of their recurrent misery. Some of them would be people I now knew slightly. They would not be swimming like mad (which of the boys had had that obscene fantasy?), only drearily rebuilding their lives after the tenth or dozenth inundation.

The front door rattled and slammed and Billy came in, dishevelled and filthy, hair in rat tails, clothes crumpled and torn, trousers rolled to the knees, shoes jammed under his belt and splayed, bony feet caked with black mud that dripped on my clean floor. He was white with fatigue, close to exhaustion.

He fell on to a chair, not speaking, and I gave him tea, holding the cup to his mouth, then wiped and dried his muddy feet and legs. When he spoke it was to ask, 'House all right?' and he closed his eyes when I nodded. It was hard work stripping him, harder still getting him to the bedroom and on to the bed. When I asked, 'Are you hurt anywhere?' he shook his head: 'Tired.'

I thought he slept immediately but he roused himself to ask, 'Store day, in't?'

Of all things to think of! 'Yes.'

Nearly asleep, he lapsed into Swill dialect but I understood that NE4 was washed out, there were no stores to be had. In a house backed by Mrs Parkes that was no great tragedy but for thousands who calculated each week down to the last meal . . .

Wondering what he had done all night in the flood water, my inexperience imagined only sentimentalities of small children rescued from drowning and old people helped to higher floors, not the organizing and slogging that had driven him to the end of his stamina. The mud on my clean floor roused a flash of annoyance that he had not wiped his feet at the door.

At the front door I saw why. In the night the water had stalked into my ambitious, inexpert little garden and trampled pansies and carnations and marigolds under black mud. Mud covered the low boards of the verandah and soaked the strip of doormat; rising another centimetre it would have been over the threshold and down the passage. The water had never threatened my home before. I thought that I would never feel safe again.

But flash floods drain away as fast as they rise and the enemy was already in retreat. I trudged through mud to the street corner to see the receding lip not twenty metres distant. The gentle slope of the road had sunk beneath a brown lake, sparkling in the promise of a cloudless day. Houses only a few doors from ours, only a few centimetres lower on the slope, had suffered a sewerlike flushing across their floors; lower still, tidemarks were at the window sills.

I splashed into half a metre of dirty water, horrified by small gardens ruined, fences broken, dwellers puttering hopelessly at the degradation of the almost nothing which was all they had. Where the towers rose to the bright sun entire floors must be submerged while the water ebbed, leaving its patterns on walls and ceilings.

The narrow-faced boy from the store appeared before me, saying carefully, like one practising a foreign language, 'Don't go down there, missus, you can't do nothing.' He gave up the struggle and reverted to familiar speech: 'S'me Dad orri'?' Something like that – spelling is helpless against it.

'Yes, he's asleep.'

He nodded. 'Fucked art, 'e wis,' and gave me an earnest instruction (probably from his mother) which I could only translate by association and guesswork. I said, 'Of course I'll look after him,' and seemed to have got it right because he gave his father's grin and splashed back downhill to join a companion on a raft of empty steel drums and push off, giving me the cheeky 'up yours' sign which had enraged me until I realized it was the regular time-of-day greeting in the towers.

I thought of him telling Vi that the Fringer woman was looking after Dad so not to worry, and I stood knee deep like a fool in the water, puzzling at the implied acceptance of things as they are. I don't know how long I stood there, cold in the warm sunlight, obsessed by my ignorance of the world of endless disaster.

A whining voice at the back of my mind insisted that while the greedy ocean rose, year by year, the real catastrophe was yet to come. Behind that again was the cowardly whisper of humanity in all ages, 'Please, not in my time.'

13

TEDDY

AD 2045–2047

1

To say that Sweet and Swill learned to understand each other would be fiddling the truth. We learned to mix without friction, but though real friendships, even a love affair or two, did straddle the social barricades, they were exceptions.

Tutorial insistence that the Swill component learn to speak correct English, be able to pass as Sweet in voice and mien, offended them: they didn't see it as an improvement and only under pressure became bilingual. (That, as it turned out, was enough to start undermining their class loyalties.)

Hardest done by in the social sense were we Fringers, seen by Swill as fake Sweet and by Sweet as Swill tainted. Stuck in the middle, looking both up and down, we realized earlier than the rest how deliberately the State fostered such attitudes. (That the State's intention was not to create division so much as to preserve an economically manageable status quo was a sophistication beyond our perception just then.)

Through all this Nick persisted under the surface of my mind, unhated. With the illogical crush-proneness of the teen years I now badly missed the hand that might have thrashed me but never did. A bad attack of father substitution.

Other teen troubles surfaced. Carol and I were fourteen when she taught me those facts of life I had known only in sniggering theory; I had sense enough, or developing self-respect enough, not to ask where she learned them. Then for a year she indulged a bitching-martinet complex, grindingly perfect in drills and regulations. She tells me I withdrew into role-playing to a point where people avoided me in their uncertainty as to who I might be at a given moment – I was unaware of it myself. We both survived our periods of ego boosting, were still together when they passed and rolling happily in the hay whenever privacy could be got.

Once or twice she tried to talk me into visiting home and we came close to quarrelling. She learned to leave the subject alone and I learned guilt as lengthening years made it ever more impossible for me to heal the break. *'Mum, I've come home.' 'Why? Is there something you forgot to take with you?'* I couldn't face it.

I heard that Kovacs had moved in with Mum; it seemed impossible, degrading. I know now that the information was fed to me and that Nick was in his shadowy way behind the feeding. It made a solid reason for accusing her of betrayal (of whom? of me?) and hardening my heart. Hearts being what they are, mine only cursed and grieved.

Word filtered through, too, of what Francis did for a living; presented to me in a manner that glossed over its criminal aspects, it seemed satisfactorily menial.

If the camp had troubled our teenage certainties, the Intelligence School destroyed them. There we had our noses rubbed in those facts that everybody knows but, as they are other people's woes, leave unattended – such as, that two-thirds of the world starves although it is easily possible with global planning, to feed everybody.

We had never set such remote facts straight in our minds. Why should we? If raised as Sweet, we had been buttressed from birth against horrors, our minds parentally turned from the abyss. If reared as Swill, taught from birth that you could have your State-given share (a frugal but scientifically calculated ration) and no more, that life meant making the most of little, that there was no way out of the Swill towers (untrue) and that the preservation of the State depended on recognizing one's place and not rocking the boat, why should they consider remote others?

We learned, in wonderment at the obvious, that the State not only encouraged these counsels of contentment but actively promulgated them. The brighter history students observed with prim surprise that both Church and State had preached this doctrine of ordained place in the scheme of things as little as two centuries ago. Our world had taken a step backward. I heard chuckling Nick query again the meaning of 'progress'.

The upshot was outrage in squad tutorial. The tutor of the day listened, curbing extravagant protest here and there but in the main agreeing with us. He sat there *agreeing* that a monstrous State kept order by lies and cozenage! His acquiescence shut us up faster than any whipcrack of authority, until a single voice was left, crying, 'But – ' and sinking into general silence.

'But – ' Larry repeated. He was a seconded policeman who treated us with genial tolerance and bouts of histrionic despair. 'But what, you outraged political nitwits? What would you do about it?'

What would we not! The air boiled with Utopias and means of confounding the State's philosophic errors. At the end Larry said, 'This uprush of well-meant poppycock takes place every year at this point in the syllabus. You are neither better nor worse than most, only noisier.'

He sat on a corner of his desk, swinging a leg and giving us the raised eyebrow that meant disillusionment coming apace. 'You will each prepare a scheme for the solution of the planetary food problem. If you feel that weather fluctuation will be the main problem, to be countered by improved meteorology, small weather-control units and better farm administration, be advised that it will not. Your concerns will be salination, education, finance, transport, religion, global politics and selfishness. For research I recommend the Governmental Procedures and Year Books of the major nations. You have surprises coming to you. Dismiss.'

As we left he had an afterthought: 'If at the end of a week anyone should despair of completing this exercise, we will weep together but no marks will be lost. That does not absolve you from trying.'

We floundered in deeper mud than ideals had dreamed of. In the end none of us completed the task; what we found in those recommended texts frightened the nonsense out of us. Police Intelligence had a major victory over social conditioning. We began blunderingly to think.

Larry believed that when ignorance had talked itself out there was room for information to enter, so the population problem followed obviously enough from the food problem. On the next day, in fact.

The squad agreed that it was, basically, one for national governments. When you have been born into a system referred to as the Concerned State, one that takes responsibility for everything, your response is to leave everything to it. Childbirth affects everyone, so the State should –

Should what?

Larry outlined the attempts that had been made in the past: reversible and non-reversible sterilization, decrees limiting family size, selective allocation of the right to breed, savage punishment for illegal conception, exhortation by charismatic leaders and such grotesque aberrations as segregation of the sexes and encouragement of homosexual relationships.

The last two we saw clearly as denials of heterosexual genetics. 'Not the others?' Larry asked. Well, yes, the others too . . . but some sort of restraint was necessary . . . 'Applied by whom?' Well, um, the prospective breeders. Contraception was, after all, freely available.

'A very respectable moral attitude for a class whose combined sexual depth wouldn't raise a breeze in a brothel doorway. What of the consequences of parenthood denied?'

We knew of those at second hand, through reading. Assessed over three generations of trial by every major nation, they were breakdown of the family unit, increases in street and domestic violence, apathy, mental depression, withdrawal from responsibility and – most seriously from a State viewpoint – unrest expressing itself in destruction of property, political dissension and outright insurrection.

'Take away the core of sexual existence, procreation, and emotional energy seeks an outlet. The alternative to creation is destruction. People *want* children.'

Sixteen is a productive age of cynicism, so it was no surprise that a voice said, 'The poor do.'

That was a kid we called Young Arry because he chose to answer to it rather than resent it as a reflection on his Swill origin; a thin skin would have started more fights than any gutter battler could survive. Besides, he was skinny and clumsy and not much good for anything but physics and distance running. I liked him in a casual way, almost against my will, but well enough to take his part when he needed support and not take it amiss when he failed to thank me for it. I suppose the dregs of vanity still showed in me, because he was the only Swill kid who would meet me half-way.

The Sweet kids in the squad didn't argue his point about the poor because Arry *was* the poor, while the Swill knew exactly what he meant. History backed his statement: poverty had always been a saddling paddock, and at the heart of our present problems were the swarming, unproductive poor.

Larry didn't give a damn for Sweet or Swill or the feelings of either. 'True,' he said, 'but why?'

'Habit,' said Arry, a laconic type.

'Indeed?'

'Lose it and you become an endangered species.'

'And that's all?'

'You need a hobby when you've got a lot of spare time.'

Larry spoiled our tittering by saying, 'That is literally true. A feature of idle poverty is a failure to develop inner resources. The poor need entertainment that costs nothing.' To the ripple of subdued catcalls he added, 'If you have to pay for it you don't deserve it.'

That set the girls squawking denunciation of prodding males treating them as sex objects.

'You mean you *should* be paid for it? Good for you, but tell me, what do you treat males as?'

Eh? Oh, as companions, prospective life partners. 'And sometimes,' said Carol, whose sense of humour played no favourites, 'as sex objects.'

'Only sometimes?'

She refused to be drawn; further gender treachery would get her a season in hell from the other girls. As things quietened down somebody asked what should have been asked earlier, 'But why does contraceptive teaching fail?'

Larry set his face in the bland innocence of the liar who refuses to be queried. 'I'm sure I don't know. It should make an interesting investigation. Let me have your ideas a week from today.'

A dozen voices asked, 'References?'

'Sex is not a subject for library research. Try thinking – or whatever.'

That was quite a gutful of challenge to absorb in two days, but it was Friday and most squaddies were going to their homes for the weekend. The population problem was left to simmer. It simmers still.

2

Squaddies raced into their civvy clothes, grabbed their bags and paused only for the regulation scan of the noticeboard. Then the small group of us who did not go home, for one reason or another, strolled to the board to see what might be new, and found nothing.

But there was a street map on the board, a big one with City Centre lined in red and the names of major buildings marked for reference. I examined it with a sting of old fascination, for in our fourth year City Centre had at last been declared 'in bounds' to us. (Permission to be grown-up!)

As kids we had talked of mysterious City Centre and its fabulous corridors of power. In time we had learned that it was just an antiquarian's delight of old buildings preserved through lack of funds to tear them down and rebuild, haunted by Small Sweet planners and programmers and secretaries and runners of messages for the Top Sweet who made the State's decisions. Longer in dying were the rumours of Swill robber gangs erupting from the sewer systems; we didn't really believe those, but you could never be sure . . .

Those who had actually seen the Centre said that nobody in his right mind would go near the musty place – 'crummy buildings and almost nobody about'. They were probably right but the glamour persisted. I wanted to see for myself.

As I peered at the map a Swill voice whined in my ear, 'Y' wanna gwin, Teddy?'

It was Arry, who could forget his Sweet speech at a fingersnap. He repeated, with apologetic care for trained elegance, 'Do you want to go in, Teddy?'

Of course I did, but civilian dress was obligatory for a City leave pass and I had none. I had outgrown my enlistment clothes and found no way to replace them; the State saw no reason to supply clothing coupons as well as uniforms.

I said briefly, 'No clothes,' hiding the hurt. Then passed the hurt to Arry. 'And where would *you* get city clothes?' The gear the Swill kids wore to go home in would not do for the Centre.

He shot me the most curious sidewise look of benevolence and complicity. 'Can get. Can borrow some for you, too.'

I didn't trust a word of that. Training or no training, Swill was Swill, and devious. But I wanted badly to see the Centre. He took my silence for assent, or pretended to. 'Twenty minutes,' he said, 'in your dosser.'

In less time than that he appeared in my cubicle with two complete outfits – trousers, shirts, belts, berets, the throatbands that were 'in' that year and two brassards identifying us as cadets. I recognized the stuff he gave me and knew it would fit, just as I knew its owner would be absent for two days and that he was a snot-nosed Sweet from whom Arry could never have cadged a loan of anything.

'Skeleton keys?'

'A loan,' Arry insisted, his grin openly conniving. 'But he's the type who wouldn't appreciate thanks.'

I had qualms.

And I had a chance to see City Centre.

I dressed.

So did Arry, with a difference. As he put on each item he studied himself in my wall mirror, entranced by the portrait of a stranger. He had never in his life worn tailored, matched clothes.

'Munt mucky,' he murmured, warning himself, and I translated, *Mustn't muck them up.*

We collected our passes and went out.

The South Gate of City Centre was a half-hour's walk away, straight down St Kilda Road with its trees and lawns and National Trust buildings, each with its descriptive plaque – Hospital, Police Barracks, Hotel, Church of Christ Scientist (what the hell?) – to Princes Bridge.

It was a hot and brilliant day with four hours of light remaining for seeing and discovering. I forgot the unease of 'borrowed' clothes and sang out, 'It's a terrific world, Arry!' Then, mocking gently, 'I mean, Harry.'

He grinned his thin grin. 'Arry's right. That's what my parents christened me. They didn't know any better.'

Parents? I came close to a social gaffe; one did not ask why another did not go home of a weekend. I would have found my own reasons impossible to make clear.

He continued as if he had heard the unspoken. 'And by the time I could have told them, they were dead.' That raised a barrage of unaskable questions but he set out, unprompted, to answer them, as if he knew that I needed his confidence before I could unlock my own. 'I was a street kid when I was seven. You know what that is?' I knew the term, no more. 'When tower folk die, others with too many in a flat will move in and take over. They won't always look after any kids left behind. Sometimes the kids run out themselves. I ran out – the lot that took over were shit.'

'So how did you live?'

'Not hard. There's thousands of street kids. Sleep anywhere – the corridors,the skirts if it isn't raining, anywhere. You join a gang, beg, steal.'

Barely comprehensible. 'But what about food, clothes when they wear out, times when you're sick?'

His answer began, I think, my understanding of the Swill sub-culture, of the order under filth and violence.

'The Tower Boss looks after his own. He sees they get what they're supposed to.' His voice held a memory of trust in that unlikely system; the Swill boy had learned to speak but hadn't shed his breeding.

I said compulsively, 'I know a Tower Boss and he's a murdering animal.'

Arry was unsurprised. 'They're all that sometimes, when they have to be. The Boss fights to be Boss and he fights to stay Boss and he fights for his people because nobody else will. You wouldn't know what the towers are like.'

True. I couldn't say a sensible word about them, only ask questions like, 'Are there schools there?'

'Not any more. But there's teachers.'

'Well, how . . . ?'

His permanent grin edged gently under my skin. 'Machines take over Sweet jobs and educated Sweet fall down into the Swill. They teach because that's all they're good for, most of them. The Bosses try to get them for smart kids. I got one who used to be a real teacher in schools.'

'But if there are no schools and records, how do you get picked for Testing?'

'Teachers tell the Tower Boss when they think they've got a good one and the Boss arranges the Test.'

That was astonishing in its implication of interaction between towers and State. One thought of the towers as limbo, ignored. I said, a bit impatiently, 'You make the Bosses sound like State servants.'

He thought seriously about that. 'No, but there's a kind of communication through the coppers, a sort of give and take, where both sides know what they can do.'

'It wouldn't work.'

He said shortly, 'It does. It's worked out between the Bosses and the coppers. The State makes the rules so everyone gets fed and housed – up to a point – but the real work of running the towers is done by coppers and Swill. It's not laws and paperwork but knowing how far you can go in one place and how you have to do it a different way in another.'

'I don't think it's possible.'

'Nobody spells it out, but that's the way of it. Sort of trial and error. How does it fit the Boss you know?'

'He's just a thieving stand-over bastard.'

'How else do you think they can work in multi-storey pigsties? What's his name?'

'Kovacs.'

'The Billygoat?' He was impressed, which riled me. 'Everybody knows about him. He's one of the old school – bust their heads first, then tell them how to behave, and keep kicking their arses till they learn. The new young ones are different – you'd almost think they've been trained.'

As simply as that, not knowing that he did, he told me with the certainty of revelation what career Nick had planned for me, explaining all his patience and his angers, everything he had said and done. It was as well that our paths had split – I was not going to be dedicated to the Swill by any high-minded do-gooder.

At the South Gate I put Nick and Kovacs out of my mind as we flashed our wristlets at the Telltale and it checked us through to City Centre.

3

From the bridge entrance we gawked at the skyline as if we had never seen it from the other side of the barrier. It was said not to have changed since the nineties, when the first crumbling of the financial basis had rocked the building industry, that old barometer of fiscal stability. That recession was a historical milepost, the beginning of the end of the old era, but we had never fully understood the tutorial explanations of the erosion of an economic system which had persisted through millennia. We saw the silliness of the basic concept that expansion was limited only by natural resources but not how the old economists had let themselves be fooled by it. Their theories had not included one for stopping the rot.

Those old buildings were not tall by comparison with the tenement towers; most were narrow and slab-sided; some had been sheathed in glass (a pretty stupid vanity) which had cracked off in places and been patched by more sensible materials that stared like blind eyes, but a few still shone brilliantly in the late sun. Most were dirty grey or deposit-streaked, standing like shabby sentries over the canyons at their feet.

Arry said, 'It makes you wonder.'

'Wonder what?'

'Why they built tall and then put up the towers taller still.' His syntax was loosening, on holiday from speech class. 'They knew it was no good. Last century, they called them high-rise workers' flats, and all they got was trouble.' I hadn't known that and it didn't seem to justify his sudden anger. He became shrill. 'They turned people into battery hens except they didn't lay.' That sounded like a book phrase and I said so, but he insisted, 'They failed once, but they started again, seventy-storey ones, and jammed 9 million people into them. People lived like pigs there but they still built up. Why?' His skinny body shook and his voice slopped over into the Swill whine. 'Wai, Teddy? Wai tay doot'us?'

What do you say to anguish you don't understand? He sniffed and with a hint of Swill savagery daring me to laugh, said with classroom care, 'Why did they do it to us?'

He wanted a slick Sweet answer he could mangle and fling back but I preferred peace. 'I suppose they couldn't think of anything better. You've seen triv pictures of Calcutta and Shanghai and South America and Africa – all shanties and lean-tos, no sewers, no taps, no way to distribute food, only street mud to walk on. We're better off than those.' So I found myself defending the State everyone knew to be a failure. 'They did the best they could.'

'So we're still the Lucky Country!'

That phrase had come down the years to haunt us, seeming to mean that we always escaped the worst of the world's troubles by luck or distance, but in Arry's mouth it was a Swill curse.

From the bridge I looked down on the river, a filthy, garbage-brown flood running bank high only a few metres below my feet, carrying branches and bottles and dead animals and clutches of nameless flotsam. Probably sewage overflow as well. It didn't quite stink but threw up the smell of Kovacs on that first day, the sharpness of Swill decay.

It was as broad as a football field, covering the platforms of the disused railway station on one bank, lapping at the walls of the derelict concert hall on the other and spreading out of sight through the abandoned streets of South Melbourne.

Arry read the gauge clipped to a lamp standard. 'Four metres of flood water. The triv'll say rain in the hills.'

Those were the years when Victoria got its share of mad weather as the Antarctic shelf melted, cooling major currents and altering their courses, raising fogbanks, changing the temperature gradients and the line of the prevailing winds, drowning untillable desert in useless water while ancient forests grew brown and bare under a brass-faced sun, giving this year and taking next, turning grassland to tinder while it poured unwanted, polluted water down the rivers.

Arry was matter-of-fact. 'Your Kovacs'll get a wet arse. Newport's right on the river flat. They'll go two floors under in this lot.'

'Cheerful sod,' I told him, but I thought of Mum with that wasted guilt I could do nothing about. Her house was high enough to escape flooding. Or was it? I did not know. I hoped in a convulsion of rage and entreaty that Kovacs was earning his mean dollars, looking after her, not shrugging his bony shoulders and walking away from trouble.

He couldn't walk away – he was living there. A swift, sick feeling that I must swallow pride and go home vanished into the smell of Kovacs and the river. *What brings you home, Teddy-boy? Your mum's safe with me. Piss off, little Sweet!*

Arry brought me back to the world. 'The Sweet all live at Balwyn Heights and such, but the bloody Swill can drown!'

But the neglect had nothing to do with caste. We could only vaguely imagine the billions it would cost to hold back the rivers and the rising sea but we knew without any vagueness that the State was broke.

We crossed the bridge into the Centre.

Crummy buildings and almost nobody. Years ago the business houses had moved out to the suburbs on the breakdown of public transport as people ceased to travel to work that did not exist. Now the business houses did not exist. In City Centre the old buildings housed State Departments employing three-quarters of the work force, so there could have been a quarter of a million people in the forty blocks of the Centre.

We did not see many of them; they were inside, running the State, appearing briefly in the street when shifts changed. The few in sight were there with purpose, moving in duty from one nexus to another; there was little for them to look at or linger over.

The streets were clean, tended by rolling robots that prowled the gutters and made forays on to footpaths when their sensors told them nobody was in the way. We amused ourselves forcing them back into the gutters, stepping in front of one as it spied a scrap of garbage and lurched after it, asking the thing's pardon and exchanging witty wonderings as to whether a machine could become frustrated. Passers-by paid no attention. Our brassards told who and what we were and they must have had a gutful of Extra cadets exhibiting their sophistication on leave.

There were few shops. You could buy magazines and snack food but only a couple of stores sold clothing or theatre bookings or anything but immediate necessities. The Centre was used, not lived in. It was inert.

Yet there were things to see. The old public library had been preserved and in a culture of tapes and data banks its contents were fabulous. More than a million books in one place was hard to credit;

believing they were all worth preserving was harder. Most were surely not worth a glance, much less the reverent handling by library staff, but a hint at this brought a curl to the antiquarian lip. No other member of the public was there, so why, if nobody used them, should they be preserved? Because they were *there*?

History was *there*, glooming uselessly in the street. Arry said, 'It's dead. There's people but they're dead too.'

Yet for all its mustiness the Centre was in use, not just dust-sheeted over for uninterested posterity. We found a cafeteria but the food was in the high-coupon range of catering for employees with generous bonus grants. I would have turned away but Arry said, 'I'll shout you.'

'What with?' He showed me, for an instant, a wad of blue bonus coupons thick enough to choke a glutton before he stuffed them back into his pocket.

'Stolen!' I must have sounded a prize prig, all shock and righteousness, but we Sweet kids were raised to believe that stealing was *out*. A precious pack of little sods we were.

'My Tower Boss sent them to me.'

I had an ungenerous vision of a Boss suckholing to an Extra who might be useful to him later on. I didn't credit the man with being proud of his ugly duckling and risking his freedom to look after him, only grunted gracelessly that they must have been stolen in the first place.

Arry explained patiently that coupons were basic exchange, passed on by police for 'favours' received. Payment for informing and betraying, sneered my holier-than-thou upbringing while my stomach thought over the food displayed on the shelves.

'There's some advantages in being Swill,' Arry said. 'Not many but some.'

We ordered a meal that might have done for a State senior in a triv drama. Morality shuddered but gorged.

Afterwards we found, right on the eastern edge, an old building with a decorative façade that stamped great age all over it, the Princess Theatre. Its plaque said it was built in the nineteenth century and was still in use. The Early Cinematograph Society was playing a season of films we had never heard of, so we used some more of Arry's coupons.

It was a peculiar experience watching what our great-grand-parents had enjoyed, probably thinking it the last word in crash-bang technology. They were short films covering a century or more of cinema 'art', if that's the word. It was all two-dimensional, pre-triv;

some had no colour and some had no sound, like cartoons where actors doubled for the drawings. Much was nearly unintelligible because acting styles have changed and notions of drama become more sophisticated. Only the early comedies, slapstick without dialogue, were wholly intelligible though primitive and idiotic, but Arry laughed himself into stitches and insisted on seeing out the whole programme. I decided that the Swill must create most of their own amusement, which doesn't make for artistic sensitivity.

When we got out into the street again, it was dark.

We walked on the floors of half-lit canyons. Windows gleamed where night shifts worked (doing what among the banked computers and automated operations?) but most were dark; upper floors vanished into a sky cloud-covered and threatening rain. The footpaths were lit at cost-saving intervals, one lamp standard in three glowing in a passage of shadows. The whole complex was so quiet that tiny noises at a distance were identifiable as footsteps or scraps of paper rustling as they blew or soft conversations between ghosts in invisible places.

We went rapidly down Bourke Street. I wànted now to get back to barracks, away from the footpaths where black lanes and alleyways dived between buildings into the silent blocks. Almost silent. Voices twittered in their darkness.

'Swill,' Arry said.

I remembered the schoolyard furphies about sewer gangs. 'What are they doing?'

'Scavenging.'

'Don't the coppers – ?'

'No law stops Swill coming to Centre or anywhere, but turn up here in bare feet with the arse out of your pants and you'll get rushed out fast, loitering or something. Night's different. Give and take. The coppers look away.'

'Muggers!'

He laughed at me. 'In Centre? You Sweet get ideas! The Bosses wouldn't stand for it – they'd have to be squaring the coppers all the time and maybe throwing them the muggers to keep them quiet. It's for scavenge.'

The accumulating picture of Swilldom as a ramshackle culture with a hierarchy and rules and a sort of grimly enforced order began to work into my imagination.

Arry grabbed my arm. 'Watch!'

All that moved in the street was a line of cleaning robots, a dozen of them, single-filing uphill towards us, deploying I thought, for a fresh sweep. 'Watch what?'

'The cleaners.'

The leading robot mounted the footpath at the mouth of a laneway, opened its hatch and tipped out the whole of its gathered garbage in a pile of assorted detritus from offices and cafés and gutters, then rolled back a pace and paused as if waiting for an activity to follow.

Scavengers erupted from the laneway and burrowed into the rubbish. Across the road from them and fifty metres away, we could not see too well in the poor light but it was plain that they knew what they wanted and worked to a method. In minutes the heap was reduced by a third and the extracted material passed by a chain of hands into the darkness. A half-naked figure operated a control on the frame of the robot; it rolled forward, sucked up what rubbish was left and moved off to the discharge depot it had been headed for. Another took its place.

'What are they taking?'

'What's useful. Bottles, cans, bits of metal, pins and clips and rags but mostly paper.'

'Paper? It would be all written on or screwed up.'

'Written on one side – the women iron it out for writing on the fair side. The rest, wrappings and stuff, gets pulped and mashed and pressed for the shapers. You can make a lot from paper, even some kinds of furniture.'

How long would a paper cupboard last? Did it matter, while you could swipe the makings of a new one?

Arry said, 'Kitchen cleaners have food in them, scraps and half-eaten stuff. It gets boiled up and mixed into messes.'

Revolting messes. But the State ration was calculated . . . Back in the Fringe Kovacs had said Swill stole from Swill, strong from weak, even adults from children . . . There would always be someone in need of food, starving amid plenty – the most ruthless Boss could not prevent it. I suffered a heaving shame at never having known hunger . . . at having known all my life of the underside of the world with no feeling for it but revulsion . . . and at now failing to understand the mind of Arry who knew and for the most part contained his rage.

Across the road the cleaners' contents were sorted with the orderliness of a State operation. Interference with State property . . . my mind was still on law. 'Don't the coppers ever stop them?'

'You don't catch on, do you? The coppers programme the cleaners to stop at scavenge points when they're full.'

In my head the structure of society shifted again.

Arry's thin face was picaroonish in the half light. 'If we can use what Sweet throw out, why not? The coppers are bastards but they aren't stupid. And in the towers a thing has to be properly busted before it's useless.'

Two men left the working party and crossed the road a little downhill from us. In the shadow of the verandah they almost disappeared.

I said, 'They've seen us.'

'They saw us when we got here. So what?'

'They're moving up on us in the shadows.'

'There's only shadows to move in – they're not sneaking.'

Nor were they: they walked openly and quickly.

'What would they want?'

Shrug. 'They'll tell us.'

They halted a few metres away. One, in the lead, was shortish and muscular but I could not see much of his face; he was heavily bearded. (Shaving, when you stop to think about it, is an expensive luxury.)

He said softly, 'Arry?'

My bleak reaction was that Swill Arry had thrown me to his Swill wolves. I accepted betrayal as an instant, unarguable fact, with no more reason than that class distrust dies hard. I stiffened in the rictus of panic. I was green and empty of experience, all intellect and no resource. Later I would learn to deal with tight corners, to take instant mental stock or explode into action as the case required, but that night I was useless. Like a hypnotized rabbit I stood there while Swill talk flew faster than I could catch. Until Arry said, 'Don't you recognize him, Teddy? Nick Nikopoulos.'

Youth is stupidly resilient. An older man, myself today for instance, with practical knowledge of violence and evil might have crumpled from sheer relief at the lifting of a threat. I, fifteen and infinitely elastic in ignorance and fast recovery, only poked my head forward to squint and say, 'I didn't know you under the beard.'

He came with his hand out and I caught the Swill stink of him, brute sweat and drains. A perfect impersonation. He wrung my hand like a blood brother and said, 'It's time I had a look at you.'

Like an idiot I could only say, 'What for?'

Some grimace behind the beard was perhaps a smile. 'To see if you are growing up yet.'

The second Swill stayed perfectly still, out of earshot but in easy reach. Back-up? Bodyguard? Something like that.

I said I thought I was doing well enough.

'But you haven't been home yet.' It was a statement, not a question, sprung with unfair suddenness.

I tested it. 'How is my mother?'

'Well. She sends her love.'

It was as indecent as a punch below the belt that he should have sought her out and that her forgiveness should stalk me so far. I blurted out hurt pride and guilt: 'I haven't asked for love.'

'I don't imagine you have but she doesn't let desertion stand in the way of it.'

I snarled, 'Kovacs stands in it.'

'Would you expect him to leave her to fend for herself? He loves her.'

That improved nothing. 'He's got a Swill wife.'

'And plenty of others. His proper name is Istvan – Stephen. The other is for Billygoat.' To my plain distress he said gently, 'Swill life is what it is, lad, not what you'd have it be. Arry, haven't you taught him anything?'

Arry said, 'Not much chance yet.'

'Dig Arry for all the Swill information you can get. Learn the words, practise the accent until you can think in it.'

It was a menacing instruction. 'You're not in charge of me.'

'When you're ready, I will be.'

'Arranged, is it? Who says so?'

He rode over the sneer. 'It's arranged.'

'In spite of – ?'

'In spite of my losing my cool with you and being taken out of secondment. You're mine, Teddy. I picked you and a couple more and I mean to have all of you.'

I said, 'You think that's a compliment, you bastard.'

'It is.'

'I'm not spending my life scrabbling among Swill.'

'Not your whole life – that would be waste.'

'Not even some of it. I'm not proud any more of being Extra but I'm not going to work the towers.'

'Not even to sieve and sift the poor buggers who'll never stand a chance unless somebody with sympathy winkles them out and gets them on to the Testing lists? We need people who can sink into the part and be Swill without ever forgetting they're Sweet. That's you, Teddy.'

'Stroking my vanity?'

He laughed. 'Indeed, indeed. How's my touch?'

More than touch he had knowledge, enough of it to know that my attitude in the camp had cloaked trust and the need for his cool interest. I had rejected my father, reacted with contempt against Kovacs and given him, Nick, only the resentful service of the coerced, all the time silently yelling for a parent to shake sense and affection into me. He knew these things because it was his business to turn kids inside out and know them, while I saw cloudily that I wanted to work with him and have him proud of me – but on my terms not his.

I said, 'Let Arry do your sifting. He knows his own.'

Arry muttered, 'I didn't come out just to go back.'

'Arry is promised to other work – physicists don't come in coupon rolls.'

'Meaning I've no choice?'

'You can always transfer out of my reach. Into the Clerical Branch, say, and be a key puncher.'

That was blackmail of a sort, the appeal disguised as a sneer. The appeal was strong enough for me to grunt that I'd worry about that when the time came, not committing myself.

He asked, 'Are you ready to go home to Newport yet?'

'No.'

'As you like. I'll keep in touch. 'Night, Arry.'

Without fuss he left us, his shadow after him.

I needed a quarrel. 'You arranged this, Arry!'

He was unrepentant. 'Nick fixed it – I only had to look out for him. We'd better get back to barracks.'

I pushed it. 'What are you, the squad's official sneak? Do you report on me to Nick? Or anyone else?'

He sighed. 'Don't be bloody stupid. He just wanted to see you. Don't take him cheap, Teddy, he's a great bloke.'

'Shit on that! Who's his mate? Another copper playing games?'

'Maybe. Or maybe one of his tower family.' He said, watching the effect, 'Nick's old man is my Tower Boss.'

It stopped me like a slap in the face. Yet it made sense of a kind while it left me with the bizarre, chastening knowledge that of the three people closest to me in my chosen life Carol was a Fringer and the other two were Swill. A psychologist might have commented that I had chosen as my instincts drove me. Anger melted as my mind revolved Swill paradoxes. 'They must know Nick's a copper.'

'The Swill? Some of them know.'

'We were always told they couldn't go into the towers.'

'Like we were told that coppers captured Swill kids and gang-raped them.'

'We had it that the Swill abducted young girls.'

He nodded wisely, my tame sociologist. 'There could be truth somewhere – things that happened and got built on.'

'So police can go into the towers?'

'Not quite. The right ones can go in but no uniformed man would risk it. On his own he wouldn't get out again.'

It seemed that nothing was black or white. 'Some can, some can't. There's anarchy, there's order. There's plenty, there's starvation. It can't work like that.'

'Can. Does. Nick's old man says it's history sorting itself out to start again.'

'Bullshit.'

'Fertilizer,' Arry agreed, 'and are we all in it!'

A smug bastard at times. At last I had to ask the basic question: 'So what is Nick doing back there?'

'You don't think he'd tell me, do you? Who says he's working? He could be visting his old man. Or maybe it's just – ' he searched for a phrase from his reading and got it wrong, ' – memory of the muck.'

Rain fell before we reached the Telltale. We got soaked and spent most of Saturday cleaning the 'borrowed' clothes.

I felt obscurely in need of more punishment than that. I had begun to see ignorance as a crime.

14

NICK

AD 2050

At seventy-one my old man thought he still ran his tower in Richmond. In fact my brothers and their grown kids did the tower's rough and tumble work and my eldest sister, who had failed her Test by a fraction, was the planner; the old man took such kudos as there was and loved himself no end. He never forgave my being a copper, refused to speak to me when I visited, but once a year signed that his paternal heart bled still for a stubborn son – he sent me a Christmas card.

In some sentimental long ago he had somehow acquired several hundred of them and each year distributed a few as tokens of favour. They were traditionally stupid, with red-coated Santa Clauses ho-hoing over the arses of grinning reindeer as they whiffled through midnight blue skies over landscapes of snow, with some verses on the inside flap by a dewy-eyed illiterate. These, for an Australian Christmas with the air like steamed pudding at 42 degrees or better!

The thought, as they say, was a kindly one and the card for 2050 had more than the usual stark *Nick, from Your Father* on it. There was a message, the first in nearly twenty years, in his inexpert script: *You never come to see me.* This was untrue – I went two or three times a year to stand around while he pretended not to see me. But I knew what he meant – I was up for official forgiveness.

I left the card on my desk while I went to see what the Colonel (Operations) wanted of me.

What he wanted was my services over the Christmas holiday period because of a confluence of weather forecasts which made Christmas Day tactically favourable, in his estimation, for a Swill raid. I might have wriggled, even argued, if the job had not been in Newport on request (through illicit channels) from Tower Twenty-three – the Billygoat.

I laid Dad's card in the drawer with all his others, thinking that I would have to find a way of explaining that duty really did come before even the most royal forgiveness, when I was struck by an idea

– concerning forgiveness – that at first only tickled my fancy, then on consideration seemed promising. It could further an aim deferred too long, it might set me in the good books of a Tower Boss whose goodwill was no mean asset, and it might be the making of a bright but directionless young PI officer.

That flash of an idea had far-reaching consequences.

Now – about corruption and Nola Parkes:

The coupon system was cumbersome but necessary. Computer rationing would have been simpler, but to have thrown the Swill to the mercy of Molecular Storage Accounting – which would have told them when and how they could have what, with no leeway for individual preference – might have been incitement to more violence than could have been controlled without slaughter. The mob was always simmering; the harassed State knew better than to remove all self-determination.

It had hoped that the coupon system would inhibit corruption; PI, with corruption part of the air we breathed, could have told them otherwise. Change the colours every month, match the serial numbers to individuals, thumbprint every one on surrender – and the wicked would still find a way. Coupons, of course, were not money . . . oh, but they were! They could not be hoarded but they could be lavishly spent. Small profit, quick return – for counter-feiters.

Also, Intelligence used them as bribes for squeals, with fine fakery to make the computers sit up and say thank you. The morality of corruption depends on which hand you are using when you say it, taking care the left doesn't know what the right is handling. We used corruption to achieve what we thought justifiable ends. Moral views, anyone? Cultural imperatives, meaning morality, change with the weather.

Real corruption flowered among the departmental heads who controlled manufacture, import and distribution of goods. Goods could be rendered untraceable and unaccountable more easily than coupons; no computer system could trace the passage of an item through a dozen hands that never hit the keys. The State didn't try. What it did was employ PI to discover who among the Very Big Sweet plundered more freely than his value to the State could justify overlooking. After which a few heads rolled down to Swilldom and the rest understood the signal.

Mrs Parkes, Superintendent under the Minister for Seaborne Import, did not need the signal – she had never been greedy.

We had never nudged her; most of us had some sympathy for her. She had taken over the business (when 'business' still meant 'finance') when her husband died because she had a sharp enough nose for decay to see that selling out and living on a fixed income could end badly in a crumbling future. What she hadn't smelt out was the network of pressure and counter-pressure, social as well as financial blackmail, in which dead Raymond Parkes had kept his business afloat in a sea of sharks. She had to conform or go under, and 'under' was Swilldom.

In classic morality she should have taken her problems to the law, trusting virtue to see justice done, but the law has never in history recognized 'virtue', preferring aseptic 'duty' and malleable 'right' to keep its verdicts untrammelled, and she knew it. Honesty would have blown sharks, networks and herself clear out of the water, into which all of them would have fallen back to sink without trace.

She chose the life of subterfuge and iron nerve. I'd have chosen it, too. We do right when the cost is bearable but morality flourishes among those who won't suffer by it.

All of which amounts to this: we knew and she knew that we knew, so she would grant me a simple favour.

Camberwell is on high ground, comfortably safe now though one day it will be part of a chain of foggy islands between the drowned city and the Dandenongs. The Parkes house is old, built when architecture still imitated English styles. This one I classified as satisfied-sedate, not the sort of place to be the centre of a spider-web with an uncomfortable but gutsy spider brooding there; intrigue and sleight of accountancy would be conducted with well-mannered aplomb. It was all old weathered walls, pillared verandah, high windows dropping to within a hair'sbreadth of green-red-yellow mosaic tiles, a hovercar pad discreetly nestled among ornamental trees and lawns, lush and green and water-greedy in a land of acute shortage. The State valued Mrs Parkes and would continue to do so while she tickled the national till without ransacking it.

She was too sensible to conduct clandestine operations in her City Centre office where jealous ears would be cocked for titbits. Double, double, toil and trouble – meaning young Francis's split-second accounting – were kept where they could be managed with Sweet delicacy, at home.

I had chosen early evening in the hope of a glimpse of Francis, whom I had never seen, before he was packed off to Quarters (a sort of barracks in the rear) for the night. The scanner didn't waste time on me when I rang – it winked on, looked, winked off. My uniform guaranteed entry.

She sent a personal servant to open to me; the house staff would have seen gossip in a police visit.

The personal servant was Francis. There was no mistaking him, though in one-to-one detail the brothers were not alike. Teddy at eighteen was stocky, strong, saturnine, with the appearance of temper tamed and disciplined but ever ready. Francis at fifteen was already the taller but slender, almost frail, with a ready-to-please expression that reached back through generations of washing hands to Uriah Heep. Each in his way resembled their mother, whom I knew only from excellent Intelligence holographs, though I had once let Teddy think otherwise. I disliked Francis on sight and wondered what childish innocence had claimed the Kovacs heart long ago. But Billy was reputed to be a sucker for kids – God knew, he had a swag of his own scattered about.

'Mrs Parkes.' I knew she was in.

The boy's disinterested expression did not change as he asked if I had an appointment. I hadn't. 'Perhaps,' he suggested, 'you should ask for one.'

'Perhaps you should tell her I have something to say concerning Kovacs.'

That should have got a reaction, but he was rock steady; being privy to secrets teaches self control. He shrugged, very slightly, with what he may have considered exquisite insolence.

'Little figureman,' – *that* reached him – 'just run to the Ma'am and tell her what the nasty copper said.'

He didn't quite dare to spit but said, 'Please wait,' and went off – to return smartly with, 'Please follow me.'

He was well trained in the spider business – he had not asked my name. Nor, it seemed had she. No names, no pack drill.

It's no use trying to describe the house. Half my life has been spent in the Swill and the other half in State offices; I don't know the proper terms for much of what I saw. Think of hand-made furniture, paintings, drapes, ornaments in metal and ceramic, rooms like jewels, carpets like pictures and lighting that revealed and caressed.

Some of my kind hate this sort of thing and talk about bread from the mouths of the needy and no person being more deserving than another. I don't give a damn about the logic of deprivation (no world will ever have enough luxury to go round) because I'd sell my soul, if it was worth anything, to possess what I saw in that house. I didn't resent the Ma'am, I envied her.

But the little office where I ended up was just an office: a desk, chairs, a communicator terminal, a built-in cally, a vocorder and a woman.

She was about fifty, dark-eyed and dark-haired, on the way to becoming heavy-bodied, not much made-up but good-looking in a way that had more to do with character than bone structure. The records said she had never had cosmetic surgery. Her gaze was not defensively expressionless, just a little quizzical. She said, 'That will be all for tonight, Francis.'

The kid shuffled, wanting to stay and listen, said, 'He mentioned Kovacs.'

'So you told me. Goodnight.'

'Goodnight, Ma'am.' He flashed me a hard look as he went, fixing my face in memory. A freak memory was listed as part of his box of tricks.

She waited. We both waited, playing the nerve game, both knowing it for a game. She sighed, not giving in, merely ending a nonsense, and said, 'Five minutes.'

I said at once, 'I am an Intelligence Officer. I am Swill born. I am a friend of Billy Kovacs.' That was a lie. I had not yet met him.

'Is he in trouble?'

That warmed me to her. Not *What does he want*? but *Is he in trouble*? From Sweet to Swill that was a lot. 'No, ma'am, and he wants no more than he already gets.' That told her pretty well how much I knew.

She nodded, the look lighting up a little, becoming more quizzical. 'So it is you who want something?'

'Nothing you'll be unwilling to give.'

She relaxed perceptibly as the unspoken word, *blackmail*, was implicitly eased out of the exchange.

I said, 'I want to give Billy and Mrs Conway a Christmas present. I want Francis home with them on Christmas Day.'

She did not ask why – the old hand knows that motives are never honestly revealed. She got straight to business. 'He will be unwilling.'

'Lean on him.'

She asked, 'What good will it do Francis?'

'I don't know. Maybe none and I don't care. But his mother deserves something. So does Kovacs, for that matter.'

'Oh, I agree. I don't know the woman but he is an excellent man, wasted in that environment.'

'Not wasted, ma'am. He's doing a job he was born for.'

179

'And he has a policeman for a friend. I can think of a dozen questions you would refuse to answer.'

'I'll answer one of them: Billy has never said a word to me concerning you and Francis.'

'Thank you. I have always trusted him.'

'Keep on trusting him. Now, about Francis?'

Her faint grimace suggested that Francis was more necessary than welcome. 'I have seven days in which to think how to go about it. Should he connect you with the matter?'

'Best not.'

'Very well. What else?'

'Nothing else, ma'am.' As I left her I thought to say, 'You can trust me, too, ma'am.'

She smiled at that, not at me, I imagine, but at all the things unspoken, a game player contemplating the board. I hurried out of the house because if I had loitered it would have had to be for hours, churning with greed. It was the only time I saw how the other one-hundredth of one per cent lives.

The reason for this meddling was Teddy. At eighteen he was through basic training and into on-the-job learning. He had done as well as expected – that is, very well – in technical studies, less well in development as a human being. He understood the social setup and the desperate reasons for preserving it against the dwindling quality of life, but he scarcely seemed to belong to it. He observed the world as though he had no part in its operation.

He had had just one sexual affair, one which seemed against all expectation to show signs of permanency, with Carol Jones. At his age it was not enough; whatever psychology and sexual convention may say, an Intelligence man needs broad and, if need be, unhappy experience of the world.

In the same way, he had made only one friend, as if one of anything was enough. That was the scrawny Swill physicist, Arry Smivvers, who had been removed to rarefied intellectual areas where a policeman would have little contact. Teddy had taken the break in sullen silence, as a personal affront from life, but they kept up an occasional contact.

He needed other, less committed contacts to teach him the multiplicity of humanity and that merely being yourself in an insulated ego is not enough and that the ego must be infinitely elastic in an evolving world. As an actor he could work faultlessly from a script; it was the ad lib situation that found him wanting in completeness.

He needed people.

He needed work.

He needed reminding that it was I who had influenced his training to make him the instrument whose rough shape I had glimpsed six years before.

The Christmas Day round-up at Newport Twenty-three needed a large team wherein the presence of a few novices would do no harm, so I asked for him to be detailed 'for experience' and added a couple of other brats to keep him nervous company on a first major operation.

15

FRANCIS
AD 2050

For years I filled in the weekends with reading and study. The departmental tutors were a revelation of what teaching could be – learning from them was no grind, more of a release, and long days lost their rigour as the world opened up with an ease that made all my past claustrophobic.

There was social learning, too. I had started badly with the senior clerk and came in for more unkindness before I discovered the value of reserve, but in the end I got on pretty well with everybody. The Fringe years faded.

Then came Christmas 2050, and the Department closed down for the traditional break. Quarters emptied on Christmas Eve as most Staff found friends to visit and the community rooms became haunts for a few murmuring ghosts like myself. I did not care; solitude was no burden.

I was surprised when the Ma'am called me to the house on Christmas morning. I thought at first that she must have a holiday task for me, which could mean a bonus gift, but anticipation evaporated when she handed me an envelope with my mother's name on it and said, 'I want you to deliver this for me, Francis.'

I don't know what jumble of words I spilled out to try to evade the impossible mission; I knew there could be no withstanding her, that I was a rat in a trap. She heard me patiently and said unmercifully, 'This is a day for reviving love; forgiveness comes easily at Christmas. You need forgiveness.'

For what? For dragging myself out of the Swill mud? But if I feared Mum's tears and Billy's hands I feared the Ma'am much more. I gave in because I must.

I dressed disconsolately for a black Christmas Day. All the long way to Newport Fringe in the hovertram I rehearsed hopeless openings, even to the simple snivelling of 'Mum, I'm sorry,' with a few tears, knowing I could not do it convincingly. Nor could I face forgiveness and a return to that squalid half-house each weekend.

I had to walk a kilometre from the hovertram stop, under a 43 degree sun; Mum's place had no air-conditioning and would be an oven. In the street outside, bringing a frightening new repulsiveness to the place, was the water. Where high tides had sometimes been visible from the back fence, on this day I saw the lapping flood at Mum's gate. In the towers whole lower storeys must have been submerged.

I felt a chill under the summer sun and the impact of a memory . . . Swill swimming like mad . . . The garden had been ravaged by water, so the tide must now have been receding but its residual mud made a filthy mess of my shoes. I hovered between apprehension and a need for yelling anger.

Knocking on the door, I felt that I stepped off a cliff.

When Billy Kovacs answered I wanted to run. My mouth dried up. He towered over my nervousness though I was now as tall as he. He wore only shorts and the skeleton that carried so much strength over thin bones made him more than ever a knob-jointed, stick-limbed spider with narrow face thrust to strike. He said nothing, just looked at me without expression as though he didn't care whether I spoke or died.

I could not pretend courage; I faced him because I had no choice. I held up the envelope with Mrs Conway printed on it and managed to say, 'I have to give this to Mum.'

He did not look at the words his weak eyes would not have been able to make out but turned on his heel to let me pass.

I saw someone in the passage behind him, a dark, thickset young man in Swill rig. He was in shadow but when he took a pace into the light I knew him.

His watching face, alive still with the certainty of his superiority, roused an instant blind hatred which until that moment I had not known was waiting in me to break and spill. The old habit of 'getting on' with him fled in recognition of humiliations and shames beaten down because too sharp to be borne. They hit my heart and head with the force of all things that made the house detestable and fearful; they made my sight dim and the world spin.

The fury must have passed in seconds, for I became sweat-cold and in command of myself and none of us had moved.

I threw the envelope down the passage to his feet and said, 'You give it to her, favourite boy!' The words must have had the effect of spittle in the eyes.

He picked it up but did not speak; the complex expression on his face, more frightened than frightening, meant nothing to my anger.

Billy seemed, for a fraction of a second, dismayed, but he did not move. I said, 'There's no need for me here now, is there?' and he made the slightest, almost stupefied shake of his head.

Triumphant, I left them standing there.

The Ma'am would have to accept the situation.

And so she did. She made no more attempts to force me back home. Perhaps Billy made some sort of explanation to her.

One thing cheered me.

Teddy – brilliant, conquering, Extra Teddy had missed his chance. He was back in the Fringe home with the number two dad he despised. Now, there was a fall!

I would not fall. The Ma'am was by then renting my talent to a small number of her departmental peers and I was making powerful friends. And making sure they needed me.

16

TEDDY
AD 2050

1

My first thought on being rostered was that the job would fill the Christmas break, my next that folklore held induction to a first 'costume' operation to be unexpected and unpleasant.

It was.

We four rookies were herded into what are called the 'Swill rooms' for six days before the job, with four old hands – two male, two female – to observe us and short-circuit disasters. Eight people was reckoned average for a Swill three-roomer; the towers had four-roomers as well but I suppose we were being offered maximum discomfort.

'When you come out,' said the ape who locked us in, 'you'll have just the teeniest idea of what being Swill means.'

The three-roomers were designed, some thirty years earlier, for at most three people. 'At most' now meant as many as could find floor space. Two of the old hands grabbed the double bed while we were still feeling depressed by the general squalor and leered at us, 'Mother and father take the snoozer, the rest of you doss where you can.'

The other old-hand woman (her name was Elsie) pushed through to claim the single bed and Freddy the Grunter (one of our old tutors) stretched on the couch. 'Floor's free,' he said and went to sleep. No one meant to be helpful.

We examined the flat. The furniture, old, worn and rickety, was in character. There was no light globe in the bedroom. ('Don't need it,' said Father smugly.) The cupboards were empty; a kitchen shelf held a few battered containers and pans and half as much crockery as we needed, all of it cracked and discoloured. The filthy windows looked out on a blank wall across an alley.

Our personal case was no better. We had the Swill rig we stood in and which we would wear for the job, plus one change of underwear. We also had a week's supply of Suss coupons for slipping under the door with a note of what we wanted.

We conferred on how to use the coupons intelligently for a week's needs. We ignored our coaches, knowing they would not help. We made very cunning outlay for food before anyone thought of detergent or toilet paper and had to do some more cunning corner cutting to squeeze them in without minimizing rations. Luckily I remembered some of the things I had heard from Arry, and thought to look at the stove. One hotplate was working. The others could have been fixed easily – if, between us, we had had a spanner or a screwdriver. That changed the food list again, increasing the order for fruit and canned supplies, which were coupon expensive. The simple matter of a sufficient diet began to look difficult, but we laughed at ourselves and coped.

We stopped laughing when, after the supplies arrived, we discovered that the fridge was not working and we had to make a few huge meals of perishables before they rotted and then go on very light rations for the final three days. The coaches did not offer to share their more experienced arrangements.

The triv screen blew out on the second night. An unhopeful call to Complaints achieved nothing.

There is no point in detailing the week's disasters: the lows were humiliating and the highs little better.

A fine low occurred when we found that the water, when it wasn't rusty, ran only at times, not always the same times and then only in half-pressure trickles. It had to be stored in the bath for lack of containers (after we had improvised a plug) and used mostly for cooking. On the second day personal cleanliness went by the board.

The flush toilet became a problem. On the fourth day we learned the consequences of flushing only when the water was 'on' instead of using some of the precious bath supply – the sewer became blocked. Forget the shifts we were put to for the rest of the time. The stench was appalling.

The coaches, of course, adapted as to the manner born. The girls taught us the reality of lack of privacy by undressing casually when the fit took them and choosing our toilet sessions to sit on the edge of the bath and chat while we relieved ourselves, not budging when it came time to reach for the toilet roll. Wiping your arse under the stare of an attractive woman is a fine inhibition breaker. Otherwise the coaches did little but observe and tut-tut when tempers ran high.

Run high they did. The first fight was on the third day after an argument about food, a shamefaced affair that petered out with no damage done. The coaches were alert observers. The second fight went the distance but was still a gentlemanly exchange. The last one, on Christmas Eve, was a yelling brawl that might have ended badly if the coaches hadn't stepped in with some smart chopping and throttling.

'Make good Swill, this pack of young thugs, won't they?' said Freddy and took no further notice.

When we were let out the fresh air in the corridor was perfume but the uniformed copper who released us said, 'Christ, but you've got the smell right.' We demanded baths but he sent us straight to Action Briefing. 'Mustn't wash off the smell when you've worked like pigs to get it.'

That, we believed (wrongly as usual) was the greater part of the reason for the filthy exercise.

There were sixty-four operators in the Briefing Room, all in costume with a general look of having picked their gear from rubbish tips. Possibly they had, but anything that was not a blocked lavatory was attar.

The Briefing Officer was Nick. I thought, *So he's reached out and grabbed me*, not sure whether to be angry or proud and certainly wary.

He looked no different from that night three years before. He nodded to me familiarly and called, 'Arry says, good luck,' re-establishing intimacy as though we had never separated. After that he treated me as just one of the task force, knowing he had picked me up right where we left off. It was a self-confidence to drive you mad.

We four rookies stayed together, brawling forgotten, seeking comfort in each other. Nick looked us over and said, 'Some fighting, I see. Who started it?'

I told him, 'I did,' trying not to sound sulky.

'Someone wouldn't let you have your own way?'

He always asked damnable questions that had to be answered. 'Something like that.'

'*Sir!*'

'Sir.'

'I'll bet it was exactly like that. In six years you haven't learned. How were they, May?'

May, who had spent much of the week in bed with Roger (who, it had eventually dawned on us, was her husband), said, 'Like rats in a pit. Bitching egos swelling like puff-adders. We had to stop one fight. About normal for the course, I think.' She added, '*Very* queasy stomachs.'

That brought a heartless laugh from our betters, having no pity; they too had had their Swill room days.

Nick made it worse. 'It's a hard way to get into the right state of BO and dirty underwear but in future you'll be able to spray it on at the last moment. The real purpose was to let you understand something of what it means to be Swill, to drive out the idea of *us* against *them*. You will be dealing with human beings, some of them monsters, others whose opportunities and intellects cannot match yours but who are none the less your equals in the sight of God, Police Intelligence and, incidentally, themselves.'

The sight of God? Nick claimed atheism, but old speech forms die hard along with the beliefs that fathered them.

He continued, 'You will not be merely ferreting out and arresting some unpleasant and dangerous people but protecting the innocent and the good, of whose demeaning environment you have gained some inkling in the past week.'

I thought he had lost his way in one of those messages from the heart with no clear idea to guide it, when he stopped dead, glanced at his notes and said, 'The operation is apprehension of a large criminal group, as many as 400 or more strong. Army Support Group will be in attendance as back-up only, on call if we need them.'

Four hundred. Or more. Sixty-four of us. *If we need them.* This was big stuff. You could feel the room rise to it.

'We will move into the area as soon as briefing is completed and the operation will commence at three a.m.'

Someone muttered, 'Christmas Day and bloody noses all round,'

'Quite so. The site is Newport Tower Twenty-three. An internal co-operating force will be directed by Tower Boss Istvan Kovacs.'

He did not glance my way, did not need to. *What else is hidden up your sleeve, Game-player?*

'Twenty-two and Twenty-four are controlled by the Swain family who seem to feel that they need Twenty-three to consolidate their grip on the north corner. They want the Kovacs connections. They used the flood warning on the eighteenth to infiltrate the lower floors, before the water rose, with thugs posing as unattached street types sleeping in the corridors.'

That was a standard move in tower feuds; nobody would question refugees from rising water or throw them out before the ebb. An invader could put in enough men to seal off the exits and stairways and terrorize the vital lower floors, then sit quietly while starvation did its work above.

A voice asked, 'And Kovacs did nothing about it?'

'But he did. He contacted us.'

'To do the work for him? Do we care? What's the bait?'

'He offers proof of two murders committed on Swain orders and evidence of two others.'

'Greatheart Kovacs, the copper's friend! Using the flood to keep them trapped till we come. Dog eats dog and sets up the meal in advance. But are a couple of killings excuse for calling the army out?'

Good question. Swill murders are rarely important in themselves. Now, if they had knocked off some Sweet . . .

Nick said, 'There's more to it than a couple of rats garrotted, a few families left in misery and a gang of wolves ruining what lives the Swill have.' He didn't fling it at us, just let it settle. It becomes too easy to take a detached view when you are thinking in terms of tactics and efficiency instead of people. 'Kovacs claims to have evidence of Swain connection with coupon forgery. It's making a shambles of Newport delivery and distribution.' He said drily, 'It's an offer we can't ignore.'

Indeed we could not. The system, the balance, the status quo must be preserved, a fact that transcended lives.

Elsie spoke up. 'We clean out his rat's nest for him, then he pays us with evidence you couldn't hang a dog on.'

'Kovacs is dependable – that's his survival trait. He wouldn't risk his tower unless he could pay hard graft. He let the Swains in to make sure of getting them cold.'

'So what does he get out of it except a bigger reputation as a copper-loving bastard?'

'What do you think he gets – Teddy?'

No problem. 'A dead enemy. Also control of Twenty-two and Twenty-four. The whole north corner to himself.'

My voice must have rasped. 'You disapprove?'

'What's to choose between him and the Swains? Perhaps he'll take over the coupon racket as well.'

'That he won't! And there's plenty of choice between him and the Swains. We might talk to him about it.'

His grin made no bones about using the job to further his private meddling.

One of the girls asked were we to draw weapons?

'No! If we find guns against us – unlikely – we'll call in the troops. However, as soon as this meeting dismisses you will draw chainmail.'

The lightweight metalloplastic undershirts were new and untried; we would be guinea-pigging as well as fighting, but karate against knives and iron bars is not unreasonable odds. You might get badly cut hands or a cracked skull if you weren't fast, but very few Swill had more than novice training in solo fighting – their forte was group tactics. They did not have the instructors or the diet for building point-directed strength and split-second reaction.

The shirts were chainmail in name only, being cut from rolled sheets, like soft calico to the touch. They were long enough to cover the genitals and cut high enough to cover the base of the throat and the arms down to the elbows; the necklines, which would be visible, were already greyed with dirt by the Quartermaster. They felt and looked less than chain armour but the strongest of us could not start a tear in them. We were marginally impressed.

2

Police Transport took us round the inland rim of Yarraville and down through the factory strip between Yarraville and Newport to the flood water's edge. Under starlight but with no moon we boarded canoes, four in each, and paddled down the flowing street towards the Newport towers, their black shapes dotted with lights like spots on dominoes. Swill may live by day but the towers are never entirely dark.

Predictably, Nick had detailed me to his canoe. Elsie was also with us; the idea seemed to be that a woman could inspire calm and confidence in the Swill women when the brawling began, so there was one with each attack group. It may have been psychologically right but I'd pity the Swill who shaped up to Elsie, taking her for a helpless maiden.

It was filthy hot, even for an Australian Christmas, and the pores in the chainmail helped little; we were live sweat boxes. Paddling was a thrusting through resistant night. No lights showed from the windowless factories locked against force and pillage; their remote hum was the only sound in a thick solitude. Floating between their automated bulks, where half a dozen Sweet employees in each watched screens and Telltales but nobody had to instruct the machines in their work, it was not hard to read the economic lesson of the fact that the buildings were raised on stilts, safe from the rising water, while the habitations of the Swill were not. Machinery must not be damaged but Swill could vacate a floor or two until the discomfort passed.

Yet the factories were not safe: floods had lapped higher than the builders had prepared against and were already a centimetre or two over the door sills in many cases. They had been raised high in the years when panic said it must be done, hoping that the water could surely rise no higher than this generous mark. The water could and had done and would rise further. It was time to shift production to the hills. If the expense could be met. Troubles beget troubles.

While the State beat its bankrupt brow Police Intelligence, uninterested in the automated props of civilization, moved on Newport Twenty-three at the call of a scheming cheapjack who had chanced his tower and all in it to enlarge his personal empire. I could see our action in no other way.

Nick, seated directly in front of me, was an outline, shoulders thickened where the cylindrical screamer bomb was slung. Its detonation would be the action signal.

I asked him, in a low voice, how Kovacs could know how soon to hold his men ready, though the answer might be obvious and the question foolish. Perhaps it was, because it seemed that Nick had had a man in there on the first day – 'wired for sound', as he put it – while the infiltration still proceeded. The Swains had never stood a chance once Kovacs had spotted them as offerings to the law and his profits.

The flood around us came alive with smooth skullcaps as army frogmen joined the advance, kicking lazily. We were close now to Twenty-two, close enough to see dimly the army floats moored in its shadow, four of them, each carrying a platoon armed with machine pistols. Their job was the collection of prisoners, possibly the whole 400; nobody wanted to call them for anything else unless the situation turned wickedly desperate. We did not want blood and deaths.

We stroked across the drowned area of cement skirting, towards Twenty-three, and on Nick's signal backpaddled to a halt. The frogmen closed in to hear final instructions. Nick spoke quietly but each word was audible just as far as he meant it to be. 'This is Twenty-three. You can see that the water is half-way up the second storey. Luck for us, that's where we'll go in. The lights showing unshaded on third, fourth and fifth storeys are ends of corridors. Swain's crew are on those floors, watching for attack by Kovacs from above. Not likely to be watching the water but could be. So we proceed from the corner, in full shadow, hugging the wall until each façade is covered by four groups. Then, in through the windows. You know what to do after that. Questions?'

'Anything for us?' That was the frogman Captain.

'Stay at the windows on the flooded second storey. Pick up anyone trying to get out. Nothing else unless I call. I don't expect heavy resistance.'

Did he not? From 400?

No other questions.

'Right. From now on, Swill-speak only. I'll slaughter the nit who talks Sweet.'

It was a necessary order. Only a few trusted Kovacs men would guess how he had produced a force of fighting Swill from the flood water to sandwich the Swains top and bottom.

My skin crawled. This was my first major operation and I was young enough to respond to the drama of thick night with the tremor of violence waiting in the air.

The actuality was not quite a let-down, rather a gradual deflation as proper planning demonstrated what planning was for. It went off like a drill movement.

Each canoe selected a point along the wall to plant its mooring suckers, well apart so that each group was handy to a different interior staircase. Nick took out an upper window pane with a gimmick I had not seen before, a glass cutter that loosened molecular cohesion to bring the pane out entire, without sound. We slipped through and into the flooded apartment. Swimming in full dress is not difficult for a short while.

At the apartment's outer door Nick duck-dived down to the lock to open it with a skeleton key. In less than half a minute we were across the corridor and into the opposite flat, which gave access to the lightwell. Nick went ahead to take out the inner window and toss the screamer bomb into the lightwell, where it floated while the acid fuse began to gnaw.

We moved to our assigned staircase. The first occupied floor was less than two metres above our heads; we heard grunts and snores. The Swains, we had reckoned, would use this as a dormitory floor, also, possibly, the one above, maintaining sentries only on the highest level.

The stench defies description. Our Swill rooms had not prepared us for the dense odour of cramped, sweating, filthy humanity and its effluents after a week's imprisonment by flood. Heaven only knew what had happened to their drainage as the tide rose but it is certain that we had swum through raw sewage. I heard behind me the sound of vomit being choked back.

'If anyone must vomit,' Nick whispered, 'dive down a metre or two first,' but nothing would have prompted me to open my mouth under that cesspool surface.

He went to the top of the stairway and peeped into the corridor, then beckoned to us to put our heads out and observe. The corridor was some 100 metres long and two and a half wide, lit only at four spaced points. The sleeping bodies lay too closely packed for an estimate of numbers; men and women were crammed like cannery fish, mostly half-naked in the stinking heat. Here and there one stirred or moaned or snored but most lay like slabs of meat in a species of exhaustion which may have had less to do with heat and tension than with blessed relief from a life-starved wakefulness.

There could have been upwards of 1,000 people on each floor of this seventy-storey termitary. The reality was much worse than Sweet fear or PI teaching – not despair or degradation but simple, brute existence. You can never decide the precise moment of a revolution in heart and head but I think it was that doss-house of the hopeless and denied that drove out of me the last spasm of contempt for the Swill. I saw the reality at the bottom of the human barrel; these were the most luckless of all, brutalized even below their hapless norm by the feuds of the Tower Bosses, kicked and held down by their own kind.

Don't imagine my bleeding heart dissolving in pity; easy senti-ment had never been strong in me and the down-to-earth years of PI training had sharpened vision rather than emotion. Yet I knew guilt because all we fortunate Sweet shared responsibility for the existence of this corridor and hundreds like it. The revolting smell of the place was the smell of our own bathed and cleansed but for ever dirty hands.

The feeling came and instantly went; it was no moment for contemplating upset philosophies.

Nick motioned us up the next stair. He checked the watch tucked up his sleeve, out of sight, counting seconds while the acid fuse ate through the plug of the bomb. He signalled us to put in our earplugs. We found the fourth storey as close-packed as the third. He signed *hurry, hurry* and we positioned ourselves until all sixteen of us on that façade were set in our groups on the upper landings of the four staircases.

On this floor a few were awake when we stepped into the corridor and a child squalled in the arms of its mother, who came instantly alert. Somewhere in the human carpet a voice called out and at once the whole place was astir. What they saw, or thought they saw at each staircase entrance, was an inflow of Swill dripping from passage through the flood; the error held them long enough to begin asking who we were and what was going on – until they saw that we stood back to back in pairs at the exits, with coshes and brass knuckles.

Whatever they might have done was frozen into shock by the screamer bomb. Dead on time, in the moment we were set and ready, the fuse pierced the plastic plug and compressed air shrieked through the siren. It began at full pitch, not whining up to it but screaming to rip the eardrums, high in the alt register. Nobody in the building could have escaped the demonic sound – it must have been heard in City Centre and in the Hampton towers across the bay. Our earplugs were good protection but the Swill were in instant pain; though it lasted no more than ten seconds it could have done damage. Then it whined down like a whimpering dog and was silent.

The Swill were held at gaze, reactions spintered by noise, puzzled at our appearance, aware of disaster and unable to move against it for lack of an order or an idea.

In the pause a woman beat at her ears with frenzied palms. As I removed my earplugs I heard her cry, 'Wozzit, wozzit?'

Nick grinned at her. 'That brain bomb, Swainey-girl!'

That, as he intended, identified us to their understanding. A man yelled, ''Em's Billy-boys!' and flung himself across the narrow hall. Nick kicked him in the kneecap and lifted his brass knuckles in threat. Anger and a rustle of intent ran through the crush and they began to move on us.

Our luck held with the instantaneous outbreak of fighting on the floors above, a tumult of thudding and yelling that rolled down the stairwells to us. Kovacs, we found later, had had his men poised practically over the Swainey-boys' heads and had closed with them in seconds. The sound spread hesitation through our corridor long enough for the trappers to see that they were the trapped and that four defenders at each stair exit, armed and determined, could hold the narrow passes indefinitely against a planless foe.

We had a moment of danger when the mob from the lower floor came racing up to discover what had happened and found themselves kicked back down by groups of what they took to be soaking wet Billy-boys sprung from nowhere.

The fighting was minimal. The disorganized opposition fell apart as Nick had foretold in briefing. Most of them took the obvious course of diving out through the windows, to be picked up by frogmen and harried to the military floats; the rest retired into sullen quiet. Not too many escaped out of a bag of over 300, of whom only three were finally arrested as the killers Kovacs fingered.

He had poured a torrent of men and not a few fighting women down the stairs so fast that they commanded the exits before the Swainey-boys realized what had hit them. Those with no nerve for the dive into the flood gave it away with only token fighting. The Swains' problem, as leaders, was that once in retreat they commanded no loyalty; their backing was too much coerced and too willing to desert if it could be done safely. Kovacs could probably have routed them without our surprise and nuisance value, but that would have left it to be done all over again on some future day. Besides, he had wanted not just a victory but a profit and a trophy. Like us pragmatically trained types, he saw clearly in his fashion.

In our corridor a few hotheads showed fight – there's always a death-or-glory element among nitwits – but I can't say that I hit anyone hard enough to do damage. Why should I? It was a police action, not a gutter brawl. In the end we herded them down to water level where the army shipped them aboard as they showed their heads. All in all, it was a clockwork operation but I was glad to pocket the cosh and brass knuckles, though I don't mind a roughhouse when the other party has some sort of a chance.

3

Kovacs came with a swaggering straggle of street brawlers at his back. He saw me standing behind Nick and knew me in spite of growth and six years separation but gave me only a flicker of a glance. He eyed the pack of us appreciatively, chewing slowly, and said, 'Frens! Good seeins! Oos Nick?' I guessed he knew well enough who Nick was but the masquerade had to be played for the ears of his unaware men.

Nick said, ' 'S'me. You'm Billy?'

' 'S'me.' He told his men, 'Em's Nick's boys fum Ya'ville. Maties.'

So our provenance was established with an easy lie and we were heroes to a well-wishing bunch who smelt as bad as we, plus the sour-sweet of chewey piercing their sweat. With introductions over, they were wholly practical; their talk was all of getting the tower operating again, particularly the sewerage. They spoke of a jobbing plumber new-tumbled into the Fringe, automated out of the Sweet life . . . he could be brought down, forcibly if need be, until he learned the facts of the gutter . . .

Kovacs would not look at me but I had no doubt that he was the reason Nick had rostered me for the job. He was shorter than I remembered – or was it that I had grown? The lines of his rat face had ploughed deeper and the hint of sadness round his mouth was a new thing. I could not know then that he had lost his eldest boy and seen a younger brother maimed for life since last we had met. He was still angular and forceful, at once muscular and skinny, alert and wholly relaxed, lively but unwasteful of movement and trying to wind foul-mouthed charm round Nick in a con man's embrace. Did he hope to fool Nick from the Richmond Towers who knew him for liar, hypocrite and killer? (But who still praised him to my face.)

I listened to them spitting the talk they had been brought up to at a speed that left me guessing at some of it. Nick was demanding the wages of interference while Kovacs weaved and ducked to reserve what he might against the need for future treacheries. But he had to give what he had promised.

When the chaffering was done Nick pushed me forward. 'Billy! 'S'Teddy Conway. Knowin'?'

Kovacs spat and rubbed his shoe over the gob, so smoothly that it might not have been a statement. 'Yuh. Knowin'.'

'Go wi'm, Teddy-boy. Ketch's bag.'

That was a new phrase to me but I dared not question it then. (To work it out: 'bag' rhyming with 'tongue-wag' equalling 'loose talk' meaning 'evidence'; alternatively, 'carry his bags' meaning 'pick up what he gives you'. It is a contorted, often ambiguous speech.)

Seeing the trap set for me to meet again with my past, I questioned, 'Go wi'm, me?' Meaning, *Why me? Get somebody else.* Nick smiled very slightly, acknowledging and overriding, and pushed me gently. 'Nuh. You.'

I could have cost him 'face' by arguing, even refusing, but I hadn't the nerve for it. Trouble now could have crabbed my whole future career. Besides – and he knew it, as he always knew – a maggot of curiosity squirmed behind my resentments.

Kovacs said nothing but started up the stairs. As he turned the first landing his sideways glance showed me at his heels and he clapped on speed. He was nearing fifty, more than twice my age, but he went up four floors at a rate that stretched me. He was one of those fleshless wonders of natural stamina who do as a matter of course what the rest of us train to exhaustion for. On the landing between floors eight and nine he stopped, surveyed me with the hungry look so much part of him and spoke quietly in his pedantic, faulty English. 'Know something? There's eight lift-shafts in the tower and once I got the whole lot working. Went three weeks before the last one broke down. Never tried again.'

I wondered how the people on the upper floors coped but was too sullen to ask. He shrugged and raced on up.

He lived on the twelfth floor, at the end of a corridor. At his door he spoke again. 'You're looking good, Teddy.' He nodded, rat-grinning. 'The copper style suits you.'

Trying to loosen my tongue? He succeeded. 'Yes,' I said. 'Never forget it.'

He raised his hands in mock horror. 'You wouldn't beat me up, mister!'

How do you handle a type like him? He opened the door and would have put an arm round my shoulders to usher me in, but I swung away. He pleaded, 'Yesterday's gone by, Teddy.'

So there it whined still, the sentimental streak of the canting crook. I said, 'Forget it. Where you are is always yesterday, stinking.' He stood back for me to enter.

It was a four-roomed flat and it was clean. Searching the Swain-held flats for stragglers we had seen some like animal pens but this was fit to exist in. That is all it was. Every fitting, every furnishing was old, worn, ready for throwing out but nothing that I could see was broken, though everything had been repaired. Apart from the inescapable smells of poverty, chewey and drains, the thing that stank worst was me. Kovacs, discounting a bruised cheekbone and split lip, was scarcely rumpled. I felt at a disadvantage, in the presence of a shabby Swill aristocracy, and out of my depth.

I don't know how many lived in that flat – there were beds and bunks wherever they could be fitted – but only one other was present, an enormously fat woman who bulged and sweated in a home-made rocking chair and surveyed me curiously.

Kovacs waved at me. ' 'S' Teddy Conway.'

Hostility flashed for a second in her eyes and vanished behind elaborate boredom. 'T'Fringy drop?'

Kovacs gave no sign of being aware of the current of her mind, as if there was no outrage in bringing his mistress's son into the family home. ' 'S'im, love. Copper tyke.' He switched to English. 'Teddy, this is my wife.'

What could I do but say, 'How do you do, Mrs Kovacs?'

She also dropped her Swill argot. 'As well as can be expected. Are you disguised or are you always filthy?'

'I dress to suit my company.'

The chair rocked to her laughter. 'A quick one, eh? Take no bloody nonsense from Swill, eh?' Her head snapped forward, striking. 'How's your mother?'

I was too furious to answer. She took a piece of sewing from her lap and lifted it to the light to jab a needle through it as she said, 'Not that I care if she's dead, mind you. But then, as Billy tells it you don't care either, eh?'

I said, with a feeling of having been clubbed, 'I care.'

'Does she know that?'

It was too much. 'Mind your own damned business.'

She waved her scrap of mending at me. 'It *is* my business. My Billy looked after muck like you and your brother' – she said this without spite, stating irreversible truth – 'when you came helpless to the Fringe, and his business is my business. I'm a Tower Wife! You two brats were a poor investment for a man who works his guts out for people who aren't worth it. Somebody has to watch his interests.'

There can be few more helpless feelings than being stood up for target practice. I turned on Kovacs, if only to get back at her. 'Did you bring me here for this?'

He said thoughtfully, 'No, but there was always the chance. The women like to have their say.'

I was angry beyond thought of right or wrong. 'And she'd have plenty to say. It must get lonely for her of a night.'

To his credit he did not take to me with that knife always handy at his belt. His face set stone hard and relaxed slowly like a mask cracking; somewhere in him was a flinder of sexual conscience. Behind me his wife tittered; somewhere in her loyalty lurked a flinder of vengefulness.

It was time to make an end before worse happened. 'Just give me what I was sent for.'

Silently he produced a sack from under one of the beds and showed me its contents – rolls of State coupons, printing samples, a corrected design layout, a thick wooden baton with a discoloration like old blood, a bundle of rags and bits of metal whose purpose I could not guess, an offcut from a roll of pulp paper and (surprisingly, for guns are not easily obtained these days) an ancient but serviceable Biretta.

'That's all?'

He nodded. 'Enough to hang 'em.'

'Enough to let us do your dirty work for you.'

His easy grin let me know the insult was cheap. 'I reckon.' He recovered fast and would not be baited.

I took up the sack. 'My people will be waiting.'

'I'll come down with you.'

'No need.'

'You think? You're off your territory, copper. Things can go wrong.'

'You care?'

'About you? A dead copper is bad for public relations.'

'Do I look like a copper?'

He agreed that few would pick me. 'But you're a foreign face and that's bad if you aren't spoken for.'

As we left Mrs Kovacs cried gaily, 'Give my regards to your mother. She'll love that.'

I felt I wanted to run and as Kovacs slammed the door behind him I would have loved to beat his head against it. But I could only croak in rage, 'Did you put her up to all that?'

'No.'

'You were always a liar.'

'Only at need. No need here. She knows her own mind.'

There were few people in the corridor, passing us in quick whiffs of sweat and chewey. Kovacs leaned against the wall, forcing me to stop, and dropped back into Swill, 'Tell yers.'

Meaning he had something to say to me. I won't try to reproduce it; no phonetics can give the *sound* of Swill. It amounted to this: a Tower Boss needs a close confidant because he has to keep so many at arm's length, and his wife, Vi, was his. What he knew, she knew. Only right, wasn't it?

And my mother?

No, that was different. She was his love, his delight, not for dirty tower business. (Love? Delight? These needed some sick thought.) *She* had to be protected.

But Vi didn't?

A bit, yes, but that was different . . . He ran out of explanation because he had none, seeing no paradox in his attitudes to the two women. It was a matter of what was due to each, right? I could see that, couldn't I?

Yes, I could see that he did what seemed suited to his needs, estimating instinctively (that is, selfishly) and never really thinking it out at all. *Yes, but that's different* . . . He was a creature of appetites with the freedom to gratify them, of instinctive responses with the egotist's ability to justify them.

Nick's canoe waited below the corridor window on the first floor above the water. I dropped the sack and he caught it. As he looked curiously at its contents I swung a leg over the sill to make my own drop but Kovacs moved coolly to thrust his arm across my chest and call down, 'Teddy's gun see t' ma.'

See my mother? Like hell! I pushed his arm away – and that was not as easy as young strength expected – and told Nick, 'No, I'm not,' as I edged forward for the jump.

Kovacs took hold of my jacket to pull me back off balance, and muttered for my ear alone, 'No guts? Haven't you learned nothing – ' and even then had to stop to make his amendment – 'learned *anything* in growing up?'

Glancing down at Nick I smelt collusion, fancied a pale, interested twitch of lips in the starlight: his meeting with Kovacs this morning had not been the first, despite their comedy of greeting. Evasion now would earn contempt from both sides; whether simulated or real seemed beside the point. Looking for a way to slip between them, stalling for time to think, I asked softly, 'Learned what?'

Kovacs surprised me. 'If you haven't got a past to fall back on then you haven't got a real life at all.'

To this day I am not sure whether or not that is nonsense. He could have appealed to filial instinct, sentiment, even reason, but instead reached so far behind all those that a shock of elemental understanding touched my unprepared mind.

'All right,' I said aloud, for both of them. 'All right.'

Nick called up cheerfully, 'It is now about five a.m. You can have eight hours special leave. Get him back to barracks on time, Kovacs. We'll give you a lift as far as the water's edge.'

Not bothering to hide the scheming.

I dropped into the water beside the canoe and Kovacs splashed down beside me; the suction grapples held it steadily to the wall as we clambered aboard. Nick headed inland in the direction of our house without asking direction, but nothing would have been gained by commenting on that; Nick always knew whatever was necessary.

We paddled up the black street between drowned houses that emerged gradually as the slope rose beneath us. All the way a question, a whole slew of questions really, occupied my mind. How did the tower dwellers manage without lifts? As many as seventy storeys down and back each day. Women loaded with stores, old people, small children. I would not ask Kovacs and my resentment against Nick then was nearly as great.

Dawn was breaking as we stepped on to the footpath. The receding flood water was below our back gate but the line of muck on the fence showed it had been higher. Twenty-four hours before it must have been swirling through the house.

I was tired and unready for an encounter. I thought *encounter* and felt defenceless. Against the past?

Some truth has to be told: I had never had much positive affection for Mum. Or for anyone – until Carol slipped through a chink and was simply there, without so much as the surprise of discovery. My parents had loved me but there had been on my side no deep sense of an emotional link. I was spoiled: I passed through childhood in a procession of benefits, knowing no reason for gratitude; what Teddy was given was rightly his and giving was a parent's duty. Our fall to the Fringe was dereliction of duty, *their fault*. I had deserted the home without a qualm.

Qualms came later – the sense of unidentifiable loss, the sharp edge of undefined feeling pricking through solitude to touch wastelands in the mind . . .

Recognizing where fault lay did not bring automatic love or yearning or repentance, it brought deep apprehension so that, at the front gate, Kovacs's hand at my back urged me, shivering, past a point of no return.

4

The garden was flattened, ruined. While my only feeling was of unpreparedness for what was being thrust upon me, Kovacs lingered over the destroyed beds. 'Two or three times a year it happens and she starts again. Makes you wonder.'

I said sharply, 'People don't give in easily.'

'Balls! Course they give in. What do you think a Tower Boss does except keep them standing up? Alison'd make a good Tower Wife.'

That was pushing it hard at me. *I'm closer to her than you are, Teddy-boy. You've got it all to learn.*

It was better to look at the house than at him. The broken boards of the verandah had been replaced; the walls had been painted; the once brown front door was now pale green. A man about the house . . .

Kovacs opened the door on to a passage whose walls were still wet with a mud line, ankle high, down their length. As lately as last night . . . The place smelled of damp and refuse. He called comfortably, 'It's me, Allie. Got a visitor.'

Her remembered voice came from the bedroom, bridging time, 'All right. Wait while I get up.'

We went to the lounge-room where nothing seemed to have changed in six years. It was inexpressibly drearier than the cool colours of my police quarters. In the kitchen Kovacs fiddled with the gas ring, said, 'I'll make a cuppa. Real tea, courtesy of your brother's Ma'am. You know her?'

'I know of her.'

I did not want chat but he was deliberately talkative. 'A good woman, looks after Francis well. There's another graceless brat that's done all right for himself.'

His ricocheting between pacification and insult showed nervous uncertainty and I should have got some advantage from it but I was too highly strung for tactics. 'What did you expect? You set him up for it.'

Spooning into the pot a more expensive tea than we ever saw in barracks, he admitted sourly, 'I make mistakes. Same as you've made a few. Not many friends, they tell me.'

'Who's *they*?' The rat face split in a comedian's smirk and at once I wanted the question answered. 'Who was the PI man under cover in your tower all last week?'

'Who do you think?'

I should have known Nick would do that job himself. The pair of them would have had a high old gossip's time with the private lives of the Conways. It was not possible for me to hate Nick but very possible to be furious with him; it would be a long time before I forgave him for Kovacs's gibing.

Then Mum came in, wearing over her pyjamas a Japanese Kimono I remembered from the Sweet home. She was looking to Kovacs but saw me and stopped dead in the doorway with an extraordinarily pensive expression, as though she must make up her mind about something and would not be hurried.

Because my nerves were jumping and my tongue could not be still I said, 'Good morning, Mum,' in a voice that would have shamed a frightened child and she frowned exactly as she used to do before chiding or punishing.

She said, but not to me, 'It's about time you showed up, Billy,' and kissed him – one of those kisses that says *this is mine* without wasting effort on it, an owned and owning kiss.

'Been busy,' he told her.

'Did it work out well? No trouble?'

'Not much. Teddy was there. He'll tell you.'

She came to where I stood by the window and I was terrified of an emotional outburst that I would not be able to match, but she had a surer sense of occasion than I. She said, 'I'll put hot water on and you can bath yourself. You'll not sit down to breakfast in my house smelling like a polecat. You can have some of your father's clothes. They won't fit but they will do for the moment.' And to my dumbness, 'Well?'

She was making it easy for me, demanding nothing. I said hoarsely, 'Yes, Mum.'

Perhaps she had after all asked too much of herself because she did something that took me apart. She played an old, private game that belonged not six years back but nearer to babyhood, placing a finger on her cheek and saying, 'If you have been a good boy you may kiss me – just there.'

Shaking a little, I did and she grabbed me and we cried. Her tears were squeezed out for a mother's reasons, mine for the release of tension. The remaking of a bond is no easy thing but at least the remaking was now possible.

That tough streak runs through all the Conways. The moment did its work and she lifted her face to say, 'My God, but you stink!' So it was over, more easily than I deserved, and I was shepherded off to the bathroom.

There wasn't much water (in floodtime!) and it wasn't very hot but it was a small bliss. My father had been taller and narrower but his clothes did well enough. Their quality surprised me. Had we been as well off as that? Or, in the creeping shabbiness of the State, had the stuff we wore deteriorated, with quality now beyond a make-do economy? It was true that we no longer said, 'When things look up a bit . . .' or 'When the bad time is over . . .'

In the kitchen I sat down to eggs and bacon, imported tea and real wheat bread – Sweet foods requiring luxury coupons. Swill got powdered egg, adulterated tea, a meat loaf that might be anything, and what they called 'stretched' bread, all calculatedly healthy but unappealing.

Training bites deep: I actually considered refusing the contraband until I realized that I would look at best a fool, at worst a hypocrite. Kovacs saw my hesitation and understood it; he had some of Nick's instinctive insight. 'Wages of sin,' he said. 'The Ma'am pays good stuff for her figure faker.' And, as I resolutely attacked the food, 'There now! A copper eating improperly procured rations! I bet that's a crime.'

Mum said, 'Don't bait him, Billy. It isn't fair.'

'He can take it.'

I might have blown up if I had not caught his expression, neither sardonic nor mischievous but oddly protective. That I could do without but I said as lightly as I could, 'I've heard of the give-and-take system,' before it occurred to me that I had heard of it from himself six years before Arry laid it out for me. 'Now I've met it.'

He told me, 'You're eating it.'

Yes, of course – eating my pride or whatever. He went on, quite gently, 'Right and wrong aren't all that easy – *easily* – told from each other.'

The bastard was trying to be fatherly. I was glad when he slurped down a second cup of tea with the sound of a pulled plug and said he had to go. 'Business won't wait in floods.' He kissed Mum, raised a jaunty finger to me and walked out like any husband off to work.

With the sound of his footsteps still in the passage I let loose the kind of silliness that animosity breeds. 'He acts as if he owns the place.'

'It is his home.'

Her coolness said that my dislike would do well to observe bounds but I had too much of it for restraint. 'He has another. I've seen it.'

She ignored the intent to hurt and said with real curiosity, 'What is it like? Is it as good as this? It can't be.'

'It isn't.'

'Dirty? No, it wouldn't be dirty.'

'Very clean but crowded, smelly. Why should you care?'

She studied me as though wondering if innocence could be taught. 'I care for his condition everywhere. I love him.'

Better than Dad? And in spite of his real wife? It was too soon for such violent questions. And there was that simple, brutalizing word: love. I thought of Carol and myself and could not equate us with Mum and Kovacs. Why is it so difficult to imagine one's mother in love, kissing and fondling and romping on the bed?

'I don't know what you see in him.' Sulky.

'Because you see nothing? What do you know that's worth an opinion?' She was not attacking, only asking.

'He's a killer.'

She replied tranquilly, 'I've been told so. It may be true. I don't know it.'

Nor did I actually know it. It was one of those things 'everybody knows' but never questions. 'And if you did know?'

'It would make no difference.' She began, casually, to clear the table. I was the flustered one. 'You can't add conditions to your choice once you've made it; there'd be no end to that sort of shilly-shally.'

I accused, 'You don't want to know.'

'I would like to know everything about him.'

'You could ask. He'd tell you, blunt as a brick.' My spite ran loose. 'You don't know where he is or who he's with right now.'

At the sink, she did not bother to look back at me. 'I don't know and I don't ask. Why trouble a man who has had little sleep for a week but goes about his work because his obligation is to his people? Do you think he'd want a querulous, questioning bitch to come home to?'

There was silence until I admitted, 'I can't help it. I hate his guts.'

'You know nothing about his guts. He was prepared to be your father when you needed one but you rejected him on sight. I won't blame you for that. I took my time about discovering him. He is a harassed, *needing* man.'

Needing? Oh, the eye of the beholder! I saw that I was not quite accepted; loved, perhaps, but not fitted in. The emotional axis had shifted in six years and it was I who must seek new balance. Mum would not bend from her choice. As she turned from the sink, wiping her hands, I saw that she had aged more than was right for her years, though still a handsome woman – but a harder one than I remembered, one who welcomed but no longer needed me. Kovacs was the needed love and mine the humiliation of knowing it.

Perhaps to break the mood, she said, 'It's Christmas Day and I haven't a present for you.'

Nor I for her. Goodwill, surely, but not my heart. We had to learn each other again.

She went to the bedroom to dress and came back looking better and fresher. I thought, *Too good for Kovacs*, and how much easier it would have been without his shadow over us.

We talked, she and I, through the morning, filling in the years until we ran down and were left with make-talk. The emotional moment was past and neither could take cover in sentiment. Whatever was to come must wait on the tolerance of time.

Kovacs came back about eleven, looking tired at last after a week that must have tested his limits. The day had developed in heat and he stripped down to shorts without any beg-pardon. Definitely the man of the house.

What did she see in him? Three-quarters naked he was a thing of knobs and sticks, scarred in half a dozen places and slashed across the stomach in a spectacular cut that must have been close to the finish of him. No doubt he took his risks with courage but so probably did his victims. And there was always the sour-sweet smell of chewey.

I wanted to leave but some residue of good manners blocked the insult of walking out as he walked in. I excused myself and went out to the back yard for a few minutes alone. Mum had made a garden there, too, and lost it to the water but the brilliant sun would dry it in a day or two for her to begin again. As she would. A lifetime of beginning again. And again.

The soft squelch of bare feet told me that Kovacs had followed me out. 'I won't go away just for you, Teddy. I won't ever leave her.'

He was not explaining or entreating, much too sure of himself for that, just making sure that I knew who stood where and which stood higher. I said between my teeth, 'You're not fit for her.'

'Don't be silly, boy. I'm what she needed when there was nobody. She didn't look down her nose.' I had done that and must pay for it. His tone took on an edge. 'I'm fit for you, too. Just as good as you.'

So he could be stung. 'You're a killer.'

He moved round to face me. 'I killed a man once. Not for myself, though – for the tower. Somebody had to do it and I don't farm out my shit work, but that don't make me a killer.' In stress he forgot to correct himself. He added in a tortuous access of honesty, 'I'd do it again if I had to.'

'Who was he?'

'That's a copper's question. Nick knows who and when and how. You mind your business.' He produced his rat grin. 'Would you turn me in if you could pin it on me? It wouldn't be all that hard to do. Would you?'

Do that to her? So soon? Be a copper with a soul of nickel steel? 'No.'

'Then you'll have to get used to me being around.'

And calling the shots, no doubt. 'I suppose so.'

'That hurt. I could hear it. You'll do all right, boy.'

His confidence drew spite out of me. 'For Christ's sake, don't give me the number-two-dad stuff. I didn't need my father and I could never need you.'

Mum came to the back door just then, floured to the elbows with whatever she was making. 'Answer the front door, please, Billy.'

'Orright.' He said to me. 'I know who this is. You'll be interested. Come on.' I followed, wondering what more this damned Christmas could do to me.

When he opened the door I could not see at first who stood there with his back to the light, only that he was a young man with good clothes cut to fit. Kovacs gave him no welcome, only waited. There seemed to be meaning in the stillness before whoever it was held out something and said, 'I have to give this to Mum.' Francis! Nick at work again?

Kovacs half turned to let him enter and I stepped forward to see him more clearly. He saw me and raised his head like an animal alerted. At fifteen he was thin and set to be tall and good-looking in a tender, slender way, but I had little chance to assess him then. Recognizing me he became absolutely still as if power had deserted him. Only his face altered in startling, furious, whole-souled rejection.

It was as if we stood at bay, until he came to jerky life to toss an envelope down the passage to my feet and cry out as if the words bubbled through spit, 'You give it to her, favourite boy!'

His look was a desire to maim. I had met dislike enough in my time but not like this. As I picked up the letter he added, like a curse, 'There's no need of me here now, is there?' and walked off and out of the gate like the ultimate Sweet scraping Swill from his shoes.

From inside Mum called, 'Who is it, Billy?' and the eternal game-player answered with just the right carelessness, 'Only somebody with a message.' To me he said, 'Not nice, not nice at all.'

'To be hated? Upsetting.' But that was not what he had meant – he was not considering my feelings.

I gave the letter to Mum, who recognized the handwriting. 'Mrs Parkes. She always remembers Christmas. She must be a good woman.'

What I had heard of her made her a corrupt, two-faced, double-dealing old fraud. Mum showed me the card, one of those old snow scene things similar to stuff I recalled vaguely from long ago.

'Silly, isn't it, but nice. We all used to exchange these once.' She read out the tinkly, stupid verse on the inside of the fold: *'Christmas cheers the family nest, Reunion sweet with loved ones blest.* Now, how could she have guessed that?'

'Psychic,' I said, because something had to be said to take away the sting of my knowledge of the misfire. Like it or leave it, I was the gift Francis should have been.

Later, while Mum cooked and we were alone for a while, Kovacs said, 'It didn't work.'

'Francis? You think Nick was trying it on?'

'I know it. Well, she got half her Christmas present.'

He did something I can never watch without a queasy disgust: pulled a quid of chewey from his mouth, flattened it between finger and thumb and stuck it behind his ear – 'for afters', as the Swill have it. A filthy habit. All he did, said or pretended was ineradicably of the gutter. So was the gross sentimentality that pursued with, 'He was a lovely kid.'

'He was a whining, lying little prick.'

'That, too. You've got no pity in you.'

Said by a Tower Boss! 'Would you want him back?'

'Yes. I'm responsible. I made him what he is.' He made one of those repellent revelations of the heart that seemed to come easily to him: 'I tried to do what a father should but I got it wrong.'

Rather than hear any more of it I left him and went to the kitchen to talk to Mum.

5

Nick sent for me as soon as I reported in to barracks.

'Well?' Meaning, *Report in detail*.

I said, 'Thank you.' If you want detail, dig for it; you command my activities but not my self-knowledge.

Drily, 'For the experience? Tell me about Kovacs.'

'He's not what I thought, but was I supposed to discover that I like him? I don't? He sickens me. Why did you do it?'

'To further your education. You'll have realized by now that the top one-tenth of one per cent of the intellects doesn't constitute much of an élite, that something more is required of a useful mind.'

The end of this imperfect day was to be a Nick tutorial. 'World awareness,' I hazarded, ready to be bored.

'Don't shit me, boy. High intelligence tends to remove itself from general considerations as though they can be left to the service classes and only the abstruse is worth its attention. Not always, though. Your friend Arry is among the top hundredth of one per cent. Did you know?'

I hadn't known and felt harshly minimized. 'The quantum cosmos is a pretty special one.'

'Just a more basic reality. He also likes people and applies his mind to them. He even likes you.'

It seemed I was ringed by do-gooders deciding who and how I should be. To divert the lecture and plant a barb of my own I said, 'The ploy with Francis fell flat,' and told him what had occurred. 'What were you trying to do?'

He was quite upset about it. 'Trying to make a gesture to bind Kovacs's confidence closer to me, and I think that worked. And trying to help prevent a crime. That didn't work.'

'A crime by Kovacs?'

'By Francis.'

I should have guessed all along that the ground was rougher than I thought. 'What crime?'

'We don't know yet. But there will be a crime, a real one, not a piddling fiddle with accounts. We aim to prevent as well as catch.'

'Where do I come in? As family Judas, planted to snoop?'

'I'm not that stupid. You were a shot in the dark. There was the chance that both of you in a reunited family might help – the deterrent of an elder brother copper always in sight. We try anything that might conceivably work. I'll have to think of something else.'

'But why Francis?'

'Because he is where he is and what he is. He's selfish, ambitious, Swill-frightened and in a position to do damage. You see that I know a lot about your brother. One day he'll see a chance and take it in order to burrow himself deeper into the ranks of the Big Sweet whom he thinks catastrophe can't hurt. So that if the Ma'am goes under the chopper Francis will have friends to shield him.'

While I was thinking, with a small tingle of surprise, how simply and nastily plain this was, he changed tack abruptly. 'Today's haul was worth the effort. Three murderers to face trial and a batch of Printing Office clerks and overseers to vanish into the Swill. Who do you think will care? Anybody besides their friends and loved ones? I sometimes think only Swill care for each other. Have you ever met a Sweet who gives a damn for anything except his own security?'

How fine the Swill, how bloody the rest of us! 'So what do you want me to be?' A phrase tickled my memory and I used it before I recalled its origin: 'Sweet with a Swill heart?'

'No. One of the new men.'

That was a new phrase from him. A new private belief, like Kovacs's cull? 'And who the hell are they?'

He said with sudden forced cheerfulness, 'I haven't a clue but they'll need to be better than the old ones if the race is to survive its stupidities. Goodnight, Teddy.'

God, they say, moves in a mysterious way to perform his little tricks – such as encompassing the fall of a sparrow. There was a crime all right, but Francis didn't commit it. I don't think even his self-serving would have connived at this one.

17

NICK
AD 2050

1

When you've pulled a real boner, leave well alone. For me that meant, hands off the Conways – but I wondered what Teddy might do about his brother. I saw no sign that he did anything, but surely he wouldn't just wash his hands of the boy? Then I thought myself into his shoes and asked what he could do – and was unable to think of a damned thing. Francis was a problem with no instant answer.

Teddy went home regularly and made a point of not telling me about it. I was not to have any credit. Nor did I use him as a messenger to Kovacs, not wanting to force that issue.

In those weeks he spoke to me only once of the towers save in line of duty, when he asked out of the blue, 'Are all tower lifts out of commission?'

'Nearly all, 'I told him.

'The man doesn't come round?' Arry must have taught him that.

'He surely doesn't. Once he did, but the lifts grew older and broke down more often and servicing became more expensive. People found their own ways of coping when the lifts were out for a month or more. They were effective ways, so the State stopped concerning itself.'

'Deliberately stopped servicing?'

'That's it. I don't know what it saved the annual budget but there are over 1,000 lifts in the towers of this city alone. A whole sub-department was eliminated. The money axe falls wherever it can.'

Every new savagery is unbelievable at first. He bit his lips, chewing this one over, to ask at last, 'How do they manage, the old, the sick, the little kids?'

Knowledge has its arid patches. 'If they're on the high levels and healthy they climb the mountain when they must. The old and sick stay put in little groups of two or three floors and live their lives there.' He shuddered and I turned the screw a little tighter. 'They're no worse off than Sweet are in a home for the permanently crippled.'

When that had sunk in he asked, 'How do they get food?'

'Lower floor groups collect all the coupons and get food for a whole floor group, than pass it hand to hand from street level to the top, five or six levels at a pass. Takes time but it works. Gives the unemployable someting to do.'

He saw some light there. 'They work like a community?'

One shouldn't be starry-eyed about people. 'It isn't love that drives them, they aren't sentimental outside the family group. If somebody won't help, his neighbours have ways of hurting him. Or her. Ostracism is the simplest. Cultures are founded on group necessities, so they co-operate and kick the shit out of anyone who won't play.'

'It would take a lot of organizing.'

'Ask your favourite Tower Boss about it. He gets the blame when the system breaks down. Ask Billy Kovacs.'

His sympathy vanished at the mention. 'Any rabbit can say *sorry, my fault*. Kovacs says the way Francis turned out is his fault but does that mean he does anything about it?'

It was than that I saw the obvious, that Billy was the ideal agent for keeping an eye on Francis.

2

Though I dressed right and smelt right and spoke right, I was never at ease moving solo in the towers except on my own family turf. A few of Billy's boys knew who I was and would lend a hand if my stranger's face started a ruckus, but going openly into Twenty-three was still a little chancy.

(Time erodes. I was no longer at ease with my family, either. They did not share the Kovacs's obsession with cleanliness, and their smell and grime set them at a distance that I dared not acknowledge. The scent of Sweetness corrupts us all.)

I made sure that Billy expected me: you'd never catch that busy grasshopper without an appointment. The flat was full of grandchildren that day, brats playing around and under the beds and greeting me in derisive Swill until Vi screamed at them not to use that talk in the house – in the street, yes, but not inside! The family was effectively bilingual. It was also present at discussions – nobody told the kids, *Go out and play*. There were no secrets in the flat: the kids had to learn from the beginning what was gossip and what was 'family talk'. The older ones were inducted into Billy's network as soon as they could be trusted, which was pretty young. He was setting up a dynasty.

This flat held his real life. I saw Alison Conway as a fantasy life that he desperately needed in order to sustain the load of leadership and doubly double-crossed morality; with her he was the man he wanted to be, with Vi the man he must be. A facile reading, perhaps, but close to the truth.

Vi made real coffee, playing hostess (courtesy the Ma'am) while the kids played around us, quietly but otherwise as if we weren't there. At first I was diffident about speaking of the Conways but she did not let bias show. She and Billy must have worked out their truce ground long ago. How, I couldn't imagine. In her place I'd have killed the bastard.

It was she who asked, after my explanation, 'But what can the Francis brat do that's dangerous?'

Billy said at once, 'Sell himself.'

'How? It's not like when there was money. Everybody knows what you should have and too much of anything is suspicious.'

'He can sell his arithmetic to somebody higher up, with more influence than the Ma'am. And then to somebody higher yet till he gets as high as he can go.'

She considered that, her fat, intelligent face working while her gross body relaxed. 'But what does he get by it? Does he want to be prime minister?'

'Security,' Billy guessed, cocking his head at me.

'Right,' I agreed. 'He was brought up Swill-frightened. Then his father – '

Billy cut in. 'There was a nasty thing his first day in the Fringe. Frightened the guts out of the poor little tyke.'

I hadn't known that, but it fitted. 'He wants a safe place that he can't be kicked down from. There's no such place but that won't stop him clawing higher and higher, and what I'm told of him suggests that he won't care who gets trampled on his way up.'

Billy showed concern. 'Like the Ma'am?'

Vi didn't see it. 'How?'

I had to explain something of the mutual dependence network that Mrs Parkes could not break out of, and of the precarious balance of corruptions – individually small but in total monstrous – underlying the administration.

That amused her. 'You mean the State puts up with it because that's easier than putting it down?'

'More advisable. The corrupt are also the talented.'

'And that scared fleabite could bring it all down by putting his boot in the wrong face?'

'Not all of it, but dislodging the Ma'am would tumble a few of her contacts, and each one of them – like dominoes.'

'Mustn't happen,' she decided. 'Things *can* get worse than they are. Lots of countries are worse off than us so there's lower to fall. Would what the Sweet get away with make any difference if it was shared out?'

Smart question. 'Among millions you wouldn't notice it.'

'Well,' she said over the lip of her cup of illegal coffee, 'we take a bit of graft ourselves.'

Billy objected, 'We earn what we get.'

She winked at me. 'Billy likes to feel honest. You'd better word the Ma'am, Billy.'

'She'll know for herself.'

'Just in case.'

'All right.'

They understood each other exactly: in four sentences discussion had taken place and agreement had been reached. I said, 'You'll have to watch him yourself, though.'

'You think I won't? What goes bad for Francis goes bad for me, doesn't it? So greedy Billy will watch it, won't he?'

Vi said, 'You say he's pretty sharp, Billy. What if *he* decides to take care of *you*? You've had a knife in your gut once before. And from a teenager.'

I needed a clearer picture of Francis. 'Would he go that far if you frightened him?'

Billy's mouth opened and shut on the shock of having to find an answer. Vi watched quizzically until he said, 'He's not that bad.' It was a mumble without conviction. 'He's my boy, after all.'

Vi said sharply, 'He was while you were useful. Children aren't pets – they're little animals that have to be watched as well as loved.'

There was muscle under her fat. I asked Billy how he would put it to the Ma'am and he turned sulky. 'Have to think about it.'

'OK. Tell me what she says.'

'I'll do that.'

We had more coffee while Vi ticked him off for being surly and I wondered how the tower folk would react to seeing their tough Boss at home.

Then Vi said, 'Tell him about the soldiers.'

I got the impression that this had been on both their minds, if only because Billy hesitated and wavered. 'Not Nick's department.'

'He can find out, though. He can ask around.'

I was to earn my pay. Push-me pull-me in action.

'All right,' he said. 'There's people getting sick. Too many.'

In the towers that could be dangerous: epidemic in the close environment was a fear the Med Section monitored constantly. 'What do the meds say?'

'They don't say anything.' Then he scared the wits out of me. 'They just take them away.'

'To the hospital at Army?'

'Out of the Enclave.'

My reflexes cried *plague* while my brain tried to concentrate on essentials. 'Vi said *soldiers*. What have they to do with it?'

'At first it was the soldiers that got sick. Next was our girls that fucked with soldiers. Then a few neighbours.'

Trust Billy to have nosed out an intelligent picture of the spread. 'How many?'

'Seventeen so far in this tower.'

'In how long?'

'About a fortnight.'

Not too bad but bad enough. 'Any quarantine?'

'In the tower? No.'

'So it's a contact infection. Venereal?'

His shoulders humped and fell. 'They don't say, but it comes from the soldiers through their pick-ups, though the army is supposed to be bio-clean. Maybe they get it through second-hand contact, the way cholera spreads through shit.'

Vi said, 'Language!' in a schoolmistress voice. Behind every successful man, somebody has said, is a stand-over woman – or something to that effect.

I asked, 'Symptoms?'

'Funny ones. Like a fever that comes and goes but the temperature goes down instead of up. Lowers the blood pressure. Then it hits the brain – they lose control of their speech and memory gets foggy. Next there's blisters round the – what was it, Vi?'

'Glands,' she said. 'Under the arm.'

'Lymph glands.'

'Yes, those.'

I could think of nothing like it among common diseases. 'How many dead?'

'Don't know. None died in the tower but how can I tell?'

'None brought back?'

'None. They may be still in hospital. Or they could be dead.'

Probably a virus. Bacteria can be cleaned up in a day or two but a new virus could require recombinant techniques to provide a phage. 'many in the other towers?'

'Some in Twenty-two and Twenty-four but I can't get figures. Nobody dead, anyway.' He complained disgustedly, 'They got no organization over there.'

I said, 'Something for you to attend to,' but he would have none of that.

'Like hell! I got them out of the shit with the Swains, didn't I? When they do something for us it will be time to help them again.'

'Very selfish people.' Vi's mouth was virtuously prim. 'Not co-operative.'

'Have you put the soldiers out of bounds to tower girls?'

'Tried, but what can you do? How do you stop a hungry kid from trading a fuck for a bit of fruit or chocolate?'

'Billy!' Vi had decided on outrage. 'I've told you before about language in front of the kids. I have to unteach them after you.'

'Sorry, love.' He didn't sound repentant.

In the silence a childish voice said from a safe hiding place, 'Fuck!' and giggled at its own thrilling impudence.

Vi's big head turned to the sound, antennae making radar search, limbs quivering in preparation for pursuit and punishment, and the room held its breath.

I said, 'I'll pick up what information I can,' and got out before the lightning struck.

It was coincidence that on the way out I passed a uniformed Med team (the only Sweet who could move unmolested in the towers) running a woman out on a mobile stretcher. Their presence was sinister and their exit more so – a Swill tower epidemic and not a single public bleat from Med Section . . . or a word to the undercover men who worked in them . . .

3

Vi's idea that I could find answers by simply asking around sprang from inexperience of administrative conduct outside the towers. Asking around, in the sense of buttonholing a prospect with *What's all the Med mystery?* would gain me only pursed lips and possibly a blast from higher up: *Police Intelligence will not, repeat not, initiate investigations into areas appropriate to other State Departments.* Med Section could be prickly about its secrets and mistakes.

I was worried by the implications of a high risk of contagion. That, in an Enclave with youngsters feeling their oats and soldiers breaking the fraternization regulations for the kind of quick nick to be bought for half a ration pack, could spread like a riot. Seventeen cases in Billy's tower could represent, if his were average, several hundred in Newport. And in other districts . . .

Not a word, not a hint in the weekly Confidential Bulletin. The PI Commissioner might know all about it but he was the kind who talked only to God and Cabinet.

If the indications were correct as I saw them, to hell with Commissioner and Cabinet. Their handling of Swill was tainted by the class fear their predecessors had created in their terror of the mob; they sat fearfully on secrets.

Ways to knowledge can be devious; private and personal contacts are useful. To siphon knowledge from the top you must sometimes insert your pipette through the bottom. Pun intentional. I sent for Teddy.

'A small job for you. Unofficial, so relax.'

'You need a message boy?'

'Don't be a brat all your life, I need your help. I'll have to tell you more than I should and trust you to keep your mouth shut.'

That pleased him. To make people trustworthy, you must first trust them. I told him what Billy had told me, without the clinical detail, emphasizing that Med shifted the patients out of the towers. 'Repeat this to nobody but the man whose name I will give you. Nobody else, not even your mother.'

He asked, 'Did Kovacs do his act when he told you about it?'

'Act?'

'The Great Cull. How the population problem will be solved by induced epidemics. Kill off all the Swill and leave the Sweet to throw parties in the brave new half-empty world. He's obsessed with it.'

He wasn't alone in that: the idea turned up every so often among the frightmongers. It was the sort of thing the half-informed Billy would come up with, but nobody with knowledge of the disgusting underside of international racism, poverty and starvation would swear that it couldn't happen. Some cunning ploys were rumoured to have been invented, such as a self-limiting gene to prevent plague recoiling on its creators . . .

It was important to discover how the army men had contracted it. There had to be a vector, a contact peculiar to them.

I said, 'Forget Billy. Are you still close with your little Ultra mate, Arry?'

'We're friendly.'

He wouldn't admit affection for anyone. For Carol, perhaps? Interesting to be a fly on the wall to hear Teddy with his sexual hair down. Or nauseating. I said, 'Ultras tend to talk mostly to each other where their specialist jargon and short-cut diction can be understood.'

He said sourly, 'Perhaps he makes an exception because I can't talk physics.'

He makes an exception for you, Snotty, because years ago he was told to instruct you informally in the practice and philosophy of Swilldom. He also likes you, I can't think why.

'I suppose not, but on the other side of his life he talks to lots of fledgling scientists like himself, and all the sciences sooner or later have to call in the physicists.'

He was ahead of me. 'So if he has Med contacts . . . and can pick up some lab gossip round the coffee dispenser . . . You know they get real coffee?' I knew – the gap between Extra and Ultra is insultingly great. 'And I report back to you.'

'*He* reports back to me. *If* he wants to do it. I can't coerce him, he's out of my reach. Don't ask him for results, leave it to him to come to me, because every additional link adds a distortion and leaves a trail.'

He took that personally, of course, always on the lookout for a snub. 'And it may turn out to be something you don't want me to know.'

'Could be.'

'Bastard.'

He liked to get that in when we were being unofficial. It was probably equivalent to *I love you too, Shithead*, but that was more than he would ever confess.

Two days later he told me Arry was interested.

For a week I heard nothing and gnawed my nails. I was dependent on Arry's goodwill, which in turn depended on such intangibles as his liking for Teddy and the distant fact that Arry and I had got along well, as instructor and squaddie, in those training days up-country after they had shifted me out of the Sweet camp and over to 'safer' ground.

Ultras can be curiosities when they open their high-powered mouths, however ordinary they look; Arry was a curiosity *until* he opened his mouth, when he reverted to the strikingly ordinary. He talked jargon only to his peers. He was one Swill who never forgot his origins: he kept up his tower contacts with genuine affection whereas many of them paid duty visits and developed a 'visitor' self to be folded up and put away on return to the Sweet world.

He was also a physical curiosity, skinny, round-shouldered and only 155 centimetres tall. He had the streetwise face of a nasty boy and streetwise he surely was but in no way nasty; he was a triumph of head over environment, absorbing training with offhand ease without drowning his Swill personality in the bath of Sweet privilege. He would be one of those 'new men' I could not define, the kind who use *all* their life experience instead of taking shelter in professionalism, one who would be useful, no matter how the culture evolved.

I was losing confidence when one day he bumped into me, literally, in the street, apologized as he dropped something slight and slippery down the front of my shirt and passed on about his business – and I about mine with a little something rubbing against my stomach just above the belt buckle. It had been a perfect drop, really streetwise.

Back at PI, I examined one of the slenderest recording filaments I had ever seen, as fine as silk. I took it to the PI deadroom, the one area in the building which we hoped was proof against electronic spying. The technicians seemed familiar with the fine wire and found me a machine to play it. I used a dead cabinet with headphones and was 99 per cent sure of privacy.

Arry is the only person I know who can speak Sweet with a Swill accent. His voice whined at me, 'Matey, have you poked your finger into something! I know you take shorthand, so stop and get yourself pencil and paper. Don't miss any because this tape will erase itself as each word is spoken.'

I had no need to stop it: I carry pen and notebook because the mnemonic training is good but not infallible. Arry went slowly enough to make transcription easy: 'This high-rise lowdown is for your jug ears only. When you're sure you remember it all, please destroy your notes.'

I remember it still.

1. The tower infection is basically an immune system depressant. It differs from last-century AIDS in its preliminary symptoms – low temperature, low blood pressure, speech interference, memory loss and lymph blisters.
2. These pass in ten to twelve days but may mask other infections lying dormant in low body temperature. With immune suppression a common cold can kill. There are also some relapses, not yet understood.

3. Vectors are not yet established. Sperm certainly, saliva maybe and just possibly sweat. If the last is true, it's an instant contact disease; would have to be because the virus dies almost at once when deprived of moisture.

4. Carriers don't show symptoms, only antibodies. This could mean a long incubation period or could indicate some natural immunity that can be tracked down and used in treatment.

5. Three strains are known so far and Med suspects a high mutation rate. Makes a nasty treatment problem.

6. Definitely carried radially outwards from army barracks in the Enclaves. Three Enclaves showing sign so far.

7. Difficult to isolate the carriers because the troops won't admit to chasing sex among Swill kids. Social choke-up! Won't admit to soiling their Sweet pricks on gutter girls! Half of them will drop into the Swill anyway when their terms are up and they can't get jobs. The answer is to blood test every serviceman in the country. This is being done.

8. Big question – where did the army get it? Not via tourists because there aren't any. You might nut something out. I want to know, too. I won't stop visiting my friends in the towers unless I absolutely must.

9. Some lab folk are muttering 'cull', that old bogey. The chiefs tell them to shut up and not be childish but my bet is that the chiefs thought of it first. But who would be culling whom? Maybe if you can find out where the soldiers pick up the virus . . . (His voice faded on the suggestion, then came back strongly:) I want some return for this. Fix a time and place and get Teddy to tell me.

He had earned whatever pound of flesh he might demand. I ran the wire back for replay. Silence. As he had said, it had cleared itself as it passed the activator head. I never did work out how that was done.

As for time and place . . . I sent for Teddy. 'Take your Ultra friend to meet your family next Sunday afternoon. I'll be there, too.'

I used the PI network to filter the appointment through to Kovacs. His presence was essential and I wasn't going into the towers until some sort of prophylaxis had been worked out.

I thought about the secrecy that kept mention of the outbreak from the news channels. It would become public knowledge as it spread – when a couple of Sweet got it and screamed the place down . . .

But how would Sweet catch it? Via the soldiers on home leave, of course. Also, PI had frequent Swill contacts . . . and if it needed only a brush against a sweaty arm while on the job, the disease could be with the Sweet already, whittling away behind Med Section silence. But Med didn't seem to know much beyond the symptoms.

On the Friday morning a General Instruction, Operational, Immediate, was promulgated by the Commissioner. All Intelligence and police penetration into tower areas was to cease forthwith. No reason given. Somebody had sense enough to be scared but not enough to be honest. The most secretive of cabals is a government pretending democracy – sometimes I think the State doesn't give a bugger about people so long as its top dogs can cower in their kennels for ever. No, that's not fair; they just don't know what to do as crisis piles on crisis.

18

NOLA PARKES
AD 2050

Familiarity makes double dealing automatic, so acceptance of my position should become easier but does not. An anomaly upsets me until it is smoothed; the unexpected sets me shivering over possibilities of mouths unstopped, cracks unsealed. I live in latent alarm.

Behind my professional expression of polite enquiry I was asking, what can he want, this 'father' of my Fringe 'nephew'? He is not frivolous; his appearances have meaning.

He seemed a little older now – hard work, profligate sexuality and the abrasions of middle age overtaking him – but his slender frame moved as smartly as ever in the suit worn to the edge of the discard but clean and mended – the Fringe impersonation was excellent. The Conway groomed her ugly duckling with an eye to characterization.

I waited for him to begin the bout. It was always a bout, gentlemanly on both sides with consensus sought rather than a points decision. I had time to note how the animal sexuality (wearing a small boy smile with wolf teeth behind the lips – virgins beware!) enlivened the unprepossessing face. As a younger woman, with less dangerous responsibilities requiring circumspection, I might have been tempted to try a fall.

He said, respectfully for a man of such authority in his own domain, 'You know Mr Nikopoulos, ma'am?'

'I remember him.' He had promised not to blackmail me. Had the promise run out?

'He sent me.'

'Could he not come himself?'

'He thought it was my job.' Were my nerves plainly jumping? He soothed quickly, 'Not trouble, ma'am,' then thought better of it. 'Not yet, anyways.'

I waited for the self-correction. A slight frown recognized the error but he let it lie. *La belle* Conway, I suspected, was coaching him into accepting his freaks of grammar instead of straining after pedantry. An intelligent woman.

He said, 'It's the boy.' Of course it was the boy. It was always the boy. I wished I had never seen Francis or let myself be talked into adding an exotic to my staff; the gain had been great but the added pressures greater.

He went on, 'You want to watch what he does,' and his voice died down to a hangdog shame. This lingering affection for Francis did not fit his toughness, but sentimentality and pragmatism are common partners of the mind, each a refuge from the tyranny of the other.

'I do watch, Mr Kovacs. What have you in mind?'

'He's got secrets, hasn't he? Your secrets.'

'Some.'

'Enough, I reckon. He can tell them.'

'To whom?'

'People with more influence than you.'

Of course, of course. 'Is this Nikopoulos's idea?'

'Yes, ma'am.' And, unwillingly, 'Mine, too.'

'You don't trust Francis?'

If he had had tears he might have shed them for the son-who-never-was. 'He's only a kid and all he's got behind him is Fringe and Swill. He's afraid of the gutter.'

'I know it.'

'Ma'am, send him home! His mum and me will straighten him out!' Billy, your grammar and your shameless pleading! Poor little Tower Boss, cursed with human weakness.

The request came too late; I had to be open with this man whom I had learned to trust. 'If I send him back to you he will run away. He knows where else he would be welcome. He would leave me today if he were not uncertain of my ability to drag him back. One day he will do it.'

'Run where?'

'To someone with, as you said, greater influence, who can protect him from the long fall. You think of me as a State servant with power but I am a very small power and can be coerced by others who also have a second set of accounts hidden from the computers. I held back his services but finally I was forced to – lend him out. Now he has connections a stratum above me.'

His teeth, greyish with the clinging chewey stain, bit into his lower lip as he suffered. 'I thought I was doing the best for him, giving him a chance to get on.'

'You were and he has taken it. But he is selfish and selfish people snatch at what they want, and make the mistakes of hurry.' He saw my drift and took in breath with a hiss. 'He could try to use his knowledge to extract concession from some less malleable employer. He hasn't the courage for that yet but it may happen as he gains confidence.'

He said, 'They'd kill him,' as if that were a commonplace.

I said, 'They would arrange his disappearance,' as if that softened the meaning.

He was awash with self-punishment. 'I got him into this!' And, like a frightened schoolboy, 'I daren't tell his mother.'

That would frighten me, too. 'I can head him off if I see trouble coming but he will take care that I don't see. And he might not listen to me. Fear and greed are not rational.'

Suddenly he seemed almost cheerful. 'I might be able to fix that – give him something to be more frightened of.'

'Yourself?'

He grinned hugely. 'No, ma'am, his brother.'

I did not like the sound of that. 'The PI man? He is young and probably still in the dedicated stage; he might double the danger for myself and others.'

'No, na, na-a-ah, ma'am!' I had not heard such a raucous Swill sound from him in years. 'Teddy's on our side. So's his boss, Nick.'

I can't pretend that the revelation shocked me; I am no more fooled than any other by ideals of official probity, but I felt that I no longer understood the give-take relationship of Swill and Sweet. The idea of Kovacs's spidery fingers reaching into the PI was unsettling. Or was PI creating a power base in the tower?

He said, 'I think that's all, ma'am,' stood and hovered in case I had more to say.

I had nothing useful to add but, moved by fellow feeling for this man as hopelessly ensnared in his world as I in mine, I offered rough common sense: 'Forget Francis. The boy you played father to no longer exists.'

'No, the past doesn't go away, ma'am. A little boy doesn't die just because he grows up.'

Hopeless. I am sure that as he left he revolved plans for the Francis who is still nine years old in his heart.

Too late I thought of the question I should have asked: who is 'our side' and what is the PI interest in Francis?

He would have told me if it had been necessary; perhaps it was better that I should not know. As for Francis, what should I watch for? I could only hope my internal alarms would sound when something was not as it should be.

19

ALISON
AD 2051

For a while after the water receded I saw little of Billy, but he had never been predictable; there had always been times when he dashed in and out again as if only to reassure me that I was not forgotten. He withheld his Swill life from me in mistaken kindness but I learned not to spend myself in worry when he came in with the effects of violence needing massage or mending. He never seemed badly hurt – one broken arm in six years was not much if I assessed his life correctly.

The absence did not worry me, but his behaviour when he did appear disturbed and then frightened me. It was not only that he had not stayed overnight in two weeks but that he had taken to kissing my cheek instead of my lips, and after a while I saw that he avoided touching my skin at all, embracing a bag of clothing rather than a body.

I thought the obvious, told myself – savagely – that six years was probably more than many women had had of him, and wondered why he hovered instead of bowing out. I had to bear with it in that hope that supposedly springs eternal.

Yet, when on a Saturday morning he popped in to inform me casually that Teddy would be bringing two friends with him the following day, I decided, without rationally choosing the moment, that enough was enough, and screamed at him that my house was not a bloody meeting hall and he could take his plot-hatching elsewhere. What, I wanted to know, was wrong with planning his bastardries in his new girlfriend's home? Or was she protected from the truth about him?

I carried on like a virago, uplifted with fury, raging to earn the backhander that pays out spitting bitches and thinking that the noisy relief of tension was worth a bruise or a loose tooth. The old pair in the other half of the house must have thought murder brewed; their door slammed and their key turned as they barricaded themselves against Armageddon.

Billy retreated from my anger with the dropped jaw of a startled boy until I realized, unbelievingly, that he did not understand what powered my ranting. In the end I planted feet apart and arms akimbo, the very cartoon of a termagant, and glared in breathless exhaustion while he mumbled and excused himself and made no sense, until I wavered in my doubtful victory. At last he told me, shamefaced as though it were his fault, of the disease in the towers, of his fear of infecting me because there was no knowing whether or not he carried it and of the rumour that it might be transmitted by the sweat of bodies in contact.

If ever there lived a brilliant, brutal idiot with a heart of soft porridge, it was my Billy.

'Why didn't you tell me, you stupid man?'

He looked old-maid-prim in his ratty way and said, 'You don't have to know about things like that.'

Protected, by God, against the awfulness of the real world! Are such moments for laughter or tears? 'I'm not cut crystal that mustn't be touched for fear of breaking.'

He said, 'You are, you know,' and I wanted to cry because in all our time together that was his nearest approach to *I love you*. Then, with an air of *Thank Christ that's over*, he demanded a cup of tea and sat himself at the table.

Without really thinking about it I put my hands under his chin from behind and pulled his head back and kissed him full on the lips before he could struggle free. 'If plague takes you off,' I told him, 'there won't be much point in my hanging about. So I'll have all of you while we're still here.'

He said, 'You're mad,' but kissed me back. Later I thought that I had been quite mad but had no regret. He stayed that night and I did not break out in blisters or run a low temperature in the following days. We did not despise Death in the Fringe or in the towers but we did not respect him either, so we took brash chances.

On the Sunday morning there was the usual trouble getting him dressed on what he called his 'day off'. His Sunday dress was at best a pair of shorts, at worst nothing at all. He would stand on the patchy back lawn in skeletal nakedness, 'soaking up some sun', while old Mrs Sanders slammed the door to her part of the house and then hovered by the window to see what might be seen. (Not so very much, to tell truth.)

I wanted him to dress, to let me make an occasion of having an Ultra in the house ('occasions' were rarities – cakes and coffee and a touch of hostessiness) but he said, ''Arry's Swill, like me.'

'Swill, but not like you.'

That started a fit of temper but brought a result – he shaved and put on trousers and shirt but no shoes or socks. Our few social arrangements usually foundered in crazy compromise.

The two boys came for midday dinner, allowing me to play housewife-hostess-mother to the limit with food that cried Parkes provisioning in every bite. At least the cooking was mine.

Teddy was, as usual, neat and reserved, still unsure how to talk easily with me and coolly polite to Billy, while his friend, Arry Smivvers (Smithers?) was barely describable. He was fully dressed despite the heat – shirt, jacket, slacks and heavy sock-shoes – and new-pin clean, but either he lacked any grain of taste or didn't care what he wore as long as it looked expensive. I don't think anyone else could have been unaware of the effect of red jacket, yellow slacks, mauve shirt and black and white sock-shoes. He was short and skinny and frail to the eye (how had he coped with those years of physical training?) and had the face of a quietly ferocious rabbit mated to the piping voice of a small boy.

He did not talk so much as natter on any- and everything; it was hard to credit that one of the finer intellects of the city was eating at my table. And he ate! He put the food away as if tomorrow held no more cakes and ale, and through it chattered like a magpie. Teddy had told me, 'He only has brains when they're needed for something,' and I believed him.

At some stage I asked did he know the Captain Nikopoulos who was to join us later. 'Nicky? Known him for years. His father was my Tower Boss. Still is, in a way.'

That was unnerving. I had adjusted to the idea of Swill intellectuals but could not readily equate them with Police Intelligence. Surely it would be to give a hoodlum a gun! Thoughts like that have to be dragged out and quashed, so strong is all that early rearing.

Teddy read my confusion and mocked me. 'Nick's a gentleman.'

Arry raised a finger. 'Sometimes! Nick's a copper first and last, and when he's being frank and open don't wonder how much is still up his sleeve because you wouldn't think one sleeve could hold that much. But in between first and last he's got his own ideas about what a copper's job is.'

'You mean he's part of the bribery circuit?'

Billy was shocked by my saying it openly but Arry snickered and looked cunning. 'He doesn't take bribes, Mrs Conway, but he gives them. He gives himself, eh, Billy? Eh, Teddy?' Billy was staidly disapproving and Teddy palely murderous. 'He impresses you with what a terrific feller he is, so you believe it and you'll do anything for him. Then he's got you for ever and he never lets go.' He crimped his skinny fingers into a fist like a closing chicken claw. 'That's Nick.'

One can have enough of dominant personalities. I said lightly, 'He won't grip me, I'm bespoke.'

'He won't need you,' said that direct little man. 'He's got Teddy. Eh, feller?'

Teddy flushed and was silent. So my self-sufficient son had a hero! So nice to know that he was still human, a romantic at heart.

I was surprised to hear myself faking the intellectualism of a woman of the world: 'Your Nick doesn't please me. One form of corruption is no more justified than another.'

Arry asked brightly, 'But where would we be without it?' then carried on in the changed tone of another side of his persona: 'Every transaction is for gain on one side or both, and the transaction that pretends to fair play is corrupt by definition. Corruption is the normal state of a society that restrains its excesses by law or morality, both of which are corrupt in effect and in intention.' He smiled at me with absolute wickedness. 'We balance our security and happiness by manipulating corruptions, so perhaps it isn't such a dirty word after all. It preserves us from the excesses of too much virtue – which is another kind of corruption.'

'So there is no purity, only compromise with good and evil?'

'And who knows which is which?'

I would not argue with a jesting Ultra, particularly as I was not sure that he jested. He was outrageous but not easily countered. I contented myself with smilingly hostessing my little cabal of corruption. If he was right (and he possibly was) then we existed in a state of scrambling from crisis to crisis, preserving our good opinions of ourselves by hailing the expedients of desperation as moral and intellectual triumphs.

In his terms, our twenty-first century made sense only as a race to stay ahead of the consequences of its own corruptions – the Greenhouse Effect among them – and hope that the future will find room for a directionless humanity.

It was a wonder that we ever found cause for laughter, but day after day we did. So, even if he was right, it didn't matter. Only when the laughter stopped would it be time for tears.

Not until later did I see that he had not been cutting an awkward exchange with a running jest but telling me that we must look straight at good and evil, right and wrong if we are to understand not only what we are but what we can be.

I was not impressed with Nikopoulos when he came after lunch. I must correct that: he *was* impressive in an animal fashion, of only middle height but obviously powerful, with the etched Mediterranean features that promise a strong personality but rarely deliver it, and the quiet voice that might have force in reserve or might not. Also, he had the cool eyes of controlled fanaticism. My instinctive reaction was 'grossly physical and intellectually devious', not a man for Teddy to look up to.

When Teddy introduced him he scanned my face, though without insolence, and seemed satisfied as if a guess had been confirmed.

I offered coffee, which he took without milk, smiled and said, 'Royal Papuan beans, Lae district. They come in through Nola Parkes's Department and don't often filter down to the Fringe.'

That was plain showing off but he was also telling me that today he was as civilian as his informal dress, not a policeman. I replied, acknowledging the message, 'The wages of sin,' and stepped plump into his net.

'The wages of Francis,' he corrected, never losing his smile, 'whom we must discuss. Teddy will have told you I am interested in him.'

'No, he hasn't.' I was at once frightened; I tried not to think too often of Francis but – I was frightened. And Teddy avoided my eyes. 'What has Francis done?'

'Why, nothing yet. It is what he may do. Billy?'

Billy had told me nothing, either. Now he described his visit to Mrs Parkes and ended with, 'She'll keep an eye on him but I reckon he's smart enough not to raise suspicion. Silly smart,' he amended, 'enough to get what he's after but not enough to see the consequences.'

He sounded practical but I knew that his not-so-rational heart bled for the Francis he had loved. Francis had never really been a lovable child but Billy, loving me, had given his affection to the boy as a step towards my acceptance of himself. Emotion drives us on twisted tracks.

'Send him home! I want him back!' That half-screech, between rage and pain, was mine but I did not care.

Billy said sadly, 'He wouldn't stay, he's too far gone. He's as scared of the Fringe as he is of the Swill.'

'I'll keep him! I'll make him stay!'

They gave me the patience of repressed pity, too well-mannered to treat me as the fool I made of myself.

'I'll make him stay,' I repeated, defying them while my throat closed on a defeated whimper because my chance to hold him had vanished in sexual haze three years before.

Nikopoulos put out his hand – a surprisingly small, delicate hand, no peasant paw – to take mine. 'Social fear is hard to overcome. Coppers call it the Sweet Dream, fear of falling.'

The fall is terrible. Even half a fall, like mine, not all the way down . . .

Arry, having no personal interest, suggested, 'Hit him with a bigger fear. Make him run home for safety.'

To him it was a simple problem in behaviour, amenable to an easy solution. Billy did not respond but Nikopoulos said, 'It's worth a thought. Save it. Let's deal with immediate things.'

My semi-hysteria rebelled at this damnable switch of attention. I squalled at him, 'I want my son!'

The sharp lines of his face shifted; he became saturnine and forceful. 'And I want you to have him. He won't be forgotten.' I liked him no better but I stopped feeling like a child offered a sweet and then denied it – until he said, 'But Francis is not the present problem,' and turned to Arry, switching me out of the circuit. 'This is your meeting, Arry. What do you want?'

The boy (so hard to remember that the urchin face was only eighteen years old) had something concealed in his skinny claw as he answered, 'I want a piece of the action.'

That old phrase, or something like it, was still current in Swill jargon but I saw no present sense in it. Nikopoulos did, because he said, 'Forget it. You'll never make a copper, Arry.' Then, watching Arry's face, he saw reason and laughed aloud. 'They caught you!' Arry turned beefsteak red. 'You've got the brains but not the field training, boy! You outsmarted yourself and they caught you at it! So now they want to use you to do a PI job for them. What is Med up to?'

Arry took it well. 'I was being cunning, turning on the big sex act – ' That was hard to imagine but the most unlikely men have spectacular love lives; Arry may have scored where physique and good looks would have got him nowhere. I wondered what the girl was like. ' – And she turned it back on me. I got the information all right, then the whole bloody Section ganged up on me and held the Research Secrecy Act over my head if I didn't tell them who was picking their brains. I had to admit it was PI but I didn't use your name, Nick. They're on to something that has to be kept quiet but they haven't the contacts to carry it through. So, if the interfering so-and-sos from PI can find out what Med needs to know there'll be no report made about interdepartmental meddling. I have to produce the goods or we all go down the drain.' He brightened to wipe an imaginary tear. 'All our young careers blighted!'

Nikopoulos said wearily, 'Bloody funny. What must I do to save your hide?'

'Yours, too.' He opened his hand to show a cylindrical tablet about two centimetres long, wrapped in clear polythene. 'Find out where this came from.'

The pale green tablet was familiar, the reason for Billy's often sweet-sour breath. Nikopoulos reached for it but Arry pulled back. Billy said, 'Chewey. So what?'

'But is it?'

'Show me.'

Arry handed it over. 'Don't open it.'

Billy examined it closely with his weak eyes and produced a tablet of his own for comparison. Arry warned, 'For Christ's sake, don't confuse them.'

'Not quite the same. Yours is more bluey-green. What's the difference inside?'

'That yours is made in State factories and distributed for coupons while mine comes from God knows where and is handled by God knows who. What Med knows is that this one came from the pockets of a dead Swill – dead from violence, not plague – and the copper who checked the body knew enough to spot the colour. He turned it in for testing because black market cheweys have to be tested for narcotic level.'

Billy said, 'The silly pricks make it too strong. Get caught every time.'

'This time they haven't been able to duplicate the colour exactly because the narcotic component is slightly different. It has to be to accommodate the culture medium.'

We all reacted sharply except Billy, who did not know the term. Nikopoulos and Teddy leaned over to look at the thing. I had to ask, 'Are you talking about this new disease?'

'Very much so. Chewey is the prime vector.' He produced another tablet with a red marker, opened the wrapping and broke it in half. 'This is a mock-up. See how it's done? The narcotic and flavouring is contained in these honeycomb cells, the chewing action bursts them open. That one – ' he nodded at the dangerous little thing in Billy's hand ' – contains also dormant viruses in a neutral medium. They come to life in the presence of saliva. They aren't natural viruses, they're laboratory constructs.'

There are ideas too large, too ramified, for immediate assimilation; you perceive their existence unemotionally, the impact comes later. So it was with a specious calm that I said, 'But that means it is being spread deliberately.'

'Doesn't it just!' He had accustomed himself to the idea, could be smart-alecky about it.

'Killing people in such horrible fashion!'

'Oh, but it isn't killing anyone.' His eyes danced with the possession of surprises. 'They all recover. Even without treatment they recover. Some low temperature, a few days out of their dizzy minds, then a high temperature that mutates the virus into a harmless form, and it's over. Some risk of secondary infection, like pneumonia, but that's no sweat.'

Billy asked, 'Then why haven't any come back that the Meds took away?'

'Quarantined for further observation. Med is into a very hush-hush operation.'

Nikopoulos muttered angrily, 'Let there be no panic! Let the little victims play!' He sniffed, lifting his head like a questing hound. 'But they recover. There are no victims.'

'Oh yes, there are! All of them, Nicky! Sterile – every last mother's son and daughter.' He made a cheerful guttersnipe's grimace at Billy. 'So there's the cull they tell me you're always on about. Very humane, too – not much worse than a bad attack of flu. And self-limiting by ensuring there's no next generation to pass it on to.' His good humour was irritating enough but what he said to Billy was horrible. 'How does it feel to be the bloke who was right all the time?'

That was cruel. Billy put the poisoned tablet on the table and said nothing. Later, with only me to see, he would cry for his unholy rightness.

20

NICK

AD 2051

The gibe at Billy was unnecessary but Arry, whatever his intellect, was street Swill and street Swill don't waste much sensitivity on each other. In any case Arry had little to waste. But Kovacs did; he was a mass of raw surfaces, forever acting tough because the man inside suffered; Alison Conway was his needed refuge.

I was not attracted by what lay below her glossy surface. A glance was enough to see what had taken Billy's ambitious but simple-hearted fancy; her handsomeness was the aftermath of beauty but her unselfconscious confidence (called, in her Sweet world, 'social poise') spoke of an underlying hardness, calculation that allowed her to hold and probably manipulate him. She must have burst on him as a dazzlement, the embodiment of 'class' dropped within his startled reach while his Swill heart thudded like a bongo drum and his avaricious loins ached in rhythm. He was stolen property; poor Vi had no chance against the glamour. But poor Vi had Billy's trust in areas Alison could not enter; Vi was the soldier's battle mate, Alison the victory whore who had to make the best of her flimsy fortune.

While I thought of all that, she showed that as well as bedworthiness she had some of Vi's ability to look to essentials. With the barest hint of hostess coolness she said, 'Arry, stop making drama and tell us why others must do your dirty work for you. Surely Med has its own field teams?'

Arry said, 'You'd think so, wouldn't you? But it won't work like that.'

'One reason,' I told them, 'is that all field teams are under a blanket order to stay out of tower areas.'

Billy banged on the table like a curse. 'That's why no meds for the past week or more.'

'Don't need 'em,' Arry said. 'Nobody'll die. It's the contact vector that worries them, makes it too likely they'll carry it back into Sweet areas.'

Alison saw nonsense in that. 'It must cross over. The soldiers go home on leave. We used to see them – '

'No more they don't, Mrs Conway, and nobody sees them. And they won't until the virology teams give the word. The soldier boys stay in barracks in the Enclaves.'

She was outraged. 'Are you saying that the Enclaves are being sealed off? To preserve the useless Sweet? Besides, we Fringers shop in the towers. It will cross.'

Arry regarded her with approval for her spirit if not for her brains. 'So the Fringe becomes Swill,' he said succinctly. 'Quarantined. Always was, really. And the Sweet aren't useless, lady – they run the show, do the work, keep it going. It's the Swill that's useless, have to be fed and housed and paid for by a bankrupt State and give nothing back.'

She said, 'I've heard the voice of desertion twice in my own family. Yours has a familiar ring.'

His quick pallor showed that she had hit low. I should have paid more attention but Billy broke in with, 'We're expendable.' He said it without animus; he had been raised in the idea. (But he and his were not expendable. Nobody was, ever.)

Arry said with gritty composure, 'The towers can't be overtly sealed off without starting a panic; they're just withdrawing every contact they can.' He looked Mrs Conway straight in the eye. 'Sealing off the Swill is just the sensible way of cutting losses where they can be best afforded.'

'Cold-blooded!'

'How would you do it, Mrs Conway? Just give the disease open slather to sterilize the best brains in the State?'

Her face said she would have loved to slap his unbridled mouth. 'I suppose I would not. But if this is where investigation must begin, what does sealing off accomplish?'

'Maybe nothing. Depends how you look at it. Government theorizes the stuff may be brought in from over the border. That's sense because what does an Australian gain from sterilizing his own? So Med thinks one of the hush-hush agencies is working that angle without needing to go to the Swill. But Med also thinks we might get a quick trace in the towers.'

She asked, 'Doesn't it all frighten you?'

'I'm Swill. I was born frightened, I just don't show it any more. Survival first – there's time to be frightened after.'

On the face of it the State position seemed reasonable but I hadn't enough facts for judgement. Still, it *could* be an inside job – there *were* possible rewards for treachery.

She appealed to me. 'Mr Nikopoulos, what does this young man want of you?'

233

Billy stood up and stretched like a lazy-tongs extending and told her, 'Make a pot of tea, Mother. He wants what he said at the start, to find where this green shit comes from. We've been saying the soldiers give it to the girls, but how if it's the girls that give chewey to the soldiers?'

Oh, how she was shocked! 'But the soldiers are Sweet. They don't chew.'

Arry told her coldly, 'They do. They always did. Bored men sit around doing nothing – and chew.'

'Depravity doesn't stop at the towers,' I said. 'It hits its real high in Sweet territory. There are Sweet who make their own chewey at four and five times strength with a deodorant incorporated so that their intimates don't catch the sniff. At that strength it's addictive and can turn nasty.'

She went to fill the kettle and, with her back to us, apologized. 'I'm still a snob. I still feel there are things Sweet don't do. Forgive me.'

Billy said, 'Sweet or Swill, shit smells the same. Sorry, love, but it does. Now, anybody got suggestions how I go about this?'

I said, 'How *we* go about it. You could run into trouble if the wrong people realize what you're up to.'

'Me in trouble? Nicky, I'm the bloke that *makes* trouble. You can't be in it, anyway. Field teams includes PI, doesn't it? So you can't go into the Enclaves without your absence being noticed. And if I make mistakes and raise a big public smell I'll need you up there using influence to get me out from under.'

His faith in me was sourly touching but he was right in saying that I could not vanish for a few days.

Arry came in eagerly. 'Most of my work is home study by terminal. I can be away with no notice taken.'

Billy took him by the belt and lofted him shoulder high, more easily than I would have guessed. 'What do you weigh? Fifty k? Maybe you're mean with a knife but you need muscle if you get caught by a mob. I'll take Teddy if Nick can cover for him.'

Mrs Conway cried out furiously, 'No!'

'Yes,' Billy said. 'It's what he's been trained for.'

'Billy, he's only a boy! Mr Nikopoulos!'

I told her, without any pleasure, 'It *is* what he has been trained for, and I can cover for him. And believe me, Mrs Conway, he is far more than a boy.'

In the strained quiet I caught Arry looking curiously from face to face, observing that alien conception, a family, with its emotional hair down.

Teddy resolved the moment. He lay back in his chair, balancing perkily on the rear legs, and said equably, 'I'll enjoy working with Dad.'

Consummate actor or not, it was a triumph. I didn't for a moment believe in the implied truce with Billy but I was proud of the way he got it exactly right. Billy's face twitched and was still; perhaps he was fooled, perhaps not.

She, I think, was not. She said dryly, accepting defeat, 'The kettle's boiling.'

She surrendered gracefully, but both her sons were out from her protecting skirts and love and authority are both hard to give up. Still, I wouldn't have cared to be Billy when she got him to herself later on.

21

TEDDY
AD 2051

1

I had to agree to the partnership. Nick could not order it but he wanted it; it was a calculated arrangement wherein he sent me to learn the Swill ropes from an old stager whom he trusted to look after me. I knew (and writhed for it) that Kovacs would raise the towers against the army rather than see me harmed; Nick knew it too. Kovacs–Conway was a team he had planned long ago and was now setting to work.

I agreed, too, because Mum wanted me not to, and I had not come home for family bondage.

I agreed because it was impossible not to, once Arry had made his excited bid. Nor could I refuse once Kovacs had fingered me for his partner; he was the last man on Earth I would let find me wanting.

Those things were plain, but why did I say 'Dad'? It was not involuntary: it was a conscious decision to communicate something. But what? Not affection. Not ever that. I think I was trying to tell Nick that I could work with the man, to tell Mum that resentments could be set aside, to tell Kovacs that I was as good a man as he (I wasn't) but that I accepted him as boss on his own turf. I was telling him – and, with a sneaking astonishment, myself – that I trusted him.

He thought I mocked him.

When the others had gone he leaned across the table, white-faced, eyes like agates raging in his head. 'Don't ever use that word to me until you mean it! I took a lot from you years back but I won't take blinding shit from an upstart Extra brat of a copper!'

With his face inches away and his anger the most honest thing I had ever seen in him – and with a sense that if it came to violence I would be half-hearted because he was in the right – I had to declare my own self-respect while placating his.

I said, 'I don't like you and I never will, but I trust you and respect you for what you are.'

236

He gave me the shark grin that was worse than a threat. 'And what I am isn't much, you think.'

I couldn't summon the cowardice to deny or evade, just enough to glare and say nothing at all. He nodded violently to himself and left the room.

Mum, who must have watched with something like horror, let out her breath and said, 'At least that clears the air,' setting a bad moment in sensible perspective. 'But he was always good to you and he's easily hurt.'

'So, I suppose, are his victims.'

'I don't know that side of him, he doesn't let me see it.' She fixed on me the sort of gaze with which I imagine the Spartan mothers sent their sons off to disasters like Thermopylae, maternal pride quelling fluttering heart. 'Look after him, Teddy, he's getting too old for this work.'

For God's sake, which one *was* she worried about? 'Mum, it's he who'll be looking after me and he's the toughest old bastard you'll ever set eyes on.'

She looked absolutely proud.

Kovacs came back more suitably dressed for his idea of Sunday – a towel round his waist – as calm as if his dam had not come close to bursting, and began to lay out his ideas for our procedure.

I became fascinated by the untrained but biddable forces he could call on and the extraordinary chances he and his tower folk could take. He could plan actions that PI, hampered by politics and regulations, dared not dream of. At one stage I said, 'With that sort of influence and the towers to call on, you could take over the city.'

'You reckon? So we could. Easy. And then what? Would we be any better off when the looting was over? Half a Tower Boss's job is stopping stupid bastards going on the riot. If we took over, we wouldn't know so much as how to run the transport, much less Med section or the food supply. Half Melbourne'd starve before we got going again. Never give people what they want – it's bad for them and everybody else.'

So I understood a little more of how the Sweet/Swill balance was maintained – the Swill maintained it because without it they would be worse off.

Kovacs asked, 'Did you know that Swill are healthier than Sweet? There's figures to prove it.'

'I didn't know. Why is it so?'

'Diet. Calories, proteins, vitamins, all that – balanced. They get enough of all the right things. The Sweet get all the luxury stuff on their bonus coupons, so they're fat and slow and sick compared with us. That's a joke for you.'

It had its funny-sour side.

'Something more,' he said, 'our Swill are better off in a lot of ways than most people ever were except for part of the last century.'

That was one of the shattering facts of our awareness of general poverty, that most historical periods would have envied our poor, who were at worst fed and sheltered and doctored. What they lacked was the expectation of ever having more.

My view of the Swill fell apart for the dozenth time as he realigned my vision of a community at once disorganized by lack of a goal yet close-knit by its own conventions and concerns. There was order because a majority insisted on order, and disorder because a minority would not be ordered; there were groups of floors where peace and community spirit ruled and there were floors that feuded in blood; there were social strata with Boss families at the apex and street kids kicked around at the bottom and, in between, self-conscious snobberies of semi-literacy, gaming groups, entertainers, valued tradesmen and even such exotics as artists. 'There's everything in the towers, rotting because there's nothing for good brains to do.'

'One thing there isn't,' I suggested. 'Hiding places.'

'For what?'

'Sex. Where do the girls and soldiers go for their hump and grunt? The soldiers can't go to the towers and the girls can hardly sneak into barracks, and all the rest is empty concrete surrounds where you couldn't hide a pencil mark.'

'You mean, where's the saddling paddock? On the assault course. You know where that is?'

I didn't know what it was, let alone where.

He dropped into Swill, mocking. 'Nunno much, Sweetyboy?'

I agreed that I didn't know all I needed to know.

'Nunno n'un. A learn yer.'

'You'll have to.'

'Swilly!' He meant, *Speak Swill.*

'Yuh. Yer learn me tops.'

We spoke Swill from then on. It was more than practice: he wittingly sniped at social barriers preserved by superior grammar and accent. He was a practical psychologist. I suppose he had to be.

He drew diagrams on scraps of paper, showing how the Newport towers fanned out from a central point with the army barracks at the pivot and behind it a stretch of wasteland reaching to the river. On that stretch was the assault course, a sort of obstacle race of trenches and entanglements and barricades used in training infantrymen. I thought it would be under water most of the time but it appeared that it was built up high enough for the sweating soldiery to use more often than they appreciated. The troops used its shadows and cavities for meeting and saddling up, Kovacs said, nine nights in ten. The girls would sneak around the side, paddling in the river overflow, and scramble up to the assault course on ropes dropped to them.

But how did they make contact to arrange their dates?

'Arrange dates?' The idea tickled him pink. (Forget our Swill; much of it would be incomprehensible.) 'You've been brought up by nice people, Sweetyboy. The girls stand in the water and whistle.'

'And take whoever answers?'

'You don't like that? Teddy, those kids are selling gash, not socializing. They're in business.'

'For food?'

'Sometimes. Depends what their pimps are telling them to ask for. Lately they're asking for chewey – the new stuff's extra strong and they go for it, God help them.'

'So we get a girl to find out where the boys get it?'

'You think he'd tell her?'

No, I didn't think he would. 'What then?'

'What we do,' Kovacs said, 'is find us a girl who'll help us snatch her soldier. He'll tell *me* who supplies him.'

I didn't like the sound of that but it was not a matter for present argument; we might manage without indecent violence. I asked, 'How do we find the girl?'

'*We* don't. We don't do anything to get us seen as taking a hand, not yet. If somebody wakes to us it's Nick that gets it in the neck. My kids'll organize the girl. They'll do it easier than you or me would.'

And they did. Two days later a message came from Vi that she had a bird in hand.

2

Returning to Twenty-three by day was a test of my fitting in. Looking right, smelling right, fluently speaking right were not enough. The shoulders straightened by years of physical drill had to be dropped into an easy slouch and the parade-ground stride loosened to an unbusy stroll. I had to be Swill without obviously working at it. On stage you can use gesture, expression, inflexion to convince a willing audience but in the corridors I had to be unnoticeably right. It was akin to that most difficult of an actor's tasks, to be unobtrusive in mid-stage.

Nervousness sharpened my observation. I saw the Swill in the light of Kovacs's instruction, observing how some showed a hard vitality and others gave in to mere existence, how some dressed while others merely covered themselves, how careful social ritual contrasted with bluntly insensitive behaviour. Most of all I noticed the children and the fact, which seemed to me paradoxical, that generally they were noisy, active and happy. ('Why shouldn't they be?' Kovacs asked. And why not? The child's-eye view is not fixed on the things it doesn't have. That comes later.) They romped in the corridors in groups and the adults gave way to them instead of pushing through or ordering them out of the way as Sweet might have done with their own. I had a hazy memory of reading that primitive societies had this attitude to kids and that psychologists spoke favourably for it. The State might learn something from its Swill.

The teenagers were less engaging, dirtier than their elders and less kempt, gathering in groups and behaving more like gangs, wearing the air of violence seeking expression. They knew Kovacs and ignored him elaborately in resentment of his authority but they were aware of his presence and that was a sign of respect, however unwilling.

They were probably responsible for the graffiti. The walls were covered – I mean packed, jammed, obscured – with scrawls and drawings accumulated from the day of the tower's opening, decades before. There were few printed words (those mostly four-letter and misspelled) and not much in the way of thought, but amidst the crudely drawn bodies and monstrous genitals were sweeps of untutored draftsmanship, designs that struck and held, juxtapositions of colour to catch and lead the eye. *Rotting because there's nothing for good brains to do.*

Climbing those stairs required usage and the leg muscles of mountain men; we arrived at Kovacs's floor with my thighs and calves beginning to grind. There we were greeted by what seemed a corridor full of children, a swoop of yells closing on Kovacs with complaint: 'Auntie Vi kicked us out!'

When he said that she must have wanted some peace, a girl about seven years old contradicted him. 'No, she didn't. She's got Bettine in there.'

'Which Bettine?'

'Bitchy Bettine from Five.'

'Ah. Well, piss off, all of you.'

They fanned back from the door in a semi-circle, not ready to go, watching him until he saw what some local artist had done to it. A crudely lined, superhuman penis had been sketched over older decorations in some sticky white medium that glittered, with under it, in shaky letters: BILLY'S BIGGY.

He bellowed at them, pleased as Punch, 'I wish it was half true, you little buggers!' The brats squealed with joy and ran off. 'No use painting it out. There'd be another one by morning.'

As he opened the door and stood back for me to pass I was charged in the pit of the stomach by a shrieking, spitting little hellcat from inside the flat. When I grabbed her she tried to kick me in the crotch, then sank her teeth into my hand. Kovacs cursed and grabbed her round the waist, carried her inside and locked the door before he dropped her.

She stayed on her knees where she fell, glaring at Vi, who sat in her rocker, interested but undisturbed. She squealed to Kovacs, 'Your bloody old slut hit me!'

Vi murmured, 'I'll hit you harder if you don't watch your mouth.'

Bettine hammered on the floor in a transport of rage that looked to me more like fright pretending courage. Kovacs looked at my bleeding hand and said, 'Wash that right away.'

Vi heaved herself out of the rocker. 'Water's off, but there's cold tea in the pot. He can use that.'

She took me to the kitchen, poured cold tea over Bettine's bite and opened an antiseptic pad (filched from who knew where?) for me to wipe it, then gave me a stickpiece to cover the toothmarks. When she wrapped the discarded pad in a screw of paper and set light to it I asked, 'Do you think her teeth could carry poison?'

'Could do. She's been trading in chewy.'

Until that moment the obvious hadn't hit me and I don't know quite how I felt. Perhaps there was nothing much to feel because there was nothing to be done. I was infected or I was not. If I was . . . my first thought was for my future with Carol, and that started cold panic.

Vi said, 'Tough luck, copper. Professional hazard, eh?'

Her easy brutality brought me back to sense and control. 'As you say.' My voice sounded steady to me.

She breathed deeply and shook through all her drapery of fat. 'I don't wish you plague though I've no love for Conways.'

'Or I for Kovacs and his brood.'

'No?' She wagged a finger in my face. 'He'll get you in the end.'

'Like fuck he will.'

She frowned, then suddenly slapped my face. 'You know I object to bad language in the home.'

In a half-daze, with my eyes on the stickpiece and my mind on what lay under it, I made some sort of apology.

Bettine had quietened down and was looking miserable. Kovacs glanced at my hand, and away, and muttered, 'I wouldn't have had that happen for anything.' The girl did not seem to gather that it seriously concerned her, but Kovacs was acutely troubled as he asked, 'How am I to tell your mother?'

His dismay let me feel stronger, superior, able to make decisions. 'Why tell her? We might have got to it in time. It's a weak organism when it's exposed.'

He shook his head, bitterly unhappy. I saw on Vi's face, before she quickly composed herself, an expression queerly compounded of malice, satisfaction and pity.

Kovacs, unable to cope, turned his attention to Bettine. 'They tell me you fuck with a soldier.' Vi opened her mouth to lay down the language law, then shut it. He said, 'Under age, aren't you?'

She spat at him, 'I'm seventeen.'

Vi interrupted. 'My record says she's fourteen. She's Sally Beech's oldest, from down on Five. They call her Bitch Bettine because she's a scrapper.'

'Good one, too,' Kovacs said. 'Fights with everything at once. Who's your soldier boy?'

'What soldier?'

'The one you fuck with. And he gives you these.' He held up a piece of blue-green chewey.

'Go stuff yourself.'

The way he smacked her mouth seemed loose and lazy but the contact cracked like a strap. I surprised a flash of shame on him as she squealed and scrambled under one of the beds, rage blazing at him out of the half-dark. 'Bastard!'

'Maybe so. Now, this soldier – '

'What soldier?'

Vi said tiredly, 'Come off it, girl. My kids saw you with him last night. You weren't the only one hanging round the assault course. That's why they suckered you up here.'

She squalled, 'Think I won't get those bastards! Just think I won't!'

Kovacs asked, 'Where's Stevie?'

'What Stevie?'

'Your pimp. The one who sends you to the soldiers to get chewey.'

She took her time deciding that he knew more than denials could evade, then said sullenly, 'He's sick.'

'How sick?'

She shrugged. 'All shivery and talking silly.'

'You fuck with him, don't you?'

'Course.'

She could be a carrier, herself immune, never sick, a spreader of sexual goodwill. My bitten hand itched.

'Well, he won't die on you.'

'Who cares? There's plenty of boys.'

'Belts you, does he?'

'Don't they all?'

'Great boyfriend!'

'They're all the same. Shits.'

Kovacs held up the chewey again. 'Does he chew?'

'Course.'

'You?'

'Course.' Then, most petulantly, 'Not the good stuff. Keeps that for himself, the mean bastard.'

'The good stuff is what made him sick.'

She said, with the boredom of disbelief, 'Balls!'

She took a lot of convincing. She took more still to come round to the idea that her generous Sweet soldier boy was doing some sort of mysterious harm, even if unintentionally. When it finally sank in that the chewey was responsible for Stevie's illness and wandering mind and perhaps for the sickness of a few dozen others, she stopped being tough and lay under the bed, crying. Vi heaved herself up to drag her out and comfort her in her enormous lap.

When it came to the point of kidding Bettine into just one more rendezvous with the soldier – he would be expecting her the following Thursday night, two from now – she was persuadable. Kovacs sold it to her as cloak-and-dagger stuff, beautiful spy leading the enemy to his doom, and it went down like chocolate. Besides, she considered she owed the bastard one for Stevie.

After he had finally sent her home, Kovacs said to me, 'You'd better get back to barracks and get your meds to look after you.'

I tried to look as if I wasn't ready to scuttle to them like a scared rabbit. 'I'll be back Thursday night.'

'No, no, stay out of it. Everything I've done with you boys has gone wrong.'

His breast-beating made me obstinate. 'I work for Nick, not you. If I haven't got the bug I'll carry on with the job and if I have, I might as well carry on as sit around waiting for symptoms and feeling sorry for myself.'

He put his face in his hands. 'It's me that's sorry.' But he did not argue. 'I'll see you down the stairs.'

My last sight as I left was of Vi's big Buddha face with its mask of mixed malice and pity.

3

I thought Nick would take it badly when I reported the bite to him that afternoon. Perhaps he did, but his response was practical. 'The girl says she doesn't get the toxic chewey?'

'That's right, but she sleeps with her pimp who's sick with it right now. She may be a carrier.'

'Sure to be.'

Through my welter of assorted feelings, I said, 'I want to get married.'

'To Carol. I know.'

Knew everything, didn't he? His existence was what love/hate meant to me. 'But if I go to Med they'll want to know how I got it and that will land you in the shit. Both of us. We'll be finished in PI.'

'No, we won't, lad. Med will keep its mouth shut. The moment we agreed to do the job Med lost its power to harm us. Connivance. We'll work through Arry since he has the contacts.'

Locating Arry by trivline was not easy. Stabs at possible venues found him either just gone or due there later. Nick persisted, outwardly unmoved, while I tried to keep the calm his example demanded and my mind sweated. The thought of Carol and an impotent future scared tears to my eyes, which Nick pretended not to notice.

It took him fifty minutes to run Arry to earth in, of all places, a cross-disciplinary seminar; the secretary agreed only after threats to call him out of session. Nor was Arry pleased; he had to be argued with.

'No, Arry, I can't, not on a public line . . . for Christ's sake, it's urgent. Teddy's in trouble . . . no, not even an hour, too much time lost already . . . I *can't* tell you . . . doesn't that give you a clue? *Yes*, that bad!'

He switched off stared sombrely at me and said, 'He'll be here.'

He was, in twenty minutes, when he wasted ten seconds in panic over me and turned at once to consideration of the meds. 'The thing is,' he said, 'that they may never have seen a case so soon after infection. They'll jump at the chance to examine him.'

I snapped that I wanted to be cured, not researched. He had the grace to be discomfited. 'With all the secrecy, we don't know how they are progressing towards a cure. My contacts don't know – or say they don't. So, catching it so early . . . Come on, we're wasting time.'

Nick called after us, 'Good luck.' His tone was concerned but how much concern could he spare? By definition the PI job must sometimes be dangerous.

We went directly to Med Section on the edge of the city, well out of Centre, in a sprawling hospital complex hung over from the last century. Arry made his contact by intercom from the ground floor and, after what turned out to be an agitated session when he gave his name, we were referred to Room 717.

We shot up to the seventh floor by express lift. Seven-seventeen was a waiting room with deep chairs, a table and a girl in nursing overall. She greeted Arry with a secretive half-smile that suggested her as the one who had trapped him in his sexual game, and said with detectable patronage, 'A result so soon?' and looked me over with a satisfied air. 'He's young for a copper, isn't he?'

Arry said, 'No result yet.'

'Sent a boy on a man's errand, did you?' She was laughing. 'So what do you want? You shouldn't be seen here.'

'He's infected.'

She took a step away from me. It may have been merely Arry's unexpectedness or it could have been a fear reaction. Arry handed back a little of her needling. 'You know it doesn't travel by air. I should have let him rub a sweaty hand over you.'

Her insolence evaporated. 'When did it happen?'

'About four hours ago. I want something done about it.'

'The treatment . . . they don't really know.' An uncertain hand crept up her cheek to twist a lock of blonde hair.

Arry snarled, 'Get Arnold!'

She went quickly, looking worried, and in a few minutes came back to lead us into a surgery. The man at the desk shooed her out with a jerk of the head. Arnold, I presumed. He stared at me so steadily that I knew he was unsure of himself, trying to get on top of a meeting that disturbed him badly. He barely nodded to Arry but addressed me with what he may have thought was a ring of authority, 'Tell me what happened.'

I did, naming no names and giving no tower number or district. He snapped irritably, 'So we're no further forward. We know about the soldiers. The question is, where do they get it?'

'We'll find that out – after I've been treated.'

'Reverse blackmail, copper?'

'We're in each other's hands.'

'True.' He cocked his head at Arry. 'You ought to bow out before it's too late.'

'Can't. Teddy's the mate. I'll see it through.'

I told him, 'No need. Get out while you can.'

'I buggered it up in the first place, so I'll stick around in case I'm needed.'

Hearing determination from that skinny frame was an uplift for my growing picture of a sturdy, bedrock Swill stratum. He would have been wiser to withdraw, but the thought faded in the warmth of having a friend at hand when I was alone in my danger and afraid of the thing inside me.

Arnold said to me, 'You may not be infected.'

'Is there a test?'

'Yes.'

'Well, then.'

He got up from the desk, said, 'Roll up your sleeve,' opened the wall cabinet and prepared to take a blood sample. Digging at a vein, he asked, 'What's your name, Officer?'

'Have I asked yours? I know "Arnold". That's enough.'

He did not answer but filled the syringe with blood and took it away through an inner door. In fifteen minutes he came back with the pale face of a man who has been bawled out with no chance of answering back. I guessed that he had had to cover himself by reporting to someone higher up, someone who was furious at the risk of exposure that I represented. He said tightly, 'You're infected.'

'So what now?'

'I suppose we'll have to do something for you.'

'You suppose?'

He threw up his arms in real distress. 'Yes – I suppose! It isn't certain but we'll try.'

I said, strung up with hope and fear and overplaying my hand, 'It'd bloody well better be certain. Let me down and I'll talk to whoever will listen. Including the Swill.'

'Come with me and don't talk like a fool.' He glowered at Arry. 'You can come and see fair play if you think that's your role.'

That was when I realized that these people could kill me as a nuisance and most likely get away with it.

Arnold informed me with angry gravity, 'I don't intend to open you up or slice anything off.' I suppose I smiled because he smiled sourly back. 'I intend to cook you.'

I said nothing to that. Best to let him have his fun and hope it was only fun. He led us into an operating theatre. 'There will be no theatre staff. The fewer people who know about this, the better. First I need to know if you are fit for cooking. Strip off.' I removed shirt, shoes and trousers. 'Underwear, the lot. You look healthy enough.'

He put me through a routine examination, including cardiograph. 'I'd hate you to collapse in the oven. Hard to explain away an unauthorized copper.'

Arry decided that was funny and giggled madly; he was a sucker for sick jokes. I stuck to sullen silence, which puts jokers off balance.

'It's no jest,' Arnold said. 'There's the oven.'

It was a steel cylinder large enough to contain a man, with a window at what I took to be the 'head' end, a snake's nest of cables plugged in along its length and a not-too-complex control board.

Arry asked through his spluttering, 'Gas or coal burner?'

'More like a microwave. In many ways, quite like.' He came at me with a syringe and I lifted my arm. Selecting a fresh vein, he asked, 'Don't you care what I do to you?'

'I care.'

'Should I tell you?'

'Keep it simple.'

Whatever was in the syringe emptied itself into my blood stream. 'The trouble with viruses is that they hide in crannies. They invade the joints, the brain, the lymph glands, the liver, and we have to flush them out of hiding. That is what the injection is for. It disturbs the organs that harbour them and they don't like it. They pop back into the veins and arteries from which the body can flush them in the normal fashion – after they're dead. Follow?'

I nodded. 'So the game is to kill them where the elimination systems can get at them. Now, you know that this virus can change its structure to deal with drugs – but it can't stand a long, hot summer. So we will create an environment some 5 degrees above normal for several minutes. About eight. That is very hot for a body to be and it is the viral equivalent of a long, hot summer. Humans can die of it if their hearts are not strong enough and your minutes will be spent on the edge of risk. I don't think it will harm a healthy youngster like you, but it could. It could even kill you. Acceptable risk?'

'Quite,' I said, very bluff and tough and shrinking inside.

He pressed a cutaneal spray against my arm and triggered it. 'A soporific.'

I said, before it should take effect, 'Arry, call the boss and tell him what's going on,' and asked Arnold, 'How long will this take?'

'If you leave at all it will be within the hour.'

'Say I'll see him tonight, Arry.'

Arnold asked idly, 'Who is your boss?'

Amateur! 'Who's yours?'

He pursed his lips. 'You will meet him before you leave.'

I couldn't let that chance pass. 'Pray to God you don't meet mine if this goes wrong.'

He said to Arry, 'Call the damned man. Let's not start a schoolyard feud.'

Pretty cheeky for the one who was making the bitching pace. As Arry went out I felt the relaxation begin.

'Tiring?'

'Yes.'

'Up on here.' He helped me on to a narrow trolley which I saw mistily would fit slots in the end of the oven, and rolled me towards it. He leaned over me to offer a last comfort. 'We have tried this on three kinds of monkeys and a resentful gorilla, so we know it works. On monkeys and gorillas. You can never be sure that the human organism will react in quite the same way – 99 per cent sure is never enough. Any last wishes? Just in case?'

Arnold must have taken a thorough going-over from higher up, but only a monster would have carried on like that unless he was sure of a successful outcome. I slipped calmly into sleep.

I woke under blankets with a headache and that striking coolness of flesh that comes after heavy sweating, and a general feeling of wanting to sleep for ever. The prick of the syringe must have wakened me – Arnold drawing more blood.

Arry came alongside with an unexpected cup of tea and I struggled to sit up. Tiredness hit like a club but I hoped it would pass. It was the cheap tea used in canteen urns, sour by comparison with our home contraband. He asked, 'All right?'

I nodded.

'I told the boss.'

'What did he say?'

'Tell him to hope his troubles will be little ones after all.'

Yes, he would, but a joke beats tears any day.

Arnold, fiddling with test tubes at a wall bench, said without looking round, 'Drink your tea and take a shower in the recess outside the door. You stink like Swill.'

'How would you know?'

I should have expected the answer: 'I was born Swill.'

Oh, the pride in origins transcended! The pride of Extrahood. Now that he had told me, I could detect it faintly in his voice. Some of the most capable men I now knew had been Swillborn. It should mean something. To be thought over later.

'When you have dressed,' he said, 'there is someone waiting to see you.'

'Your nameless boss?'

'Somebody.' He stacked test tubes in a rack, each with a fingernail of fluid of a different colour, shading from veinous scarlet to bluish to clear.

I asked, 'Is the guinea pig clean?'

'There still has to be microscopic examination and a count.'

'At least I'm alive.'

'Yes,' sounding as though it hurt him. 'Take your shower.'

The water cleansed me but I still felt like the wrath of an avenging God. Arnold seemed to think that I looked like it, too, because he gave me a sharp-tasting draught of some kind and had me sit down for five minutes. Whatever it was helped.

'Temporary only,' he said. 'You've had a grilling, if that's the phrase, but you'll pick up quickly.' He instructed Arry, 'Don't leave him until you've delivered him home.'

Said Arry, 'Bet on it, mister. I wouldn't miss a bar of this.'

So at least one of us was enjoying himself.

An intercom buzzed and Arnold answered it. 'The gentleman is ready for you.' To Arry, who stood with me, 'Not you. You wait here. This way, cloak-and-dagger boy.'

He left me in an interrogation cubicle, actually a Diagnostic Interview Room, little different from a PI setup with recording equipment and cameras.

The man behind the desk was in his fifties, sallow-faced, square-faced and blank-faced in the way of inquisitors who would have you think them disinterested. I did not recognize him; there was no reason why I should recognize one of hundreds of civil servants but I filed him, item by item, for identification – grey-green eyes, mouth generously wide but ungenerously thin in the lips, hair basin-cropped in the Sweet fashion of the moment, ears flat to the skull, chin unexpectedly loose and deep lines – not laughter lines – beside the mouth.

The interview was bewilderingly short.

He said, with no apparent bias for or against, 'You're lucky to be alive. You have served as test subject for a highly debatable experimental treatment and survived.' His voice was cool, his speech precise, his expression null. 'I permitted the test because it wouldn't have mattered if it had killed you.'

Cadet training is a time of shaming put-downs and impersonal diminishments but nothing in those years matched the impact of the equable, incontrovertible statement that I did not matter, that my life was of no moment to anyone but myself. We accept that only one person in a million has real importance to the race but each of us remains the centre of his universe, the pivot of energy and mind. That man told me in a single sentence that the world would not flicker if I ceased to exist, that it would have affected nothing if I had never existed and that my continued existence would affect nothing in the stream of time.

It was with the piping hate of a midget that I assumed defiance to save myself from tears. 'Using disposable oddments saves qualms of conscience.'

'Yes.' Just that, *Yes*.

'And since I have survived?'

'You can save me time. Who is your immediate superior?'

'Find out. Who are you?' Schoolboy stuff perhaps, but it's a style of defiance that rankles.

He peered, not owlishly but as one recognizing a familiar brand of intransigence. 'Of course I will find out – faster than you will identify me.'

So he would, with my face already videoed from every angle and my voice recorded for prints, but that would not lead him to Nick because junior PI have no group allocation but form a training pool to be called on by senior officers as required. He had not bothered to ask my name; perhaps he knew it, perhaps he did not care. He stabbed at his desk panel and my voice spoke clearly out of the air, threatening Arnold that I would spread what I knew among the Swill.

He cut it off. 'Gutter stirring! Would you do it?'

At that moment I did not know what I might do but played it safe. 'I don't think so. If the sufferers are treated by the meds and the supply of doctored chewey dries up there will be no need to tell anyone.'

Nonsense, of course, and he knew it. 'To that, two things. One, the immediate origin of the doctored narcotic is known and drying up of the supply is in progress. For your interest, it is brought in from over the border. The Indons also are infected and the ultimate source is uncertain.'

'But they push it to us?'

'Not wittingly. There is some fraternization between border patrols which is very difficult to prevent.'

That explained the soldiers. Or did it? To question it would only reveal that I knew more than he guessed. I asked, 'And the other thing?'

'New therapies must be designed. Quickly, I hope. The virus is vulnerable, but though nobody dies of the infection, many might succumb to the heat cure.'

That rang true, but why tell me? So that I would carry it back and render further investigation unnecessary? To let PI know that international relations were involved and that Med Section had the game in control?

He said, as if I bored him, 'You can go now.' There is no smallness like that of a nonentity.

In the theatre Arnold told me my tests were negative. 'You'll live with your balls working.' His spite was worth getting away from.

Going down in the lift, I asked what Arnold Whatever could have against me. Arry sighed and explained to the class dummy, 'The fact that you copped a dose of virus and had to come to Med making threats, that's what. It was a complication he couldn't see the end of, so he reported it to cover himself and in about two minutes flat all the wrong people knew that some Med Section juniors had been trying a little undercover work where silence is golden. Now a lot of meds will be disciplined with loss of seniority and all that, Arnold among them. Also the nurse you saw first up. You're as popular as the disease.'

He was happy about it. Humiliation by his bit of failed nursing sex would have had something to do with that.

'I should have thought of all that.'

'Your mind was otherwise engaged. Now you can lift it above your crotch and let it operate.'

That sounded more like asperity than good humour.

We took a hovertram back to City Centre and the journey gave my mind time to grind into gear. Whatever the boss man had wanted of that interview and had not obtained (or had he?) I was sure that he would be seeking the name of the PI officer who had run an illicit Swill expedition. So I would be tailed in some fashion until I reported. So immediate reporting was out.

Tailed?

I had been out of my clothes for some time in the theatre. Arnold could have slipped a pinhead mike and bleeper into the weft of my trousers – the tiny things could defy an hour of search without a detector.

I scribbled a note and passed it to Arry. *I may be bugged.* He thought about it and nodded, understanding that I could not report to Nick until I was clean. Worse, if I skipped the barracks and went to Mum in Newport, the trail would lead straight to Kovacs.

I wrote again: *Give me a password for Richmond.*

He saw at once where Richmond fitted, tracing my moves in his mind, testing each one before he agreed. He wrote: *Say you have a message from Arry the Sprat for Top Nick. Tower Eleven.*

I replied: *Warn Nick.*

He put the scraps of paper in his pocket. I believe that later he shredded them into confetti and let them flutter into the river. The most ardent operator could not have collected and collated the sodden scraps.

I asked, aloud, because it was something any listeners to my hypothetical bug would expect me to ask, 'What will happen to you?'

He held up crossed fingers. 'Nothing much, I reckon. Good physicists are scarce. I'm good.'

He did not sound wholly confident of that. I know now that he had begun to have second thoughts. But he did get a message through to Nick.

4

I went back to barracks and missed the evening meal through snatching two hours of sleep while the day faded. What I had to do needed darkness but the lost meal was a regret; the night could turn out long and active and the effects of that horrendous fever were still with me.

I stripped off everything I wore and combed my hair out thoroughly; pinhead mikes could be planted in the hair. Then I dressed in minimal Swill clothing, a sleeveless shirt and a pair of thin shorts which were in fact old trousers cut off half-way down the thigh. They were appropriately filthy but did not smell; I took a small stink spray for use when the time came. Over the Swill gear I pulled long trousers and a sleeved shirt, added sockshoes and a throatband and was at once a randy young feller preparing for a night with the girlfriend.

I called Carol and arranged to meet her at her Admin Section in East Melbourne. She would be upset when I failed to show up but if computer snoops were monitoring me, the rendezvous would make my movements plausible. East Melbourne is half-way to Richmond.

I signed out for the evening and walked into City Centre, wondering if a bug in my clothing back at barracks was holding surveillance at a halt or whether I was being physically tailed. I made no attempt to check but walked straight up Flinders Street towards East Melbourne with the old disused railway yard on my right, ten or fifteen metres below street level. The river regularly overflowed here to cover the rusting lines and some lonely rolling stock that had rotted there for half a century. Rotted was the word, for the area smelt foul when the water shrank to quagmires between floods.

I headed for the point where the old West Richmond line splits off from the main yard and runs for a mile or so through a cutting. There are big, spreading, ancient trees where the line runs beneath the road to enter the cutting; I was able to stand motionless in their shadow for ten minutes, watching for sign of a tail. It was just after eight, which is not a shift-change hour, and few people were on the footpaths on this edge of City Centre. What few there were seemed intent on their business and none were loitering. I decided that the moment was safe and went over the picket fence and into the railway cutting.

The cutting was six or seven metres deep here and thick with weeds and shrubbery growing almost impenetrably wild, but the line was on an upgrade and free of water; in the noiseless sockshoes I made good time by stepping on the rotting sleepers to avoid the sharp stone filling. I thought I should reach West Richmond station undetected.

The line surfaced in the middle of the weed-grown, abandoned Jolimont Park but the shrubbery along the fences was thick enough for cover. I passed the tumbledown, forgotten Jolimont station, weed-smothered and buried under its fallen verandah, without incident and entered the long tunnel that runs under the hill to emerge near West Richmond.

Walking in the dark was slower but I was well into the tunnel when I saw the pale gleam of a masked torch and heard wooden sabots crunching on the stone filling.

I should have realized that this easy ingress to Richmond would be to the Swill an easy egress for night foraging in City Centre. I backed out of the tunnel at speed, scrambled up the bank, dragged off my Sweet overclothes, doused myself with stink spray, threw away the can, shoved the discarded clothes out of sight among the weeds and scrambled back to the line. All that took less than a minute.

Barefoot, in torn shorts and shirt, I waited in the middle of the line, arms spread in the signal meaning *friendly stranger*.

Sudden silence said they saw me. Then they were all round me, a dozen or more of them. One lifted the muffled torch and peered into my face. I had not shaved and a two-day beard was something no Sweet would wear.

'Whoya?'

The voice was not inimical; quizzing a stranger was routine. I said, 'Newport feller. Matey.'

'Goin'?'

'Richmon'. Tah 'leven.'

'Who dere?'

'Top Nick. Knowin' Billy Kovacs.'

They had heard of Kovacs, a legend among Bosses.

'So?'

'I got info to Top Nick.'

'What info?'

I shook my head violently. 'No tellins. Tellins Top Nick, not youse.'

They grumbled but took refusal better than I had hoped. Old Nikopoulos apparently commanded some respect and nobody was anxious to interfere. Still, they played safe: three were detached to walk me to Tower Eleven, one holding each hand in the dark and the third coming behind. And so I got to Richmond Towers.

The Richmond Enclave had a powerful advantage over Newport: it was above the floodline. It was a decade older than Newport, built on a slightly different plan and notably lower than the monsters erected later, when crumbling economies had ruined the working majority and deepened the gulf between rich and poor. Those were surface differences: the walls were smothered in the same graffiti and the smell of drains and crowded humanity was equally present.

An addition in Eleven was a pungent odour of decay on the ground floor; I guessed that Top Nick was in trouble with his garbage disposal and that tonnes of rotting matter clogged an overloaded destructor system. I wondered briefly if Kovacs had a specialist who could be ferried across on an aid mission.

The Nikopoulos flat was located on the ground floor; the old man had less demanding strategic ideas than Kovacs.

My escorts held my arms until the door was opened, taking no chances with a stranger. A skinny, teenage girl with furious Greek eyes peered through the slit-opened door and cased me with inquisitive impudence before she let it a little wider. I think I was approved for later attention but we never came to grips.

She screamed, 'Grampa!' and continued her inspection under the eyes of my grinning warders until an old, craggy, bald and testy man with unmistakable Nikopoulos features shoved his face into mine as though hostilities should begin at once and demanded with cracked menace what I wanted.

I asked, 'You'm Top Nick?'

'S'me. S'wot?'

'Got 'ot talk fum Arry ter Sprat.'

From inside Nick's voice called, 'That's my boy. Let him in, Poppa.'

Top Nick said evilly, 'Nunna fu'n copper!' and to my escort, 'Piss it!'

Not one to be gracious to guests or doers of a kindness, Top Nick. (I found later that he was all bawl and bluster, flattering himself that he was still the all-powerful Tower Boss while the family operated without consulting him.) The escort gave me parting stares that added up to *Lucky youse we din case youse copper*, while I tried not to make it obvious that my heart was coming down out of my mouth after an uncertain hour.

The Nikopoulos flat resembled the Kovacs's in that it plainly housed more people than it could reasonably hold but unlike theirs it was dirty. I had seen much filthier places in my brief entries into the Newport tower and Top Nick's was probably about par for people who had given up most kinds of pretence; it took a Kovacs with social climbing instincts to battle the odds in parading a gimcrack gentility.

Nick said, 'About time you showed up.'

Another man was with him, also in Swill rig, a copper whom I knew by sight but not by name. Nick introduced me to his father, who nodded with a graceless assumption of superiority. His son might be a copper and might have vouched for his assistant and myself but that did not mean that he enjoyed having us in his home. Taking advantage of the bastards was one thing but entertaining them strained good Greek protocol.

Nick did not introduce me to the other PI man, who also was defying regulations by being here. No names, no reprisals.

Only the five of us were present, speaking Swill because, it soon appeared, old Top Nick had trouble understanding Sweet English. Then there were only four because Nick said to the girl, 'Piss it, Lissa!' She protested that she was sixteen and fit for family councils, until Top Nick pushed her to the door and repeated his son's 'Piss it!'

Nick told me that Arry had contacted him through a chain of intermediaries, enough of them to cover his tracks, and that he had come straight here to wait for me. The other PI man spoke not a word during the entire meeting.

Nick got down to business right away, making me reproduce every word spoken by Arnold and his boss. Recall training had sharpened a natural ear for dialogue to the point of being near eidetic – there was no problem there. Arnold's talk held no interest for him but to one of the boss man's statements he came back time and again: *One, the immediate origin of the doctored narcotic is known and drying up of the supply is in progress. For your interest it is brought in from over the border. The Indons also are infected and the ultimate source is uncertain . . . There is some fraternization between border patrols which is difficult to prevent.*

Top Nick understood little of this foreign tongue but pretended alert comprehension while Nick had me repeat it to terminal boredom as he examined every word.

'Can you give me his voice, Teddy? The accent, the sound?'

The boss man's neutral quality was less easy to imitate than an individual tone would have been; it took me a dozen attempts before I felt I was somewhere near it. Nick cocked a glance at the other PI man, who shook his head, not recognizing it.

Nick asked, 'Do you think he was telling the truth?'

'It was a give-nothing-away tone – truth and lie would have sounded much the same.'

'So he was probably lying. I want to identify him. Describe him.'

I went through the major points – sallow skin, grey-green eyes, wide mouth, thinnish lips, flat ears, basin crop, deep lines at the mouth corners.

'Long face? Wide? Narrow?'

'Square face with a puffy jaw.'

The anonymous man sketched rapidly on a scratch pad and turned the result for me to see. Nick asked, 'Like that?'

'Something. Higher forehead. Jaw a bit rounder. Mouth wider. Cheekbones very high. Mouth lines much deeper – very deep.'

The second sketch contained definite elements of the man but only elements. The PI artist began again, creating an Identikit. I had seen this done with superimposed basics on a computer screen but had never considered it possible by hand. This man sketched at lightning speed, never fudging a line. At the end of twenty minutes we had a protrait as nearly like the boss man as my memory could construct.

Nick said thoughtfully, 'That identifies him. He can be big trouble.'

I asked, 'Do you really think he was lying?'

'Yes and no. He's one who believes that truth is whatever serves the State. A patriot of sorts, but an honest patriot? If so, why did he tell you those things?'

As usual he expected an answer. 'So that I'd repeat it to my superior, who would then conclude that there was no point in PI continuing to interfere.'

'What if he lied?'

'To cover up something? Same result – to make PI drop its interest.'

'And if he thought PI might identify him and suspect that he lied?'

'Then it would be a warning to PI to lay off.'

'Lay off or else?'

Or else what? I had no idea what administrative revenge could encompass; the State seemed to be housed in boxes with little communication between them.

'But why,' Nick continued, 'should our prodding worry them so?'

All the possible answers to that were as unreal as triv plots. I could only say, 'We'll never know if we stop now.'

'So?'

'We carry on.'

He should have cried *Good man*! or some such, straight from the triv scripts, but what he said was, 'Make sure Billy knows just what he's getting into.'

'I don't think he'll pull out.'

Nick did not bother to answer that. One of his less lovable traits was his conviction that we would always do as he wanted. We always did.

He sent the lightning sketcher away with an escort Top Nick called up for him. After midnight he said to me, 'Come on,' and we slipped out of the tower with a scavenging gang. With them he made arrangements for me to be passed across the city, from group to group, to Newport, knowing that neither of us would be safe so long as I was visible in barracks.

At the last minute I asked who was the boss man but he shook his head and would not tell me. The less I knew . . .

The Swill who passed me from Enclave to Enclave in a wide quarter-circle round City Centre, through Kensington to Newport, did not pretend friendliness; they were doing a reciprocal job for a known PI contact whose reputation guaranteed the necessity of what he asked, but that did not include loving the bastard. The trip, about ten kilometres on foot, opened my eyes to the ways of travelling unseen through the city, via Fringe areas and Sweet areas and Enclaves, using back lanes, forgotten railway cuttings, transport tunnels, factory areas where little but automation moved, public gardens, overgrown allotments and some unsuspected and ghostly blocks of ancient, mildewed, tumbled, abandoned houses.

They turned me loose in Newport just before dawn and turned back without farewell. I was tempted to go to Mum's place for a shower and a sleep but I had to assume that my identity was known by now and that covert closed. 'They' might connect me there with Kovacs, but winkling a man out of a tower, one protected by a Boss, could cause precisely the public uproar – involving an army peacekeeping squad – that 'they' would wish to avoid. I could be safe with Kovacs for a few days before 'they' found a means of flushing me out, time enough to get our soldier and our information.

So I went downhill to the riverside levels where river and sea combined to keep the streets permanently under a half-metre of water, and splashed my way to Twenty-three. Climbing the twelve flights to the Kovacs flat left me close to exhaustion; Arnold's cookery had taken more out of me than I had guessed.

Vi answered the knock, mountainous in a dressing gown and bedraggled with sleep. 'Thought it might be you. Been up all night by the look of you. What about the bug?'

'I'm clean.'

'Just as well. You'll have to doss on the floor.'

In the middle of the day Kovacs came home and shook me awake and sat by me on the floor, three-quarters naked as he usually was in the flat, spidery and knobbly and worried.

'What's this about, boy? What're you doing here?' Before I could answer he asked, 'What about the bug? You got it or not?'

'I had it but Med Section has a cure. Rough but quick.' When I described it to him his relief was so genuine that I wished I could think as well of him as he wanted me to. At times the wolf beneath the skin seemed an illusion but it was never far away. A caring wolf was still no fireside pet.

I told him the story of my day and night, ending as Nick had instructed, 'He said I should be sure you knew what you were getting into.'

The risks were not on his mind. He said, 'The Med man – that's if he was Med – says the Indons are passing the stuff to the border patrols. Right?'

I thought over the wording as I had repeated it for Nick. 'Not exactly. He suggested it. He said they are sick with it, too, so perhaps it comes from somewhere else. But I'm not sure I believe it.'

'Nor me.' He was suddenly sombre. 'But why don't you?'

'Why did he bother to tell me anything? It might have been just a blind to stop further questions from PI.'

'So where does it come from?'

I knew what was in his mind, his 'cull' bugbear, and I didn't want to get into an argument over something that only seemed wilder the more you thought about it. I said I had no idea and he let it drop.

Vi gave us soup for lunch. Soups formed a large part of Swill diet because everything had to be used up – wasting food was the unforgiven sin, unused scraps were unknown.

All that Wednesday and the next day I stayed in the flat, browsing among Kovacs's old books, very curious some of them, that he kept stacked under the beds, all the time wishing for word from Nick though common sense dictated that he should lie low.

On the Thursday night, late, we picked up Bettine, all self-important with her role as *femme fatale* scheming to bring the scheming soldiery undone, and went out into the night – Bettine and Kovacs and I plus Gordy and Jim, Kovacs's streetwise, fightwise twin sons, sixteen years old, burgeoning replicas of their father.

From the moment we stepped into the water at the foot of the tower stairs we knew we would be wading all the way, save for what we hoped would be no more than a minute or two on the assault course. The youngsters, tough-soled through a lifetime on concrete and in water, went barefoot; Kovacs and I wore rubber shoes. The moon was high but dim behind drifting clouds. Once in the street we depended on the youngsters for guidance and they were as unerring as homing birds.

5

Taking the soldier was disgracefully easy; the work lay in getting there and back.

It was as well that the darkness made it difficult to identify the filth in the water. We tripped over submerged snags and ran into floating, nameless debris, stinking rubbish carried down from the backblocks; we stumbled into potholes that the knowledgeable youngsters could not always save us from, and fought up out of them against soft slops of slime that touched and clung.

The kids headed straight for the old river embankment, now permanently under water, well beyond the purlieus of the towers. There we turned south towards the barracks. The army complex was brightly visible, alive with window lights, its two- and three-storey structures glittering at the feet of the monstrous Swill blocks. It seemed to float on its built-up mound; when the moon dodged clouds for a few seconds we could discern the unlit bulk of the assault course running out into the water, a huge, man-made promontory.

Walking along what was once the embankment, in forty minutes we reached the assault course, every minute of it waist deep.

The water was cold – despite enduring summer it was always cold, fed by the new currents sweeping up from the melting ice. Shivering as I waded, a thought that would not go away was of the kids who made this disgusting, punishing trip night after night to trade their bodies for what they could get. As for the callous hunger of the young pimps who drove them . . . but I was passing beyond moral judgements where Swill were in question, perhaps where human beings of any kind were in question. Their need drove.

The wall of the assault course became palely visible in the thin light, a hundred-metre length heaving itself five metres out of the water, its grey cement flanks crowned with strands of barbed wire barely visible against the clouded sky. The blank sides seemed featureless but Bettine knew precisely where she was leading and fetched us up at a point very close to a rough black arrow, the marker that some lover – hungry Swill or itching soldier – had aerosoled on the cement, pointing up to the saddling paddock.

Drilled in what we must do, we left Bettine there and moved well away from her and sank into the water to eye level. My teeth chattered. Her business was to go up first and engage the man's attention, ours to follow while he was distracted. She had understood, giggling, that we did *not* want him with his pants down, which would only cause delay. We wanted to be in and out with speed.

When we were in position she put two fingers in her mouth and split the night with a whistle. It seemed there was nothing furtive about these transactions, which meant that they were known to and tacitly ignored by military authority. After tonight they would not be ignored.

A voice on the height answered, 'That you, Betty?'

Another, some way off in the night, called quietly, 'Jonno's bit of sniggle's showed. Half your luck, Sarge!'

She had not said he was a sergeant. A good-tempered sergeant, too, who called back, 'Fuck your fist, laddie! This is man's work.' It was just possible to see his form at the wire.

Bettine said, 'Ya, feller. 'S'me.'

He was not entirely careless. A powerful torch beam lit her for a moment and swept the area, but we were well out of the way. He snapped it off and the wire rattled as he flung something over it to make a bridge. A folded blanket, I hazarded. He called, 'Coming down!' and I guessed at a rope snaking down the wall though I could not see it.

We moved in towards Bettine, who was already swarming up. It was an easy pull for her in bare feet, a 60 degree slope in rough cement. For a moment she loomed against the sky as she went over the wire like a small monkey.

Her method of concentrating the sergeant's attention was simplicity's self: she started a quarrel as soon as she hit the ground. Not all of it was acting – she was raging angry for her beastly Stevie and more than a little frightened, and she went for him like a squalling termagant. Not much was distinguishable but the word chewey came through in furious repetition and it sounded as though she accused him of all the plagues of Egypt.

I was half-way up the rope with Kovacs behind me before the man edged a word in to ask what in Christ's name she was talking about, to be answered with a fresh flood of gutter Swill. With my head just above ground level I saw that she had moved round so that the sergeant's back was towards us; I reached for Kovacs's hand to ease him over the lip of the mound.

What lover-boy had flung over the wire was a field mattress, soft rubber thick enough to muffle the spikes. As the bedevilled man lost his temper and began calling Bettine all the stupid bitches he could lay a cursing tongue to, I put my hand on the mattress and vaulted over.

The wire squealed and rattled as Kovacs came after me and the man could not fail too hear it but he was within touching distance and his turning head laid him wide open. It does not take strength to knock a man out, only a knowledge of exactly where to hit him. Besides, I was wearing a knuckle sheath, and he went down without a sound. That was a bonus of fortune; so was the luck that made the guards roving pickets instead of stationed sentries, on the move and getting further away. I thought we deserved some luck for sheer nerve. Kovacs was ready with the gag and we tied his wrists in front of him rather than behind because there was a long, stumbling walk ahead of him.

Kovacs hissed at Bettine and she slipped back over the wire and down the rope. We lifted the sergeant on to the mattress and the twins took him off on the other side. Getting him down the wall was an affair of holding his dead weight with the straining muscles of one arm – he was a bigger man than any of us – and the rope with the other. The need for silence made the job twice as long as it might have been and all of us were breathless and sore when we hit the water.

The sudden cold brought the sergeant round and he struggled and grunted behind the gag. There was nothing for it but to hit him again. Then we had to carry him, holding his face out of the water, until we were beyond earshot of the assault course. We set him on his feet and Kovacs told him that he would have to walk because the distance was too great for carrying. He promptly dropped to his knees, leaving only his head and shoulders above the water, and made it plain that he intended to stay there.

Kovacs said in his ear, 'We can always go back and get another one.' The sergeant glanced at him but did not move. 'We can't leave you behind, though, can we now?' And he shoved the man's head under the water and leaned on his shoulders. The sergeant was a strong man but with his hands bound he had no chance. He heaved like a threshing horse but his breath only ran out the sooner. His struggles became twitchings and I protested, 'Let up, man, you're drowning him!' Kovacs spat at me, 'Shut up, copper gentleman!' and held the poor brute down until the twitching slackened and almost stopped. Then he pulled the man's head up by the hair and held him while he struggled all over again to breathe. I would have loosened the gag but Kovacs snarled, 'Leave it! This is business and he better know it.'

In a vagrant spear of moonlight I saw Kovacs's face for a moment and it seemed incongruously that *he* was suffering. I remembered that childhood canard, *It hurts me more than it hurts you*, and wondered if Kovacs would go the distance and drown the man if he did not capitulate – suffering, no doubt, all the while. And whether or not I would stand by and let him do it. I was not sure. Believe me, I was not sure.

The kids seemed interested but unmoved. What sort of brutality had they learned to absorb in growing up?

When we hauled the sergeant to his feet he stood with drooping head, not looking at us. The fight was gone out of him; only a fool dies for sheer defiance. Kovacs said, 'There's a long walk ahead of us, Sarge. Don't make it hard on me.'

Hard on *him*.

We went slowly with the half-exhausted man. At some stage we heard shouting behind us and saw the flash of torches atop the assault course, but we were well away by then. If they had had a mobile searchlight, now . . . but at a picket post, why should they?

In an hour we splashed into the lobby of Twenty-three. It was still pitch dark. The operation had been almost stupidly easy and I said so to Kovacs, who replied, 'What sort of shit do they teach you in PI?' *That* made the sergeant's head snap up. 'Success is knowing what you're about and not taking silly chances.'

The enterprise had seemed to me an accumulation of chances but I had to admit that he had known what he was about and that he had what it took to earn a reputation among Tower Bosses.

But I would have preferred him without crocodile tears.

6

Kovacs had a small torch. We splashed through the dark lobby to a door under the stairway, behind the inoperative liftwell. As he opened it a sweetish, pungent odour was carried on a waft of warm air. The twins stepped back and Bettine made noisy play of being sick at the stomach. The sergeant was surprised and repelled but he stood still, waiting, body alert and eyes alive.

Kovacs said, as on some ordinary night at home, 'Bed, you kids.'

His twins were unwilling but knew better than to argue. Bettine, unfamiliar with Kovacs-clan discipline, stood her ground when he jerked a thumb at her and ordered, 'Get!'

Her young-old face hardened. ' 'S'mine!'

'Eh?'

' 'S'my meat now. Orf, you!'

She argued with her own nasty logic that she had a right to see! She got him, didn't she? She had a right to see Kovacs hurt him! She knew what was on and she wanted to see!

The sergeant darted a startled glance at the angry Kovacs and at Bettine a look of creeping horror. Kovacs said, 'She's only fourteen. They're animals at that age.'

The sergeant thought he lied. 'She told me – '

'Sixteen? Age of consent? They get old fast in the towers. Bettine, get!' In the end he had to tell the boys to drag her off while she shrieked her disappointment in a tirade which centred, peculiarly, on revenge for her sick Stevie, the pimp who beat and ran her. All drama and no sense.

The sergeant watched her out of sight. He repeated, 'Fourteen!' as if he feared we held it against him.

Kovacs pushed him to the door. 'In there.' We splashed down a short corridor to another door; when he opened it the sickly smell flooded out full blast and I recognized the stench of the garbage well. There were a dozen of them in the tower, deep slurry-pits that reduced everything but glass, plastic and metal to a thick sludge to be precipitated into the sewers and spat out by the city's pumping units somewhere in the polluted bay.

The smell of decomposing matter, with an added sourness suggesting that the toilet flush system was leaking into it, was as much as I could stand without gagging. The sergeant was suddenly and desperately sick. Kovacs watched him, grinning and winking at me. I had been about to protest at use of this room until his wink reminded me of the psychological advantage given us by physical sickness in an already frightened man.

The place was windowless and the torch lit only glimpses of shapes but Kovacs moved familiarly, lighting hurricane lamps which revealed broken and bulbless electric brackets. The lamps added a fresh burden of stench to the fetor – God knows what was in them, probably a mixture of sump oils and greases filched from the factory discharges and home-processed in some tower-devised way.

Aside from some makeshift tools – rakes, hooks, shovels – leaning against the wall, the perimeter of the well was bare. The central sump was guarded by a wall of sandbags a metre or so high, a necessity where the floor level was permanently calf deep in water; in flood time the whole area would become a sewer but little could be done about that. The garbage chute descended from the ceiling nearly to the level of the bags and I looked over them to see a steel grille covering the well and over it a litter of all the bottles, tins and plasticware that should have gone to recycling instead of down the chute. The tools would be for Kovacs's men to clear them away as they clogged the grille. Far down below I heard the rushing of outlets; when the storms rose most of their cargo would come pelting back to wash through the stinking streets.

The sergeant peered at the sandbags. 'Army supplies.'

Kovacs nodded. 'Have to get them somewhere, don't we?'

'Steal them?' He had control of his voice as he played the scared man's game of pretending interest in trivia.

'Bought and paid for – after a fashion. Quartermasters like a good screw as much as picket sergeants and they pay in their own coin.'

'Ah!' The reference seemed to strike home.

'Very corrupt, the army.'

No answer to that. The abominable smell of the place seemed stronger in silence.

'I'm going to untie your hands, Sarge. Don't dash for the door. The lad here'll only have to flatten you again.'

I was not sure I could do it so easily to a man prepared for it. He was twenty kilos bigger than my seventy-odd and he had the unmistakable trained-down look; he could be faster than one expected of big men and if he were karate trained I could be in trouble. Still, there was Kovacs, with no guessing at his brand of fighting save that it would be nasty and effective.

The sergeant summed me up and nodded slightly; his assay of Kovacs took longer and he was not fool enough to discount slenderness or age or the knife with which Kovacs sliced his bonds. He leaned against the sandbags, breathing gently, waiting for us to make a mistake.

He was not the rough, tough drillmaster of military legend but a man in his mid-twenties, fair-haired and fair-skinned with the gentle profile my slender experience coupled with artists and writers, and full, red, almost girlish lips. He was, none the less, a strong, instructed fighting machine.

The poor light with upward slanting shadows gave Kovacs's narrow skull and prominent bones the face of Satan. I think he knew it as he knew everything he could make use of. He produced a couple of chewey tablets, held them close to a lamp before he stripped the wrapping from one and popped it into his mouth.

He held out the other to the sergeant, who shook his head.

'Don't chew, Sarge?'

'No.'

'Dirty habit, eh?'

'I didn't say that.'

'Then try this.'

'Why?'

'So you can experience first hand what you're handing out to Swill kids in exchange for a bit of gash.'

The man frowned. 'I don't follow. Is there something wrong with the stuff? It's supposed to be high quality.'

'Who says that?'

'It says so on the carton.'

'What carton?'

That was the right question because chewey is packed, for cheapness, in disposable pulp bags. It was the wrong question because Kovacs had leapt in too eagerly, homing in on the nature of his interest, alerting the sergeant that here was something of importance.

He said rapidly and clearly, 'Sykes, John Phillip, Sergeant, Stores Security, Second Grade, V3472688,' then clamped his mouth tight as a trap and stared defiantly at us.

Kovacs said, 'That's buggered it,' berating himself.

I was surprised that he knew what had happened because use of the hypnotic trigger was not common knowledge. An army prisoner under questioning is required by international law to reveal only his name, rank and number, but our army had booby-trapped the prisoner's brain by implanting 'name, rank, number' as a key to lock all other answers into a psycho-physical straitjacket. It was a routine hypno operation on all who served on border patrols.

Kovacs asked me, 'You know what this is?'

'I've heard of it.'

'How much?'

'He can't answer any questions relating to military matters.'

'That's right.' He grinned wickedly at Sykes. 'What happens if he tries?'

'Blinding migraine, nausea, muscle cramps, constriction of the throat muscles. He *can't* answer.'

Sykes felt that he now had some control of the situation. He said to me, 'He called you PI. What are you doing with Swill? It's time *you* talked to *me*.'

266

As if he had not spoken Kovacs held out the toxic chewey a second time. 'Chew, soldier.'

'What's wrong with it?'

'Who knows? Maybe nothing. If there's nothing wrong a little chew won't hurt you.'

'I don't use the stuff.'

Without warning, without any tensing of the body that I saw, Kovacs hit him with a smashing right hook in the middle of his face. I heard his nose break and in the lamplight black blood flowed from his lips and nostrils. He slammed back so hard against the sandbags that I thought he would go over on to the grille but he leaned there, bent back, hands to his face, crying something unintelligible so distorted was it with pain.

I cried out, 'Man, go easy on him!'

Kovacs snarled at me, 'Shut your fucking mouth!' and if ever lamps lit a demon's eyes it was then. He held out the tablet. 'Chew, you bastard!'

Sykes brought his hands down and behind the blood his expression was blank unbelief that this could have been done to him for so small a purpose. In patent bewilderment he took the tablet and his hands trembled as he stripped away the wrapper. With a last look of helpless enquiry at Kovacs he lifted the thing to his mouth.

I yelled, 'No!' but Kovacs was before me, slapping it out of his hand. It flipped over and over in the lamplight and dropped into the sewer.

Kovacs said, 'He's honest. He doesn't know.'

It was impossible not to feel pity for Sykes as he listened to what Kovacs told him; there can be few horrors to equal being informed in bitter, squalid detail how you have been used to visit disease on the innocent while taking your own pleasure. I watched his face in that well of shadows as what was told him slotted into the items of his own undisclosable knowledge. In minutes he became the one of us who now knew both sides of the affair and could not tell what he knew.

He cried, and that was something I had not seen in a man since my father charged from the kitchen to the bedroom in the last despair of his life. Once I would have despised him but Carol and Nick and Arry had purged me of contempt; I ached for the poor brute trapped in his psycho-physical prison, alone.

Kovacs seemed immune to everything but a self-lacerating fury for having precipitated the block, complaining that all he had wanted to know was the source of the stuff. 'And you know! You're on Quarter staff, so you know!'

Sykes laughed through his mask of blood. 'I would have told you. Now I can't.'

Kovacs said very sharply, 'I think you can.'

An adroit, clever, oblique questioner can sometimes penetrate a block by eliciting replies on only vaguely related subjects until an outline of the suppressed information shows through the mass of disparate answers, but neither of us had the psychiatrist's expertise for that sinuous process.

Kovacs meant something else, something quite different, and Sykes knew what it was; he held Kovacs's eyes in understanding and fear. I would have known, too, if it had not been a thing so at odds with every instinct that it did not at once enter my mind. I was struck by the fear on their faces; Sykes no doubt had cause for apprehension but I could not guess what afflicted Kovacs and did not understand his feeling until after it was all over. I had come early to the conclusion that he feared and felt nothing.

He took up a lamp and pushed his face close to Sykes's, with the light in the soldier's eyes. 'How long since they put the hook in you?'

I said, 'He can't answer that. It's military.'

Kovacs took no notice of me. Perhaps he saw some reaction the voice was inhibited from expressing, for he looked fleetingly as though something had been understood. 'Some time back, eh? On border patrol?'

He lowered the lamp and said to me, 'It weakens with time. It gets so a man can break his own conditioning – if he's hurt enough or terrified enough.'

Understanding the unthinkable, I protested, 'That's barbaric.'

He erupted in instant, violent rage. He screamed at me, 'Run back to your mother if you can't face it!'

Sykes seized the moment to burst between us like a thunderbolt but bungled it badly in the half-light and narrow space. His weight tossed me out of his way and on my back in the water; it was his sheer ill luck that my flailing feet tangled in his ankles and he went momentarily to his knees. Even so he contrived to hit me on the cheekbone, harder than I had ever been hit in my life before, as he scrambled up.

Kovacs came at him from behind and did something so cold-blooded that it still spikes my dreams. He grabbed Sykes's right arm as the man rose to one knee, pulled it straight out and slightly back, then slammed his foot down hard on the shoulder joint.

Sykes shrieked – there is no other word for it – with the agony of dislocation and remained kneeling, head down, breath rasping in sobs of pain and shock. Kovacs stood over him, yelling like a madman, utterly out of his mind, 'You'll tell me! Tell me! Everything you know you'll tell me!' He thumped the outraged shoulder and Sykes whined, and it was the face of insanity that sometimes bawled and sometimes pleaded like a child, 'You'll tell me, soldier. Oh, you'll tell me, tell me, tell me.'

I shouted, 'Kovacs, stop it!' and sounded in my own ears only horrified and futile.

He shot me a glance of blind hatred. 'If you're not man enough, go and hide!' Then, watching me with rage in his eyes in case I should try to interfere, he wrenched Sykes's other arm from its socket and the man's howling echoed round the walls.

I heard voices as the outer door flew open and half a dozen men crashed into the narrow passage, calling, 'Wha's on? Wha' doon?'

What was on, what was doing, was nothing they had not seen before, Billy Kovacs getting some answers. They would have stayed to watch, like the kids, if he had not gestured them out, his face demoniac. They went without question, curiosity satisfied, not quite joking over the sight but not disturbed by it, either. They came in, looked and went out and I had seen at last the blunting of the soul that comes to those whose lives are without change or hope of change. They came and went like an irrelevance, the inconsistent piece that memory puzzles over and forgets.

So we were as we were, Sykes on his knees in the polluted water, whining like a sick dog, his useless arms hanging from his shoulders while the thin, demented figure of Kovacs kneeled with him, mouth at the man's ear, articulating threats in a failing, strained voice like a cracking twig. And I – I watched as if I were the one hypnotized and unable to break a block.

I could have stopped it, could have torn Kovacs away and knocked him out. And what would I have done then with the tortured man whose agony I could observe but not relieve? That was an emotional dilemma. There were others. There was the conviction that if the knowledge could be obtained, we must have it and that the eyes of conscience must be blind to the manner of getting it. I plead for myself that I was eighteen, a boy at large in the world's viciousness, still the creature of what training had drummed into me, that it was necessary that some suffer for the general good. I was still in training, still under pressure, not yet stuffed so full of horrors as to question what was rammed into my eager head, so I watched with revulsion, loathing what Kovacs did, loathing him for what he was and telling myself that it must continue because the end was the safety of all the people. Looking back, the excuses leave me feeling no better about it.

Grotesque and wrenching was the fact that Sykes was trying to answer, now that he knew the truth behind the game of tablets for sex. He wanted to answer and could not. Part of the hoarse, strangled breathing was his attempt to speak against the conditioned stricture of his throat. He wanted to answer not because his courage had run out but because he knew that for right or wrong he *should* answer; his kneeling was not surrender but the torment of stomach spasms contingent on the effort to tell. Kovacs was in fact holding him from falling to drown on the floor.

Eerily, Kovacs's voice changed to a new mode of whispering persuasion. I could just hear his murmuring. 'Don't try so hard, soldier, just let it come. You try to tell it and your body knots up. Just let it come . . . when it's ready . . . when it falls out because there's nothing left to stop it.'

Sykes lifted his head to search his tormentor's eyes and made raw noise in his throat like struggling speech. He nodded slightly and uttered somewhere near the low threshold of my hearing, 'Yes . . .'

I felt then that I knew nothing at all about people or what the human mind could do, when madman and victim agreed on brutality and the manner of it, Sykes saying, 'Hurts . . .' as his breath ran out on a sigh, and Kovacs murmuring a kind of loving encouragement, 'A little pain . . . and then it's over . . . good soldier, good man . . . a little pain . . .'

His face changed again as he spoke, into the mindless absorption of a moron at play, dreaming of the next anguish.

He must be, I thought, at bottom insane.

What he did was startling in its implication of his capacities, something I would not have known how to do. He took each of Sykes's arms in turn, pulled the limb out straight as the man moaned, steadied the shoulder joint with spider fingers and jerked it back into the socket. All the time his splintering voice crackled and whispered.

A man cannot break modern conditioning by his own will; it must be relieved by the implanting operator or drain away gradually with time – or be rejected by a body fighting for its life and sanity. The tormented body-mind, driven to self-preservation can, in unbearable extremity, achieve what the will cannot. The two of them were devoted to the simple proposition, in one murderous and in the other unimaginably courageous, that the man had not yet been badly enough hurt. Resetting the shoulders had relieved no pain – the arms would be useless for days, hanging from a mass of torn ligaments and black, bruised flesh. As yet they were only a continuing agony for reinforcement.

Expert torture requires implements, refinements centred on specific nerves; there are limits to what can be done with bare hands. Kovacs knew what could be done. Without warning he let go of Sykes and stood up.

The sergeant fell face down into the shallow water and stayed there, drowning, legs scrambling for a non-existent hold, body writhing, arms twitching uselessly because he could not force them to work, to raise him. He was barely able to squirm his mouth above water, to gulp a breath before Kovacs pushed him down again. He was being killed slowly and he knew it, killed with the maximum infliction of despair; the time came when he no longer struggled to raise his head.

Perhaps by then he wanted to die and might have done if his great courage had not wanted to live and talk; there was a terrifying sense of co-operation between them. Kovacs seized him by the hair, dragged him upright and set him against the wall, holding him steady with one hand leaning at arm's length on his chest, inhibiting further the laboured breathing.

Still with that moronic emptiness in his eyes he prised Sykes's legs apart with his knee and said, 'I'm going to crush your balls.'

That threat penetrates where other pains can be withstood; it hits psychic depths. Sykes, near-drowned, was almost incapable of reaction but he shook his head weakly and tried to move his helpless arms across his body. Kovacs nodded violently, endorsing his promise and with all his strength drove his knuckles into the exposed crotch.

Sykes was too strong, too fit, too outright brave to faint and he was beyond screaming. He slipped gently down the wall to sit like a collapsed puppet, whimpering. Kovacs dragged him upright, savaging the agonized arms, never ceasing his compulsive questioning, and again prised the legs apart.

As he drew back his fist Sykes cried out what might have been, 'Please, no!' in absolute terror. Kovacs hesitated, craning close to the sergeant's face where, unbelievably, something like the flicker of a smile crossed the blood and strain. The damaged mouth began jerkily to speak.

It was over.

Kovacs held him like a baby, loving his handiwork, hugging triumph to his heart and asking, asking, asking the questions.

My relief was so great that at first the words were only dribbled sounds in the lamplight, until he dropped a name and even Kovacs's absorption livened in a spasm of shock.

I listened then in a web of shock of my own, discovering that if the sergeant's purgatory was over, a door to another purgatory of a different kind was opening for me.

My first thought was that I must protect my brother, whatever miserable thing he had done or had become; second thought showed me why I must protect him – so that Mum should never know what Francis had become involved in.

There was a long silence when Sykes had done. Kovacs sat back on his haunches, knowing what my thought must be. He looked old in that unkind light, a mask of sharp bones and deep creases, the demon in him gone away, leaving the ageing poseur who faked and conned and tortured in the name of his empire, Twenty-three. Perhaps he was remembering his entry into our lives as we struggled with our belongings on the footpath. In Francis the team of Kovacs and Conway had produced its end product.

He half rose, leaning towards me, reaching to lay a hand on my shoulder. Comforting me, by Christ! He said softly, 'Teddy.'

I struck his hand away so hard that his knuckles cracked against the wall like a stick breaking and he fell forwards into the water. I cursed at him, 'Animal! Barbarian animal!'

He put his hands up in a gesture like fear, not physical fear but a pleading against rejection. It was so unexpected that it cut across my instinct to kick and maim. There seemed no end to his store of pleas and persuasions.

'I had to, Teddy.'

Horribly, there was truth in this. There may have been other methods, had we known of them, but in his terms he had had to do what he could. Uneasily, in my terms also.

He said, 'You couldn't do it, boy, but I had to.'

No, I could not have done it. I can fight better than most in a competitive way and I could fight savagely for my life if need be but I could never have done what he had done. He had called up the killer and harnessed it to his will but I had no killer in me. I was Sweet reared, civilized, aware of the beating heart of humanity; I had no defence against the Swill kind of reality. I was, in the gutter world of necessity, incompetent.

The knowledge improved nothing; that my companion dog, Kovacs, needed patting made him no less feral or untrustworthy.

My reactions were so chaotic that I said what must be the stupidest thing you could say to an unbalanced man, 'You aren't human. You're insane.'

I might have triggered more blind rage, but he shook his head like

272

an animal scattering water and said strongly, 'It isn't mad to see clear what you have to do.'

He had Nick's ability to throw up statements that challenged my certainties, opening up areas of the mind that loomed and threatened because I could not see into them. Some remnant of stubbornness prompted the thought, *But you have to be insane to do it*, but the sense of uneasy ignorance stopped me saying it. Instead, I nodded at Sykes, lying with his head against the sandbags, incredibly asleep and violently snoring.

'What about him? There's no meds in the towers now.'

'He'll be right.'

'How will he? You can't just leave him to recover on his own.'

'Why can't I?' That savagery was meant only to jerk me into mental gear. He said with harsh weariness, 'Start your brains working instead of your feelings,' and went splashing outside into the lobby.

He came back with four of the ruffians who had appeared earlier in search of spectator sport. They carried a rough stretcher of poles and bags. They lifted Sykes, with the care of those who had handled broken men before, on to the sandbag parapet. He woke and cried out and one of them said, 'Sorry, mate, we got no dope.' They eased his trousers down, padded his crotch with rags and fixed the pad with strips of clothing that had been sewn into bandages.

For his outraged shoulders they could do nothing and no expertise could prevent pain as they folded his hands over his stomach. He wept and two of them made the soothing noises of helplessness as they lifted the stretcher above the water and the others manoeuvred him on to it.

He breathed like an exhausted runner as Kovacs bent over him. 'If we stood you up could you walk a bit?'

Sykes asked hoarsely, 'Far?'

'Maybe fifty metres.'

The sergeant made a slight movement of his chin, the sketch of a nod. 'Try . . . try.'

Kovacs laid his fingers on the man's cheek. 'Good soldier! Terrific soldier!' In Sykes's contorted smile I recognized some manner of basic communication, wordless understanding. Now that they both knew the same things, the personal slate was clean. In Kovacs's place I would have been pleading for forgiveness, but they knew it was not necessary, did not matter.

Kovacs said to the stretcher party, 'Drop him as close to the barracks gate as you can get. Set him on his feet and let him walk in. Help him if you have to but don't get caught. If he falls, shout for the sentry and run. You have to get there while it's still dark, so make it fast.'

They took Sykes away and I never saw him again, which was as well because I could not have looked in his eyes.

I felt I could stand no more of Kovacs. I said to him as a farewell, ridding myself of him, 'I'm going to Mum's place.'

'No!'

'Your part is over,' I told him. 'Mine begins now.'

'Not with your mother. Not till we've worked something out. A story.'

'We don't tell her anything, that's all.'

'You aren't thinking, Teddy. Francis has to be got out of there. He's got to disappear.'

Kovacs in his emotional welter had grasped the point my bright Extra mind had not, that not only was Francis his beloved woman's son but that the trail leading to him would also lead to the power behind him once Nick took action.

'They'll kill him,' Kovacs said. 'Whoever it is will kill him. We can hide him, we can hide anyone in the towers. Come upstairs, we've got to talk it over.'

He was right. We needed a plan of some sort before I talked to Nick, which must be very soon.

It was still dark outside. The savagery in the garbage well had occupied less than half an hour but I needed urgently to get out of the unbearable tower. At the top of the first flight I said, 'There's nobody around, we can talk here.'

There was a weak globe on the landing; they tried to keep the stairs lit at night. In its little radiance I dare say I seemed as drawn and ill as Kovacs. He seemed ready to collapse. I thought vaguely of emotional reaction as he, a step above me, looked down and I saw that he was crying. He said in a shocking gabble, 'Don't desert me, Teddy.'

He did not mean now, this minute. He meant ever, and I was enraged by the vanity of the demand. I knew what would come next. *I did my best, I tried to be a father to you,* and my insulted stomach would turn completely sour.

As so often in this terrible new world, I was wrong. He clutched the stair rail and slid down the wall like a man fainting until he sat on the top step with his head against a poisonously obscene graffito. He said, 'I'm too old, I can't take it any more.' The tears did not run but squeezed out one by one, reluctantly, while I wondered what the devil to do with him. I could not just walk away. I said, 'You still do a bloody good imitation.'

274

He dropped his head and shoulders and became the most wretchedly forlorn thing in my experience. I felt that I had hit a helpless child who had nothing in common with the demon in the garbage well. I tried to help him up. 'Come on, now. I'll see you home.'

He would not move. He said, 'I have to do it, Teddy. I can't ask anyone else to do what I won't do myself.'

This was something I had heard spoken of but had never known, the immense, empty loneliness at the top. It meant more than the solitude of a leader daring neither intimate nor favourite; it meant being the one who must do whatever needs doing, able to give orders only to those who cannot match him. It was the sort of comprehension against which personal vanity falters.

He said, 'I am not mad,' and I don't know which of us he was trying to convince, but I needed to be firm against pity.

I said to him in the hardest, most clipped tone I could summon, 'It wasn't sanity I watched dribbling sympathy while it planned the next torture. I saw your butcher face when you hurt him.' Once started I could not stop the attempt to clear the whole slaughter-house from my mind. 'Your blood was cold. You played at humanity in moments between, but the truth was in your mad eyes. You loved what you did.'

For a long time he said nothing, only leaned in a heap against the wall while I wondered what I was achieving aside from some unworthy release of a twelve-year-old's spite.

At last he muttered, 'You young ones are hard. Haven't been hurt enough.'

It seemed I would have to wait until he ran out of self-pity, but he rallied in a spurt of hard, energetic speech.

'I'm not mad, Teddy. Things have to be done and they aren't easy things. I have to work up to them, pretend to myself that they're right good things, think what sort of man I have to be and get under his skin. *Be* him for a little while.'

He seemed to think that made everything plain. In a way, it did. He could search in himself for what he was and let it loose, like an animal . . . Then in seven words he stripped my thinking bare, 'Nick says you're an actor. You'd know.'

I did know. I knew how often I had stood in Kovacs's footprints, calling myself Macbeth and screwing my courage to the sticking point, Brutus while I sweated my soul away in the intention of murdering the man who had made himself my father, Hamlet in his final rage, his one moment of true insanity when he killed like a

275

hacking vandalizer of flesh – and how, in moments of transformed intensity, I had looked out on the scenery and other players in dazed recognition that they were real and I the imitation who must find its way back to human conduct.

If my possessed eyes had looked out on a corresponding reality instead of painted props, would the stage murderings have been pursued to their end?

We can convince ourselves of strangeness because the possibilities are in us; there are realities at the bottom of the mind that can be called on to power the pretence. Any man, given the need, can do anything, *be* anything. Any man – or woman – can kill. Insanity is when you can't stop, can't slow down, can't withdraw from the final blow.

Looking into the capacities of my own mind was like peering into some parallel universe where the laws of sense did not operate and anything was possible. The measure of Kovacs was his ability to enter as far as need drove, and retreat at will.

It was becoming plain what damage these experiences did to him. He had earned his right to be a freakish and difficult man.

He asked, as if I were judge and jury, 'Don't you understand at all?'

With a feeling of burning some crucial bridge behind me, I said, 'I can try, Dad.'

He howled at me, 'I told you never to say that!' and I had to back from his swinging fist.

I said desperately, 'Until I meant it.' His eyes blazed at me out of his huddle. 'Come on, Dad. It's a long way up.'

Did some part of me mean it? I didn't know. I was feeling very small and confused about my intentions and it was a damnably long way up.

7

Vi let us in, looming in a sack of a nightgown, not pleased at being wakened and warning us not to disturb the children. There was little chance of that – living so many to a cramped space, I thought they'd sleep through anything. The beds seemed full of them, packed like small, blanketed sardines. Gordy and Jim were swaddled on the floor.

Billy's bed had been left vacant for him (king's privilege), a narrow affair of planks with a decrepit sleeping bag. He collapsed on it like another empty bag and asked for tea.

Vi said softly, with venom, 'You bloody would! At this time of the morning! Feeling sorry for yourself, are you?' He looked away, not answering. 'One of those nights, eh? You, copper! Who's he been beating up?' When I did not speak, because I did not then recognize her approach to therapy, she reverted to complaint. 'Tea at this time!' She settled herself in her rocker.

I said, 'I'll make it!'

She surveyed me with quizzical amusement. 'You will? Didn't I say he'd get you in the finish?'

I had that to think over while I made tea in the Kovacs kitchen. Rightly or wrongly, it seemed I was committed in a puzzlingly schizophrenic loyalty to him and the end of it could only be conflict of interests and duties. Mum would be happy about it and Nick would be proud of a manipulation successfully brought off. Francis would be contemptuous if I read him rightly, but how he felt scarcely mattered for during the climb we had decided what must be done about him.

When I gave Vi her tea she carried on her tirade. 'You'll see plenty of this before you're through – the Tower Boss without a heart who gets sick for a week after tanning some brat's arse and comes home to weep over it.'

I said it had been more than an arse tanning.

'Bones broken? Some blood on the floor? What's the difference? You know something? He got religion once and found a priest to confess him. Then he decided that God couldn't stand him and gave it away!' She rocked slowly, suddenly desolate. 'It was good for a laugh. There has to be something to laugh at.'

I protested, 'You can't say he's short of courage.'

'Courage?' She heaved with unvoiced amusement, or perhaps unshed tears. 'Knight-in-armour stuff? You mean, plain old guts, the stuff Tower Bosses are made of? You begin to wonder after twenty-eight years of watching this one's guts run out like water as soon as the pressure's off.'

I got out as soon as I could, thinking that Billy paid a stiff price for one wife's loyalty and another's love. Thinking, too, that my education in human relationships was bringing only jolting reverses and that anything you might think of people, good or bad, was likely to be true inside the same inconsistent heart and mind.

A figure came racing up the stairs to meet me. Nick, saying, 'Caught you in time.'

I must have been stupid with strain and lack of sleep. 'How did you know I was here?'

'Where else would you be? Where are you off to?'

'To Mum's. For Sweet clothes. I need them.'

'You don't. Stay away from your mother's. Don't you think it's watched? Now, did you get the story?'

'Yes. The stuff comes in with Canteen stores – '

'Later! Need I see Billy? Does he know anything you don't?'

'No. I was with him all night.'

'Good. Out of here!'

From the lobby we waded out into broad daylight but it was still too early for many to be about. Swill streets empty of milling crowds were strange, alien. The huge skirts surrounding each tower set them apart from each other as silent strangers, mute slaves supporting the arch of the sky. The morning brooded between them in cathedral quiet.

Nick led, not out of the Newport area but deeper into the Enclave, taking a route where the ground rose clear of the water and we could make speed. He said, very quietly, though no one was within hearing, 'You're being looked for by people pretending casual interest. You were supposed to lead the pursuit to your principal but you slipped the net. You're hot. Very hot.'

When I had nothing to say he asked impatiently, 'Do you understand just why you are a centre of activity?'

I did understand and had been suppressing the memory, wincing in advance at the anger I had earned. 'Do you?' he persisted, as ever, demanding self-abasement.

'I opened my mouth too wide.'

'Yes?'

'I threatened to tell the Swill what I knew.'

'You didn't know a damned thing that could be proved but the boss man couldn't be sure of that. He could have had it drugged out of you, but – ' he stopped dead and grabbed my shoulder and glared into my face, ' – but then he would have had to kill you, rather than send you back to PI and the departmental storm that would have been roused.'

I protested that I had told him I wouldn't really do it, that I had changed my mind.

'And could change it back again if the pressure got too strong. He's not an idiot. So he had to risk letting you go, to see where you would lead him. He's a risk taker but he lost you and he'll be bitter. Your home and every place you frequent will be staked out. They'll be searching Twenty-three within hours.'

I asked timidly, 'Then where do we go?'

'Where I take you. Tell me about last night.'

He was coolly impatient with the details of the kidnapping, to him routine stuff that anybody could bring off, but he cursed Billy for tripping the sergeant's block. I said it was accidental but he said Billy must know blocks were routine and had bungled it. He was furious. Then, gravely, because he knew the only possible answer, he asked, 'What did he do?' and listened impassively to my account of the mauling, asking only, 'Did you help him?'

'I couldn't. I haven't got it in me. Billy hasn't, really, either. He's just about in collapse.'

Nick was neither surprised nor sympathetic. 'He's notorious for it – the thug who weeps for his victims.'

'No,' I said. 'Billy weeps for himself.'

Nick was savage, with Billy, with me, with the whole sick operation. ' "Billy" now, is it? A touch of reality does make a difference! Do you know that forcing a block can bring on a heart attack? What did the poor bastard tell you?'

To me the shock had been my brother's involvement; stripped of that, the rest amounted to little. The stuff was delivered in cartons direct to the Stores, addressed personal care of the Unit Intelligence Officer – Nick interjected a satisfied 'Ah!' – who made it available to the troops as sexual bait. The cover story was that this was a softening-up exercise to get the little Swill sexpots thoroughly hooked on super-strength narcotic and so open up an information line for some higher-up purpose unstated. 'It goes in by special delivery from Eastern Imports.'

'That's part of the Ma'am Parkes's demesne.'

'Yes. And it is carried by special messenger.'

'Did you get a name?'

At the look on my face his sour mood lifted. He slapped his thigh and spluttered, 'Wouldn't you know it? So young Francis has a tiger by the tail! To him they'd be only boxes of chewey, filthy stuff the lower classes use. Swill's delight.'

I said with that special patience of restrained anger, 'He's in danger. Now that Sykes knows what the stuff really is he'll talk and the troops will take it out on Francis as the only one they can get at. Kill the evil messenger! Some of them have used the chewey themselves – '

'Are you telling me Billy has sent that man back to his unit? Is he out of his mind?'

'What else could he do? The man was in terrible shape and where else could he go? If Billy hadn't sent him back to his MO he'd have been lamed for life.'

279

Nick said thoughtfully, 'I might have let him rot. Think what will happen when this story gets round the regiments.'

'Nothing worse than if it got round the Swill.'

'Think, boy! The Swill can be kept under by soldiers but who can keep the soldiers under?'

For once he did not expect a reply and my sick feeling of having walked blindly over a precipice was no comfort. He was silent as we crossed the far edge of the Enclave and moved into a Fringe area I had not known existed. We stopped at a grimy dwelling with a boarded-up shop front, a design that had not been built in a hundred years, with shop and store space below and a small dwelling above. The ground floor, Nick said, was a 'safe house', one of several PI kept for emergency use. I did not ask who lived above. He would not have told me.

The musty, uncleanly shop section contained an old counter, a cupboard, a table and a few chairs; it was purely for birds of passage. Nick opened a large carryall that stood on the table. 'Our uniforms.' He dragged them out. 'Towel. Shaving gear. There's a cold water gulley trap at the back door. Hurry it up.'

I spotted, in a shed at the bottom of the back yard, the snout of a small patrol hovercar. 'Our transport,' Nick said. 'Hurry.'

I did not ask why, simply hurried. In something under five minutes we were shaved and in uniform. Pulling on my pants, I asked, 'How much trouble am I in?'

He was blunt. 'Your career is over unless I can salvage it. That sergeant! Christ almighty!'

'And you?'

'They'll have more trouble with me.'

That I could believe. 'Who's they?'

'In the last analysis, the whole damned government.' He swept up the bag with our Swill rags in it. 'Out!'

By seven thirty we were on our way. 'Where to, Nick?'

'To get Francis. We can hide him in the towers – '

'Billy thought that. He'd die of fright.'

Nick continued across me, ' – we'll have a pawn for bargain and blackmail.'

'To do what?'

'Mainly to save our own skins. Once that's attended to we can look ahead.'

'What about Francis afterwards?'

He fished in the dashboard locker and brought out a packet of sandwiches. 'Hungry?'

'Yes. About Francis . . .'

'The more I hear of him the less I care what happens to him.'

I said without much conviction, 'The way he's turned out isn't all his fault.' He stared ahead at the road; I tried again, wondering how well I knew Nick after all. 'Mum cares. She doesn't talk about it but she cares.'

'Mothers are impenetrable.' He gave me the ghost of a grin. 'How you do love suffering humanity all of a sudden. Your brother has to be snatched, whether he deserves it or not. After that the finest crystal ball couldn't see what will happen. If we don't take him, and quickly, they may well get rid of him before the soldiers pick him up.'

Eighteen is no great age; I felt helplessly young amid the realities of a world I had thought I was learning about but had only taken for granted.

'Who would – get rid of him?'

'Kill him? The executive division of Political Security. What the triv calls the Secret Service. The boss man you saw at Med Section was Arthur Derrick, Superintendent, Confidential, Internal Affairs. See how important you have become!'

I saw and was shocked into petrifaction. It took time for the implications to show themselves. 'All this means that our own people are spreading the chewey. It doesn't come from outside.'

'It may come from outside but our people are surely using it.'

'Billy's cull.'

'I think not. That's a last resort idea. More likely a try-out to see what can be done and how, if it ever becomes necessary. We've made it go badly wrong for them.'

He patted my knee and I thought he was about to make some useless apology for getting me into this dangerous affair, but what he said was, 'Always be sensibly afraid but short of shit scared. Eat your sandwich.'

22

NOLA PARKES AND ARTHUR DERRICK
AD 2051

1   Nola Parkes

At seven, dressing-gowned, waiting for my morning tea to cool, I called, 'Come in,' expecting Gwen with my outfit for the day, but it was Tallis, still wearing his pantry apron. 'I thought it better to come myself, ma'am, than to risk staff gossip.'

Strange. In twenty years he had never come beyond the outer door of the private suite. 'About what, Tallis?'

'A caller, ma'am. A Mr Arthur Derrick.'

Only a stupid woman would not have been alarmed by that name at this hour, but half a lifetime of dissimulation pretended only mild interest. 'Thank you for the thought, Tallis, but I am not about to be arrested.' Was I not? 'You recognized him?'

He allowed himself the knowledgeable half-smile that can make a private servant unbearable. 'In society service, ma'am, a useful memory may avoid a contretemps.'

The years had earned him the right to a little gratuitous insolence. 'Ask him to wait ten minutes.'

'He is urgent, ma'am, and there are others with him. Plain-clothes policemen, I think.'

I cried with an ageing woman's assumption of gaiety, 'No woman of fifty delays an *urgent* gentleman.' Fifty-six, in fact and he knew it. 'But must I receive him *en déshabille?'*

Tallis was not amused. 'His haste might recommend it, ma'am.'

A suave cynic, my Tallis, but he had had the sense to bypass the staff. 'In the office,' I said, 'in three minutes.'

I ran a washer over my face and a comb through my hair, donned a hairnet and slippers and took the cup of tea with me as a stage property to fiddle with if nerves failed – and received him in character as a working woman taking the day as it comes. And, to my surprise, without a tremor.

He left his four policemen (even my inexperience could identify their large frames and set, slightly overfed faces) in the small library, dropped himself into the client's chair and remarked coolly, 'You haven't changed much, Nola.'

I found myself retorting with sincere sharpness, 'In a dozen years I have changed considerably. So have you. What do you want? Tea and a chat?' Why do we imagine that aggressiveness shows self-possession and innocence?

The dozen years was the time since we had been – almost – lovers. It was for the best, I believed, that his departmental ambitions and my clandestine dealings warned me that the liaison could be a dangerous one. I had managed the disengagement clumsily and now his easy use of my first name rankled and accused.

He had changed in more than appearance. His thin body was as stiff now as then, his hair a little greyer, his generously wide mouth the same deceptive slit, his green-grey eyes as coolly lively – and his vanity less hidden. Success had relaxed the caution that once disguised self-love as enthusiasm, had exposed the mental preening of a man proud of his status and appearance and forever conscious of both. I suppressed the temptation to tell him that the youthful basin crop was a mistake on a man edging sixty.

'I could thank you for tea later, Nola, but not yet. You can expect a visitor, I think.'

'Another? You think?'

'I am almost sure. I have put myself in the other's place and asked what should I do. The answer? Come here, swiftly.'

'Other?' Parroting, I thought at once of Kovacs, of some error betraying our unspoken friendship. For it was that.

'Captain Nikopoulos.'

My surprise was genuine. 'What on earth could he want?'

He laughed at me. 'Not you, Nola, not you. Francis Conway is his necessity.' That struck below the belt. Francis was a vulnerability I should have discarded long ago. Had I known how. Derrick's amusement was the knowingness of a nasty boy. His pleasure was to spy out the signs of fear, mine to deny him.

'Don't make mystery, Arthur. What is going on?'

'I can tell you a little. The rest will have to come from Nikopoulos.' He leaned forward, projecting intimacy. 'We don't want you, Nola – at any rate, not yet. I don't give a damn about your petty thieving. It is accepted while you avoid outright greed. What a disgusting clique you commercials are.'

That, from the so-called Secret Service, was too much. 'Your cabal peddles no honesties.' I was more brazen than brave. The auditors knew and were bland but Political Security was a more subtle terror.

He ignored the insult but snapped his fingers for a blank-faced acolyte to hand him a carton and step woodenly back into place. I had staged such demonstrations myself on occasion. Arthur – no, the Superintendent, Confidential – laid the carton on my desk.

'Do you recognize it, ma'am?'

Now we were official; the real dialogue had begun.

I told him: 'Imported extra-strength chewing sweet. Of course I recognize it. It is forwarded, I suspect, through your Department, for distribution through mine.'

'Suspect?'

'Why not? It is a restricted distribution item consigned directly to Intelligence Officers of army units, via the Canteen Service, in tower areas.' My steadiness gave me heart.

He raised his eyebrows, pretending surprise. 'I believe some 30,000 items pass through your Department, yet you pay attention to one as minimal as this.'

'I pay attention to the unusual, especially when tied to a revolting story involving deliberate addiction of Swill girls. Is it true?'

'Perhaps, perhaps. What of it?'

'In God's name, Arthur, what can your spiteful files derive from the helpless Swill?'

'Are people like your friend, Kovacs, helpless? Have you become a Swill lover?'

'Don't be vulgar.'

'Vulgar? They are the pulse of the world. It is essential to know how they think and what they think and what they as a collective animal may do.'

His tone had altered; he had said something I believed, but I was not gulled. 'So that you may stop them doing it.'

He frowned as though I had said a foolish thing. 'Sometimes. And sometimes encourage. Most of the time, just worry about it. In the long run they are the world, not we Sweet.'

It was a proper rebuke. Under other circumstances his answer would have piqued my curiosity about the human being lurking within the bureaucrat, but he realized the irrelevance and returned to business. 'If I gauge him rightly, Nikopoulos will be here within the hour. Have young Conway available. And please make sure that all staff are kept from this part of the house. I don't want Nikopoulos alerted by some unexpected friend.'

'There are no police spies in my household.'

He stood. 'Don't be too sure of it.'

I was shaken; he would know better than I if I harboured snakes unawares. To cover confusion I said, 'One member of staff must stay in the front of the house. Not even a policeman would expect me to open my own front door.'

'Of course not.' He beamed at me. 'The excellent Tallis must be with us to open the door.'

I was sure he had named the snake.

He repeated the fingersnapping display. Another police flunkey came forward with a roll of transparent material which he spread over a pane of the window, trimmed to fit and smoothed with a little roller. Applied, it was invisible. He returned silently to his place, a non-person. He should have been rewarded with a piece of sugar.

But Derrick was in explanatory mood. 'A sneak's toy, an invisible microphone, powered by the voice. Now, if my men and I retire to the kitchen, may we take up your offer of tea?'

I said, 'Take what you want and be damned.'

It was small and cheap but it cracked the edge of his composure. 'You always had the making of a mean-tongued bitch.'

We had been reduced in a moment to spitefulness. So much for our yesterdays – each had seen what the other had become.

I sent for Tallis and told him that the staff must keep to their work areas, but I could think of no reason for the order. 'Invent something, Tallis.' Let him earn his cumshaw.

I do not know how he explained the presence of police in the kitchen, or if he bothered to explain anything.

I dressed slowly, wondering, concluding that the chewing sweet had flushed an unexpected quarry and that a trap was laid for Nikopoulos. What could he have done? I was accustomed to the honest masks of public servants concealing dishonest minds but I had read the Captain as one of the rare incorruptible.

I was returning to the office, still in the corridor, when Tallis opened the front door to yet another group of police thugs bringing a prisoner. It was not Nikopoulos.

Billy had been terribly beaten. A thug at each arm held him erect. His face was barely recognizable, blood and bruises framing bloodshot, hating eyes. Even the backs of his hands were blackened as though boots had stamped on them.

I cried out something useless, like, 'Oh, no!' and he spat at me. Or tried to. The spittle clung in muck to his torn, uncontrollable lips. I burst into tears, not knowing what I might have done wrong.

Derrick emerged from the service corridor, saying, 'No, no, Mr

Kovacs, the Ma'am is not at fault. Your connections made you obvious game.'

Billy seemed to see truth in that; his eyes lost their blaze. I had wept for shock on seeing him, now I wept for one of the few good men I had known and raged at Derrick, 'Did your animals have to treat him like this?'

He eyed me with smiling speculation and asked his men, 'Did you?'

One answered, full of grievance, 'He was hard to take, sir. If the soldiers hadn't been with us we mightn't have got out alive.'

Billy said with care, manipulating words in his ruined mouth, 'Bastard hit Vi.'

One of them raised a bandaged hand. 'The woman bit me, sir, and hung on.'

I heard my voice without dignity or restraint, 'Why, why? He's a good man.'

Derrick shook my arm furiously. 'If you knew what he did to a wretched army sergeant last night you would think differently. Have you a first-aid kit?' I nodded and he ordered the hovering Tallis, 'Take him away and patch him up.'

I said, 'Billy, I am so sorry,' and I think that the new agony on his face was intended to be a smile. He was the one I should have met years ago.

They vanished into the Staff areas and I went to the office to stare at the wall, at the untouched cup of tea and at the still not understood web of circumstance centred on my home.

It seemed only a flash of time from Tallis knocking at my bedroom to the moment when, through the transparent microphone, I saw Nikopoulos's hovercar skim the low garden fence and settle on the path.

Derrick reappeared as if the success of his prediction had catapulted him into instant existence. 'Let him tell what he wants, Nola. I need to know how much he knows.' He stared hard into my eyes as though to penetrate my mind. 'Don't warn him. Don't dare. I would take no pleasure in tossing you to the towers.'

He went away, leaving me with the threat only the Little Sweet, the disposable Sweet, commonly feared. The suddenness of his malice drove into me the nature of their fear. We had created the class gap as an economic necessity for control of the crumbling world, not seeing it as a garbage tip that could swallow us alive.

My anger boiled with all the conventional urges to rebellion and defiance but I knew that I would do what Derrick required. A lifetime of privilege found no courage for the towers.

Tallis came, smooth-faced. 'Captain Nikopoulos, ma'am, with a younger officer. A cadet, I imagine.'

'Also in dire urgency?'

'I suspect so, ma'am. He has asked for Francis Conway.'

The Captain was direct; sometimes it scores. 'His reason?'

'The police don't commonly offer reasons, ma'am.'

'Do they not? Well, show them in here.'

'And the lad, ma'am? Conway?'

'Hasn't Mr Derrick given you your orders?' He remained a fraction too impassive; self-control involves knowing when to relax. 'Keep him handy but out of sight.'

'Yes, ma'am.' He went away.

It is unlikely that I impressed Nikopoulos as calm and untroubled. The sight of Billy had shattered my staunchness. It is one thing to know that abominations are practised behind the screens of power, altogether another to meet with them in the beaten body of a friend. There was, too, the microphone; I was burdened with deceit. If my hands were steady my spirit shook and I suppose my voice also as I talked commonplaces. 'Captain Nikopoulos! I hardly expected you again so soon.'

He made an officer's brief gesture of coming half to attention for the greeting. 'Ma'am.' If the voice was expressionless the face was not. His intention was ice cold and his eyes held me in suspicion. Of what?

I talked across nervousness. 'By the look of him your colleague might be the other Conway boy.' I talked at random but there was a superficial resemblance to Francis.

The boy came to attention like the rookie he was, not yet schooled in quick sketching of the social forms. 'I am Edward Conway, ma'am.'

As surly-faced as Francis was incipiently handsome.

Nikopoulos laid a scribbled note on my desk. *For all our sakes, turn off your recording gear.*

'I have none on.' Not quite a lie, wholly an evasion. My shame was sure that he must detect the effort it cost me not to turn my head to the window.

He made no bones about coming round the desk to check the control panel, and said abruptly, 'I'll be taking Francis away. He's in trouble and it would be better that well-wishers deal with him before others do.'

'Have you a warrant of arrest?'

He smiled sourly. 'Ma'am, don't fence with me. Your safety also is in question. Send for Francis,' and added unwillingly, preserving the forms, 'if you please.'

'I do not please, Captain, without an explanation of the implied threat.' Oh, very haughty, the Ma'am.

He seemed to restrain himself from an outburst of ruthless haste; the other, Edward, watched me with the expectant malignance of youth. Nikopoulos fumbled in his pocket to produce what I should have expected if my wits had been less scattered, a tablet of extra-strength chewing sweet, its blue tinge unmistakable. 'The new stuff,' he said.

'Quite so.'

He stripped the wrapping from the thing and held it out to me. 'Chew it, ma'am.'

'Are you drunk?'

'No, ma'am. Chew it!'

'I certainly will not.' I had always held the habit an unclean one, involving much spitting, and had heard that users store the half-chewed mass behind their ears.

'Sweet don't chew, ma'am? Believe me, they do.'

I said resolutely, 'This one does not.'

He wheedled unpleasantly. 'One little chew can't hurt, ma'am. Can it, now?' He dropped pretence. 'You know what this is, don't you?'

I tried to be cool and steady. 'It contains an extra-strength narcotic. I do not approve but it has been issued for special distribution and I have no authority to refuse.'

'Special distribution?'

'To Army Intelligence. I assume you already know that.'

'Yes, I know. Chew it, ma'am.'

His determination was daunting. I attempted a useless asperity. 'You're raving. The stuff is habit forming.'

'Not in one little chew, surely?' He leaned across the desk to overawe. 'You will chew this, ma'am, if I have to force it into your mouth and champ your jaws between my hands.'

He took my wrist and slapped the tablet into the palm. I could only ask, querulously, 'Is this some manner of test?'

'Now, there's a question!' There was no hate in him, only an absence of mercy. I remembered that Arthur Derrick, in the kitchen, listened to all this. And would not interfere? Perhaps it was not yet time. He would not let some evil thing happen to me. Or would he not?

Trusting in protection at hand, I said, 'Very well,' and put the tablet in my mouth. It was pleasantly sweet.

Instantly Nikopoulos's hand was at my jaw, not forcing me to chew but clamping tightly so that I could not. He pulled my head forward and down. 'Spit it out!'

I spat it into his open palm and he wrapped it in a handkerchief. I felt degraded and soiled.

He sighed, 'I'm prepared to believe that you don't know.'

Then he told me what it was and what it did.

Nikopoulos was a professional who kept his humanity in some desk drawer of his life, to be indulged secretly; for the rest, he was all calculation, not to be liked or disliked, only feared – and perhaps trusted for what he was. It was not kindness that kept him silent while I sat stunned by what he had told me, but the awareness that a response jerked out of me would be useless. What response could be adequate?

In his good time, Nikopoulos said, 'The story is that these tablets are imported from outside, from the orientals. Should I believe that?'

That could be answered without thought. 'You should not. Imported samples would have been subjected to analysis for purity and possible side effects of the supposedly stronger narcotic. The culture would have been detected at once.'

'So – two possibilities. The tablets are imported with full knowledge of their properties or they are manufactured here and distributed with – um – malice aforethought.'

His urgency had gone; it might not have been genuine in the first place. Now he was conversational and of course I asked like a puppet, 'But why?'

'Billy Kovacs would say that's common knowledge. Has he never punished you with his ultimate solution of the population problem, the cull?'

He had, and had dropped the subject when he saw that I did not take him seriously. 'I thought it was his private rattle, his King Charles's head.'

'And now?'

How could I imagine that my own people would set out deliberately to sterilize a huge sector of the population? I thought of why they would not do it. 'The risk is too great. If there is no vaccine, and if it penetrates Sweet areas it could recoil on its distributors.'

'There's a possible answer to that. It may help your peace of mind if you don't hear it yet awhile. Again, there is a treatment for the disease and young Teddy here has had it, but it's one that might kill as many as it cures.'

'Young Teddy' listened like a terrier to its master; this empty-souled man could attract hero worship.

'That's by the by,' Nikopoulos continued. 'An urgent question, ma'am, is what you will do with your knowledge.'

I answered that very carefully. 'I will need to speak to some colleagues, in confidence. It may be possible to discover where pressure can be applied.'

Young Conway said, 'I threatened to tell the Swill, but that wasn't a good idea. It would cause riots and death and save nobody.'

That was good thinking from one at the age of urgent enthusiasm and thoughtless action. I asked, 'Whom did you threaten?'

He looked to his Captain. 'What's the man's name?'

'Arthur Derrick.'

All the activities of the morning fell into their pattern. 'What did he say to that?'

'He asked, "Would you?" and when I thought about it I knew I wouldn't.'

Nikopoulos stood. 'You know the situation, ma'am. Now, I want to get Francis out of here.'

'I don't understand why.'

'Look,' he said, 'you used him for special delivery of the cartons. His presence was the signal to the Intelligence Officer that what he was delivering was the special stuff. In sanity's name, why did you pick him for the job?'

Because I had, in a muddled way, tried to do something useful. 'All his personal problems arise from fear of the towers. I thought it could do him good to become used slowly to the Swill ambience. He would be perfectly safe because the truck would not stop save inside the regimental area.'

Edward said, 'Just riding through the towers would frighten the shit out of him,' and coloured and muttered an apology.

'I've heard the word before. I still don't understand why Francis must go.'

Nikopoulos told me about a sergeant who had discovered the nature of the tablets (Arthur had said something about a sergeant and Billy) and by now would have spread the word throughout his unit. Francis, the messenger, would be the focus of the anger of the men. Unfair? What has fairness to do with outrage? The danger that he could be traced to Quarters was real. Wondering how long this charade must continue, I said, 'I'll send for him.'

Derrick's 'sneak's toy' was something more than a microphone. It could speak to us. It said, 'No need, Nola, I have him here.'

Nikopoulos's gaze communicated nothing but his body surged with rage and contempt for me. He went to the window, examined it, ran his fingers over it – it crackled and hissed – nodded to himself and said, 'You bitch!'

Now the resolution was at hand I could ask composedly, 'What could I have done? He was here an hour before you, with menaces. There are men with him. Had I warned you, you could not have escaped.'

'Who?'

'Derrick.'

'Ah!' He said to the boy, 'Chin up, kid! And don't talk until you have to.'

2 Arthur Derrick

Now that I have them all under my hand, what am I to do with them? Some of my departmental officers would dispose of them, wipe them out . . . *It is expedient that one man (or half a dozen) should die for the good* . . . and think no more of it, or bother to tell me. File 'em and forget 'em. Murder is easy when control is absolute, communications not only censored but *accepted* as being censored and the people split by mutual antagonisms. Anything is easy. However monstrous. As with random seeding of infection.

How my political masters would be horrified by knowledge of expedient murders! Not by the murders but by having their publicly stainless noses rubbed into the news of them. *Surely, Derrick, something less – um – absolute . . . ?*

Have I done wrong? Then punish me, my masters! Let justice reign and the State rot! But the State will reign and justice will rot while your dilemmas need me as my cowardice needs you.

Ah, well, now . . . Perhaps, after all, one understands the pressures of necessity . . . the pragmatic viewpoint . . .

And so, the end of it.

Nola looks, or thinks she looks, into my soul to see there an iceberg, because only icebergs survive in the frigid sea of policy. One hint of warmth in the blood and the suckerfish gather, cold mouths hungry for weakness.

But I am, like so many more, only a counterfeit iceberg with the fear of falling at my heart. And some warmth, some hidden, frightened warmth.

We of the Civil Service executive grades are the frozen ghosts of the youngsters who started out to be idealistic pillars of the State. So much for moral courage. The suicide rate among us is instructive: it sorts the human beings from the icemen.

I don't yet despise myself enough for that, but it will come.

I have never ordered a killing.

Nor will I.

But the price of pity is a chilled gaze hiding the fear of falling.

So, what shall I do with them?

Sykes I have dealt with. And shudder for it. The Intelligence Officer had the sense to call me direct when they found the man in a state of collapse and raving at a scatterwitted gate sentry, telling of plots and horrors, plainly out of his mind with pain and shock. No trouble there: Hypno Section has him and will keep him blocked – for life if necessary. His incubation period is over and his temperature fluctuations have begun; he will have ongoing psychological problems when he realizes that he is irreversibly sterile (Irreversibly? Some research there . . .) and that his mind harbours an uneasy gap.

I should weep for poor Sykes but cannot remember where my tears are kept.

I should weep for Kovacs, the best of them, the one irreplaceable soul, contorted and wasted but irreplaceable. The fools didn't need to beat him half-way to the Med ward but the smell of blood fuels violence in small-souled men. Only a fool would kill Kovacs. Without his kind there would not even be the glacial State, only a crumbling bedlam.

Nikopoulos is intelligent and cool-blooded (not cold-blooded) and dangerous when crossed. What is the price of his silence? Something may emerge. He talks, they tell me, of 'New Men' . . .

Edward Conway is just a young lout but it appears that Nikopoulos is his private godling, so the Captain is the key to him. And Extras are a national resource. We hope.

His disgusting brother – I have sat in this Staff Common Room for half an hour, listening with my earpiece to Nikopoulos and Nola floundering in their quicksand while at the unencumbered ear this grovelling figure-spitter tries to win my approbation. He doesn't know yet why he has been summoned but he has fastened on me, unerringly, as the power to be cultivated.

Who cares what happens to him?

His unfortunate mother, I suppose.

Could she be the key to his silence?

Then there is poor Nola. Have no fear, Nola, your place in the glacier is assured. Training replacements takes too long. You will stay quiet for fear of me. I will see to it. Not the vengeance of the spurned, my ex-darling, but the self-regard of the cured.

And bright little Arry Smivvers with his fatal flaw, seduced by however many pieces of silver it takes to maintain the Ultra lifestyle to which he has grown accustomed so quickly – what of him? He will tell nothing – but what will life with a small, gnawing shame do to him? Why, it will sap his self-confidence and keep both of us safe.

But Francis is a fool and a frightened fool. It is his undeserved fortune that I balk at ordering a death. On the day I do so, I will have reached the end of my emotional tether, have given in to the lure of the easy way out.

Well, on with it: 'No need, Nola. I have him here.'

I lead my little cavalcade of problems to her office.

3 Nola Parkes

The policemen came to the office door with guns, Derrick pushing Francis ahead of him. The brothers glared at each other with the hard anger you see in fanatics and the uninhibited young. The sight of Francis mind-naked left me amazed that I had not recognized the power of repressed passion in him. He had the opportunist's talent for blandness but the sight of his brother surprised an instant of truth out of him. It disappeared as he came to the desk, declaring stoutly, 'I've done nothing wrong, ma'am.'

Nor had he, but Derrick slapped his ear smartly. 'Shut up!'

'Why should I shut up? I – '

He gasped as Derrick threw him into the arms of a policeman. 'If he talks before I require it, break a couple of teeth for him.' He considered the boy with an expert's distaste. 'You are the only innocent party here and the only one for whom I feel no glimmer of respect.'

He must have made use of his time in the Staff area, and he had never been a slouch at probing personalities. He turned to Nikopoulos. 'Captain, you can't play spur of the moment games without leaving a trail. Taking a patrol car into the Fringe identified you as soon as I heard the Sykes report.' Nikopoulos acknowledged the point with a twitch of lips. Derrick was genial. 'You had no choice, I realize that. You depended on speed to carry you through but you didn't know that I knew about Sykes.'

He moved aside to let Billy be pushed in. Billy's bright eyes told me he had been given a stimulant of some kind but he limped badly; that he stood without assistance was more pride than strength. His hands had been bandaged and his face cleaned and steristripped. I could only guess at the bruises under his clothes.

Derrick said, 'Mr Kovacs has more heart than sense. He let Sykes go back to barracks. Between the lot of you, you could only take chances and multiply errors after that.'

I tired of his gamesmanship, though there was probably some player's point to it, and said as sharply as my uncertain voice allowed, 'Find Mr Kovacs a chair! Young Conway!' Edward had been staring at Billy with fascinated horror; he jumped as though I had stung him. 'Get up and let the man sit!'

A most cryptic look of affection, doubt and complicity passed between the man and the boy who put his arm round Billy's shoulders and said softly, 'Sit down, Dad.'

That last word set off a series of reactions. Derrick's eyebrows rose in disapproval of Sweet/Swill rapprochement, Nikopoulos looked unaccountably like a golfer who has sunk an improbable putt and Francis emitted half a laugh before a hand was clapped over his mouth. I had no idea what it all meant but Billy had his chair, which was the least I could do for him. And, I feared, the most.

Derrick remained tiresomely jocular. 'All comfortable? May we proceed?'

Billy said through thickened lips, 'Shitmouth!'

A policeman moved to strike him but Derrick pushed the man's arm down. His joviality vanished; he surveyed Billy with the same brooding concern that had surfaced earlier when he spoke of the Swill. 'Mr Kovacs may be the one honourable human being among us – in his fashion. He may even be aware of his stature – in his fashion. I, at any rate, respect him – up to a point. Captain?'

Nikopoulos nodded. Francis was a study in disgust but I felt the little glow that comes with having one's conviction upheld. Edward showed the youth he had not grown out of by flashing Billy an approving, comforting wink. Billy did not relax his surly, pensive expression. I thought he knew exactly how good and how evil he was, how intuitively competent and how short of greater wisdom. And I wondered why Derrick used such a blatantly lubricating approach.

He continued amiably, as though he had heard my thought, 'Now we should test his stature. Eh, Captain?'

Nikopoulos frowned, making play of taking this spider-and-fly game seriously. 'You can't,' he said. 'You're an amateur.'

It was not the moment I would have chosen to launch an insult but I supposed he thought he had nothing left to lose. I think now that he was putting Derrick off balance, seeking the word or hint he could turn to advantage.

Derrick reacted intelligently: he stood perfectly still for perhaps half a minute, swallowing anger. Then he spoke to his police: 'Strip that thing off the window.'

One of them lifted an edge with a fingernail and pulled it away.

'All of you retire to the Staff area.'

The arrogance of the order, with no hint of explanation, was breathtaking. The man holding Francis began to ask, 'Sir, are you sure – '

'Quite sure. They won't attack me. Their play is over. They have nowhere left to run.'

He gave a little frozen smile as the policemen went. It was an impressive demonstration of confidence, to say openly that he wanted no witnesses of what was now to be said and done, that he did not care what might be said, hinted, sneered afterwards behind his back.

With the little smile still on ice he asked, 'Nola, are you sure you want to listen to dangerous information?'

I was not, but neither would I be casually dismissed. 'I want to know how and why I have been used.'

'So you shall but it won't amount to much.' He turned to Francis. 'Tell me about extra-strength chewing sweet.'

The boy's assessments had done their work, fixing on Derrick as the power to be courted. He recited submissively, 'It's a new small-quantity line for delivery to selected army bases only. It comes special delivery from Department One, Internal Affairs . . .'

'My Department,' Derrick said.

Francis dried up, startled and unable to decide how that affected him.

'Come on, Francis. Why is it being distributed?'

Francis shook. 'I'm not supposed to tell.'

'You're not supposed to know. Now, tell.'

'It's for soldiers to feed their Swill girls so they'll tell what goes on in the towers in return for more. They get addicted.'

'The fool who told you that is under arrest. He can't help you. Did you protest against delivering the product?'

'I couldn't.'

'Though it meant keeping facts from your Ma'am? You thought a senior man's confidences declared his interest in you and could be to your advantage. You had no doubts?'

'About telling the Ma'am? He would have . . .'

'He would have killed you. That wouldn't have mattered to anyone but yourself. I meant, did you have any doubts about making addicts of teenage girls?'

He did not understand, actually did not understand. 'Why? They're only Swill.'

I have never sat through anything quite like the silence that followed. He searched our faces for agreement. 'Well, aren't they?' He fixed on Derrick for support. 'That's right, isn't it? It's your Department that puts the chewey out. So it has to be all right.'

Derrick nodded and spoke again in that brooding, inward-looking tone. 'Like you, lad, I do what I must. The penalty for standing up for conscience is too high.'

There it was. He, too, was caught in the web of Sweet survival and afraid to struggle, wearing authority as a mask for the activities of despair. I saw again something of what had attracted me in the years before he reached the eminence where corruption is the only path to continuance. Acquiesce, aid and abet – or drop from sight. How well I understood.

He returned to cold-blooded statement: 'Control Series XC 42 is an immune system repressant activated by contact with saliva. It produces strong symptoms which pass quickly and are dangerous only to persons with cardiac weaknesses. Random infections incurred during the twelve days of symptom expression are easily buffered by routine treatments without affecting the virus, which is a tailored recombinant product with a built-in progressive mutation that renders it harmless in twelve days. During that time it can be transmitted by intimate contact, as in kissing, biting or coitus. In its active stage it can be killed by fairly heroic methods, as Officer Conway is aware, but these are not dangerous to the life of a normally healthy patient.' His cold stare relaxed into a crocodile smile at the young man. 'He was bitten by an infected girl who seems to be a natural immune but a carrier. He was no doubt concerned for his future in the marriage market but after treatment his spermatozoa remain in the full operative eagerness of bouncing youth. No other patient can boast of that. All the others are sterile. That is the end result of the infection. It is also, as the military might express it, the purpose of the exercise.' He turned his bleakness on Billy. 'As a proponent of the cull theory, what do you think of the method?'

Billy matched him, ice for ice. 'Less trouble than shooting 'em. No mass disposal problem. We get enough trouble with the sewers as it is.' He licked his lips because speaking hurt them. 'There'd be room to flush you and your kind, though.'

He spoke for all of us. Time stopped, I think, while we tried to take in a legend come to murderous life. Nikopoulos had had time to assimilate and consider; his brittle pragmatism (a necessity of his trade, I suppose) had looked all round it. He asked, 'Can you control it?'

'It controls itself. The mutations render it harmless even in carriers after two weeks. The chewey is being withdrawn, so the outbreak is effectively over.'

Nikopoulos laughed. 'Just a trial run! We're not for the chop this time round. Now you can count up the cases, draw the proliferation graphs and make the demographic estimates.'

All this coolness roused my gorge; I could not hold in some expression of horror. 'Arthur, how could our own people do this? I can understand an enemy . . . awful things are done in wartime . . . but this is barbaric.'

He gave me what I deserved. 'Doing it to somebody else's people is not barbaric? Isn't it better than the nuclear winter we have held off for a century and which nobody would survive? No plague in history ever killed off the whole of even an enclosed community. If there has to be a cull – and you know damned well that sooner or later there has to be – let's at least learn to do it with a minimum of suffering for the culled.'

The arguments of bleakness are hard to counter. The heart rejects them, the mind rejects them but the intellect cringes before the intimations of the inevitable. He had not done with me. Something of the lost man behind the bureaucrat cried plaintively in his voice.

'We *are* barbarians. With survival the only moral touchstone, we show what we are. We kill in order to live. Our final decency is the ability to see what we are and exercise some rational control over it. The world's survivors will be the ruthless, not the holy meek.'

I asked, 'Is that the best philosophy can devise for the future of us all?'

'Don't be catty, Nola. Philosophy devises nothing, so we get ready to ride out the storm. It's too late for bitching. It was always too late.'

Billy said thickly, 'Three hundred million years we've got.'

Derrick understood the odd interruption. 'Ah, a reader! That's one calculation of how long life may exist on this planet. There are others but they all tell the same tale. We are only the beginning of humanity, the larval stage, the species preparing for its discovery of

297

what intelligence is for. We will survive and develop, each crest a little higher than the one before. Time will take care of us – one way or another.'

Francis had followed all this in bewitched silence. Now he said with an air of having extracted the essential meaning, 'That's all in the future. We aren't going to die now.'

Derrick growled, '*You* may if you don't take care.'

The boy came astonishingly alert, an animal in terror, questing for the enemy. 'I haven't done anything!'

'You have become a symbol – that's worse than doing. The Newport soldiers know what has been done to them. A dozen are sterile and you can guarantee their vengefulness.'

'But I didn't do it.'

'They know the face of the delivery boy and his name. They can find you. You are marked.'

Francis spoke in what I can call only a muted scream. 'But I don't have to go there again! I don't, ma'am, do I?'

He had no strength to fall back on; inside him was a void free of everything but his overriding need. He cared only that Francis should persist, scot free. After all, he was only fifteen. I said hurriedly because I could not bear the total selfishness of his fear, 'No, not again. It is over.'

Derrick continued, ignoring us, 'The army will find you. When it does you will try to implicate others and possibly precipitate the chaos your brother had sense enough to retreat from. You will leave the Ma'am's service at once.'

Nikopoulos nodded vigorously – those two saw eye to eye.

With a side glance at me Francis chattered, 'There's others want me. Other Departments. I know a lot of people.'

Derrick shook him lightly. 'No names! You are a dangerous young time bomb and I won't have you exploding at will. It's time to take your headful of knowledge out of play.' He cocked a cynical eye at me. 'Poor Nola. You didn't realize what you were taking on. You created a market in child prodigies. There are at least two others operating. This one can go home to his mother. He'll be out of the way there with his family for keepers.'

Francis shrieked and flung himself on the floor, literally at Derrick's feet, pleading unintelligibly. Derrick stepped back and the boy followed, clawing for his ankles. The brother, Edward, with a grimace of ancient scorn, kicked him in the ribs, took him by the hair and an armpit and dragged him to his feet. He shook Francis's head back and forth and snarled at him, 'Shut up, you shit!'

Amazingly, Francis became quite still, blinking as if trying to focus the face. Edward let go of him and Francis flung himself on the tougher, stronger boy who, taken off balance, crashed his head against the wall and slumped to the floor. He lay momentarily unconscious and Francis was a total flare of triumphant hatred. He had discovered in himself a force to throw even fear aside. I could not doubt that he had taken a revenge that had waited all his life.

Derrick grabbed him before he could begin on his plain intention of kicking his brother into cripplehood. Nikopoulos went on his knees to attend his stunned officer, who stirred and sat up quickly. Billy reached out with what looked like timidity to take Francis from Derrick, who pushed him away. The boy gazed at Billy with a fresh fright, expecting retribution, and tried to pull away, but Billy held him fast. 'It'll be all right, boy. No harm'll come.'

Francis shook like a leaf while very young tears ran down his cheeks – and took instant advantage of the opportunity to mumble, 'I didn't mean it, Billy. I never hated you.'

I wished Billy had been in condition to give him the merciless belting he had earned. And knew he would not have done it. His brother said derisively, 'Oh, for Christ's sake!' and climbed to his feet.

Derrick was intrigued. 'I don't know what all that was about but if it gets the brat home without further drama, well and good. He will be safe there so long as nobody reveals his address. And so long as he stays away from the soldiery.'

Edward laughed without pleasure. 'He won't have the guts to walk through a Swill street.'

Billy was suddenly angry. '*You* had to learn! Half his trouble is your bloody big opinion of yourself.'

'And the other half was you selling him to the ma'am!'

Derrick observed that nothing cleared the air like a family brawl, but would they please keep it for later? 'We have more important moves to discuss, haven't we, Captain?'

Nikopoulos shook his head. 'No, it's over. You won't touch any of us.'

Derrick seemed to have expected no less. 'I like a man who can keep his head. My Department can use you.'

'No. Sooner or later you would give me an intolerable order "for the good of the State" and I would be sick over your boots. I haven't given in to necessity so thoroughly as you. I was born Swill and can go back there where useful things wait to be done.'

'By your New Men?'

For once the Captain was taken aback. 'Where did you hear that?'

'From your friend, Arry Smivvers. I sat up half the night listening to his shameful confidences.' He made a mollifying gesture to Edward's breath of dismay. 'Don't call him traitor, he did all he could to make saints of both of you and the complicated Mr Kovacs, though I must say the Kovacs image faded when the Sykes story came through just after dawn.'

Edward asked savagely, 'What did you do to make Arry talk?'

'Nothing, young feller, nothing. He is very intelligent. He saw what the end must be and decided on a clean breast, which might save him from penalties for his part in the adventure. That's all it was, really – he couldn't face the possibility of relegation. As we say in the Department, *There's no Sweet like an old Swill*. Add to his intelligence that he is an excellent advocate who argued very convincingly that I should take no action against any of you. That way took some of the stigma from his pleading for himself. And all the time Captain Nikopoulos had foreseen his arguments! Eh, Captain?'

I did not know then who Smivvers was, but the explanation of betrayal, which was in some manner not a betrayal, seemed of a piece with the sad moralities that held our lives together with darns and patches.

Derrick said cheerfully, 'I do nothing and you all keep your mouths shut on what you know. Agreed?'

Nikopoulos grunted, 'Agreed,' and Billy muttered, 'Right.'

That might have been the tame, stand-off ending of it, save that Edward seemed unable to believe what he heard. He cried out, 'Nick, you mean to let him get away with it? Treating people like laboratory animals!'

Nikopoulos snapped at him, 'Use your head, boy!'

It was Derrick who showed his teeth without reserve. 'Talk and I'll have you killed! Judicially if necessary. That's the threat, boy. Now here's the sense behind it. Yesterday you saw the foolishness of talking to the Swill. Today, tell me what would be gained by talking to the softer-hearted Sweet?'

'They could pull your bloody-minded State down in ruins!'

'Doubtful. Captain?'

'Very doubtful. You have the armed forces. The Swill might not rally to help Sweet, and if they did they are packed into easily controllable ghettos.'

'Say they succeeded. Who would be better off?'

'Nobody.'

Edward said desperately, 'We could have human beings in power instead of robots.'

Derrick showed reasonableness, an honest effort to instruct in his fashion. 'They would soon be the same robots as their predecessors. Government means doing what you must, not what you would. This country and every country has survived the nuclear century by keeping on talking and never taking an irreversible step. It will survive the next decades of secret biological warfare by constant vigilance and defensive research and everything else will be subservient to those. After that, what? War by weather control, with toxic rains? I don't know, but if it is sufficiently horrendous and won't slaughter its perpetrators, it will arrive. States will survive by doing what they must. Throw a government out and its successors will be constrained to repeat the monstrous actions they rebelled against. The State that breaks the status quo may destroy the planet. Mr Kovacs, do you agree?'

'Every Tower Boss knows those things. The ones that don't, don't last long.'

'You get rid of them?'

'We surely do.'

'Just like the embattled State preserving the balance?'

'Like that.'

It seemed that only platitudes remained, running in circles.

Derrick said, 'Why don't you all go home? We're finished here.'

And they did, with a flurry of little behavioural flourishes.

Edward looked from Nikopoulos to Billy as if idols had fallen. The Captain rested a comforting hand on his shoulder and grimaced as it was shrugged off; a great structure of young idealism had been blown away like cobweb. That misery would not last. Nikopoulos and PI held him fast and would provide new goals.

Billy stood up, slowly, a joint at a time as his stiffening bruises cried aloud. 'I'll be limping a bit.' He put out his arm. 'Give me a shoulder, Francis.' Francis hesitated, probably revolving doubts and fancies about the nature of his welcome, then gingerly moved under the waiting hand.

I'll swear that what I saw briefly in his brother's eyes was affronted jealousy. Billy had his second family together again. He was welcome to them.

I said, 'Goodbye, Francis,' startling him, bringing him face to face with the immediate fact of turning his back on the Sweet life. It was best that he break cleanly and at once. 'I'll send your belongings after you.'

'Thank you, ma'am. Goodbye, ma'am.' It was a desolate sound on which he went out of my life suddenly and for ever. Mrs Conway must have been a surprised woman that day.

Which reminded me . . . 'Billy, come and see me when you feel better.'

He smiled as best he could, understanding that I would not stop his 'pay'. I could at least continue that as a hostage to human decency.

In watching Billy I nearly missed one other last exchange: there was a hesitation, the merest slowing as Nikopoulos passed Derrick at the door, a quick, cool meeting of glances. I am not sure that the Captain did not give the faintest of nods to Derrick's mask of an empty smile. I am sure a message passed, an understanding was admitted.

4   Arthur Derrick

Nikopoulos did not foresee the Smivvers arguments. How could he? I gave him the public credit rather than have the truth about Sykes pop out in front of Francis. The Captain – nobody's fool, this jumped-up Greek peasant – knew that I would have had Sykes shut up before the rank and file troops were alerted to anything but delirious ravings, and would surely have perceived the obvious action taken. So he knew that I lied.

And, because he knew, he saw that the lie told to gag and frighten Francis – a lie supplied by the peasant himself via my sneak's toy – was the amnesty for all of them.

He did not know why, but he is an opportunist. (Aren't we all?) So, 'You won't touch any of us,' taunts he, impudent as you like, while only he and I know the unspoken question, *What will this forbearance cost and how will I use the screw?*

I tell him, not too obliquely, that I will have use for him and he makes the token refusal that saves face before his friends. In mentioning the New Men I go as far as I dare without knowing what the words mean, and he sees – I think he sees – that in the corridors of ice there are some who may discern a hopeful flame in the seething mob and fan it . . . discreetly.

Professional game-playing has made both of us adept at subliminal conversation.

5   Nola Parkes

I wished only that he would go and leave me alone with all this beastliness, and he knew it, but he sat himself on the edge of my desk to say, 'Now you have seen the State at work,' as if I should acknowledge a special treat.

I said, 'Don't be disgusting. A State that strikes its own, at random, for experiment, is past hope.'

'Hope caused the experiment, hope of survival. As the great nations break up, each new little statelet shrinks behind its boundaries in new distrust of its neighbours. Piddling little bang-bang wars keep morale afloat while they empty treasuries and spread starvation. The big one will come when someone has a weapon that he thinks won't recoil on him, so, like everyone else, we keep up with the latest.'

'I've had enough popular cynicism for one morning.'

He said with insulting patience, 'Not cynicism. Depopulation is a future necessity and we're in the survival race along with the rest. We could spread the chewey back among the Veets – we stole it from them if that helps your perspective – but we can't send squads there to count cases and observe progress. We have to practise at home. And, as that disgraceful brat remarked, "They're only Swill."'

'Whom an hour ago you called the pulse of the world.'

'And meant it. They'll be the survivors. We top dogs, all plot and plan and devious cunning – like Nola and her mates – will hold the place together as long as we can and then go down with it, but they'll survive. They get the training every day of their lives, learning to do more with less.'

'Survival by brute endurance!'

'In evolutionary terms it might outpoint intellect.'

He brandished his policy-sanctified necessities and I had no alternatives to offer. It was mere sulkiness that made me say, 'You infected Sweet as well. Did you count on sterile soldiers?'

He refused to be stung. 'No. We did not know that chewing was prevalent among them. That's the sort of small but significant information that fails to reach the planners. Poor Sykes could have told us, if he'd known there was anything to tell.'

'The sergeant? What happened to him?'

He told me, in awful detail. 'That's the other face of your friend Kovacs.' I could say nothing to that. 'The joke, if your sense of humour can stand it, is that Sykes, once he realized the setup, was

quite willing to have the information tortured out of him because
that was the only way to get at it quickly. And all for nothing! But
there's a man for you!'

'You suggest we turn ourselves into dumb beasts?'

'Nola, Nola, idealism was for the last century, when there was
still time. Everyone has his vision of the world one and indivisible
– if only the other bloke will play the same game. But everybody
wants to be the one to make the rules. No, we're down to more
primitive needs. The sea will rise, the cities will grind to a halt and
the people will desert them. What then? A hunter-gatherer period
while the ecology licks its wounds? I don't know. I do know that
with these things in mind the State has no time to concern itself
with moral quibbles or – ' he slipped of the desk ' – your petty
pilfering.'

He called his policemen and left.

Tallis came to tell me that the household was running normally
again. I told him to pack Francis's belongings and he said that was
already in hand; he was attending to it personally. And removing
anything useful, no doubt. I no longer had the power to punish
presumption.

I never saw the brothers again, or Nikopoulos. Or Derrick. Billy
visits occasionally, as a friend, quite openly. He comes by the front
door and we giggle together like children at Tallis's prim disapproval.

6   Arthur Derrick

To think that I wanted to marry her! I didn't have the excuse of
youth or first love, only of middle-aged madness howling at the
moon. How we would have loathed and exacerbated each other's
self-disgust! Thank you, Nola, for losing your nerve; I, after a year
or two, would have lost my sanity.

Go back to running your junk-store satrapy with the added chore
of doing your own complicated books. I hope, as you should,
never to see that whining boy again; at another time I might begin
to kick his grovelling arse and find myself unable to stop.

Nor do I want to see Kovacs, though I probably shall. His jugger-
naut virtue humbles me unbearably. He does appalling things
because he believes in their necessity; I do worse, believing only in
the vengeance of my political masters. I fear falling.

The police brat doesn't matter but his household god is something else: Nikopoulos is a planner and he has something in mind. He has too much sense to be a revolutionary (our history has slipped too far for revolution to change anything except for the worse) but little Arry's talk of the New Men alerts my sense of activity impending.

I must watch. It may be necessary to stop him.

Or to help him.

I would like to leave behind me at least one action that does not make me feel that I should join Sykes in the hypnotist's hall of fancies and forgetfulness. Until then I must apply myself to the crude, stopgap politics of the despairing State – keeping a game-player's eye on all our Nolas and Arrys.

23

FRANCIS
From his diary – AD 2056–2061

11 February 2056

Five years back in the Fringe and resigned to it. Not reconciled, never that. What a hopeless, helpless lot the Swill are. I've lost fear of them but I can't feel for them as Teddy seems to. I used to be afraid of their violence but that can be avoided; now I just detest their dirt, their whining voices and their lack of interest in anything but enduring through the night to the following day.

4 March 2056

Drama! Nikopoulos has resigned from PI and gone to live in Twenty-three. Swilldom is heaving with the story. Nobody has ever thrown away status like that before. Billy knows the score but isn't telling. Nor is Teddy.

10 July 2056

Bit by bit the silly saga emerges. Crazy Nikopoulos heads a group of do-gooders – *Swill*, for God's sake – who call themselves the New Men. What good they do is yet to be seen. One thing certain is that Nick is teaching Billy new tricks about organization and will probably take over Twenty-three one day – if the Kovacs kids don't slit his throat first. There are rumours of similar happenings in other Enclaves. Richmond and Elwood are mentioned.

22 March 2057

We need a new home. Three times this month the water has raced through the house. Sea water, salt and cold. We pay now for our

great-grandparents' refusal to admit that tomorrow would eventually come. The riverside towers are a full storey deep, permanently.
Rafts and home-made boats form a daily regatta of misery.

1 September 2057

Our new home is on high ground on the other side of Newport, in
another Fringe. At least it is dry. Teddy found it or scrounged it or
'persuaded' some poor devil. It's a queer old place which once had a
shop on the ground floor and living quarters above. Very rackety and
inconvenient but Maria loves it (she has the antiquarian pretensions
that make a Fringer excuse for putting up with second best) and it may
see our lives out if it doesn't fall down before the sea rises to claim it.

16 September 2057

Something's up and I want nothing to do with it. Our big ground-
floor room, once a shop, is a meeting place. That's why Teddy did
whatever he did to get this house. Who and what are the New Men?
There seems to be no definition, but Nick is their leader. Billy is
involved, too, and Mum is taking an interest. Billy wants me to join
but I've lost any taste for involvements.

3 October 2057

To stop Mum's nagging I attended a New Men meeting. It is not,
thank sanity, a secret society but a talkfest of the discontented. Oh,
the intellectualizing and the barbershop philosophy! Idealistic stuff
about educating the Swill, preparing them to outlast the end of our
culture. The poor dimwits *are* the end of it. Maria has joined and
pesters me but I tell her to leave me alone, she can do as she pleases.
We are drifting apart already and neither cares greatly. It hasn't been
much of a marriage; my fault mainly, but so be it. I had my fling at
preparing a shining future; now I'd rather others bang their heads
against stone walls of reality.

22 February 2059

Today I went with Maria to pick up groceries and on the skirting of

Tower Four caught sight of something which turned out to be quite astonishing – a big group of Swill watching something in rapt *silence*. Maria, who seems to be known by an extraordinary number of them, coaxed a passage for us, dragging me unwillingly, my nose rebelling.

In the middle on a low, knocked-together dais, was Teddy, in dirty Swill rig, enacting what seemed to be a dance. In a while I saw that he was in fact miming a play, taking all the parts, switching from character to character with a twist of the features, a defining gesture, a change of deportment. He told, without words, a tale of a Sweet electrician being superannuated down to the towers and there looking after the internal power lines, vetting the outdated trivs and – this was the most emphatic section – teaching children to be electricians. Not the teenagers – his impersonation of a ratbag teenager drawing graffiti brought the crowd to laughter and a few teenagers to spitting fury they dared not express in violence – whom he portrayed as feckless, unteachable and already lost, *like their parents* (that roused some muttering), but the very young, the seven- and eight-year-olds, girls as well as boys. He did a hilariously crude sketch of Grandma blundering round the flat when the lights fused, then standing by in puzzled wonder when seven-year-old Junior did a running repair with an improvised fuse wire. Then he gave them a quick reprise of the electrician teaching young kids.

It was tremendously impressive and the crowd applauded. And so they damned well should have – he was brilliant. He was more than brilliant; I can recognize flowering genius when I see it and a pared-down, unfussy technique that has been rehearsed to perfection and drives every point home. When, afterwards, he melted into the crowd they clotted in groups, discussing what he had told them.

So that is what my policeman brother is actually good for. Like myself he has a talent. But his is admired. Too late, of course. Everything is always too late. Nothing can save this crumbling planet except elimination of three-quarters of its people.

And we know that can happen.

25 February 2059

It's a sad, mad world. Teddy and Carol have resigned from PI and gone to live with the Kovacs tribe in Twenty-three. He means to spend the rest of his life in mimed propaganda. Is he just stagestruck or is an achievement possible?

13 July 2059

The meeting room has become a kindergarten for a dozen smelly Swill brats being taught to do things with their hands while a gaggle of *ci-devant* tradesmen get them interested in making things work. The tradesmen, having no teaching expertise, aren't very good at it but the kids seem to enjoy it. At least it keeps them off the streets. Mum is teaching some to read and write; they're not so keen on that but they might be when they discover story books. (The Ma'am has a lot of these. Must remind Billy.)

Billy wants me to teach arithmetic but I won't do it. I don't understand arithmetic. I can switch the light on but I don't understand electricity; I can manipulate figures but I don't understand them. And I'm sick of figures.

Contact with Swill depresses me. I am condemned to life here but I don't have to join in it.

4 November 2059

They have roped me in at last. Not as a teacher; I will *not* stand for Swill clustered about me. Billy and his fallen technicians have collected some technical manuals which they don't know how to reduce to simple tools of instruction. It's quite easy to simplify them. I once saw a military Small Arms Manual, designed for the teaching of nitwits, and I can see that it has an ideal instructor's layout. You can learn from it without an instructor. That's the model I will use. It will occupy the endless days.

So I am doing something 'useful'. Maria, who had, as she put it, 'given me away', seems to think this makes me respectable again. As though I care.

11 February 2060

Word processors! Seven of them! Old models, prone to breakdown, but *here*. In a million years Billy could never have brought off that haul. When I asked who provided the stuff, he said, 'Arthur Derrick,' uncomfortably, aware of stirring unwelcome memories. (I clutched his ankles and wept over his feet. That I was fifteen and stupid, another person, does not ease the shame.) Why Derrick? Is he another frustrated, do-gooding, bleeding heart? Hard to imagine.

Perhaps a political spy disguised as Santa Claus, lulling the Trojans with gifts? Billy thinks it isn't important, so long as the loot rolls in. He says Derrick *likes* Nick's ideas. Perhaps pigs grow wings and the world really is flat.

23 August 2060

Derrick was here today. Actually here. So was a huge consignment of paper, literally millions of sheets. And cases of books, basic technical stuff in the main. He saw me but did not speak. He looks older and has had the sense to let his hair grow but still resembles a waiting crocodile. He contemplated a working classroom for ten minutes in reptilian silence before he said to Billy, 'I was intrigued by Nick's New Men because I didn't know what he meant.' Billy told him, 'Neither did Nick, then.' I still don't know.

24 August 2060

I asked what he meant by New Men. He said they are people who do what they can instead of sitting on their arses waiting for time to roll over them. Smart bastard. So that's why all these dreary books have to be extracted, boiled down and turned into learning texts for duplication in thousands. Stuff like farming, cloth-making, hygiene – much more ambitious than the simple home-tradesman manuals of last year. 'A legacy for the dark years coming,' says Billy, who is a sucker for a catchphrase.

4 March 2061

Mum is not well, losing weight and not retaining food. The meds seem puzzled.

13 March 2061

Catching 'em young seems to bring results. Those ten-year-olds can make processors do anything but sing and dance. Even Derrick, on his occasional visits, cracks open a narrow slit of approval. Today I cracked a bit more than that, his silence. We passed each other in the hallway and on impulse I jeered at his departing back, 'Why bother? Your arse is safe from the rising damp.' Without turning, he said, 'Yes, that's why.' What is he after? Forgiveness of sins?

Mum no better. She is *thin*. We begin to hear tales of other women in similar case. Why only women?

17 March 2061

Mum will die. She knows it and speaks of it calmly. Billy pretends he is not distraught; the meds don't pretend to be anything else. It seems there are dozens of cases, all women. Another experiment? Derrick doesn't know. Or says he doesn't. But he looks like a man pursued.

20 March 2061

Mum is dead of this anorexic wasting. So are others. I sat with her last night while her consciousness came and went. Once she said, very forcefully, 'I've had a *good* life, Francis. So full.' Full, I thought, of what would have been avoided in a saner world. Or is it a matter of knowing what you want, irrespective of the nature of the world? I thought once that I knew what I wanted. Billy came in later, but by then she was rambling about the past, about summertime and the glistening sea.

THE AUTUMN PEOPLE – 3

Andra to Lenna

. . . So, after three years and a dozen attempts, I realize that this play is unwritable. I have given it up. After a year of wrestling with a psychiatrist to find a satisfactory central source for Billy's inconsistencies, after switching my attention to Teddy and taking endless lessons in the techniques of mime (which will, at least, be professionally useful), after trying to refocus the whole period through the eyes of Derrick, I have given it up.

Your novel is not at fault. I should have seen from the beginning that these people struggled in the nets of local culture and their own personalities; they did not represent the collapsing world. It might be impossible, I feel, to create a group that *could* represent it.

It is too easy to fall into the trap of seeing history in terms of human movement, as though all else is ancillary, as though *we* make history. It is history that makes *us*. The Greenhouse years should have shown that plainly; the Long Winter will render it inescapable. The Greenhouse years made a shortish downward curve in human fortunes; the Long Winter may make a longer but, because we are better prepared, shallower dip.

Or, are these no more than necessary experiences in the life of the species, not peaks and depths at all, but interruptions comparable to the rainstorms and frosts we learn to deal with by changing our clothes for the duration of discomfort? In the enormous stretch of history to come the Greenhouse years will rate as little more than an unseasonably hot day . . .

She filed the letter among the documents which would, on her death, become part of the university archive, along with the academic reviews which disapproved of attempts to reduce history to flashes of insight through narrow tower windows.

But, she thought, the novel gained me some recognition in the larger world outside the campus and since I, unlike history, am not here for ever, that is an acceptable pleasure. The little human glimpses *do* help, if only in confirming our confidence in steadfast courage.

POSTSCRIPT

Nobody can foretell the future. In a world of disparate aims, philosophies and physical conditions the possible permutations are endless; few guesses aimed beyond a decade from today are likely to be correct, even by accident. So, this novel cannot be regarded as prophetic; it is not offered as a dire warning. Its purpose is simply to highlight a number of possibilities that deserve urgent thought if some of them are not to come to pass in one form or another.

1. *Population*.   This is a present problem in many areas and may soon be a problem in all areas, with special emphasis on those with little arable land. Demographic forecasts suggest a slowing of the birthrate, but that prediction is based on assessment of possible/probable future trends which are not really amenable to assessment. It is possible that the planet's population will double within three to four decades.

2. *Food*.   How shall we feed a planet with twice its present population? We know that it is possible in terms of food production, yet already about half the population is underfed and much of it actually starved. Why?

3. *Employment*.   Long-range predictions of the results of automation are cautious and conservative and limited to a very few years. The factors that cannot be assessed are managerial greed, stresses of competition and the ability of rising Third World technologies to undercut a productivity geared to profit instead of usefulness.

4. *Finance*.   In this novel I have placed the collapse of the money system in the fifth decade of the new century. Some thinkers have suggested the second decade as crucial. The reason? Lack of markets caused by unemployment beyond previous nightmares of recession, bankrupt governments and the collapse of the Third World market for shoddy.

None of these things need happen. All of them can if we ignore the warnings of Sir Macfarlane Burnett that we 'must plan for five years ahead and twenty years and a hundred years.' No country in the present world is likely to do this because no government can, by the nature of its provenance, plan beyond its own tenure. All governments busy themselves with preserving and continuing their own power. They do little else. There are no votes in projects twenty years in the future, let alone a hundred.

Two other major matters must be considered by today's futurologist:

1. *Nuclear war.* My opinion, for what it may be worth, is that this is an unlikely occurrence. Those capable of it know the cost: nobody left to loot the losers. Fanaticism cannot be discounted as a possible, demented impulse but there we can only take refuge in optimism.

2. *The Greenhouse effect.* It is unlikely that we will have definite information on the extent of this before the turn of this century. It could be a comparatively mild matter of gently changing climates (but not therefore to be ignored) or it could be a global disaster, striking with great suddenness.

We can be sure only that enormous changes will take place in the next two or three generations, all of them caused by ourselves, and that we will not be ready for them. How can we be? We *talk* of leaving a better world to our children but in fact do little more than rub along with day-to-day problems and hope that the longer-range catastrophes will never happen.

Sooner or later some of them will.

Drowning Towers is about the possible cost of complacency.

Sleep well.